SACRAMENTO PUBLIC LIBRARY

3 3029 05568 6471

SACRAMENTO PUBLIC LIBRARY

T

95814

3/2005

THE MAN WHO
LOST THE SEA

Theodore Sturgeon playing guitar to entertain fellow conventioneers at the 1962 World Science Fiction Convention in Chicago, at which he was Guest of Honor. Photograph by Dean Grennell.

THE MAN WHO LOST THE SEA

Volume X:

The Complete Stories of

Theodore Sturgeon

Edited by
Paul Williams

Foreword by
Jonathan Lethem

North Atlantic Books
Berkeley, California

Copyright © 2005 the Theodore Sturgeon Literary Trust. Previously published
materials copyright © 1958, 1959, 1960, 1961 by Theodore Sturgeon and the
Theodore Sturgeon Literary Trust, except "The Man Who Figured Everything,"
which is copyright © 1959 by Don Ward and Theodore Sturgeon and the
Theodore Sturgeon Literary Trust. All rights reserved. No portion of this book,
except for brief review, may be reproduced, stored in a retrieval system, or
transmitted in any form or by any means—electronic, mechanical, photo-
copying, recording, or otherwise—without written permission of the publisher.

Published by
North Atlantic Books
P.O. Box 12327
Berkeley, California 94712

Cover and book design by Paula Morrison

Printed in the United States of America

The Man Who Lost the Sea is sponsored by the Society for the Study of Native
Arts and Sciences, a nonprofit educational corporation whose goals are to
develop an educational and crosscultural perspective linking various scientific,
social, and artistic fields; to nurture a holistic view of arts, sciences, humani-
ties, and healing; and to publish and distribute literature on the relationship
of mind, body, and nature.

Library of Congress Cataloging-in-Publication Data
Sturgeon, Theodore.
    The man who lost the sea/ by Theodore Sturgeon ; edited by Paul Williams
; foreword by Jonathan Lethem.
        p. cm.—(The complete stories of Theodore Sturgeon ; v. 10)
    Summary: "The tenth in a series of volumes of collected stories by noted
science fiction writer Theodore Sturgeon. Features stories written between
1958 and 1961"—Provided by publisher.
    ISBN 1-55643-519-3 (cloth)
    1. Science fiction, American. I. Williams, Paul, 1948– II. Title.
PS3569.T875A6 2004
813'.54—dc22

                                                    2004024132

        1 2 3 4 5 6 7 8 9 MALLOY 10 09 08 07 06 05

EDITOR'S NOTE

THEODORE HAMILTON STURGEON was born February 26, 1918, and died May 8, 1985. This is the tenth of a series of volumes that will collect all of his short fiction of all types and all lengths shorter than a novel. The volumes and the stories within the volumes are organized chronologically by order of composition (insofar as it can be determined). This tenth volume contains stories written between spring 1957 and autumn 1960.

Preparation of each of these volumes would not be possible without the hard work and invaluable participation of Noël Sturgeon, Debbie Notkin, and our publishers, Lindy Hough and Richard Grossinger. I would also like to thank, for their significant assistance with this volume, Jonathan Lethem, the Theodore Sturgeon Literary Trust, Marion Sturgeon, Jayne Williams, Ralph Vicinanza, Tina Krauss, Dixon Chandler, Cindy Lee Berryhill, T. V. Reed, and all of you who have expressed your interest and support. For those who would like more information about Theodore Sturgeon and the Theodore Sturgeon Literary Trust, the website address for the Trust is: http://www.physics.emory.edu/~weeks/sturgeon/

BOOKS BY THEODORE STURGEON

Without Sorcery (1948)

The Dreaming Jewels [aka
    The Synthetic Man] (1950)

More Than Human (1953)

E Pluribus Unicorn (1953)

Caviar (1955)

A Way Home (1955)

The King and Four Queens
    (1956)

I, Libertine (1956)

A Touch of Strange (1958)

The Cosmic Rape [aka *To
    Marry Medusa*] (1958)

Aliens 4 (1959)

Venus Plus X (1960)

Beyond (1960)

Some of Your Blood (1961)

*Voyage to the Bottom of the
    Sea* (1961)

The Player on the Other Side
    (1963)

Sturgeon in Orbit (1964)

Starshine (1966)

The Rare Breed (1966)

Sturgeon Is Alive and Well . . .
    (1971)

*The Worlds of Theodore
    Sturgeon* (1972)

Sturgeon's West (with Don
    Ward) (1973)

Case and the Dreamer (1974)

Visions and Venturers (1978)

Maturity (1979)

The Stars Are the Styx (1979)

The Golden Helix (1979)

Alien Cargo (1984)

Godbody (1986)

A Touch of Sturgeon (1987)

*The [Widget], the [Wadget],
    and Boff* (1989)

Argyll (1993)

The Ultimate Egoist (1994)

Microcosmic God (1995)

Killdozer! (1996)

Star Trek, The Joy Machine
    (with James Gunn) (1996)

Thunder and Roses (1997)

The Perfect Host (1998)

Baby Is Three (1999)

A Saucer of Loneliness (2000)

Bright Segment (2002)

And Now the News . . . (2003)

CONTENTS

Foreword

By Jonathan Lethem

I never met Theodore Sturgeon, but I did have a chance to introduce him to my father, in a Sturgeonish fashion. Paul Williams and I were visiting Woodstock, New York, on our way from a science fiction convention in Massachusetts. In Woodstock we were to meet my father, who had driven to pick me up from and return me to his cabin in the Catskills. In Woodstock Paul and I met Noël Sturgeon, Theodore Sturgeon's daughter. We were an hour or so early for the rendezvous with my dad, and, of course, more than a decade late to hope for an encounter in the flesh with Theodore Sturgeon.

This was in 1993, at the start of North Atlantic Books' noble publishing marathon *The Complete Stories of Theodore Sturgeon*, of which this is the tenth volume. At that time the project was a whisper or a promise. Or perhaps I should say it was a drive in the woods, for that is what it was that day. We went for a drive in the woods and Paul and I contemplated the territory of Sturgeon's life in his Woodstock years, with Noël's eloquent guidance, her narration and her silences. She led us down backroads to contemplate the place where Sturgeon's writing shack had been hidden. We absorbed the presence of his absence, and I absorbed the delicate weight of his daughter's spoken and unspoken memories, and those of her father's friend Paul. I remembered what I knew of Sturgeon, the stories when I'd first read them as a kid. Noël spoke of her childhood with an artist father, and I thought of my own.

Then we went back into Woodstock and met my father in a café. By the time I was able to introduce Noël to my father I felt I was returning a favor, or at least trying to. I felt that I was completing a circle. Leaving Paul and Noël behind, driving off into the Catskills,

I spoke to my father of Sturgeon, and I spoke to him differently. That night I slept beside my father in two sleeping bags in a cabin lit only by candles and by the stars, and told him more of my life as an adult than I ever had. I was still with Sturgeon, though I was alone with my father and had never been with Sturgeon at all.

These stories are like that: they speak of human beings connecting with other human beings or attempting to do so at great odds, and at odd angles; of human beings failing at or sabotaging their own best efforts for fear that what they want most doesn't make any sense, or that the odds are too great; of human beings learning again and again that their thin howling selves are part of a chorus which stands shoulder to shoulder in a traffic jam, a mob scene of lonely selves, of members of a great estranged family of beings. Sturgeon wrote miraculous short stories. Some fly, some stumble, but all are miraculous. By that I mean he always wrote of miracles, of deliverance and miracles and of a lust for completion in an incomplete world. He wrote of needs and their denial, with such undisguised longing and anger that his stories are caustic with emotion. His stories are carved in need. Many of the fine examples gathered here in Volume 10 are by happy coincidence the first ones Sturgeon wrote in those woods; he moved his family to Woodstock in 1959.

Paul Williams once said, in conversation, that Sturgeon's "only method was the tour de force." That has long seemed to me the only critical remark on Sturgeon's art that needs making. It is impossible to imagine the work arising from anything but the peculiar circumstances of its making. Sturgeon found his urgency directed in becoming, in bursts of stylistic juice, the John Dos Passos, the William Faulkner, the Ring Lardner, the James Thurber, the Virginia Woolf of science fiction. The pulp form gave him the motifs of transcendence and metamorphosis, and the imperative of optimism, he needed to cut against what seems to me an instinctive morbidity. See how his imagination collapses into the gothic in the non-SF tales; alternately, consider how *The Man Who Lost The Sea*, the finest literary fugue this side of James Salter's *Dusk,* relies on its rocket. Yet Sturgeon's work is the opposite of Pop Art; he never predicted much; his cheerleading's embarrassing. He can seem misplaced in science fiction; I'd argue he'd have been misplaced anywhere. And would he have written his masterpieces without that form to write against? I doubt it.

The results—well, they're as impossible as the foregoing suggests. Theodore Sturgeon's best stories are triumphant Golems. They stride tall while they shake off the entreaties of the clay of the battleground of which they were formed. They have nothing but their voices.

—Jonathan Lethem
Brooklyn, New York

A Crime for Llewellyn

He had a grey little job clerking in the free clinic at the hospital, doing what he'd done the day he started, and that was nineteen years back. His name was Llewellyn, and Ivy Shoots called him Lulu.

Ivy took care of him. He'd lived with Ivy ever since she was an owlish intellectual with an uncertain, almost little girl look about her and he was a scared, mixed up adolescent wilting in the interim between high-school and his first job. Ivy was in several senses his maiden experience—first date, first drink, first drunk, and first hangover in a strange hotel in a strange city accompanied by a strange girl. Strange or not—and she was—she was his Secret.

A man like Lulu needs a Secret. A sheltered background consisting of positive morality, tea-cozies, spinster aunts and the violent contrast of eighteen months as a public charge—after the aunts had burned to death, uninsured—had convinced him that he was totally incapable of coping with a world in which everybody else knew all the angles. So he fell joyfully into the arrangement with Ivy Shoots and the Secret that went with it.

He was small and he was pudgy, and he wasn't bright, and his eyes weren't too good, and the very idea of his stealing a nickel or crossing in the middle of the block was ridiculous. It seemed to him that all the men around him emanated the virtue of sin—the winks and whistles at the girls, the Monday tales (*boy did I tie one on Saturday night)*, the legends of easy conquests and looseness and casual infidelity, the dirty jokes, and the oaths and expletives—and because they seemed to have no scruples they kept their stature as men in a world of men.

In this, Lulu could easily have drowned. Only his Secret kept him afloat. He told it to no one, partly because he sensed instinctively that he would treasure it more if he kept it to himself, and partly because he knew he would not be believed even if he proved it. He could listen contentedly to the boasting of the men he envied, thinking *if you only knew!* and *you think that's something!* hugging to himself all the while the realization that not one among them had committed the enormity of living in sin as he was doing.

When he first went to work at the hospital, he was the youngest clerk in the crowd. He had felt enormously superior to the other sinners who with all their triumphs had not been able to dye themselves as black as he had succeeded in doing. As the years went by, and he became one of the older ones, he patronized the young ones instead and pitied his contemporaries.

All this, of course, took place in his most inward self. On the surface he was an inconspicuous individual who was laughed at when noticed—which was seldom—and he took both the laughter and the anonymity as envious compliments. *You don't know it and you'd never guess, but you're talking to a pretty gay dog.*

Life with Ivy was, in some respects, as methodically guarded, as hedged about with limitations as his infancy with the aunts had been. In all their years together it never occurred to him that there was anything very unusual about the fact that they never entertained at home nor, for that matter, went anywhere together. She had her friends, and he had his acquaintances, and they seldom discussed them.

As a matter of fact they talked about very little. Ivy Shoots was a statistical typist, a strange breed to begin with. She was capable of meticulous accuracy without concentration and she spent her days rapidly typing long lists of bond issues and proofing drafts of catalogue numbers and patent listings.

She would arrive home within a few seconds of 5:45 each evening. Lulu, who went to work at six in the morning, would be waiting, with no variation in the pattern. Unvaryingly the potatoes would be on to boil. He had done the marketing; she cooked. They ate; he washed up. It was all very painless and almost completely automatic. He had eight shopping lists and she had eight menus, so that by using one each day they never ate the same food on successive Wednesdays.

He took out the laundry on Mondays, the dry-cleaning on Tuesdays and picked both bundles up on Fridays. She made the bed and handled all of the money. He dusted and swept and put the garbage out. On Saturday mornings she left the house at eight. Sunday evenings precisely at nine she returned.

He spent Saturday mornings cleaning the house, Saturday afternoons at the movies (a children's matinee, with 5 Cartoons 5), and all day Sunday listening to the radio tuned in loud. Ivy couldn't abide the radio, so out of consideration for her he used earphones on weekday evenings. And on weekday evenings she read novels—each a book club selection—from the lending library in the drugstore downstairs.

There were two things in all his life with her which he never opened. They were his pay envelope and the black steel box on the night table. Opening the first was unthinkable, and the second impossible, since she kept the key on a ribbon around her neck. Each of these closed matters was indicative of the total way her mind worked.

She pooled her wages with his pay envelope and kept track of every penny. Lulu neither smoked nor drank. He walked to and from work and brought his lunch in a paper bag. He had no use for cash and—except for his movie money on Saturdays—never touched it. Laundry and groceries were handled by monthly bill—and paid for by mail. It is the literal truth that on nine hundred and ninety-one successive weeks he never once broke the seal on his pay envelope.

There was nothing in such self-control not compatible with the effortless routine of his life, and he put all temptation behind and away from him—along with U.S. foreign policy, baseball games, and the mating of the sapsucker, Ivy's whereabouts on weekends, and all the other world's works in which he did not participate. Perhaps it would be more correct to say he simply filed it away, not so much forgotten as simply unremembered.

So life proceeded for nineteen years while wars and seasons crept by unnoticed, touching him no more than ambition or variety did. His life was a quiet succession of children's matinees, with 5 Cartoons 5, of work in the morning and potatoes to peel at five in the afternoon, and, it may even be noted, the perfunctory performance, in the speechless dark, on three Tuesdays and three Fridays in each month, of an activity most essential to his secret status.

Evening after quiet evening was spent simply with the radio droning through the earphones into Lulu's lethargic and semi-conscious mind, while Ivy Shoots sat across the room from him in a straight-backed chair with her novel in one hand and her balsam inhalator—she was perpetually entering or leaving a head-cold—in the other. Whether or not they were happy is an argument for people who like definitions, but it can hardly be denied that a good many of the less restricted are unhappier than Lulu Llewellyn and Ivy Shoots.

In the nineteenth year of their arrangement, Ivy Shoots had a sort of colic of the conscience. Maybe it had something to do with the poor-man's Yoga she was hobbying at the time—a pseudo-mystic cult which dictated that the higher self, being chained to earth by lies and sin, must confess All to be cleaned and truly free itself. Anyway, she started to brood, and she brooded for three days and nights, and then one evening she began breathing hard—which made her cough—and at last came out with it: "Lulu, you're a good man. A *really* good man. You've never done anything wrong in your whole life. You couldn't. So you needn't be ashamed."

Lulu was, of course, no end startled. He pushed back his left earphone and blinked. "I'm not ashamed," he said. Then, in utter amazement, he watched her leap up, and go scrabbling for the key of her black box. In a moment she had opened the box and was fanning through the papers it contained. In another moment she had found the paper that was to explode a bomb-shell in Lulu's quiet life. She simply crossed the room and handed it to him.

"Well, read it," she said.

He blinked and did as he was told. And he honestly couldn't understand it, it was a legal form, apparently—all filled out with names and dates and witnesses and the like. He got as far as realizing that and then his mind refused to go on. He waved the paper and said inanely, "What's this?"

She expelled her breath slowly, looked up at the ceiling as if to remind herself that she could not expect him to understand all at once, and them gently took the certificate from him. She held it so that he could see it clearly, while she pointed out its significance. She explained each part to him—his signature, hers, the witnesses, the place, the official stamp, and finally the date, some nineteen years before. He nodded as each brick of structure fell into place, right up until she said, "... so you see, we were married that night." At that last point he looked up.

"No we weren't," he said. "It's some kind of mistake!"

"But I tell you we were, Lulu." She tapped the paper. "We were."

"No we weren't," he said again, but now with all of the assurance gone from his voice.

"Do you remember that night? Try to remember. Think back."

"Well, it was a long time ago."

"The very next day when you woke up there in the hotel. Start then."

"Well ..." He tapped the paper, his eyes wide, and she nodded. He said, "Oh." And after a bit, his only defense, his only reference: "Fellow on the radio said ..." He stopped, trying to remember exactly what the fellow had said. "He said you can't do that get married all at once, drinking and all."

"It happened nineteen years ago, Lulu."

Lulu sat looking at the marriage certificate. It began to blur before his eyes. He whispered, "Why did you do it, Ivy?"

"I wanted to get married, that's all. I couldn't ... do it any other way."

It wasn't really an answer to the question he had asked her, which concerned only him and an old piece of paper—not her at all. But he found he could not repeat the question and after a moment he didn't even try. She was nineteen years in the past, saying, "I was going to tell you, but I was afraid. I didn't know you, Lulu—the way I do now. I didn't know if you'd be angry or hate me, or leave, or what. I was going to tell you," she added after a pause, "but I waited so I could be sure you wouldn't be angry. And in a week ..." She closed her eyes. "... you were glad. You said that. It was the only thing bad you ever did, or thought you did. It was the only thing. And now you see you didn't do anything bad after all. I—I know it must be a shock, but . . ." She shrugged then, opened her eyes, and smiled at him.

"Well!" she said briskly, "I'm glad you know now. At least you won't have that on your conscience. You!" she added, with the completely sincere but naive fondness that often seems only a hair's breadth from scorn. "You doing *anything* bad. The very idea!"

He sat in his usual chair in his usual plump slump, with his feet in his shoes—he wiggled them to be sure—and his heart going not much faster than usual. He was all the parts of a man, alive and feeling, with the same name as before and the same weight cradled the same way on the bent springs of the same chair. Yet he could not have been more different had he become six feet tall or shrunk to midget size, or even if he had changed species and become a squirrel or a philodendron.

He just sat there wondering numbly where he had changed, and why so drastic a change seemed not to show somewhere. Something inside him had crumpled, but its precise nature eluded him. He put his hand on his round little stomach as if to find it, but everything felt the same to his touch.

Why did you do it, Ivy?

But he couldn't ask the question aloud. Instead he stood up suddenly, and because of some freak lack of control, his voice came out harsh, whiplike. "Ivy, you let me think . . ."

She whirled to face him, paling.

He was sorry his voice had done that, he was sorry he had frightened her. He was bewildered by the fact that he felt fright too. He opened his lips to speak, and saw the absolute attention her sudden fright had gained him. He knew then that his next words would be words she would never forget. They came, and they were, "I guess I might's well turn in now." He shambled past her, saw the fright leave, and the color return to her face.

"Yes, you must be tired," she said cheerfully. "I felt funny there for a second. I guess what I need is a bite to eat!" She began to trim the crusts off some bread slices and to hum a no-tune she was fond of. Lulu had heard it for so long he was unaware of whether or not he liked it. It was a random sequence of notes within a range of about

6

four tones. But unlike any other music, it was phrased not by bars nor melodic units, but by ladylike sniffs from her perpetually dripping nose.

Lulu found himself watching that nose as he slowly undressed. It was slightly bulbous at the tip, reddened and highly flexible, the results of years of blotting and mopping and repeated testing during the rare times when the drip was absent. He looked at the nose and he said to himself, *nineteen years,* and somehow that made sense to him. He got into bed and lay down to stare up at the ceiling until she retired.

She stopped by the bedroom door. She had the black box nestling in the crook of one elbow and a small sandwich in the other hand. She chewed and swallowed and then patted the black steel affectionately with the sandwich.

"Don't you ever forget, Lulu! Anybody tries to make out you did a wrong thing in your whole life, this box has all the proof in the world it's not so."

She came in and put the box down on the night table, and patted it again. She hummed for a moment longer, then took another bite out of the sandwich and said, "My, I feel so *good* now that it's in the open. Lulu, I'm filing that paper under M in the writing-desk. Don't forget—in case you ever need it for anything. It doesn't need to be in the box any more."

She washed up her things and put them on the rack to dry and after a while she came to bed. It wasn't Tuesday night or Friday night. It was Sunday night. They went to sleep without talking.

Lulu went to work on Monday. It was pretty bad. The talk was the same as every Monday and that was what made it so bad.

. . . about the ninth beer I was . . .

. . . only a high-school kid, Joe, but she . . .

. . . summagun rolled just one too many nines, so I . . .

. . . so I . . .

. . . pair of . . .

. . . Roseland . . .

Pretty bad. It washed and splashed and flooded around him, trickled away, and then came back, foaming and roaring to engulf him for the second time. He found that the Secret, in taking its departure, had left all its reflexes behind. He couldn't unlearn his defenses. Any anecdote which dealt in coarse, boastful fashion with sex, sin or scandal, he had been accustomed to counterbalance with a hidden loftiness, and from that take his pleasure.

But how could he experience pleasure when he had to remember that black steel box with its damnable certificate? Each time it happened he was emptied, and emptied again, and each time, it all had to happen again. *But we got married, we got married,* he told and told himself, and was then without sin to call his own.

Tuesday was much worse. The hairy-chested histories were fewer, of course, having nothing as eventful as a Saturday night to draw upon. But they were, by contrast, more unusual and unexpected. Lulu never knew when a charity-patient's face would appear in the grated arch above his desk, and give evidence of some riotous sin solely by its scars and contours, or drop before him some virile obscenity which he might repeat but could never hope to conceive. And when these things happened he was caught up in his hellish little chain and reflex, the lofty pleasure, the recollection and the emptying.

What made it so much worse was that, unlike Monday, Tuesday's misery continued after quitting time. To be strictly accurate, the misery *re-emerged* after quitting time, after everything else, the homecoming, the potatoes, the dinner, the dishes, the radio and the reading. His last activity with Ivy on Tuesdays—and Fridays, except for every fourth—had regularized itself into a commonplace, and destroyed all piquancies but one. And that one had been Lulu's alone, his own special creation. It was the core crystal of his Secret.

He was able to conceal the change from himself until the very moment arrived, in its usual form of two firm taps on his shoulder as he lay in bed with his back to Ivy. He immediately, and with conscious decision, shook his head. The gesture in darkness was invisible, but conveyed itself quite clearly through the bed; Ivy's response was to stop breathing for a time. When she resumed, the sniffs which punctuated it were no more frequent, but they were much fuller in body, the oboe (as it were) replacing the clarinet.

This departure from routine was demoralizing in the extreme, and brought to Lulu his first dim awareness that the future was going to be quite different from the past. A miserable hour or two later he made the further distressing discovery that he missed tormentingly that which he had just refused, such being the tyranny of the habitual.

You, too? he demanded wistfully of his body as he had for two days of his mind. *Can't you understand that it's all changed now?* Somehow his body couldn't. He lay rigid and miserable until the window-sashes showed darker than the panes, and then got up and dressed and went to work. Ivy, who frequently showed signs of life when he got up in the morning, now lay with her eyes closed, too still to be asleep.

As might have been expected, Wednesday was a quiet day containing a stretch of hell. As quitting time approached, a couple of orderlies started horsing around in the employees' locker room which adjoined Lulu's office. Custom demanded that they have but one thing on their minds and three ways of getting rid of it—through comedy, insult, and loud-mouthed boasting. The location of their lockers—diagonally across from each other in the big room—made them fire their expletives at the tops of their voices. The position of the main exit set their course inevitably past the back of Lulu's chair.

They boiled out of the locker room into the office. Lulu didn't turn to look at them, even when one said, "Do you know what we ought to do some payday? We ought to take old Llewellyn out an' get his ashes hauled."

"He wouldn't know what to look for unless you dressed it up to look like a ledger book."

"Maybe he fool you. Maybe he set so quiet around here 'cause he keepin' all he can handle around home."

Lulu did not move, and his stillness seemed to force the orderlies' attention on him. One wisecrack, one grin over his shoulder, and they would have moved away. But he had no wisecrack and he didn't know how to make a grin. He could only sit still with his back to them.

"Nah. I'll tell you somethin'. He just ain't alive. Man don't chase a little ain't really livin'."

The uproarious laugh. Apparently the heartiness of their mirth was a good substitute for the missing reaction from Lulu, for they turned abruptly and moved to the exit.

Suddenly Lulu got to his feet excitedly. "I know what I'll do. I'll go out and pick up some actress," he told himself. And suddenly felt fine. He felt better than he had at any time since the night when he had first seen the marriage certificate. He couldn't explain why the idea had come so abruptly into his head—only that it had.

I'll pick up this actress, he told his image in the washroom mirror five minutes later. The image nodded encouragingly back at him. No matter what happens then, I'll have it to tell. Maybe I'll tell them and maybe I won't. Maybe it'll be all about how she steals my wallet and my watch, and that's funny. Or maybe it'll be about how she can't get enough of me, how she gives me her money and sells her ring.

I won't tell them a thing, he decided firmly as he left the hospital. I'll make it happen, that's all. They don't have to know. I'll know.

Halfway home he said to himself, I don't even have a wallet. I'll have to buy one first.

On the steps at home he added, a watch too.

Considerably sobered, he let himself into the apartment, hung up his jacket, and got the potatoes and the knife and a pan of water and a paper bag for the peels, and stood in front of the counter in the kitchenette.

How much money is a wallet and a watch ...

He didn't know. It would have to be a whole lot, because he'd have to have money for the actress too.

He put down the potato he was peeling and pulled on his lower lip. There was one thing he could do—he could quit going to the movies on Saturdays.

"That's a lot of Saturdays," he murmured.

The idea of holding on to his own pay envelope simply did not occur to him; anyway, when he thought about money he thought about Ivy. In fact, it took him quite a while to dispose of the very direct idea of getting the money from her simply by asking for it. He decided against that very direct solution only because he didn't think she'd have any. He just couldn't erase from his mind the picture he had of her paying out money every month for electricity and gas and other household expenses.

The amount of money that could be accumulated by two people with steady jobs and a medium-low standard of living over nineteen uninterrupted years of employment, was completely beyond his comprehension. When he began to search her writing desk it was only with some vague recollection of one of his painful overheard anecdotes at the hospital—something about a boy who was eighty cents short rummaging in his mother's purse and finding forty dollars. "Lift it from the old lady's shopping money," he murmured.

Well, there wasn't any shopping money. There wasn't a thing in Ivy's desk but painfully neat stacks of writing paper and envelopes and the file of cancelled checks cross-indexed by number, date and alphabet—he recalled the incomprehensible ritual each New Year's Day when she burned every check seven years old—little boxes of paper clips, three sizes; rubber bands, two sizes; first and fourth class package labels; bottles of ink, red and blue-black; forty-two thousand dollars in bonds, three unopened boxes of pencils, and a file of correspondence. Lulu turned away in disappointment and went back to peeling the potatoes.

He sighed and turned on the radio and went on peeling the potatoes. He heard a commercial advertising wristwatches and paused midway in his task to listen to it. The man said they started at only $49.95. That didn't sound so "only" to Lulu. That much money would amount to—uh—He closed his eyes and moved his lips while he worked it out—about two years and nine months worth of Saturday movies. After that he'd have to get a wallet, and then more money—to give to the actress. He wandered how much money you had to give actresses. Oh well. He could certainly manage to find out in the next three years, or four—or however long it took him.

Bulletin. Five-state alarm for two men who had only an hour before held up a suite of offices on High Street. The robbers had made off with four thousand in cash and negotiable bonds and twelve thousand in securities.

All that money would be enough, thought Lulu. Good heavens! Imagine it—wanting money real bad, and going out and getting it, *just like that.* Imagine having a story like that to tell about yourself (whether you kept it to yourself or not.) *So I took out the gun and said all right, let's have them there securities.* He didn't quite know what securities were, but they sounded like fine things to have twelve thousand dollars invested in. Anyone with enough spunk to do a thing like that could make up for a good many years of sinlessness.

He wouldn't have to wait around for years counting every penny until he had enough money set aside to pick up an actress. (Much of Lulu's radio listening was in mid-afternoon, and the disruptive elements in the lives of decent people in the serials was very frequently an actress.) Matter of fact, if you could steal like that, you wouldn't even need the actress. The stealing would be sin enough. *All right, you, let's have those negotiable bonds.* He didn't know what bonds were either. And he didn't have a gun.

Suddenly his hands stopped moving and he looked down at them and the long curl of potato skin depending from the paring-knife, and he said aloud, "I do so know what bonds are and I don't even need a gun."

At half past two on Thursday afternoon he was standing timidly at the edge of a wide expanse of polished marble inside the First National Bank. He no longer carried the folder next to his skin, with his undershirt and outer shirt tucked over it. (Ivy had said, as he left, "Lulu, I do believe you're putting on more weight.") He had secured one of the hospital's big manila envelopes and crammed the bonds into it. The envelope was wet now where his hand grasped it. He peered all around and just didn't know what to do.

A man in a policeman's uniform—but grey instead of blue—crossed over to where Lulu was standing. He had a gun. "Can I help you, sir?" he asked.

Lulu swallowed heavily and tried to say, "I got some bonds." But no sound came out. He coughed and tried again.

"You want to talk to somebody about some securities," the guard almost miraculously divined.

Lulu managed to nod. The guard smiled and said, "All right, sir. Just step this way."

Lulu followed the guard to a low shiny wall with a mahogany gate that swung open both ways. Beyond the gate was an area containing a half-dozen desks and a half-dozen chairs, all very far apart like small islands in a big river. The guard pointed at one of the chairs beside one of the desks.

"Just sit down there, sir. Mr. Skerry will take care of you in a moment."

The guard turned away.

Lulu sidled through the gate, wondering with mounting alarm what "take care of" might lead to, and sat down on the edge of the chair with the envelope on his lap. The man behind the desk was huge. He had snow-white hair and ice-blue eyes and nobody in the world could have had a collar that clean. He finished doing something with a ruled card on the desk and then hit the card hard with a rubber stamp. Then he looked at Lulu, who shrank under the impact of a truly frightening smile. The man asked, "What can I do for you?"

"Uh," said Lulu. He dropped his eyes, saw the envelope, and remembered the bonds. He gave the envelope to the oversized Mr. Skerry.

Mr. Skerry looked at him almost accusingly before he took out the bonds, and after he took out the bonds, and a third time after he had riffled through the stack, and that final scrutiny was the worst. He said, "What are these?"

"Well," said Lulu. "Bonds."

"Hmm, I see."

Mr. Skerry took a glass-case out of his waistcoat and opened it with a snap and took out a pair of glasses and put them on. They hung to his face by biting the bridge of his nose with little gold lips. Lulu was fascinated. Mr. Skerry bent his iceberg of a head and looked at Lulu between the tops of the lenses and a frown. "Are these bonds yours?"

"Oh yes," said Lulu.

"Hmph," said Mr. Skerry to the bonds. He lifted them a little and let them fall to the desk and looked at the stack again.

"What I wanted," said Lulu timidly, "is the money."

"Oh?" said Mr. Skerry.

The phrase from the radio bulletin came to Lulu, and he pointed his finger. "They're *negotiable* bonds," he said, his voice quavering a little.

"Oh yes, they certainly are, Mr. Er-ump."

"Llewellyn," Lulu supplied.

"Llewellyn. Of course, naturally. Excuse me." Mr. Skerry picked up a yellow sheet with some very black typing on it, made three quick motions with his finger on the telephone dial, and said into the instrument, "I've got BW listing No. three seventy-eight. Is that the latest? You're sure, now? Very well." He hung up, and studied the yellow sheet, and then put it down beside the bonds and began methodically to go through them, comparing numbers on the bonds with numbers on the list. "Well," he said after a while, "that part's all right, anyway."

He picked up the yellow sheet again and waved it at Lulu and smiled. Over the smile his eyes were precision-aimed—as ready as a pair of steel drills. "This is the latest list of stolen bonds," he said. "We always know."

He then did nothing for a moment but watch Lulu's face. Lulu's face remained utterly expressionless, because Lulu had gone utterly numb.

"Now then, you want to liquidate all of these bonds, Mr. Llewellyn? I see. Well, I'm afraid it will take a while. If you'd be kind enough to wait over there . . ." Lulu looked up at the big clock on the wall in panic. It was a minute or so of the bank's closing time. A brassy clang had started echoes all up and down the vast marble interior, and when he glanced towards the big door where he had came in he saw that the brass gates had been closed. The guard was herding people out a smaller door at the side of the building.

"Oh dear, I can't. I can't," he gasped. "I've got to get the potatoes on!"

"Miss Fisher," said Mr. Skerry flatly.

Startled, Lulu said, "What?"

But before he could make a more disastrous blunder a homely ageless fat girl with thick glasses appeared at the other end of the desk and said, "Yes, sir?"

"Take these bonds and list the numbers on a receipt for Mr. Llewellyn here," said Mr. Skerry. "Mr. Llewellyn, can you come back tomorrow at about this time? We'll have everything taken care of by then." He added quickly, as if to override a protest (which Lulu would not have dared to interpose) "Not today, not today. There just isn't time. These things take a while, you understand? Miss Fisher, get his address. You can wait over there," he said to Lulu and pointed with his frown.

Lulu went 'over there,' which was a long leather bench against the opposite wall. Near it was a much smaller desk than Mr. Skerry's, where Miss Fisher sat enthroned. In front of her was an electric typewriter. She had the bonds at her elbow and was turning them over one by one with her left hand while her right danced frantically and apparently unnoticed on the top rows of keys.

Lulu watched her with awe. She had a flexible bulbous nose almost exactly like Ivy's, and he felt comforted. The tip of Miss Fisher's nose was the only remotely familiar thing in this cold busy place.

Much sooner than he would have thought possible, she was finished. She took down his name and home address and work address and asked him if he had a car registration—which gratified him— or any identification at all. He showed her his pay signature card, and she seemed satisfied. Then the guard with the grey uniform let him out the small door, and he hurried home to peel the potatoes.

It took Mr. Skerry just three phone calls and forty minutes of his costly time to discover the identity of the bonds' rightful owner. Shortly after that Ivy Shoots sat in the chair at the end of his desk. He had to tell her three times in a row and then show her the bonds before she could believe her ears.

Lulu got up and dressed as quietly as he could. Maybe the difference was all in him, but Ivy had seemed painfully quiet all evening and he didn't like it and he wanted to get out of the apartment before he had to talk to her. But he got only as far as the bedroom door when her voice brought him up short.

"Lulu."

Slowly he turned back. He said, "I'm late already. It's half past . . ."

"That's all right. I want to talk to you." She turned on the lamp on the night table. "Lulu, anything to do with money, you ought to ask me first."

He didn't say anything. He found that he felt no fear, but only a fierce secret happiness. The money wasn't important, getting caught wasn't important. The important thing was stealing the bonds, and she couldn't change that. He hoped she would hurry up and get through accusing him, because he wanted to be at his cage at the hospital. He wanted to hear the people all around him talking, and be able to say silently, how long has it been since you stole three and a half pounds of negotiable bonds?

"It was really too silly of you. You just don't understand these things, Lulu. Do you know you came *that* close"—she showed him how close with a thumb and forefinger—"to getting arrested for *stealing* those bonds?"

Lulu made no reply, offered no defense. He simply poked out his lower lip and looked at his shoes. He didn't know what to say.

"You told yourself I was keeping all that money for myself, didn't you?" she said. "Isn't that what you thought?"

He remained silent.

"Oh dear, I suppose I can't blame you. I just never dreamed you'd misunderstand and you never said anything. It seemed the best way. You've got to believe me, Lulu! You do believe me?" She looked at him and sniffed unhappily, and blew her nose. "No—I guess you don't. Wait—I'll prove it."

He looked at her, and what she read in his face he had no way of knowing. But she scrabbled at her throat so roughly and suddenly that she tore off one of her shoulder-straps. She pulled out the key to the steel box by its ribbon, and put it in the keyhole and opened the box, and took out the top paper without looking at what she was doing and gave it to him.

"You take this with you when you go back there this afternoon, and give it to Mr. Skerry. He's a nice man, and he'll take care of everything."

Lulu looked down at the paper, and then quickly back at her. "It's called an assignment form. It signs over most of the bonds to you, Lulu. They're yours. Don't you understand? I worked it out to the penny—how much I've made, how much you've made, and all the expenses we shared. That's your money, Lulu. Only you've got to believe I wanted you to have it all along."

He looked at the assignment form, and slowly put it away in his breast pocket with the receipt that Miss Fisher had given him at the bank.

"You could have gone to jail, Lulu, you silly. For stealing your own money. Imagine you—*stealing!*"

He looked at her and at the black box. Suddenly he began to tremble. Something about him made Ivy pick up the bed-clothes and clutch them to her breast. "Lulu!"

He whirled and ran out. He was panting even before he began to run. He pursed up his lips painfully and his cheeks went round and flat, round and flat, like a little plump bellows. His eyes began to water and his throat hurt him.

He hadn't stolen anything. He felt cheated, betrayed, lost.

And Mr. Skerry was nicer to him on Friday afternoon than any-one had ever been since his aunts died. He told Lulu that he now possessed a very respectable sum of money which he'd do well to—direct quote—"let that fine woman take care of for you." When he got no reaction from Lulu—who had gone numb again—he sighed and helped him deposit most of the money in a savings account and some of it in a checking account.

He even showed him how to make out a check and keep up the stubs. He really took a lot of trouble over Lulu, who absorbed per-haps a fifth of what he was saying and ultimately escaped into the sunlight again.

He found Friday's shopping list and blindly went through the routine of marketing and getting home, the stairs, the key, the putting away of the groceries. Then he went into the living room and sat, or collapsed, into his chair in the corner by the radio.

He was confused and despairing, lost especially in the once securely-blueprinted stretches of the future. More than anything else, he wanted back what he had lost—this apartment, this routine, Ivy's protective handling of everything. His hand strayed to the radio dial but he could not switch it on because of the envelope which was propped against it. The envelope had his name on it in Ivy's quick accurate handwriting. Wondering, he tore it open and unfolded the sheet of letter paper within and squared himself away to read the communication through. He read every word in quick succession without grasping the letter's meaning at all. He was just getting the feel of the words the first time around. Then he started over, reading each sentence slowly for the meaning alone.

Dear Lulu:

I am going away right from work today instead of tomorrow morning. So don't do so many potatoes and be sure to put my half of the liver in the freezer part.

I am going away early this week because I want to think about things. What happened about the bonds opened my eyes a whole lot, and I have to look around with my eyes open. You must believe me when I say I never meant to keep the savings away from you. You have got to believe me. Please. It's just that in arranging everything to suit myself I never thought you might feel hurt and not understand. It was all done to make everything simple for you but now I want to arrange everything to make it fair. I am very sorry Lulu. Don't worry if what I'm saying doesn't make sense right now. It will later. You'll see.

Lulu please, please don't do anything silly. Don't go away and leave me whatever you do. You don't know how to take care of yourself. If you want to go later, well, all right. But give me a chance to teach you how to do for yourself. I am so afraid you will get yourself into some awful trouble.

Lulu you are a good person, a very good person who could not do a bad thing if you tried. I don't like myself very much just now, and I am not surprised if you don't either. I want to help you and do some things over I have done wrong. So please don't go away. I'll be worried sick. Believe me about the bonds, it's the truth. Now you have your share you can believe me, can't you? Only just don't go away anywhere.

Ivy

The last paragraph contained several crooked lines and words crossed out here and there and squinched up so that reading them took time. Lulu read the last part four times, and then he drew down the paper and glared at the radio. "I am not!" he barked in the same furious voice with which he had frightened Ivy by accident once.

... *a very good person who could not do a bad thing if you tried.* "I am *not!*" he shouted for the second time. He stamped across the room and back again, and what he felt uncurling somewhere in the region of his solar plexus was a new thing, a frightening thing. It was anger—and nothing that he had ever experienced in his entire life up to that instant had made him feel enraged before.

He scooped up the letter and glared at it. Next to that one infuriating statement—which he again denied out loud—the only other thing the letter had to say to him was the desperate, pleading request that urged him not to go away.

Leaving Ivy—leaving the only home he had—was something that would never have crossed his mind in thirty years' trying. But when Ivy said it, and said it over and over, it exploded inside him. "I will so," he told the piece of paper solemnly. "I will so leave."

And he did. He really did. He filled two paper shopping bags with his clothes and left on Saturday afternoon instead of going to the movies as he had planned. He got a furnished room right across the street from the hospital and down the street from the bank and up the street from the movies.

On Monday they called him in to the main office arid sat him down, in front of a telephone with the receiver off. He picked the receiver up and listened to it, and sure enough it was Ivy, calling him up at work for the very first time. She sounded terrible, with her squeaky pleading, her frequent sobbing, and another one of her head colds. He just listened in complete silence until there was a pause, unable to think of anything to tell her that would make even a little sense to himself.

He finally said, "No, no, I can't. You hear, I can't no more." He put the receiver on its cradle and sat there looking at it. He found he was trembling. He thought he ought to tell her at least that he wasn't sick or in any awful trouble. He picked up the phone again but it only buzzed at him. Ivy was gone out of it. He recradled the receiver.

The hospital cashier glanced at him, and then came over. "Anything wrong?" he asked.

Lulu stood up and wiped his upper lip with the hack of his hand. "I can take care of myself," he said almost belligerently.

"Why, sure you can," said the cashier, backing off a pace. "You just didn't look so good, that's all."

"Well, I'm not going back there," said Lulu.

"Okay, okay," said the cashier, holding up placating hands. "I just wanted to help."

"No sense ever asking me no more," said Lulu. He shambled back to the receiving desk, leaving a very puzzled young man staring after him.

For a few weeks, getting adjusted to living alone took up so much of Lulu's life and thoughts that he had no time for his sins. Living in furnished rooms and eating in restaurants are not always completely simple matters even to the intelligent, and Lulu was a babe in. the woods almost from the first. Keeping cash on his person was a habit he found complicated and very difficult to acquire.

He used his checkbook constantly, for a ten-cent cup of coffee, a sandwich, and once even for a newspaper so he could check the radio programs. Finally the manager of the restaurant where he ate came over to him with a sheaf of his checks and asked him plaintively to cut it out.

"Write a big one any time, and keep the cash in your pocket and use what you want. Okay? You got my girl spendin' a hour and a half every week listin' your checks in the deposit slip."

Lulu blushed painfully and promised to do better. To his amazement he found that he could. He tried the same thing at the grocery, where he had been writing a check every night for two soft rolls and six slices of liverwurst for his lunch. He wrote a check for ten dollars, and used the cash for a week. The proprietor was pleased and even increased the thickness of the liverwurst slices as a token of his esteem.

He passed Ivy twice in the street. She did not speak to him, and he was speechless even at the thought of her.

His new life wove in one unexpected thread. The second day of his liberation he was in a booth in the restaurant, and had just finished his soup when he became aware of someone standing next to the table. He looked up and there was Miss Fisher from the bank.

She said timidly, "I do beg your pardon. But I thought perhaps you wouldn't mind if I shared this table with you. There are no other seats in the restaurant ..."

He got up hastily and made room at the little table and saw that she had the salt and he even stacked her cafeteria tray on top of his out of the way. When she was organized she looked at him with a wan thank-you smile that became recognition. "Why, it's Mr. Llewellyn!"

He didn't say anything more to her that evening—he couldn't. But the next night she was there ahead of him and when he came along with his tray, she called out to him and patted the table across from her. After that they always had dinner together. She was quiet and nice, and she let him be silent for as long as he wanted to be.

Six or seven weeks later something happened at the hospital that made a deep impression on Lulu. A furious young female face appeared at his wicket and demanded: "Where is George Hickenwaller? Where is he? I got to see him right away."

Lulu stared dumbly until she banged the palm of her hand on the shelf by the wicket, and repeated the question. Her face started darkening ominously and the blood-vessels on the sides of her neck began to stand out in the most alarming fashion.

He remembered then. George Hickenwaller was the married orderly who had annoyed him more than most of the others—although he wasn't quite sure why. "I'll find him. Just wait a minute," he promised. He got up, and went over to the doorway of the locker room, and saw at once that George Hickenwaller was in there with his back to the wall. He was making wild signals of distress and prayer, and moving his mouth strangely, giving vent to some exaggerated, silent, pleading syllables which Lulu could not understand.

He went back to his wicket. "He's in there," he said, thumbing at the door.

"In there, is he?" said the young woman. She turned angrily to the man behind her. Lulu saw that the man was a policeman. "He's in there," she relayed.

"In there, is he?" the policeman countered. He ran around to the front, to the general office door, and went sprinting across behind Lulu and into the locker room.

There came sounds of the chase and a cry for mercy, and then poor Hickenwaller was walked abjectly out by the policeman. The big, red-faced cop had a meaty hand on his collar and another in the back of his belt.

Quite a crowd had gathered by this time and Lulu found himself standing next to Hickenwaller's friend, the other orderly. This man shook his head sadly. "I tol' him he wasn't goin' to get away with it. 'I know what I'm doin',' he says. 'I got it made.'" The orderly shook his head again. "He got it made *now* all right, but good."

"What did he do?" Lulu asked.

"Got married."

"To that one?" Lulu pointed at the angry woman, who was ducking under the policeman's guard to punch Hickenwaller solidly on the ear.

"Yeah, an' another one too. I tol' him she'd find out."

"Two wives?"

"Bigamy," said the orderly knowledgeably.

"Is that very bad?" Lulu asked, really wanting to know.

The orderly cocked his head and squinted at him. "Lew old man, let me tell you. *One* is very bad."

"Yes, but this—uh—bigamy. It's *really* bad, huh."

"No way to get to heaven."

"Well," said Lulu, and got back to work.

Dinnertime, comfortable with Miss Fisher in the booth. He wondered why she seemed so glad to have dinner with him all the time. What did she get out of it. He didn't ask her. But he continued to wonder.

"Oh, *there* you are!" someone said at his elbow. It was the manager. He half-filled the booth and loomed over them. "I thought I had all the trouble with you I was goin' to," he growled at Lulu.

Lulu went speechless. He made himself smaller in his seat, while Miss Fisher looked frightened at the manager and anxious at Lulu.

The manager banged a check with a bank slip stapled to it, banged it down directly in front of Lulu. "After all that trouble, now they're bouncing."

Lulu didn't know what to say. Miss Fisher stared at him, while the manager continued to glare. People began to crane and peer at them. Lulu slipped down another notch in his seat.

Suddenly Miss Shelly Fisher snatched up the check, "Just a minute, Mr. Grossman," she said firmly, "I'm sure this can be straightened out. Mr. Llewellyn, didn't you make a large deposit at the First National just a few weeks ago?"

Lulu nodded.

"Have you put any more money in the checking account since then?"

He shook his head sheepishly. "I didn't know I had to," he mumbled.

"Well, have you taken anything out of the savings account?"

He shook his head. Miss Fisher said, "I'll vouch for him, Mr. Grossman. He just isn't used to a checking account yet. He has a good balance in savings. You can take my word for it."

"You work at the bank?"

"You've seen me there."

He nodded slowly. "Well, all right then," he growled. He picked up the check and waved it in front of Lulu's nose. "You take care of it by this time tomorrow, you hear?"

"Of course he will. Of course," said Miss Fisher soothingly. She put her hand over Lulu's as he slipped yet another inch down in his chair, which put the table about breast-high to him. Grossman went away.

"It's all right now," she said. "It's all right. Sit up, Mr. Llewellyn."

He did, shamefaced. "I didn't know," he said feebly.

"You'd better let someone look over your checkbook. Do you want me to?"

"It's home," he said, regretfully, feeling that the simple statement had disposed of the matter.

"I don't mind," she said, surprisingly. "I have nothing else to do."

"You mean, you'd come to . . ."

She nodded while he fought his unwilling tongue. After a moment she got up. "Come on," she said.

Unbelievingly he followed her out of the restaurant, and then led the way to his rooming house.

The room was so small he had to sit on the bed if she was going to sit at the table. He kept it neat enough, but places that crummy are unconquerable. He found the checkbook and gave it to her. She riffled through the stubs, finding not a single entry.

"Well," she said, "No *wonder!*" Very carefully she explained to him how he must keep his record in the stubs and make an effort not to let checks bounce. He nodded humbly every three seconds while she talked. She did it kindly and did not laugh at him, or sneer.

"Yes, Mr. Skerry told me. I guess it didn't stick."

"*Lots* of people don't understand it at first."

This is a very fine lady, he told himself, and wished he could say it out loud.

"What are those?" She pointed to the top of the chest, where eleven cash envelopes lay in a neat row.

"Oh, that's my paydays," he said.

She picked one of the envelopes up, pressed it, shook it, and finally read the data typed on it. "Cash, my goodness. They pay you in cash. You shouldn't leave cash around."

He could only manage to get out a faltering, "I'm sorry."

"My, you do need someone to look after you." She counted the envelopes. "Don't you see, if you put these in your checking account every week you'd always have money to write checks against?"

He didn't see. He just waved at the envelopes and said unhappily, "I just never knew *what* to do with 'em."

He intercepted her look of astonishment and said abjectly, "I never could understand all this. You want to help me with it?"

So Miss Fisher began taking care of Lulu Llewellyn.

He began to be happier. Yet his relationship with Miss Fisher was so innocent, and she herself so different from any woman he'd ever met that some of his old torment began to return, and he found himself cringing again under the assault of other people's sins. Now, however, as his philosophy of sin began a slow evolution, there was a slightly different reaction. Instead of considering himself totally unfit and excluded, he began to match what he knew of himself against each of the sins he heard recounted. Could I do *that*? Could he ever gamble? Seduce? Steal, swear, assault, outwit? Always no and no and no, and the words in Ivy's letter trailing across his clear conscience: *a very good man who couldn't do a bad thing if he tried.*

And then one day he saw the face of Hickenwaller's friend go past his wicket—just that, a reminder. And belatedly, as all things did, the solution came to Lulu Llewellyn.

He went to Miss Fisher and asked her, and she cried. Then she said yes, she would marry him. Then she cried again and said pathetically that she had made up her mind when she was eight years old that nobody would ever want her and she might as well face it.

So they went down to City Hall and got a license, and three days later they were married. He chittered and jittered like the most eager of grooms. He was eager about something else than that which plagues most grooms, however, and it was more important—to him, at least.

That very evening he marched to Ivy's apartment and up the one flight of stairs. It made him feel a little strange to be knocking on the door instead of using his key, but somehow he felt that he should knock, that he owed her that courtesy. He waited happily, feeling the crackling comfort of the marriage license in his breast pocket.

The door opened.

"Lulu! Oh—Lulu, I'm so glad." She looked worn, sallow-cheeked, but her eyes were shining. She pulled him inside and shut the dear. "I just knew you'd come back. I just knew you would, you had to."

He cleared his throat. "I . . ."

"Don't talk. Don't say anything. I've had a chance to think things out clearly. And oh, Lulu, it's all so senseless and I'm so sorry."

"But I didn't . . ."

"Don't say another word. You're going to listen to me now. I've waited too long. You just stay right there where you belong."

Half playfully but very firmly she nudged him over to his old chair and crowded him until he had to sit down.

"I won't be a second," she said, and ran out of the room. He sat there, his backsides liking the old chair, and thought excitedly. You're the first. Miss Fisher—she's the second. He wondered how that would sound if he ever told it at the hospital. He put the speculation aside to think about later.

After a moment she came out of the bedroom carrying the black metal box. "I'm not a stupid woman, Lulu," she said. "Really I'm not. I read and I think and I can keep my end up when I talk with well-educated people. But sometimes the brightest of us can be more stupid than the slowest witted. Well, anyway, I'll admit it. I finally had to talk it out with someone. I did, Lulu—and I got the answer." She inserted the key in the box, turned it, raised the black metal lid. "He's a dear man, a brilliant man. He's a psychiatrist. I told him everything, but you mustn't worry about that, Lulu. They're like *priests*. Anyway, I didn't even tell him your name."

She rummaged in the box and found a paper and began to gesture with it while she talked.

"There it was, right in front of my silly old eyes, and I never even saw it. He explained to me that it was *terribly* important to you to thank we were living together *without* being married. He said it made a man of you. He said you had been very strictly brought up and that you had—well, he called it a 'black-and-white' morality. He said you took it so seriously when you were a child that you had nothing at all on the black side—not so much as cheating on a school examination, or hitting a puppy in your whole life. That's why, he said, when I finally told you that our living together was a 'white' thing, and had been from the beginning, it was a terrible blow to your self-confidence. You just couldn't stand it."

"Now I'm going to tell you something I never thought I'd ever tell to a living soul. I was on my own when I was fourteen, and I always had to think things out for myself. Sometimes I did well at that, and sometimes I failed. But I always thought things out for myself first—not for laws or anyone else or customs or anything like that, but just for myself alone. Well, never mind all that now. One of the main things was—I thought I had to have freedom. I made up my mind I'd do what I wanted with whom I wanted, just as long as I was discreet. As long as I put a partition that was like a high wall between the one thing and the other. You don't understand this, do you? Well, that's all right, You'll understand all you need to in just one more minute."

"Didn't you ever wonder what I did with my weekends for nineteen years, Lulu? Didn't you *care?*"

He started to answer, but she gave him no chance. "No; I don't suppose it ever occurred to you to wonder. It was just the way things were—like water running downhill and the sun coming up. You knew I was going to be away Saturday and Sunday, and you just accepted it. Poor Lulu! Well. I see I've get to tell you then. I was taking a course in economics for a while. Let me see that would be about six years ago. Oh, I've done all sorts of things on weekends—and anyway, there was this man. You see, and I don't know what happened to me at all, but I'd never felt like that in my life before. And I guess I never will again," she added in a whisper, tragically.

Then she blew her nose. "I have the most awful cold, Lulu. I think I'm a bit feverish. So there I was, feeling like that about this man, you see, and for a while I thought he might feel the same way about me. So I saw a lawyer and showed him my papers, and I got this. Here, Lulu, this is yours. This is for you." She handed him the paper.

The whole episode was so reminiscent of the one which had blasted his quiet life once before that he took the paper without even glancing at it. He simply closed his eyes, and got up and stood trembling, waiting for he knew not what.

She understood and laughed happily. Then she coughed, and laughed again and took the paper away from him. "You're afraid of it, and I don't blame you. Here, I'll read it to you." Her hand touched his, and he felt the paper slip out of his fingers.

"'There came before me in the County Court in the township of . . .' Oh, let's skip all that lawyers' talk. Here it is. 'Therefore by weight of evidence in camera'—that means secret and confidential—'the marriage of said L. Llewellyn and said Ivy Shoots is hereby annulled and held to be void and without existence.'"

She pushed the paper triumphantly back into his lap. "You understand that, Lulu? It isn't a divorce. A divorce says a marriage was and is no more. This says that in the eyes of the law and in my eyes, Lulu, and in your eyes, Lulu, the wedding never took place. You see? You see? So if that was what was bothering you, it needn't any longer. It's gone. We're without benefit of clergy if that's how you'd like it to be. We can call it common-law if you want that instead. Lulu I just don't know—?"

He lay in a pressing welter of thoughts and scraps of thoughts. The one which came swirling to the top first had to do with the nature of the certificate in a modern culture. The thought wasn't quite that lucid in him, of course. He saw the blasting of his painless existence by a piece of paper. He saw people breaking the law and being broken by it—a piece of paper for each. A piece of paper for everything you did or didn't do, even the things which were truly and really done, just by changing the paper.

"Lulu," she whispered, "If you should want to—you can even m-marry someone else. You're free to do that, to hurt me that much if . . ." And then she began to cough. The wracking, all-too-familiar quality of the cough made him shift uneasily in his chair, and over his heart his new marriage license crackled gently.

Somewhere deep within him stirred the bitter, despairing thought that he was going to have to pick up an actress after all. Pick one up and marry her—or he would never be a bigamist. He put his knuckles slowly up to his forehead and closed his eyes. He stood like that for a long time while his lips tried futilely to shape words. Finally a half-sentence came. "Think about," he said. He went to the door. "Think about it, I'll . . . think about it."

"Come back . . . soon," she said. "It's not—good here now, Lulu. I didn't know what I—well, come back soon." She did not accompany him to the door. He knew she was going to cough, or cry, or let go again in some even more distressing way. He got out quickly.

Lulu went upstairs to the pharmacy and said, "Joe, I don't sleep so good."

Joe said, "How long you want to sleep?"

"Just once, twelve hours. Like a cold shower couldn't wake me up."

"Can do, Lew. Take two of . . ."

"That's the trouble, Joe. Pills choke me up. You got powder that don't taste so bad?"

"I got better'n that. I got a liquid don't taste at all. Only, Lew, don't talk it around, right?"

"Me? Joe, I wouldn't do that."

"That's good. That's fine, Lew."

An hour later Lulu said, "Drink your milk."

Obediently, Shelly Fisher Llewellyn drank her milk. She was quite unhappy for a four-week bride. For the time being she was trying to escape from her unhappiness by doing everything she could think of that might please her husband. Lulu got up and stretched. "I don't know what you're going to do, but I'm going to turn in," he said. "Don't come now if you don't want to. Good night."

"Oh," she said, "I'll come."

He embraced her while she fell asleep. He said, "I'm going to hold you just like this all night long."

Just after two in the morning he silently mounted the steps at Ivy's place and let himself in with his key. She never had asked him for the key and never would. The chain lock wasn't on either.

He was wearing gloves and sneakers. It was dark inside and he was as quiet as all the rest of it. He knew where it creaked and where it bumped. He drifted through the place and into the bedroom like a searching of wind.

She was peacefully in bed on her back, her lips slightly parted.

He couldn't really see her, but he could sense her there, lying very, very still.

He got the second pillow, *his* pillow, from the bed, just the way he had thought about it. She wasn't touching it with her cheek or left hand, and she didn't stir when he lifted it away. Very carefully he tucked the end of the pillow under his chin, so that it hung down over the front of his chest like a bib. Then he fell across the bed with the pillow over her face and leaned his whole weight on it, with both hands pulling upwards on the bed rail. Far a couple of seconds it was as if the woman and the bed and even the floor were fighting back, but it passed quickly. He clung there, heavy on her, for a long time, till he was sure.

Panting, he rose and stood and held his breath and listened. The whole world was asleep.

It's done, he said silently. She always had an answer in her black box, she always made me lose. But I fooled her. Now I've done the biggest one of all.

The box. There it was. He crossed to it and tried the lid, feeling sure it would be locked. To his surprise, it wasn't.

He opened it. There was only one paper in it.

He began to tremble. If she'd had one paper she'd kept away from him, he told himself, it was a paper he didn't want to see. He took it in the dark and carried it to the bathroom and tore it into fragments and flushed it away.

Then he left—not by the front door, but by the fire escape. He left the bedroom window open and the lower section of the fire escape lowered—swung down and held by a tilted ash can.

When he got back to his room he undressed quickly, silently, and climbed into bed. He was exalted, beside himself, a giant. Shelly said in the morning, very shyly, "Quite a man, aren't you?"

The detective sergeant had an old face and brand new eyes. He came to Lulu's window at the hospital and peered through the bars and said, "You're Llewellyn?"

Lulu said: "That's my name."

"Where were you at last night?" the detective asked.

"Home; asleep."

"Well, that's all right. We checked already. You got an ex-wife who called herself Ivy Shoots?"

Whatever showed on Lulu's face must have looked all right to the detective, for he paused for only an instant before he said: "Well, she's dead."

I killed her, said Lulu. But to his own amazement he didn't say it aloud. He wanted to, but somehow he couldn't. He couldn't say anything.

"Don't take it so hard," said the detective. "We all got to go some time. What I want to know is—you goin' to plant her? The doctor, he didn't know who to notify, so he called us. We had to go through her stuff, and that's how we found your address. She didn't have much, but she left it all to you."

"Oh."

"You better get right down there, and check up. Somebody broke in there last night. Only thing we can find is missing is her death certificate. The doc says he wrote one and stuck it in a lockbox beside the bed. But we found only the box."

"Death certificate?" Lulu whispered.

"Yeah, there she lays stiff as a plank, dead of pneumonia. And somebody comes in and puts a pillow over her face and swipes the exit ticket. Must've took it in the dark, thinking it was worth something. Joke on him. But you better get down there and check."

"I killed her," said Llewellyn. "I did, I killed her."

"Cut it out," said the detective.

"Well. I did," said Lulu.

'There's a nice legal duplicate piece of paper says you didn't," said the detective, and drove Lulu down to the apartment, where there were lots of people to tell him all the things he had to do. He did them and he died.

He's still working at the hospital behind his little iron grating, and he takes the laundry out on Mondays and the cleaning on Tuesdays and picks them all up on Fridays, and he has the potatoes on by the time his missus gets home from work every day. But he's dead all right.

It Opens the Sky

Opportunity knocked again, this time right on the eyeball, making him blink.

Deeming had stopped at a crosswalk—he lived in one of the few parts of town where streets still crossed on the same level and was waiting for the light to change, when on the post by his head, right at eye level, a hand appeared. It wore a thin gold band and a watch. It was the watch that made him blink. He'd seen only one like it in his life before, a beautifully made little thing with slender carved-ruby numerals and, instead of hands, the ability to make its rubies glow one at a time for the hours, and a ruddy-amber pip of light float mysteriously at the right minute. It was geomagnetically powered and wouldn't wear out or run down for a thousand years. It came from some place in the Crab Nebulae, where the smallest intelligent life form yet known to man did a brisk trade in precision engineering.

Deeming tore his gaze away from the watch and followed its wrist and arm down to its owner. Deeming was not especially fond of animals, but he categorized his women with a zoological code. They were chicks, fillies, bunnies, and dogs, in descending order of appeal.

This one was a goat.

She looked as if she had packed sixty years of living into thirty-five plus. She had half a bag on already, though it was still early in the evening, which accounted for her holding the pole up while she waited with him for the light to change. She had not noticed him, which was fine, and he acted just as abstracted as she was.

I'll give it two hours, he thought, and then, as she sagged slightly and caught her balance too quickly and too much, as befits any drunk passing through dignity on the way to sloppiness, he made it ninety minutes. That watch is mine in ninety minutes. Bet?

The light changed and he strode out ahead of her. Just past the corner he stopped to look in a display window and see her reflection as she approached, stiff but listing a bit to port. He let her pass him and then to his delight saw her step into a cocktail bar. He went the other way, rounded the corner, entered a restaurant, and went straight back to the men's room. He had it to himself for the moment, and a moment was all he needed. Off came the stiff, clipped moustache; out came the golden-brown contact lenses, so that now his eyes were blue. He combed the parting out of his flat black hair and set up waves. Half-inch inserts came out of his side pockets and were slipped into his heels, to change his gait and increase his already considerable height. He took off his jacket and turned it inside out, so that he was no longer drab and monochrome, as befitted Mr. Deeming, second assistant to the assistant desk man at the Rotoril Hotel, but sport-jacketed and cocky the way Jimmy the Flick ought to be. Jimmy the Flick always emerged and disappeared in men's rooms, not only because of their privacy, but because that was the one place you could count on not to see one of those damned Angels, who didn't eat, either.

Deeming was pleasantly certain, as he left the place, that no one had noticed him going in or Jimmy coming out. He went around the corner and into the cocktail joint.

Deeming sat on the edge of his bed, feeling glum. He tossed the watch up in the air and caught it.

It hadn't been ninety minutes after all—it had taken him nearly two and a half hours. He hadn't planned on her caring quite that much for the watch. She wouldn't take it off for him to admire and wouldn't agree that it was out of kilter and he could adjust it in just a second, so he had to use the old midnight-swim gimmick. He'd got her into the car all right, without her seeing the number plate, and he'd done a good clean job of parking by the river where it wouldn't be noticed. It was hard to judge how drunk she was. When she talked about her husband—the watch was all that she had of her husband's any more—she sobered up altogether too much, and it took a lot of oil and easy chatter to get her off the subject. But anyway he'd got the clothes off her and at last the watch, down there by the river, and then had managed to scoop up the lot and sprint back to the car before she could bleat, "Oh, Jimmy—Jimmy, you can't!" more than twice. He didn't know how she'd get back to town and it didn't worry him. He found six and a half in her pouch, and an I.D. card. He pocketed the money—it about covered the price of her drinks—and incinerated the rest of her stuff with the clothes. A good clean job, carrying the special virtue of being totally unlike anything he had ever done before; if there was anything in the cosmos that would bring a swarm of Angels down on a citizen, it was the habitual crime habitually performed. He should be proud.

He was, too, but he was also glum, and this irritated him. Both the glumness and the irritation were familiar feelings with him, and he could not for the life of him figure out why he always felt this way after a job. He had so much to be glad about. He was big and handsome and smart as an Angel—he might even say smarter; he'd been doing this for years now and they'd never come close to picking him up. Damn zombies. Some said they were robots. Some said supermen. People touched their cloaks for luck, or to help a sick child get better. They didn't eat. They didn't sleep. They carried no weapons. Just went around smiling and being helpful and reminding people to be kind to one another. There used to be police and soldiery, according to the books. Not any more. Not with the Angels popping up whenever they weren't wanted by the people concerned, with their sanctimony and their bullet-proof hides.

Sure, Deeming thought, I'm smarter than an Angel. What's an Angel anyway? Somebody with rules to abide by. (I've got a little more elbow room than that.) Somebody who is remarkable to begin with and makes himself more so with magic tricks and golden cloaks and all that jazz. (I'm an invisible clerk at a low-level fleabag, or a disappearing cockerel with a line like lightning and sticky fingers— whichever I want.)

He tossed the watch and caught it and looked at it and felt glum. He always felt glum when he succeeded, and he always succeeded. He never tried anything where he wouldn't succeed.

Maybe that's the trouble, he thought, falling back on the bed and looking up at the ceiling. I got all this stuff and never use but a fraction of it.

Never thought of it like that before.

I break all the rules but I do it by playing safe. I play it safer than a civil servant buying trip insurance for a ride on a bus. I walk under a closed sky, he thought, like a bug under a rock. Course, I put the tight lid on myself, which is better than having a lid put on, even a large lid, by society or religion. But even so ... my sky is closed. What I need, I need *reach,* that's what.

Or maybe, he thought, sitting up to glower at the watch in his hand, maybe I need a pay-off that's worth what brains and speed I put into it. How long have I been working respectably for peanuts and robbing carefully for—well, no more'n an occasional walnut?

Which reminds me, I better get this thing fenced out before that spaceman's relict finds herself a fig leaf and somebody with a whistle to blow.

He got up, slowly shaking his head in disgust and wishing that one time—just one lousy time—he could make a touch and feel as good as he had a right to feel.

He put out a hand to the door and it knocked at him.

Now, you see? he told himself out of the same sort of disgust, you see? Anybody else would freeze now, turn pale, start to sweat, throw the watch into the reclaimer, run up the wall like a rat in a box. But look at you, standing absolutely still thinking three times as fast as a Class Eight computer, checking everything, including all the things you have already done to handle just this situation—the moustache back on, the brown eyes again, the shorter stature again, the heel pads hidden in the reversible jacket and the jacket hidden in the secret panel behind the closet.

"Who is it?"

... And your voice steady and your pulse firm—yes, Deeming's voice and the pulse of innocence, not the jaunty Jimmy's tone or his rutty heartbeat. So what's to feel glum about, boy? What's the matter with you, to dislike yourself and every situation you get into, purely because you know before you start that you'll handle it so well?

"May I see you for a moment, Mr. Deeming?"

He didn't recognize the voice. That was good, or it was bad, depending. If good, why worry? And why worry if it was bad?

He dropped the watch into his side pocket and opened the door.

"I hope I'm not bothering you," said the pudgy man who stood there.

"Come in," Deeming left the door open and turned his back. "Sit down." He laughed the minor assistant's timid little laugh. "I hope you're selling something. I wouldn't be able to buy it but it's nice to have somebody to talk to for a change."

He heard the door close carefully. The pudgy man did not sit down and he did not laugh. Deeming did not care for the silence so he turned to look at the man, which was apparently what the man was waiting for. "You can have somebody to talk to," he said quietly. "You can talk to Richard E. Rockhard."

"Great," said Deeming. "Who might Richard E. Rockhard be?"

"You haven't . . . well, that isn't really surprising. When they're big, everybody knows them. When they're hiring and firing the big ones, they tend to be almost as quiet as assistant clerks, Mr. Deeming . . . You know Antares Trading? And the Lunar and Outer Orbit Lines? And Galactic Mines?"

"You mean this Rockhard is—"

"In part, Mr. Deeming. In part."

Jimmy the Flick would have bugged his eyes and made a low whistle. Deeming put his fingertips together and whispered, "Oh, my goodness."

"Well?" said the man, after waiting for something more and not getting it. "Will you come and see him?"

"You mean, Mr. Rockhard? You mean—me? You mean—now?"

"I mean all those things."

"Why does he . . . what—well, why me?" asked Deeming, with becoming modesty.

"He needs your help."

"Oh, my goodness. I don't know what I could possibly do to help a man like . . . well, can you tell me what it's about?"

"No," said the man.

"No?"

"No, except that it's urgent, it's big, and it will be more worth your while than anything you have ever done in your life."

"Oh, my goodness," said Deeming again. `What you'd better do is go find an Angel. They help people. I can't—"

"You can do things an Angel couldn't do, Mr. Deeming."

Deeming affected a laugh. It said a thousand words about the place and function of the Little Men of the world.

"Mr. Rockhard thinks you can, Mr. Deeming. Mr. Rockhard knows you can."

"He knows ... about *me?*"

"Everything," said the pudgy man, absolutely without inflection.

Deeming had a vague swift wish that he had atomized the watch after all. It seemed to be as big and as spillable and as hot as a bowl of soup wedged into his side pocket. "Better get an Angel," he suggested again.

The man glanced at the door and then took a step closer. He dropped his voice and said earnestly, "I assure you, Mr. Deeming, Mr. Rockhard will not and cannot do that in this matter."

"It sounds like something I'd better not do," said Deeming grimly.

The man shrugged. "Very well. If you don't want it, you don't want it." He turned to the door.

Deeming couldn't, for once, help himself. He blurted out, "What happens if I refuse?"

The pudgy man did not quite turn back to face him. "You promise me you will forget this interchange," he said casually, "especially if asked by one of the gentlemen in the pretty cloaks."

"And that's all?"

For the first time a glint of amusement crossed the bland features. "Except for wondering, for all the days of your life, what you might have missed."

Deeming wet his lips. "Just tell me one thing. If I go see your Mr. Rockhard, and have a talk, and still want to refuse. . . ?"

"Then of course you may. If you want to."

"Let's go," said Deeming. They were high over the city in a luxurious helicopter before it occurred to him that "If you want to," said the way the man had said it, might have many meanings. He turned to speak, but the man's face, by its very placidity, said that this was a man whose job was done and who would not add one syllable to cap it.

Richard E. Rockhard had blue-white hair and ice-blue eyes and a way of speaking that licked out and struck deep like a series of sharp skilled axe blows, cutting deep, careless of the chips. This tool's edge was honed so fine it was a gentleness. Deeming could well believe that this man was Galactic Mines and all those other things. He could also believe that Rockhard needed help. He was etched with anxiety and the scarlet webs of capillaries in his eyeballs were bloated with sleeplessness. He was a man who was telling the truth because he had not time to lie. "I need you, Deeming. I am supposing that you will help me and will speak my piece accordingly," he said, as soon as they were alone in a fabulous study in an unbelievable penthouse. "I give you my word that you will be in no danger from me unless and until you do help me. If you do proceed with it, you may be sure the danger is sizeable." He nodded to himself and said again, "Sizeable."

Deeming, the hotel clerk, got just this far with his clerkly posture: "Mr. Rockhard, I am absolutely mystified as to why you should turn to a man like me for any . . ." because Rockhard brought both hands down with a crash and leaned half across his desk. "Mr. Deeming," he said, in his gentle, edged voice, with all the power in the world throttled way back and idling at the ready, "I know about you. I know it because I needed to find such a man as you and I have the resources to do it. You may wear that common-man pose if it makes you comfortable, but do not deceive yourself that it deceives me. You are not a common man or—to put it on the very simplest terms—you would not be in this room at this moment, because the common man will not be tempted by anything which he knows offends the Angels."

So Deeming dropped the invisibility, the diffidence, the courtesy and deference of an assistant to an associate, and said, "It is hardly safe for even an uncommon man to offend them."

"You mean me? I'm perfectly safe from you, Deeming. You wouldn't report me, even if you knew I couldn't strike back. You don't *like* Angels. You never met another man before who didn't like them. Therefore you like me."

Deeming had to smile. He nodded. He thought, but when is he going to point out that if I don't help him he will blackmail me?

"I will not blackmail you," said the old man surprisingly. "I will pull you into this with rewards, not push you into it with penalties. You are a man whose greed speaks higher than his fear." But he smiled when he said it. Then without waiting for any response at all, he made his proposition.

He began to speak of his son. "When you have unlimited credit and an only son, you begin by being quite certain that you can extend yourself through him to the future; for he is your blood and bone, and he will of course want to follow in your footsteps. And if it occurs to you that he might veer from that course—it never does occur to you until late in the game, too late—then you let the situation get past curing by the smug assumption that the pressures you can put on him will accomplish what your genes could not."

"Ultimately you realize that you have a choice—not the choice of keeping or losing him; you've lost that already; but the choice of throwing him out or letting him go. If you care more for yourself and what you've built than you do for your son, you throw him out, and good riddance. I"—he stopped to wet his lips and glanced quickly at Deeming's face and back to his folded hands—"I let him go."

He was still a moment and then suddenly wrenched his hands apart and then laid them carefully and silently side by side before him. "I don't regret it, because we are friends. We are good friends, and I helped him in every way I could, including not helping him when he wanted to make his own way, and giving him whatever he asked me for whether or not I thought it was valuable." He smiled suddenly, and whispered more to his sleeping hands than to Deeming, "For a son like that, if he wants to paint his belly blue, you buy the paint."

He looked at Deeming. "The blue paint is archaeology, and I bought it for him. Dead diggings, pure knowledge, nothing that will make a dime to buy a bun with. That isn't my kind of work or my kind of thinking, but it's all Donald wants."

"There's glory," said Deeming.

"Not this trip. Now hear me out. That boy is willing to disappear, cease to exist, become nothing at all, just to follow a thread which almost certainly leads nowhere, but which, if it leads somewhere, can become only an erudite curiosity like the Rosetta stone or the Dead Sea scrolls or the frozen language in the piezo-crystals of Phygmo IV." He spread his hands and immediately put them back to bed. "Blue paint. And I bought it."

"What do you mean 'cease to exist—become nothing'? You don't mean 'die,' you mean something else."

"Good, good, Deeming. Very perceptive. What it means is that in order to pursue this Grail of his, he must expose himself to the Angels. They can't stop him, but they can wait for him to come back. And I bought him another bucket of paint for that. He has a paid-up ticket to Grebd."

Deeming unhesitatingly released the low whistle. Grebd was the name of a sun, a planet and a city in the Coalsack matrix, where certain of the inhabitants had developed a method of pseudosurgery unthinkably far in advance of anything in the known cosmos. They could take virtually any living thing and change it as drastically as it wanted to be changed, even from carbon-base to boron-chain, or as subtly as it might want, like an alteration of all detectible brainwave characteristics or retinal patterns, or even a new nose. They could graft (or grow?) most of a whole man from a tattered lump, providing it lived. Most important, they could make these alterations, however drastic, and (if requested) leave the conscious mind intact.

But the cost of a major overhaul of this nature was beyond reason—unless a man had a reason compelling enough. Deeming looked at the old man with unconcealed awe. Not only had he been able to pay such a price, he had been willing—willing in a cause in which he could have no sympathy. To care that much for a son—to care so very much that the most he could ever hope for now would be to meet a total stranger in an unexpected place who might take him aside and whisper, *"Hello—Dad!"* but for whom he could do nothing further. For if he had transgressed some ruling of the Angels so drastically as to need a trip to Grebd, the Angels would have an eye on the old man for all time to come, and he would not dare even to smile at the new stranger. Such a transgression meant death. Could a father so much as clasp his son's hand under such circumstances?

"In the name of all that's holy," Deeming breathed, "What did he want so badly?"

Rockhard snorted. "Some sort of a glyph. There's a theory that the Aldebaranian stock sprang from the same ethnic roots as those in the Masson planets. It sounds like nonsense to me, and even if it's true, it's still nonsense. But certain vague evidence points to a planet called Revelo. There may be artifacts there to prove the point."

"Never heard of it," said Deeming. "Revelo ... n-no. And so he makes his discovery. And goes to Grebd. And gets his total disguise. And forever after, he can't claim the discovery he made."

"Now you know about Donald," said the old man wryly. "He just wants the discovery made. He doesn't care who makes it."

They looked at each other in shared bafflement. At last Deeming nodded slightly to convey the thought that it didn't matter if he understood. If Donald Rockhard was crazy, that was beside the point. He said, "Now where do the Angels come into this?"

"Revelo," said the old man, "is—Proscribed."

Well then, Deeming thought instantly, that seems to be that, and where's the problem? A Proscribed planet was surrounded by a field of such a nature that if it was penetrated by a flickership, anything organic aboard would instantly and totally cease to live. If Donald had gone to Revelo, Donald was dead. If he had been snapped out of hyperspace on the way there by the outer-limit warning field, and had heeded the warning, then he hadn't landed on Revelo, hadn't broken an Angel dictate, and wasn't in trouble. Deeming said so.

Slowly Rockhard shook his head. "He's on Revelo right now, and alive. Far as I know," he added.

"Not possible," said Deeming flatly. "You just don't penetrate the field around a Proscribed planet and live."

"Very well," said the old man, "nevertheless he's there. Look, I'll tell you something that only four other men know. There is a way to get through to a Proscribed planet."

"About thirty years ago one of my ships happened on a derelict.

God alone knows where it came from. It was a mess, but it contained two lifeboats intact. Lifeboats with flicker drive."

"Boats? They must be big as ships, then."

"Not these. They do the same thing as our flicks, but they don't do it the same way. It isn't understood yet just how, though I have a man working on it. The captain of my freighter brought 'em back for me, for my spacecraft collection, never knowing just what he had. We found that out by accident. We fitted them out with Earth-type controls, but although we know what button to push, we don't know what happens when we push it. It worked no better than our own flicks, so there was no point in filing the information with the Improvement Section. And when we found out the ships would penetrate the Proscribed planets, we just kept our mouths shut. I have my opinion of the Angels, but I will say that when they proscribe a planet, they do it for a good reason. It may have rock-plague aboard, or, worse still, yinyang weed. Or it may be just that the planet is deadly to humans, because of its sun's radiation or the presence of some hormone poison."

"Yeah," agreed Deeming, "Nantha, Sirione, and that devil's world Keth." He shuddered. "Glad they keep us off that one. Guess you're right—the Angels know what they're doing just this once.... What's so special about Revelo, that it's Proscribed?"

"As usual, the Angels won't say. It might be anything. As I say, I trust them for that, and I'm not going to be the one who spreads around a device to make it possible for anyone to penetrate any of 'em."

"Except Donald."

"Except Donald," Rockhard conceded. "For that I have no excuse. If something there kills him, it's a chance he was willing to take. If he brings something out inadvertently, it will be taken care of on Grebd. And I know he won't bring out anything on purpose, like yinyang seeds. Explain it all away, don't I?" His voice changed, as if some internal organist had shut down all the stops and grouped out new ones. "Don't tell me I shouldn't have done it. I know that. I knew it then. But I'd do it again, hear? I'd do it again if it was what he wanted."

43

There was silence for a time and Deeming turned his head away as a decent person might, offering privacy to another. Rockhard said, "We found out how the little alien flickers penetrate the Proscribed planets. They turn it inside out. An analogue might be the way a surge of current will reverse the polarity on a DC generator. We found out," he said bleakly, "that if that happens, the flicker goes in harmlessly. And then when it comes out, the field will kill anyone aboard." He raised his head and looked at Deeming blindly. "Don doesn't know that," he whispered.

Deeming said, "Oh."

After a while he spoke again, incredulously. "I think you're saying that I . . . that somebody has to go there and tell him."

"Tell him? What would he do if you told him?"

"Wouldn't the flicker reverse the polarity a second time?"

"Not from the inside. Besides, that polarity reverse is only an analogy, Deeming. No, what has to be done is to take him this," and from the desk drawer, he scooped two tiny cylindrical objects. Both together were less than the length of his little finger, smaller in diameter than a pen. Deeming rose and went to the desk and took one of them up. There were four separate coils rigidly mounted on the cylinder, toroids, each wound with what seemed to be thousands of precise turns of microscopically fine wire. At one end was an octagonal recess, meant apparently to receive a rotating shaft, as well as a spring collar designed to clamp the device down. The other end faded to insubstantiality, neither transparent nor opaque, but both and neither, and acutely unsettling to watch for more than a second or two.

"Replacement freak coils for the flickerfield," he diagnosed. "But I never saw them this tiny. Are they models?"

"The real thing," said Rockhard tiredly. "And actually an improvement on the one the aliens put on those boats. Apparently they never encountered the kind of deathtrap the Angels use, or they might well have designed one like this."

"What do they do?"

"Put a certain randomness in the frequency of the flickerfield, when it approaches a Proscribed area. Just as a flickerfield works by making a ship, in effect, exist and cease to exist in normal space, so that it doesn't exist at any measurable time as real mass, and can therefore exceed the velocity C, so this coil detects and analyses the frequency of the Angel's death-field, and phases with it. The death-field doesn't kill anything because the approaching ship ceases to exist before it enters the field and does not exist again until it is through it. Unlike the one Donald tried, it doesn't affect the field or reverse its direction."

"So if Donald gets one of these and replaces his frequency coil with it . . ."

"He can forget the existence of the Angel's field."

"On Revelo or any other Proscribed planet." Deeming tossed the coil and caught it. He held it up and sighted past it at Rockhard. "I've got a whole cosmos full of bad trouble here in my hand," he said steadily.

"You have every rotten plague and dangerous plant pest known to xenology, right here in your hand," agreed Rockhard.

"And yinyang weed. Lots of money in yinyang weed," said Deeming reflectively. Yinyang (derived from the old Chinese yin and yang), the two-colored disc divided by an S-shaped line, and representing all opposites—good and evil, light and dark, male and female, and so on—as well as the surprising fact that the flowers were an almost perfect representation of the symbol in red and blue, was by far the most vicious addictive drug ever known, because not only was it potent and virtually incurable, it increased the addict's intelligence fivefold and his physical strength two to three times, and he became an inhuman behemoth with the sole desire to destroy anything and everything between himself and his source of supply, able to outlast, outthink, outfight and outrun anyone of his species.

"If you're really thinking about making money out of yinyang, you're a swine," said Rockhard evenly, "and if that was meant as a joke, you're an oaf."

Deeming locked eyes with him for a moment, then dropped his eyes. "You're right," he muttered. He put the coil carefully down on the desk next to its mate.

Rockhard said, "You worry me, Deeming. If I thought you'd use these coils for any such thing I'd ... well, Donald can die. He'd die gladly, if he knew."

Deeming said soberly, "Can you find a man willing to breach an Angel's command who is not also willing to take anything that comes his way?"

"*Touché,*" said Rockhard, with a bitter and reluctant grin. "You have a head on your neck. Well, have you got the picture? You're to go to Revelo in the other alien lifeboat, equipped with this coil. Slip through the field, locate Donald, tell him what's happened, and see that his coil is replaced with this other one. Then off he goes to Grebd for his—his camouflage job."

"And what do I do?"

"Come back with a message from Don. He'll know which one. When I hear it I'll know if you've done the job."

"If I haven't I won't come back," said Deeming bluntly, and realized as he said it that, incredibly, he had at some point decided to do this crazy thing. "And what do you do if I come back and say 'Mission accomplished'?"

"I'm not going to name a figure. It's a little like the way top executives get paid, Deeming. After a certain point you stop talking salary, and a man begins drawing what he needs for expenses—any expenses—against the value of his holdings. When his holdings go up to a certain level the company stops keeping books on what he draws. It'll be like that with you. You just take what you want, as often as you like, for as long as you live. One man might break up this organization by throwing assets away, but he'd have to work all day every day for a good long while to do it."

"We ... ah ... have no contract, Mr. Rockhard."

"That's right, Mr. Deeming."

He's saying, thought Deeming, you can trust me. And I can. But I can't say that to him. He'd have to answer no. He said cruelly, "You ought to let him die."

"I know," said Rockhard.

"I'm a damn fool," said Deeming. "I'll do it."

Rockhard held out his hand and Deeming took it. It was a warm firm hand and when it let go it withdrew slowly as if it regretted the loss of contact, instead (like some) of falling away in relief. This was a man who meant what he said.

Which of course, he thought, is only another species of damn fool, when you get down to it.

Why me?

That was the base thought, the kingpin thought, the keystone thought of everything that happened between that first meeting and the day he coined off for Revelo. By that time he knew the answer.

Begin at Earth, go to Revelo, do a little job, and return. If it had been just that, and that's all, there wouldn't have been a reason for Deeming's presence in the matter. The nameless pudgy man could have done it; the old man could have done it himself. But there were—details.

There were the two interminable briefing sessions. He had the new coil; all he had to do was plug it into the alien ship.

But the alien ship was hidden far from Earth.

All right; given the ship, all he needed was to drop a Revelo course-coin into his autopilot and push the button.

But he didn't have a Revelo course-coin. Nobody had a Revelo course-coin. Few people even knew where it was. There was a coin, certainly. In the files at Astro City on Ybo. He'd have to get that one. The files ...

The files were in the Angel Headquarters building.

Well, if he got the ship, and if he got the coin, and if Rockhard was right and the new coil worked properly, not only to get him through the death-field but back out again, and if this could be done without alerting an Angel (Rockhard's reasoning was that by turning the field inside out, Don had almost certainly alerted them, but that the new design, which would not—he hoped—touch or affect the field, would permit Deeming to get in and both of them to get out again without activating any alarms. So that for an indeterminate time the Angels must operate on their original information—that one ship had gone in, none come out), and if Donald Rockhard were alive, and if he knew what message to give Deeming and if Deeming got back all right and if Rockhard understood the message properly and if, after all this, Rockhard paid off, why then, this looked like a pretty good deal. And also clearly something that only a man like Deeming could possibly accomplish.

So there were the two long briefings with Rockhard and his scientific assistant Pawling (of whose discourse Deeming caught not one word in nine), and a hurried trip back to his own quarters, where he wrote suitable letters to the hotel and to his housing and food depots and maintenance and communications services and so on and on, including the mailing of the goat's wrist-watch where it would do him the most good, and the paying of bills for liquor and clothing and garage, and, and . . . ("How doth the little busy bee/Keep from flipping his lid like me?" he sang insanely to himself as he did all the things that would assure the hive that it could rest easy, nobody was doing anything unusual around here, honest.) When he was finished with it his affairs were ready for him to resume in a couple of weeks, or, if not, a small secondary wave of assurances to the trades, comforts, and services would go out announcing a minor accident, and making arrangements for another two weeks' absence, and then another ripple reporting a new job on Bluebutter, which was somewhere among the Crabs, and at last a line to a bartender, *How are you Joe?* to be mailed at the end of two years. If that one ever got mailed, he'd be eighteen months dead, and if he thought he had cold feet before, he was afraid to bend his toes when he wrote it.

The day came (was it really only four days since he started out to fence a watch and faced a knocking door?) for departure. Rockhard shook his hand, and Deeming for the second time felt that warm contact and, along with it, a thing in the old cold eyes that could only be covered by the word 'pleading.' If the pleading had words, what would they be? *Bring my boy out.* Or, *Let me trust you.* Or maybe, *Don't doubt me: don't ever doubt me.* Perhaps, *You're my kind, boy—a pretty sleazy edition, but anyway my kind, so . . . take care of yourself, whatever.* He handed Deeming more cash money than he had had in his hand since the night he gathered up the big pot at the poker game and handed it over to the guy who won it from him on the next hand. But this time it was only expense money, not even figured in. Rockhard probably never knew how close he came to losing his man by the size of that pittance. Or maybe he did. The pudgy man and the chauffeur were about as easy to shake from that moment until coin-off as a coat of shellac.

And did he lean back in cozy cushions and watch a band of loving friends waving from the blockhouse? He did not. He left the house in the back of a utility truck, which pulled up in utter darkness inside a building somewhere. He was hustled wordlessly into a side room, shoehorned into a power suit, and rammed into a space fully as tall as the underneath of a studio couch and round—torturously, about two hand-breadths less than he was tall, so that he couldn't straighten out. They welded him in, at which point he discovered that his honey-pipe had not been given the quarter turn necessary to open it to the converters. He spent almost the entire night trying to grip it with his southern cheeks, which he found indifferently prehensile and, as time went on, demanding of differential subtleties that he would have sworn were beyond his control. He was wrong; he succeeded by laborious fractions and got it open and at last lay sweat-drenched and limp with effort and relief. And then more time flowed through his prison than any small space ought to hold, when he had nothing to do but think.

And the only thing he could think about, and that over and over, was that he really wasn't too uncomfortable or distressed by this imprisonment, because he seemed to be conditioned to it. He had, after all, for some years lived huddled in mediocrity with his hotel job pulled no less tight around him than this welded steel pillbox. His excursions as the disappearing Jimmy the Flick were no less confined; confined by limited time, limited targets, and the ubiquitous golden Angels with their wise kind faces and understanding voices, God burn 'em all. They were supposed to be unkillable, but he'd sure like to get one for Christmas and make some simple tests lasting till, say, Midsummer Eve. They, more than anyone, kept the sky closed over him, so he had to walk everywhere with his head bent. He tried to imagine what it would be like to walk in a place where his personal sky had room for a whee of a jump and a holler that anyone could hear and the hell with them; but the wish was too far from his conditioning and bounced him right back to the uncomfortable thought that he was not uncomfortable here, and so around he went again on the synapse-closed box, closed sky. Damned strong gentle Angels—how would it be to run tall someplace? But I can't quite grasp that, here in this closed sky.

And then he slept, and then the surface under him rumbled and tipped, and, lo and behold, it was only the next morning after all.

He switched on his penetroscope and waited impatiently while the pseudo-hard radiation fumbled its way through the beryl hull metal and the image cleared. His prison was being lifted by a crane onto a lowboy trailer, which began to move as soon as it had its load. It tumbled out to the apron where the ship waited, belly down like some wingless insect, with its six jointed jacks, one of which was footless and supported by a tall gantry which had thrust out a boom to hold up the limb, like a groom holding up a horse's split hoof while the stableboy runs for the liniment.

The lowboy was positioned under the leg, and Deeming blinked at the pounding and screeching going on above him as his tomb was bolted to the landing jack and became a part of it. Then there was a quiet time as tools and ground hands got clear, ports and locks were battened, and the crew assumed coin-off stations. Somewhere a whistle was blowing; Deeming could hear it through his radio, picking it from the intercom, which in turn had it from an outside microphone in the hull. It stopped, and there was a rumbling purr as all six legs began to straighten, pushing the ship up off the ground so that most of the terrestrial matter included in its flicker-field would be air.

Then without warning the earth was gone, the vanished ship lightyears away already before the gut-bumping boom of its air-implosion could sound. Deeming's stomach lurched, and then there was gravity again and a scene in his 'scope—a rolling grey-green landscape, with a few cylindrical buildings and a half-dozen docking pads.

That's the trouble with space travel nowadays, he thought glumly. They've taken all the space out of it.

The ship hovered perhaps a thousand feet high, drawing antigrav power from the beam generator down below. It drifted slowly downwards, positioning itself over one of the empty pads.

Pad 4.

According to his briefing, the correct pad was number 6. With rising anxiety he saw that 6 was already occupied by a small sport flicker.

There was only one way he would ever get out of here, and that was in Pad 6. Nobody in the ship knew he was there. He was not even sure of the origin or destination of the ship, or on which planet they were now landing. If it set down in the wrong pad, he would stay right where he was, leave with the ship, and either starve or set up a howl with his radio and get dragged out at the wrong place at the wrong time by the wrong people.

He turned on his transmitter, fingered it to docking frequency, and said authoritatively, "Wear off, skipper. Pad 6 is ours." He waited tensely. He hoped the ground control would think it was hearing a crewman speaking to the captain while the captain thought he was hearing ground control.

He heard murmurs in the intercom but could not pick them up clearly. The ship steadied, then began to sink again. He waited tensely, begging his brains to come up with something, anything, then literally sobbed with relief as a space-suited figure tumbled out of the blockhouse and sprinted for the sportster in Pad 6. The little ship lifted and slid into 4, and Deeming's ship settled into its assigned berth.

For a moment Deeming lay trembling with reaction, and then grinned. He wondered if the captain and the control officer, sitting over a beer later, would think to ask each other who had called out to wear off. That, he said, is how fights start in bars.

He scanned once around him with the 'scope and thereafter ignored the scene. He grasped the metal ring in the center of the floor of his prison and turned it. Faintly, he felt the slight tapping of a relay sequence, and then the surface on which he lay began to descend. Down it went to ground level and still down. He snapped on his helmet light confidently; nothing would be seen from outside but the great round jack foot pressed solidly against the concrete pad. Who could know that its sole pressed a matched disc of concrete down into the ground?

The movement stopped and Deeming saw the niche in the concrete wall to his right. He swiftly rolled into it, the surface which had carried him down already starting back up. Silently it slid by him—he had not realized it was so thick—until it formed a roof for the underground room which now was revealed. He dropped down to the floor. The space was tiny, just enough for himself and the tiny alien lifeboat which lay welcoming him with glitters of gold from its polished, dust-bloomed surface.

It was a sphere, at first sight far too small to be good for anything. The single bucket seat had been designed for a being considerably shorter than he, and narrower too, he realized, grunting, as he wedged himself into it. The controls were few and simple. The hull material was, from inside, totally transparent. The entire power plant must be under the seat.

He thumbed the sensors at his waist, and settled back to wait. In a moment he heard the hiss of air as his power suit flooded the tiny cabin, and then the sensors, having analyzed the atmosphere and pressure-checked the seals, tinkled cheerfully. With a sigh of relief he wrung his helmet off and unclamped his gauntlets. From his pouch he found the course-coin for Ybo, an osmium disc with irregular edges like a particularly complicated cam. He dropped it in the slot of the course box, and confidently thumbed the red button.

There was no sound. The boat seemed to settle a little, and there was a measurable flash of that indescribable, discomfiting greyness to be seen outside. Deeming was not worried about the sudden vacuum he had created in the hole. It would hardly be noticed amid the rumblings and scrapings of dockside, and the chances were that air would seep in slowly enough to make the whole thing unnoticed.

He looked around him with pleasure. Rockhard's people had really set things up properly. Though a flickership could coin off from anywhere, on, over, or under the surface, planet falls were generally made high. Contact with anything on the ground from a child's toy to an innocent bystander could be unpleasant. It wouldn't hurt the ship, which would flick out of existence and remove itself automatically at the slightest sign of coexistent matter, but the less resilient planet-bound object would not be so fortunate. One solution was a landing plate, and that was what had been supplied here. It beamed the ship in and brought it to contact unless there was enough heavy matter in the way to be dangerous, in which case the beam operated but the landing guide did not, and the craft would appear with good safe altitude. The device was no larger than a dinner plate, and buried under a sprinkling of topsoil it was undetectable.

The lifeboat nestled near the bottom of a deep narrow cut in hilly land. It was night. A brook burbled pleasantly somewhere close by. Weeds nodded and swayed all about; a searcher would have to fall over the ship before he could see it. Deeming unhesitatingly unbuttoned the canopy and swung it back. He had been on Ybo before and knew it as one of the few "perfect" Terran planets. He breathed the soft rich air with real pleasure, then rose and shucked out of his power suit and stowed it on the seat. He pulled the creases out of his trustworthy reversible jacket, checked his pockets to see that he had everything he needed, closed and locked the canopy, and climbed the steep side of the gully.

He found himself at the edge of a meadow. A beautiful planet, he told himself cheerfully. He stretched, for a moment capturing that open-sky fantasy of his. Then he saw moving lights and shrank down into the long grass, and his personal sky was tight down over him again.

It was only a ground car, and he certainly could not be seen. He watched it veer closer to him and then pass not thirty paces away. Good; a road was just what he was looking for.

He took careful bearings of the bank on which he stood, and then followed the crest of it down to the road. He was gratified to see a milepost by the coping of a stone bridge which carried the road over the brook he had heard. Finding this place again would not be difficult.

He strode cheerfully along the road towards the loom of city lights that limned the wooded hills close ahead. He was still in his *why me?* phase, and he had a moment of real regret that Rockhard could not have shared this adventure with him, or even done it alone. Well . . . if he wanted to give away unlimited chunks of credit for work as pleasant as this, it was his hard luck.

He mounted the hill and suddenly the city was all around him. His landing spot wasn't at the edge of town—it was in Astro City's huge Median Park. Why, there was the Astro Center, not five minutes away!

It was an impressive building, one of those low, winged structures which seem to be so much larger on the inside than they are outside. Wide shallow steps led up to the multiple doors. It must have been early in their evening; the place was still busy, and ablaze with lights. Deeming knew it was open all night, but later the crowds of spacemen, shipping clerks, students of navigation, flicker techs and school children would thin out. Wonderful, he thought. If he needed crowds, here they were. If not, not.

At the top of the steps a slender girl in her mid-teens emerged from the door and stopped to answer his automatic smile radiantly. And to his intense astonishment she sank to one knee and bowed her head.

"Ah, don't, my child—please don't," said a resonant voice behind him, and a tall Angel swept by him and lifted the girl to her feet. He touched her cheek playfully, smiled, and went into the building. The girl stood looking after him, her hand pressed to her cheek and her eyes bright. "Oh," she murmured, "Oh, I wish . . ." Then she seemed to become aware of Deeming standing beside and behind her, and stepped to the side in confusion. "I'm so sorry. I'm in your way."

In spite of the fact that he wore the brown uniform of mediocrity—his nondescript suit and pathetic crisp moustache—he said with the voice of Jimmy the Flick, "Finish your wish, pretty. You'll never get a wish that you break in the middle." And he smiled the glittering happy smile that never belonged with the small silly moustache and desk clerk Deeming's invisible unnoticeable crowd's face. Inwardly he seethed. He had been frightened by the sudden appearance of the Angel; captivated by the girl and the utter adoration which for a crazy moment he had thought was his; intoxicated by the nearness of this last barrier to his quest, hyperalert because of it. And so for the very first time Jimmy the Flick smiled from the desk drudge's face, creating a new person whose actions he could not quite predict. Like the swift glance he threw upwards. Why that? Why, the sky, of course: he had felt the shuttering sky move upwards a bit to give him room to move. Well, *sure,* he thought in a burst of astonishment, *there's much more room to move when you don't know what move you might make next.* A crazy moment, all this in a click of time, and the girl was taking from him his astonished smile in its mismatched face and giving it back to him hued with all the tints of herself, saying, "Breaking my wish . . . ? Oh, I did, didn't I?"

She put her hand to her hot throat and looked swiftly into the building where the Angel had disappeared. "I wish I were a boy."

He laughed so abruptly and so loudly that everyone on the steps stopped to catch a piece of it and go on, smiling. "That's a wish that deserves breaking," he said, making no slightest attempt to hide his admiration of her. She was slender and tall and had one of those rare gentle faces which can move untouched through any violence.

"But who ever heard of a girl Angel?" she said.

"Oh, so that's your trouble. Now why would you want to be an Angel?"

"To do what they do. I never yet saw an Angel do a thing I wouldn't want to be doing. To help, to be kind and wise and strong for people who need something strong."

"You don't have to be one of them to learn all those things."

"Oh yes, you do!" she said, in a tone that would accept no argument or discussion. He understood, and grudgingly agreed. Thinking like an Angel did not give one the sheer strength nor the resources to act like one. "Well, even if you could become a man, that wouldn't make you an Angel."

"But then I could get to be one," she said, craning her neck to look far out over the plaza where there was a glimpse of gold from the cloak of another of the creatures. She glowed when she saw it, even so distantly, and brought the glow full on Deeming when she faced him again. It was unsettling as hyperspace.

"Are you sure of that? Were they just plain men before they were Angels?"

"Of course they were," she said with that devoted positiveness. "They couldn't be so much to humans without being human first of all."

"And how do they get to be Angels?" he bantered.

"No one knows that," she conceded. "But, you see, if a man can become one, and if I was a man, I'd find out and do it."

He stood in the full radiation of her intense feeling and irrationally admitted that if she were a man and wanted to be an Angel, or wanted anything else that much, she'd probably make it.

"I'd like to think they were just men, at that," he said.

"You can be sure of it. What's your name?"

"What? Uh ..." The strange first fusion of Deeming the Invisible with Jimmy the Flick had him disoriented, and he could not answer. He covered it with a cough, and said, "I've just come in from Bravado to this place I've heard so much about."

If she noticed that he had avoided her question, or wondered about such a place as Bravado, she gave no sign. The worlds were full of slightly odd people these days and the sky full of names. She said, "Oh, may I show it to you? I work here. I'm just off duty, and I really have nothing else to do."

He wished he knew what her name was. He soaked up this eagerness of hers, this total defenselessness, trust, earnest generosity, and felt a great choking wash of feeling of a kind quite alien to him. He cared suddenly, cared desperately about what might happen to her in the years to come, and wished he could spare her whatever would be wrong for her; wished he could run before her and remove anything over which she might stumble, kill anything which might sting her; guard her, warn her ... He wanted to grip her shoulders and shake her and shout, look out for me, beware the stranger; trust no one, help no one, just look out for yourself! The feeling passed, and he did not touch her or speak of it. He glanced into the building and remembered that there was something he needed in there and must have, no matter what he had to use to get it. He would use this girl if he had to; he knew that too. He didn't like knowing it, but know it he most painfully did. He said, "Well, thanks! It's very kind of you."

"No it isn't," she said, with that faithful ardor of hers. "I love this place. Thank *you*," and she turned and went in. He followed humbly.

Hours later he had what he wanted. Or, at least, he knew where it was. Among a hundred sections, a hundred thousand file banks, dozens of vista rooms with their three-dimensional map of all corners of the known cosmos, among museum halls with their displays of artifacts of great, strange, dead, new, dangerous, utterly mysterious cultures of the past and present, there was a course-coin for Revelo—a little button of a thing which a man could hide in his hand, and which bore the skills to pilot him to the Proscribed planet, and through which, like light through a pinhole, all his being must now pass, to fan out on the other side and place him in a picture of wealth beyond imagining. He glanced at the girl walking so confidently beside him and knew again that whatever she was worth, she wasn't important enough to turn him aside, precious enough to spare if she got in his way. And this made him inexpressibly sad.

He saw the banks of course-coin dispensers, where any planet's coin could be acquired by anyone ... well, almost any planet by almost anyone. Spell out the name of the planet on a keyboard, and in seconds the coin would drop into a glass chamber below the board. Inspect it through the glass, and if it bore the right name, press your thumb into a depression at the right (your thumb would identify you for billing later) and the chamber opened. Or if you'd miscued it and saw the wrong coin, or changed your mind, hit the reject button and the coin would be returned to the bank.

So he punched out K-E-T-H, and a blank disc dropped into the chamber. *Proscribed,* a lighted sign under the chamber announced.

"Oh, my goodness, you don't want that one!" cried the girl.

"No," said Deeming truthfully—of all planets in the universe, Keth was the most unspeakable. `I just wanted to see what happened if you punched for it."

"You draw a blank," said the girl, touching the reject button and clearing the chamber. "Proscribed coins aren't even in this area. They're kept separately in a guarded file room. Do you want to see it? Angel Abdasel is the guard; he's so nice."

Deeming's heart leaped. "Yes, I'd like that. But ... don't make me talk to an Angel. They make me feel ... you're not going to like this ..."

"Tell me."

"They make me feel small."

"I'm not angry at that!" She laughed. "They make me feel small too! Well, come on."

They took a grey tube and floated to the upper level of the low building, then walked through a labyrinth of corridors and through a door marked STAFF ONLY, which the girl opened for him, waving him through with mock gestures of pride and privilege. At the end of the corridor was a stairway leading down; Deeming could see the corner of an outer exit down there, and floodlit shrubbery. Near the top of the stairs was an open doorway; through it Deeming got a glimpse of gold. There was an Angel in there. Deeming stepped close to the wall, out of the Angel's line of sight. "Is this the place?"

"Yes," she said. "Come on—don't be shy; Abdasel's ever so nice." She tapped at the doorpost. "Abdasel ..."

The resonant voice in the room was warm and welcoming. "Tandy! Come in, child."

So her name's Tandy, thought Deeming dully.

She said, "I've brought a friend. Could we ...?"

"Any friend of ..."

Deeming had Rockhard's specially designed needler out before he moved to the doorway. He rested it against the doorframe and put his head forwards only far enough to sight it with one eye. He fired, and the needle disappeared silently into the broad golden chest. There had been no warning for the Angel, and no time. He bent his head in amazement as if to look at his chest while a hand rose to touch it. The hand simply stopped. The whole Angel stopped.

"Abdasel ...?" whispered the girl, puzzled. She stepped into the room. "Angel Ab ..." She must then have sensed something new in her companion's tense posture. She turned to him and eyed the needler in his hand, and the frozen Angel. "Did ... did you—?"

"Too bad, Tandy," he rasped. "Too damn bad." He was breathing hard and his eyes burned. He dashed tears away from them with his free hand furiously.

"You hurt him," she said dazedly.

"He never felt a thing. He'll get over it. You know I have to kill you?" he blurted in sudden agony.

She didn't scream, or faint, or even look horrified. She simply said, "Do you?" in open puzzlement.

He got her out of the way then, not daring to wait a second more for fear he might debate the matter. He closed his mind down to a single icy purpose and lived solely with it while he pawed over the Angel's desk for an index. He found it—a complete list of Proscribed planets. He recognized the small keyboard beside the computer for what it was, a junior version of the dispensers downstairs, lacking the thumb plate which identified the purchaser.

He took the Angel's hand. The long arm was heavy, stiff, and noticeably cold—not surprising considering the amount of heat absorbing *athermine* particles which the needle was even yet feeding into his bloodstream. It was enough to freeze an ordinary human solid in minutes, but he had Rockhard's assurance that it would not kill an Angel. Not that he cared, or Rockhard either. For his purposes, the special needle was just as good either way.

He lifted the heavy hand and used one of its fingers to punch out the names of eight Proscribed planets, among then, of course, Revelo. He scooped them out of the receiving chute and dropped them in his pocket. Then he went to the door and stood holding his breath and listening intently. No sign of anyone in the corridor.

He whipped off his jacket and reversed it, slipped the inserts in his heels, removed the moustache and contact lenses, and stepped out into the corridor. He did not look back (because all he could see whether he looked or not was what lay crumpled on the floor smiling. Smiling, through some accident of spasm—a cruel accident which would mark his inner eye, his inner self, forever).

He went downstairs and out into the night, not hurrying.

He walked towards the park, numb inside except for that old, cold unhappiness which always signaled his successes. He remembered thinking that this was only because the take was so small.

Well, he needed to think of a better one than that now.

His sky pressed down on his skull and nape. He watched each step he took and knew which step to take next.

It was very dark.

He found the road and then the milepost by the bridge. The people he had passed paid him no attention. When he was quite sure he was unobserved he slipped into the underbrush and through it to the meadow. He found the sloping ridge at the lip of the gully and moved along it, seeing mostly with his leg muscles and his semi-circular canals. He drew his needler because it was better to have it and not need it than to need it and not have it; he moved silently because there was such a thing as a statistical improbability, and when he reached the point over the hiding place of his boat, he got down on his stomach and lay still, listening.

He heard only the gurgle of the water.

He got out his pencil torch, and held it in the same hand as the needler, clamping them tightly together and parallel, so that anywhere the light beam struck could be the exact target for a needle. Then walking his elbows, worming his abdomen, he crept to the edge and looked down.

Pitch black. Nothing.

He aimed the needler and torch as close as he could to where the ship ought to be, put his thumb ready on the stud, and with his other hand found the light switch and clicked it on.

The narrow beam shot downwards. He was well oriented. The circle of white picked out the boat and the ground around it, and the figure of the Angel who sat in a patient posture on top of the boat.

The angel looked up and smiled. "Hello, friend."

"Hello," said Deeming, and shot him. The Angel sat where he was, smiling up into the light, his eyes puckered from the glare. For a long moment nothing happened, and then, with head still up, and still smiling, the Angel toppled rigidly off the lifeboat and pitched backwards into the rocky streambed.

Deeming turned out the light and clambered slowly down into the dark. He fumbled his way to the boat, unlocked the canopy with the pre-set palm pattern, and climbed in. Then he cursed and climbed out again and found the water's edge and fumbled along it until his hands found the soft, strong folds of the golden cloak. He blinked his light once, briefly, and studied the scene as it faded from his retinas. The Angel lay on his back, turned from the hips so that his legs still held the sitting position he had been in when shot. His head was still back, but Deeming had not seen the head; it was under water.

He heaved the big body, lifted it, shifted it until he was sure it was placed the way he wanted it. A man as big as this Angel would have been a sizeable load to move around; the Angel was a third again as heavy as that. (What *are* they, anyway?)

Then he got back into the boat and buttoned it up. He took his stolen course-coins and racked them neatly with the ones the ship already had. And for a while he sat and thought.

Hello, friend.

Her name was Tandy.

(Old eyes, pleading.)

"There's a lot of money in yinyang weed."

He shifted in annoyance and pressed his thumbs to his eyes until he saw sparks. These weren't the thoughts he was after.

He ran his hand over the coin rack and slipped his fingers behind it to touch the new flicker-frequency coil which he had plugged in back there. In these tiny objects he had a potential possessed probably by no human being since time began. He had free and secret access to eight Proscribed planets, on some of which there was certainly material that someone, somewhere, would pay for exorbitantly—completely aside from yinyang weed. He could assume that he could not be traced from Ybo ... no—no he couldn't. Say rather that as far as he knew he couldn't be traced; as far as he knew he had not been observed. The stories that were told about the Angels, how they could read minds, even newly dead minds ... and then, for all their strength and confidence, for all their public stature, did they really feel that one Angel guarding the Proscribed coins would by his sole presence be sufficient to protect such potential devastation as those little discs represented? If he, Deeming, were setting up that office, Angels or no Angels, he'd put in cameras and alarms and various interlocks, like a particular rhythm pattern for keying the wanted discs which no outsider could know about.

The more he pursued this line of thought, the less confidence he had that his trail was cold. The more he thought of this, the more sure he became that even if they could not follow immediately, they would have nets spread in more places than even his growing fear could conjure up.

What would he do if he were an Angel and wanted to catch the likes of Deeming?

First of all, he'd cordon off the Proscribed planets (assuming that the keyboard had made a record of what coins were taken; and it was unthinkable that it had not).

Then he'd put a watch on every place known to have been a haunt of the criminal—on the growing assumption that they could very soon find out who he was.

If they found out who he was, then special watches would be put on Rockhard, because the deal with Rockhard would certainly be discovered; it was too complex and involved too many people to be hidden for long, once the Angels had any lead at all.

Which meant that Earth was out, the Proscribed planets were out, Ybo and Bluebutter and anywhere else he'd ever been were out. He had to go to a new place, somewhere he had never been, where no one would know him, where there were lots of people to disappear among. Somehow, some way, he could think his way through to Don Rockhard and some, anyway, of the riches the old man had promised him.

He sighed and pawed through the coins on the rack until he came to the one marked Iolanthe. A big planet, a little hard on the muscles for comfort, but well crowded and totally new to him.

He dropped it into the slot and coined out of there.

Iolanthe was really up to the minute. He came out of flicker with about a mile of altitude and took a quick look around before he flicked to the nightside. With a design as unique as the ship's, he wouldn't want to leave it where it would cause comment. So he hung in the sky and fanned through the communications the planet had to offer.

They were plenty. There was a fine relief map of the planet on perpetual emanation in conjunction with the space beacon, and a wonderful radio grid, so it was easy to place himself. There was an entertainment band and best of all, a news band—a broad one, set up in video frames, each with its audio loop of comment. He could tune in any page of the entire sequence. It was indexed and extremely well edited to cover both current news and background, local and intercultural events.

He started with the most recent bulletins and worked backwards. There was nothing, and nothing, and nothing that might apply to him, not even a date line from anywhere he'd been. Until suddenly he found himself gaping into the face of Richard E. Rockhard.

He turned up the audio.

"... indicted yesterday by C Jury of Earth High Court," said the announcer suavely, "on one hundred and eleven counts of restraint of trade, illegal interlocked directorates, price pegging, monopoly, market manipulation ..." on and on and on. Apparently the old pirate had blown his balloon too big. "... estimated value of Mr. Rockhard's estate and holdings has been estimated in excess of two and three quarter billions, but in the face of these charges it is evident that the satisfaction of invoices outstanding, accounts receivable, taxes and penalties will in all likelihood total to a far higher figure than the assets. These assets are, of course, in government hands pending a detailed accounting."

Slowly, his hands shaking, Deeming reached for the control and turned the communicator off. He watched, fascinated, as the ruddy, cold-eyed face of the old man faded away under his hand, distorted suddenly, and was gone. A trick of his mind, or of the fading electrons, shattered the picture as it was extinguished, and for the tiniest fraction of a second it assumed the wordless pleading which had moved him so deeply before.

"Stupid, clumsy old swine," he growled, too shocked to think of anything really foul to say.

No money. There wasn't anything except what the government held. He could see himself going to the government with a claim like his.

He pawed through the money the old man had given him for incidentals. He had used none of it so far, but it no longer looked like a lot. He crammed it back into his pocket and then shook himself hard.

I got to do something. I got to get down there and disappear.

He cut in the penetroscope and switched it to the video. The instrument resolved night views considerably better than it did images through beryl steel. He aimed it downwards and got a good sharp focus on the ground and began hunting out a place to hide his boat. He would want hilly or rocky ground, a lot of vegetative cover, access to road or river, and perhaps ...

Something golden flashed across the screen.

Deeming grunted and slapped at a control. He caught them, lost them, caught and hung on to them—three Angels, flying in V formation close to the ground, with their backpack geo-gravs. They were swiftly covering the ground in a most efficient area search looking for—well, something concealed down there, small enough to justify that close scrutiny, sitting mum enough to justify a visual hunt. Something, say, about the size of his boat.

On impulse he cut in the ship detectors. The picture reeled and steadied and reeled again as the detectors scanned and selected, and then gave him a quick rundown of everything it had found, in order of closest estimated arrival time at a collision point with him.

To the north and north-east, two small golden ships converging.

To the east, another, and directly above it, another, apparently maneuvering to fly cover on its partner.

To the south, a large—no, that was nothing, just a freighter minding its own business. But no—it was launching boats. He zoomed the video on them. Fighter boats streaking towards him.

To the south-east ... The hell with the south-east! He pawed the Revelo coin out of the rack and banged it down on the slot of the coin box. It bounced out of his fingers and fell to the deck. He pounced on it and scrabbled it wildly into his hand.

A luminescent pink cloud bloomed suddenly to his right, another just behind him. Its significance: stand by for questioning, or else.

His hull began to hum, and, impressed on this vibration as a signal on a carrier, his whole craft spoke hoarsely to him: "Halt in the name of Angels. Stand by for tow beam."

"Yeah, sure," said Deeming, and this time got the coin to the slot. He banged the button, and the scene through ports and video alike disappeared.

He switched off everything he didn't need and lay back, sweating.

He wouldn't even glance at the remote, wanly hopeful possibility that they had mistaken him for someone else. They knew who he was, all right. And how long had it taken them to draw a bead on him on a planet to which they could not possibly have known he was going? Thirty minutes?

He found himself staring out of the port, and became shockingly aware that he was still in hyperspace. He had never been in the grey so long before; where in time was this Revelo place anyway?

He began to sweat again. Was something wrong with the field generator? According to the tell tales on the control panel, no; it seemed all right.

Still the queasy, deeply frightening grey. He blanked out the ports and shivered in his seat, hugging himself.

What had made him pick Revelo anyhow?

Only an unconfirmed guess that one man had managed to stay alive there. The other Proscribed planets were death for humans in one form or another; he had no idea which. Revelo probably was too, for that matter, but Don Rockhard would hardly have chanced it if it was certain death.

And then maybe—just barely maybe—the new flicker coil really would work so well in the Revelo death-field that he could slip through without detection. Maybe, for a while, for a very little while, he could be in a sheltered place where he could think.

There was a shrill rushing sound from the hull. He stared at the ports but could see nothing. He switched on the detector and then remembered the port blanks. He opened them and let the light of Revelo flood in.

He had never seen a sky like this. Masses of color, blue, blue-green, pink, drifted above him. The dim zenith was alive with shooting sparks. A great soft purple flame reached from the eastern horizon and wavered to invisibility almost directly overhead. It pulsed hypnotically.

Deeming shuddered. He set the detector to the task of finding Don Rockhard's boat and let it cruise. He started the exterior air analyzer and sat back to wait.

Since the missing boat was so small and the planet so large, he had to set his detector's discriminator very wide and its sensitivity high. And it found all sorts of things for him—great shining lumps of metallic copper and molybdenum jutting from the ragged hills, a long wavering row of circular pools of molten lead, and even the Angel's warning beacon and death-field generator. It was obviously untended, and understandably so; it was self-powered, foolproof, and set in a case that a hydrogen explosion wouldn't nick.

He had to sleep after a while, so he set the buzzer to its loudest and lay back to sleep. It seemed that each time he slept he dreamed and each time he dreamed, no matter how it began, it always ended with his coming face to face with a smiling Angel, unarmed, pleasant, just sitting waiting for him. Each time the buzzer sounded, he leaped frantically to see what it was reporting. The need to spend a moment with someone else beside himself, someone else's ideas besides his turgid miasmas of flight and dead smiles and kind relentless Angels became urgent, hysterical, frantic. Each time the buzzer sounded it was rich ore or a strange electrical fog between two iron crags, or nothing at all, and, at last, Donald Rockhard's lifeboat.

By the time he found it he was in a numb and miserable state, the retreat which lives on the other side of hysteria. He was riding a habit pattern of sleep and dream, wake and stare; hear the buzzer, lurch at the screen, get the disappointment, slap the reject button, and go on. He actually rejected the other lifeboat twice before he realized it, but his craft began to circle it and the strong fix made it impossible for the buzzer to be silent. He switched it off at last and hovered, staring dully at the tiny bronze ball below, and pulling himself back to reality.

He landed. The craziest thing of all about this crazy place was that the atmosphere at ground level was Earth normal, though a bit warm for real comfort. He buttoned the canopy and climbed stiffly out.

There was no sign of Donald Rockhard.

He walked over to the other boat and stooped to look in. The canopy was closed but not locked. He opened it and leaned inside. There were only three course-coins in the rack, Earth and Bootes II and Cabrini in Beta Centauri. He fumbled behind the rack and his fingers found a flat packet. He opened it.

It contained a fortune—a real fortune in large notes. And a card. And a course-coin.

The card was of indestructible hellenite, and bore the famous symbol of the surgeons of Grebd, and in hand script, by some means penetrating all the way through the impenetrable plastic, like ink through a paper towel, the legend: *Class A. Paid in full. Accept bearer without interrogation.* It was signed by an authoritative squiggle and over-stamped with the well-known pattern of the Grebdan Surgical Society.

The coin was, of course, to Grebd.

Deeming clutched the treasure into his lap and bent over it, hugging it, and then laughed until he cried—which he did almost immediately.

To Grebd, for a new face, a new mind if he wanted it—a tail, wings, who cares? The sky's the limit.

(The sky—your sky—has always been the limit.)

And then, new face and all, with that packet of loot, to any place in the cosmos that I think is good enough for me.

"Hey! Who are you? What do you think you're doing? Get out of my boat! And drop those things!"

Deeming did not turn. He put up his hands and stopped his ears like a little child in the birdhouse at the zoo.

"Out, I said!"

Deeming lifted the treasure in shaking hands, rumpling and spilling it. "Out!" barked the voice, and out he came, not attempting to pick anything up. He turned tiredly with his hands raised somewhat less than shoulder height, as if they were much, much too heavy for him.

He faced a hollow-cheeked, weather-beaten young man with the wide-set frosty eyes of Richard Rockhard. At his feet a cloth sack lay where he had dropped it on seeing someone in his boat. In his hand, steady as an I-beam, rested a sonic disrupter aimed at Deeming's midsection.

Deeming said, "Donald Rockhard."

Rockhard said, "So?"

Deeming put down his hands, and croaked, "I've come to paint your belly blue."

Rockhard was absolutely motionless for a long moment, and then as if they were operated from the same string, his gun arm slowly lowered while slowly his smile spread. "Well, damn me up and back!" he said. "Father sent you!"

"Man," said Deeming exhaustedly, "I'm sure glad you ask questions first and shoot later."

"Oh, I wouldn't've shot you, whoever you were. I'm so glad to see another face that I ... Who are you, anyway?"

Deeming told him his name. "Your father found out that when a boat like yours busts through the Angel's death-field, it turns it inside out. Or some such. Anyway, if you'd coined out of here you never would have come down anywhere."

Donald Rockhard looked up into the mad sky, paling. "You don't say." He wet his lips and laughed nervously. It was not a funny sound. "And now that you've come to tell me, how do you get out?"

"Don't look at me like no hero," said Deeming with the shade of a grin. "It's only a matter of plugging in a new freak coil. That's what I was doing when I bumped into all that cabbage. I know I had no business looking it over, but then how often do you bump into four million in negotiable good cash money?"

"Can't blame you, at that," Rockhard admitted. "I suppose you saw what else was in there."

"I saw it."

"The theory is that if you plan to go to Grebd, no living soul should know about it."

Deeming glanced at the disrupter hanging from the young man's hand. The hand was slack, but then, he hadn't pulled the weapon away either. He said, "That's up to you. Your father trusted me with the information, though; you ought to know that."

"Well, all right," said Rockhard. He put the gun away. "How is he?"

"Your father? Not so good. I'd say he needs you about now."

"Needs me? Why, if I showed up in the same solar system and the Angels found out, it'd cost him."

"No, it wouldn't," said Deeming. He told him what had happened to the old man's towering structure of businesses. "Not that a lousy four million'd do much good."

Rockhard bit his lip. "What do you think I could get for the card?"

Deeming closed his eyes. "That might help," he nodded.

"I've got to get out of here," said young Rockhard. "You finished with that coil?"

"Just got the old one out."

"Finish it up, will you? I'll just sort out one or two of these." He dumped the contents of his sack on the ground and hunkered down over them.

"That what you're looking for?" asked Deeming, going to his own boat for the coil.

The other snorted. "Who knows? They might be potsherds and then again they might be fossilized mud puddles. I'll just take the best of 'em for analysis. You think archaeologists are crazy, Deeming?"

"Sure," said Deeming from the other boat. "But then, I also think everybody's crazy." He lay belly down on the seat of Rockhard's boat and began picking up money. He got it all and the card and stacked them neatly and slipped them into their packet. Rockhard glanced in at him.

"You taking some of that for yourself?"

Deeming shook his head. He put the packet on its shelf behind the coin rack. "I've been taken care of." He got out of the boat.

Rockhard got in, and looked up over his shoulder at him. "You better take some. A lot."

"I won't be needing it," said Deeming tiredly.

"You're a funny guy, Deeming!"

"Yuk, yuk."

"Will I see you again?"

"No."

When Rockhard had no answer to that flat syllable Deeming said, "I'll swing your canopy." Under cover of reaching for the canopy, he got out his needler and concealed it in his sleeve, with the snout just protruding between the fingers of his closed fist. His little finger rested comfortably on the stud. He leaned on the fist, resting on the cowling right back of Rockhard's ear.

He said, "Goodbye, Rockhard."

Rockhard didn't say anything.

Deeming stood for a long time looking down at the needler in a kind of dull astonishment. *Why didn't I shoot?* Then, when Rockhard's ship had flickered and gone, he let his shoulders hang and he slogged through the hot sand to his boat.

God he was tired.

"Why didn't you shoot?"

Deeming stopped where he was, not even finishing a stride; one foot forward, the other back. Slowly he raised his head and faced the golden giant who leaned casually, smiling, against his boat.

Deeming took a deep breath and held it and let it out painfully. Then in a harsh flat voice he said, "By God, I can't even say I'm surprised."

"Take it easy," said the Angel. `You're going to be all right now."

"Oh sure," said Deeming bitterly. They'd scrape out his brains and fill his head with cool delicious yogurt, and he'd spend the rest of his placid life mopping out the Angels' H.Q., wherever that might be. "Here," he said, "I guess you won this fair and square," and he tossed his needler to the Angel, who waved a negligent hand. The weapon ceased to exist in mid-air halfway between them. Deeming said, "You have a whole bag of tricks."

"Sure," said the Angel agreeably. "Why didn't you shoot young Rockhard?"

"You know," said Deeming, "I've been wondering about that myself. I meant to. I was sure I meant to." He raised hollow, bewildered eyes to the Angel. "What's the matter with me? I had it made, and I threw it away."

"Tell me some more things," said the Angel. "When you shot that

Angel on Ybo and he fell with his head underwater, why did you take the trouble to drag him out and stretch him on the bank?"

"I didn't."

"I saw you. I was right there watching you!"

"The hell you were," said Deeming, looked at the Angel's eyes, and knew that the Angel meant what he said. "Well, I—I don't know. I just did it, that's all."

"Now tell me why you knocked out that girl with your fist instead of killing her and covering your tracks."

"Her name was Tandy," said Deeming reflectively. "That's all I remember about it."

"Let's go way back," said the Angel easily. "When you left old Rockhard's place for an evening to clean up your affairs, you put a watch in a package and put it in the mail. Who'd you send it to?"

"Can't recall."

"I can. You mailed it back to the woman you stole it from. Why, Deeming?"

"Why, why, why! I always did that, that's why!"

"Not always. Only when it was a watch which was all the woman had left of her dead husband, or when it was something of equal value. You know what you are, Deeming? You're a softy."

"You're having yourself a time."

"I'm sorry," said the giant gently. "Deeming, I didn't win, as you just put it. You've won."

"Look," said Deeming, "you've caught up with me and I'll get mine. Let's let it go at that and skip the preaching, all right? Right. Let's go. I'm tired."

The Angel put out both hands, fingers slightly spread. Deeming tingled. He distinctly heard two sharp cracks as his spine stretched and reseated itself. He looked up sharply.

"Tired now?" smiled the Angel.

Deeming touched his own forearms, his eyelids. "No," he breathed, "By God, no, I'm not." He cocked his head and said reluctantly, "That's the first one of your tricks I've liked, shorty." He looked again at the jovial golden man. "Just what are you guys, anyway? Oh, all right," he said immediately, "I know, I know. That's

71

the question you never answer. Skip it."

"*You* can ask it." Disregarding Deeming's slack-jawed astonishment at that, the Angel said, "Once we were a strong-arm squad. Sort of a small private army, if you can understand that. All through history there've been mercenaries. Once there was a thug called the Pinkerton man. You wouldn't know about that—it was before your time. Our outfit was operated originally by a man called Angell— with two Ls, and we were called Angell's, with an apostrophe S. So the name really came before the fancy clothes and the Sunday-school kind of activity we go in for now."

"And as time went on we recruited more carefully and improved our rank and file more, and in the meantime our management became less and less, until finally we didn't have a management. Just us, and an idea that we could stop a lot of trouble if we could make people be kind to one another."

"You've sometimes got an offbeat way of being kind!"

"People used to shoot a horse with a broken leg. It was kind," said the Angel.

"So why do you tell me all this?"

"I'm recruiting."

"What?

"Recruiting," the Angel said clearly. "Mustering new men. Making new Angels. Like you, if you want to."

"Aw, now wait a mucking minute here," said Deeming. "You're not going to stand there and tell me you can turn me into an Angel! Not me, you're not."

"Why not?"

"Not me," said Deeming doggedly. "I'm not the Angel type."

"You're not? What type is a man so big he can't live one life at a time but has to play the inverted *and* upside-down Robin Hood for the people? Were you aware that you never stole from anyone who did not, in the long run, benefit by it, learn something from it, and, if he'd lost something of real importance, he always got it back?"

"Is that really so?"

"I can show you a case history of every single one of them."

"You've been on to me for that long?"

"Since you were in third grade."

"Cut it out," said Deeming. "You'd have to be invisible."

The Angel disappeared. Blinking, Deeming walked slowly over to the hull and ran his hand over it.

"Not that that's so marvelous, once you know how it's done. Do you know any reason why a flicker-field shouldn't be refined down to something the size of your fist?" demanded the Angel's voice from mid-air. Deeming whirled and saw nothing. He backed against the boat, wide-eyed. "Over here," said the Angel cheerfully, and reappeared to the right. He drew back his cloak and turned down his waist-band. Deeming briefly glimpsed a small, curved, flat plastic pack of some kind.

"You've got to understand," said the Angel, "that human beings, by and large, are by nature both superstitious and reverent. If you substitute science for their theology, they'll just get reverent about their science. All we do is give them what they want anyway. We never pretend to be anything special, but neither do we deny anything they think about us. If they think we're power-hungry slave traders, we prove they're wrong. If they think we're demigods or something, we don't say anything at all.

"It works out. There hasn't been a war in so long that half the population couldn't define the word. And we came along when we were needed most, believe me. When man was expanding against and through extra-terrestrial cultures. The word had to be spread, or damn well else."

"Just exactly what is the word? What are you really after?"

"I've already told you, but it sounds so confounded simple that nobody will believe it until they see it in action, and then they find something else to describe it. I'll try you again," said the Angel, chuckling. "The word is, *be kind to each other*. It opened the sky."

"I have to think about that," said Deeming, overwhelmed. He shook it off. "Later, I'll think about it ... I hear things about you people. I hear you don't eat."

"That's so."

"Or sleep."

"True. We don't breed either; we haven't been able to get our treatment to take on women, though we'll make it someday. We're not a species or a race, or supermen, or anything like that. We're descendants, out of sadism by technology, of the yinyang weed."

"Yinyang!"

"Our dark and deadly secret," said the Angel, laughing. `You know what the stuff does to people who take it uncontrolled. In the right hands, it's no more addictive than any other medicine. And you see, Deeming, you don't, you just *don't* increase intelligence by a factor of five and fail to see that people must be kind to one another. So the word, as I've called it, isn't a doctrine as such, or a philosophy, but simply a logical dictate. By the way, if you decide against joining us, don't go clacking in public about yinyang, or you'll get yourself clobbered out of thin air."

"What did you say? What?" shouted Deeming. "If I decide against ... Have I a choice?"

"Can you honestly conceive of our forcing you to get people to be kind to each other?" asked the Angel soberly.

Deeming walked away and walked back again, eyes closed, pounding a fist into his other hand. "Well, you don't force me; fine. But I still have no choice. I'll take your word for it—though it'll be months before it really sinks in—that you boys are off my back. But I can't go back to that mess on Earth, with all old Rockhard's affairs churning around and the government poking into all his associations, and ..."

"What mess did you say?" asked the Angel, and laughed. "Deeming, there isn't any mess."

"But Rockhard ..."

"There isn't any Rockhard. Did you ever hear of any Rockhard before that fat boy called on you that night?"

"Well, no, but that doesn't mean- Oh, by golly, it *does* mean ... yeah, but what about the big smash-up, all Rockhard's affairs; it was in all the newscasts, it said right there ..."

"In how many newscasts?"

"When I was on Iolanthe! I saw it myself when—oh. Oh. A private showing."

"You were in no position to be suspicious," the Angel excused him kindly.

"I'll say I wasn't. Your flyboys were about to knock me out of the sky. I could've been killed."

"Right."

"Matter of fact, suppose I'd kept my mouth shut when I was welded up in the landing foot of that ship? I might be there yet!"

"Correct."

"And if I'd bobbled that job on Ybo I could have caught a disrupter beam."

"Just get used to it and you won't be so indignant. Certainly you were in danger. Everything was set up so that you had right and wrong choices to make, and a great deal of freedom in between. You made the right choices and you're here. We can use you. We couldn't use a man who might jump the wrong way in an emergency."

"They say you're immortal," said Deeming abruptly.

"Nonsense!" said the Angel. "That's just a rumor, probably based on the fact that none of us has died yet. I don't doubt that we will."

"Oh," said Deeming, and started to think of something else. Then the full impact of what he had just heard reached him. He whispered, "But there have been gold-cloaked Angels around for two thousand years!"

"Twenty-three hundred," said the Angel.

"For that you stop breeding," said Deeming, and added rudely, "tell me, Gramps, is it worth it?"

"In all kindness," beamed the Angel, "I do believe you should have three of your teeth knocked down your throat, to guard you against making such remarks in the presence of someone who might take it less kindly than I do."

"I withdraw the remark," said Deeming, bowing low; and when he straightened up his face was puckered up like that of a child wanting to cry but hanging on tight. "I have to make gags about it, sir. Can't you see that? Or I—I ..."

"All right, boy. Don't let it worry you ... it's a big thing to meet without warning. D'ye think I've forgotten that?"

They stood for a while in companionable silence. Then, "How long do I have to make up my mind?"

"As much time as it takes. You've qualified, you understand that?

75

Your invitation is permanent. You can only lose it by breaking faith with me."

"I can't see myself starting a movement to persuade people to hate each other. Not after this. And I'm not likely to talk. Who'd listen?"

"An Angel," said the golden one softly, "no matter whom you were talking to. Now—what do you want to do?"

"I want to go back to Earth."

The Angel waved at the boat. "Help yourself."

Deeming looked at him and bit his lip. "Don't you want to know why?"

The Angel silently smiled.

"It's just that I have to," blurted Deeming protestingly. "I mean, all my damn miserable years I've been afraid to live more than half a life at a time. Even when I created a new one, for kicks, I shut off the original while it was going on. I want to go back the way I am, and learn how to be as big as I am." He leaned forward and tapped the Angel's broad chest. "That—is—pretty damn big. If I let you make me into what you are, I'd go back larger than life size. I want to be life size for a time. I think that's what I mean. You don't have to be an Angel to be big. You don't have to be any more than a man to live by the word, for that matter." He fell silent.

"How do you know what it's like to be what you call 'life size'?"

"I did it for about three minutes, standing on the steps of the Astro Central on Ybo. I was talking to . . ."

"You could go back by way of Ybo."

"She wouldn't look my way, except to have me arrested," said Deeming. "She saw me shoot an Angel."

"Then we'll have that same Angel arrest you, and restore her faith in us."

Deeming never reached Earth. He was arrested on Ybo and the arresting Angel draped him over a thick forearm and displayed him to the girl Tandy. She watched him stride off with his prisoner and ran after them.

"What are you going to do with him?"

"What would you do?"

They looked at each other for a time, until the Angel said to Deeming, "Can you tell me honestly that you have something to learn from this girl, and that you're willing to learn it?"

"Oh yes," said Deeming.

"Teach him what?" cried the girl, in a panic. "Teach him how?"

"By being yourself," Deeming said, and when he said that the Angel let go of him.

"Come see me," the Angel said to Deeming, "three days after this is over."

It was over when she died and after they had lived together on Ybo for seventy-four years, and in three days he was able to sit among his great-grandchildren and decide what to do next.

A Touch of Strange

He left his clothes in the car and slipped down to the beach.

Moonrise, she'd said.

He glanced at the eastern horizon and was informed of nothing. It was a night to drink the very airglow, and the stars lay lightless like scattered talc on the background.

"Moonrise," he muttered.

Easy enough for her. Moonrise was something, in her cosmos, that one simply knew about. He'd had to look it up. You don't realize—certainly *she'd* never realize—how hard it is, when you don't know anything about it, to find out exactly what time moonrise is supposed to be, at the dark of the moon. He still wasn't positive, so he'd come early, and would wait.

He shuffled down to the whispering water, finding it with ears and toes. "Woo." Catch m' death, he thought. But it never occurred to him to keep *her* waiting. It wasn't in her to understand human frailties.

He glanced once again at the sky, then waded in and gave himself to the sea. It was chilly, but by the time he had taken ten of the fine strong strokes which had first attracted her, he felt wonderful. He thought, oh well, by the time I've learned to breathe under water, it should be no trick at all to find moonrise without an almanac.

He struck out silently for the blackened and broken teeth of rock they call Harpy's Jaw, with their gums of foam and the floss of tide-risen weed bitten up and hung for the birds to pick. It was oily calm everywhere but by the Jaw, which mumbled and munched on every wave and spit the pieces into the air. He was therefore very close before he heard the singing. What with the surf and his concentration on flanking the Jaw without cracking a kneecap the way he had that first time, he was in deep water on the seaward side before he noticed the new quality in the singing: Delighted, he trod water and listened to be sure; and sure enough, he was right.

It sounded terrible.

"Get your flukes out of your mouth," he bellowed joyfully, "you baggy old guano-guzzler."

"You don't sound so hot yourself, chum," came the shrill falsetto answer, "and you know what type fish-gut chum I mean."

He swam closer. Oh, this was fine. It wasn't easy to find a for-real something like this to clobber her with. Mostly, she was so darn perfect, he had to make it up whole, like the time he told her her eyes weren't the same color. Imagine, he thought, *they* get head-colds too! And then he thought, well, why not? "You mind your big bony bottom-feeding mouth," he called cheerfully, "or I'll curry your tail with a scaling-tool." He could barely make her out, sprawled on the narrow seaward ledge—something piebald dark in the darkness. "Was that really you singin' or are you sitting on a blowfish?"

"You creak no better'n a straight-gut skua gull in a sewer sump," she cried raucously. "Whyn'cha swallow that seaslug or spit it out, one?"

"Ah, go soak your head in a paddlewheel," he laughed. He got a hand on the ledge and heaved himself out of the water. Instantly there was a high-pitched squeak and a clumsy splash, and she was gone. The particoloured mass of shadow-in-shade had passed him in mid-air too swiftly for him to determine just what it was, but he knew with a shocked certainty what it was not.

He wriggled a bare (i.e. mere) buttock-clutch on the short narrow shelf of rock and leaned over as far as he could to peer into the night-stained sea. In a moment there was a feeble commotion and then a bleached oval so faint that he must avert his eyes two points to leeward like a sailor seeing a far light, to make it out at all. Again, seeing virtually nothing, he could be sure of the things it was not. That close cap of darkness, night or no night, was not the web of floating gold for which he had once bought a Florentine comb. Those two dim blotches were not the luminous, over-long, wide-spaced (almost side-set) green eyes which, laughing, devoured his sleep. Those hints of shoulders were not broad and fair, but slender. That salt-spasmed weak sobbing cough was unlike any sound he had heard on these rocks before; and the (by this time) unnecessary final proof was the narrow hand he reached for and grasped. It was delicate, not splayed; it was unwebbed; its smoothness was that of the plum and not the articulated magic of a fine wrought golden watchband. It was, in short, human, and for a long devastated moment their hands clung together while their minds, in panic, prepared to do battle with the truth.

At last they said in unison, "But you're not . . ."

And let a wave pass, and chorused, "I didn't know there was anybod . . ."

And opened and closed their mouths, and said together, "Y'see, I was waiting for . . ." "Look!" he said abruptly, because he had found something he could say that she couldn't at the moment. "Get a good grip, I'll pull you out. Ready? One, two . . ."

"No!" she said, outraged, and pulled back abruptly. He lost her hand, and down she went in mid-gasp, and up she came strangling. He reached down to help, and missed, though he brushed her arm. "Don't touch me!" she cried, and doggy-paddled frantically to the rock on which he sat, and got a hand on it. She hung there coughing until he stirred, whereupon: "Don't touch me!" she cried again.

"Well all right," he said in an injured tone.

She said, aloud but obviously to herself, "Oh, *dear* . . ."

Somehow this made him want to explain himself. "I only thought you should come out, coughing like that, I mean it's silly you should be bobbing around in the water and I'm sitting up here on the . . ." He started a sentence about he was only trying to be . . . and another about he was not trying to be . . . and was unable to finish either. They stared at one another, two panting sightless blots on a spume-slick rock.

"The way I was talking before, you've got to understand . . ."

They stopped as soon as they realized they were in chorus again. In a sudden surge of understanding he laughed—it was like relief— and said, "You mean that you're not the kind of girl who talks the way you were talking just before I got here. I believe you . . . And I'm not the kind of guy who does it either. I thought you were a—

thought you were someone else, that's all. Come on out. I won't touch you."

"Well ..."

"I'm still waiting for the—for my friend. That's all."

"Well ..."

A wave came and she took sudden advantage of it and surged upward, falling across the ledge on her stomach. "I'll manage, I'll manage," she said rapidly, and did. He stayed where he was. They stayed where they were in the hollow of the rock, out of the wind, four feet apart, in darkness so absolute that the red of tight-closed eyes was a lightening.

She said, "Uh ..." and then sat silently masticating something she wanted to say, and swallowing versions of it. At last: "I'm not trying to be nosy."

"I didn't think you ... Nosy? You haven't asked me anything."

"I mean staying here," she said primly. "I'm not just trying to be in the way, I mean. I mean, I'm waiting for someone too."

"Make yourself at home," he said expansively, and then felt like a fool. He was sure he had sounded cynical, sarcastic, and unbelieving. Her protracted silence made it worse. It became unbearable. There was only one thing he could think of to say, but he found himself unaccountably reluctant to bring out into the open the only possible explanation for her presence here. His mouth asked (as it were) while he wasn't watching it, inanely, "Is your uh friend coming out in uh a boat?"

"Is yours?" she asked shyly; and suddenly they were laughing together like a brace of loons. It was one of those crazy sessions people will at times find themselves conducting, laughing explosively, achingly, without a specific punchline over which to hang the fabric of the situation. When it had spent itself, they sat quietly. They had not moved nor exchanged anything, and yet they now sat together, and not merely side-by-side. The understood attachment to someone—something—else had paradoxically dissolved a barrier between them.

It was she who took the plunge, exposed the Word, the code attachment by which they might grasp and handle their preoccupation.

She said, dreamily, "I never saw a mermaid."

And he responded, quite as dreamily but instantly too: "Beautiful." And that was question and answer. And when he said, "I never saw a . . ." she said immediately, "Beautiful." And that was reciprocity. They looked at each other again in the dark and laughed, quietly this time.

After a friendly silence, she asked, "What's her name?"

He snorted in self-surprise. "Why, I don't know. I really don't. When I'm away from her I think of her as *she,* and when I'm with her she's just . . . *you.* Not you," he added with a childish giggle.

She gave him back the giggle and then sobered reflectively. "Now that's the strangest thing. I don't know his name either. I don't even know if they have names."

"Maybe they don't need them. She—uh—they're sort of different, if you know what I mean. I mean, they know things we don't know, sort of . . . feel them. Like if people are coming to the beach, long before they're in sight. And what the weather will be like, and where to sit behind a rock on the bottom of the sea so a fish swims right into their hands."

"And what time's moonrise."

"Yes," he said, thinking, you suppose they know each other? you think they're out there in the dark watching? you suppose *he'll* come first, and what will he say to me? Or what if *she* comes first?

"I don't think they need names," the girl was saying. "They know one person from another, or just who they're talking about, by the feel of it. What's your name?"

"John Smith," he said. "Honest to God."

She was silent, and then suddenly giggled.

He made a questioning sound.

"I bet you say "Honest to God" like that every single time you tell anyone your name. I bet you've said it thousands and thousands of times," she said.

"Well, yes. Nobody ever noticed it before, though."

"I would. My name is Jane Dow. Dee owe doubleyou, not Doe."

"Jane Dow. Oh! and you have to spell it out like that every single time?"

"Honest to God," she said, and they laughed.

He said, "John Smith, Jane Dow. Golly. Pretty ordinary people."

"Ordinary. You and your mermaid."

He wished he could see her face. He wondered if the merpeople were as great a pressure on her as they were on him. He had never told a soul about it—who'd listen?

Who'd believe? Or, listening, believing, who would not interfere? Such a wonder . . . and had she told all her girlfriends and boyfriends and the boss and what-not? He doubted it. He could not have said why, but he doubted it.

"Ordinary," he said assertively, "yes." And he began to talk, really talk about it because he had not, because he had to. "That has a whole lot to do with it. Well, it has everything to do with it. Look, nothing ever happened in my whole entire life. Know what I mean? I mean, nothing. I never skipped a grade in school and I never got left back. I never won a prize. I never broke a bone. I was never rich and never hungry. I got a job and kept it and I won't ever go very high in the company and I won't ever get canned. You know what I mean?"

"Oh, yes."

"So then," he said exultantly, "along comes this mermaid. I mean, to *me* comes a mermaid. Not just a glimpse, no maybe I did and maybe I didn't see a mermaid: this is a real live mermaid who wants me back again, time and again, and makes dates and keeps 'em too, for all she's all the time late."

"So is *he*," she said in intense agreement.

"What I call it," he said, leaning an inch closer and lowering his voice confidentially, "is a touch of strange. A touch of strange. I mean, that's what I call it to myself, you see? I mean, a person is a person all his life, he's good to his mother, he never gets arrested, if he drinks too much he doesn't get in trouble he just gets, excuse the expression, sick to his stomach. He does a day's good work for a day's pay and nobody hates him or, for that matter, nobody likes him either. Now a man like that has no *life;* what I mean, he isn't *real.* But just take an ordinary guy-by-the-millions like that, and add a touch of strange, you see? Some little something he does, or has, or that happens to him, even once. Then for all the rest of his life he's *real*. Golly. I talk too much."

"No you don't. I think that's real nice, Mr. Smith. A touch of strange. A touch ... you know, you just told the story of my life. Yes you did. I was born and brought up and went to school and got a job all right there in Springfield, and ..."

"Springfield? You mean Springfield, Massachusetts? That's my town!" he blurted excitedly, and fell off the ledge into the sea. He came up instantly and sprang up beside her, blowing like a manatee.

"Well no," she said gently. "It was Springfield, Illinois."

"Oh," he said, deflated.

She went on, "I wasn't ever a pretty girl, what you'd call, you know, pretty. I wasn't repulsive either, I don't mean that. Well, when they had the school dances in the gymnasium, and they told all the boys to go one by one and choose a partner, I never got to be the first one. I was never the last one left either, but sometimes I was afraid I'd be. I got a job the day after I graduated from high school. Not a good one, but not bad, and I still work there. I like some people more than other people, but not very much, you know? ... A touch of strange. I always knew there was a name for the thing I never had, and you gave it a good one. Thank you, Mr. Smith."

"Oh that's all right," he said shyly. "And anyway, you have it now ... how was it you happened to meet your ... him, I mean?"

"Oh, I was scared to *death*, I really was. It was the company picnic, and I was swimming, and I—well, to tell you the actual truth, if you'll forgive me, Mr. Smith, I had a strap on my bathing suit that was, well, slippy. Please, I don't mean too *bad*, you know, or I wouldn't ever have worn it. But I was uncomfortable about it, and I just slipped around the rocks here to fix it and ... there he was."

"In the daytime?"

"With the sun on him. It was like ... like ... There's nothing it was like. He was just lying here on this very rock, out of the water. Like he was waiting for me. He didn't try to get away or look surprised or anything, just lay there smiling. Waiting. He has a beautiful soft big voice and the longest green eyes, and long golden hair."

"Yes, yes. *She* has, too."

"He was so beautiful. And then all the rest, well, I don't have to tell you. Shiny silver scales and the big curvy flippers."

"Oh," said John Smith.

"I was scared, oh yes. But not *afraid*. He didn't try to come near me and I sort of knew he couldn't ever hurt me . . . and then he spoke to me, and I promised to come back again, and I did, a lot, and that's the story." She touched his shoulder gently and embarrassedly snatched her hand away. "I never told anyone before. Not a single living soul," she whispered. "I'm so glad to be able to talk about it."

"Yeah." He felt insanely pleased. "Yeah."

"How did you . . ."

He laughed. "Well, I have to sort of tell something on myself: This swimming, it's the only thing I was ever any good at, only I never found out until I was grown. I mean, we had no swimming pools and all that when I went to school. So I never show off about it or anything. I just swim when there's nobody around much. And I came here one day, it was in the evening in summer when most everyone had gone home to dinner, and I swam past the reef line, way out away from the Jaw, here. And there's a place there where it's only a couple of feet deep and I hit my knee."

Jane Dow inhaled with a sharp sympathetic hiss.

Smith chuckled. "Now I'm not one for bad language. I mean I never feel right about using it. But you hear it all the time, and I guess it sticks without you knowing it. So sometimes when I'm by myself and bump my head or whatnot I hear this rough talk, you know, and I suddenly realize it's me doing it. And that's what happened this day, when I hurt my knee. I mean, I really hurt it: So I sort of scrounched down holding on to my knee and I like to boil up the water for a yard around with what I said. I didn't know anyone was around or I'd never."

"And all of a sudden there she was, laughing at me. She came porpoising up out of deep water to seaward of the reef and jumped up into that sunlight, the sun was low then, and red; and she fell flat on her back loud as your tooth breaking on a cherry-pip. When she hit, the water rose up all around her, and for that one second she lay

86

in it like something in a jewel box, you know, pink satin all around and her deep in it."

"I was that hurt and confused and startled I couldn't believe what I saw, and I remember thinking this was some la ... I mean, woman, girl like you hear about, living the life and bathing in the altogether. And I turned my back on her to show her what I thought of that kind of goings-on, but looking over my shoulder to see if she got the message, and I thought then I'd made it all up, because there was nothing there but her suds where she splashed, and they disappeared before I really saw them."

"About then my knee gave another twinge and I looked dawn and saw it wasn't just bumped, it was cut too and bleeding all down my leg, and only when I heard her laughing louder than I was cussing did I realize what I was saying. She swam round and round me, laughing, but you know? there's a way of laughing *at* and a way of laughing *with,* and there was no bad feeling in what she was doing."

"So I forgot my knee altogether and began to swim, and I think she liked that; she stopped laughing and began to sing, and it was ..." Smith was quiet for a time, and Jane Dow had nothing to say. It was as if she were listening for that singing, or to it.

"She can sing with anything that moves, if it's alive, or even if it isn't alive, if it's big enough, like a storm wind or neaptide rollers. The way she sang, it was to my arms stroking the water and my hands cutting it, and me in it, and being scared and wondering, the way I was ... and the water on me, and the blood from my knee, it was all what she was singing, and before I knew it it was all the other way round, and I was swimming to what she sang. I think I never swam in my life the way I did then, and may never again, I don't know; because there's a way of moving where every twitch and wiggle is exactly right, and does twice what it could do before; there isn't a thing in you fighting anything else of yours ..." His voice trailed off.

Jane Dow sighed.

He said, "She went for the rocks like a torpedo and just where she had to bash her brains out, she churned up a fountain of white-water and shot out of the top of it and up on the rocks—right where she wanted to be and not breathing hard at all. She reached her hand into a crack without stretching and took out a big old comb and began running it through her hair, still humming that music and smiling at me like—well, just the way you said *he* did, waiting, not ready to run. I swam to the rocks and climbed up and sat down near her, the way she wanted."

Jane Dow spoke after a time, shyly, but quite obviously from a conviction that in his silence Smith had spent quite enough time on these remembered rocks. "What . . . did she want, Mr. Smith?"

Smith laughed.

"Oh," she said. "I do beg your pardon. I shouldn't have asked."

"Oh please," he said quickly, "it's all right. What I was laughing about was that she should pick on me—me of all people in the world . . ." He stopped again, and shook his head invisibly. No, I'm not going to tell her about that, he decided. Whatever she thinks about me is bad enough. Sitting on a rock half the night with a mermaid, teaching her to cuss . . . He said, "They have a way of getting you to do what they want."

It is possible, Smith found, even while surf whispers virtually underfoot, to detect the cessation of someone's breathing; to be curious, wondering, alarmed, then relieved as it begins again, all without hearing it or seeing anything. *What'd I say?* he thought, perplexed; but he could not recall exactly, except to be sure he had begun to describe the scene with the mermaid on the rocks, and had then decided against it and said something or other else instead. Oh. Pleasing the mermaid. "When you come right down to it," he said, "they're not hard to please. Once you understand what they want."

"Oh yes," she said in a controlled tone. "I found that out."

"You did?"

Enough silence for a nod from her.

He wondered what pleased a merman. He knew nothing about them—nothing. His mermaid liked to sing and to be listened to, to be watched, to comb her hair, and to be cussed at. "And whatever it is, it's worth doing," he added, "because when they're happy, they're happy up to the sky."

"Whatever it is," she said, disagreeably agreeing.

A strange corrosive thought drifted against his consciousness. He batted it away before he could identify it. It was strange, and corrosive, because of his knowledge of and feeling for, his mermaid. There is a popular conception of what joy with a mermaid might be, and he had shared it—if he had thought of mermaids at all—with the populace ... up until the day he met one. You listen to mermaids, watch them, give them little presents, cuss at them, and perhaps learn certain dexterities unknown, or forgotten, to most of us, like breathing under water—or, to be more accurate, storing more oxygen than you thought you could, and finding still more (however little) extractable from small amounts of water admitted to your lungs and vaporized by practiced contractions of the diaphragm, whereby some of the dissolved oxygen could be coaxed out of the vapor. Or so Smith had theorized after practicing certain of the mermaid's ritual exercises. And then there was fishing to be eating, and fishing to be fishing, and hypnotizing eels, and other innocent pleasures.

But innocent.

For your mermaid is as oviparous as a carp, though rather more mammalian than an echidna. Her eggs are tiny, by honored mammalian precedent, and in their season are placed in their glittering clusters (for each egg looks like a tiny pearl embedded in a miniature moonstone) in secret, guarded grottos, and cared for with much ritual. One of the rituals takes place after the eggs are well rafted and have plated themselves to the inner lip of their hidden nest; and this is the finding and courting of a merman to come and, in the only way he can, father the eggs.

This embryological sequence, unusual though it may be, is hardly unique in complexity in a world which contains such marvels as the pelagic phalange of the cephalopods and the simultaneity of disparate appetites exhibited by certain arachnids. Suffice it to say, regarding mermaids, that the legendary monosyllable of greeting used by the ribald Indian is answered herewith; and since design follows function in such matters, one has a guide to one's conduct with the lovely creatures, and they, brother, with you, and with you, sister.

"So gentle," Jane Dow was saying, "but then, so rough."

"Oh?" said Smith. The corrosive thought nudged at him. He flung it somewhere else, and it nudged him there, too. . . . It was at one time the custom in the Old South to quiet babies by smearing their hands liberally with molasses and giving them a chicken feather. Smith's corrosive thought behaved like such a feather, and pass it about as he would he could not put it down.

The mer*man* now, he thought wildly . . . "I suppose," said Jane Dow, "I really am in no position to criticize."

Smith was too busy with his figurative feather to answer.

"The way I talked to you when I thought you were . . . when you came out here. Why, I never in my life . . ."

"That's all right. You heard *me,* didn't you?" Oh, he thought, suddenly disgusted with himself, it's the same way with her and her friend as it is with me and mine. Smith, you have an evil mind. This is a nice girl, this Jane Dow.

It never occurred to him to wonder what was going through her mind. Not for a moment did he imagine that she might have less information on mermaids than he had, even while he yearned for more information on mermen.

"They *make* you do it," she said. "You just have to. I admit it; I lie awake nights thinking up new nasty names to call him. It makes him so happy. And he loves to do it too. The . . . things he says. He calls me 'alligator bait.' He says I'm his squashy little bucket of roe. Isn't that awful? He says I'm a milt-and-water type. What's milt, Mr. Smith?"

"I can't say," hoarsely said Smith, who couldn't, making a silent resolution not to look it up. He found himself getting very upset. She seemed like such a nice girl . . . He found himself getting angry. She unquestionably *had* been a nice girl.

Monster, he thought redly. "I wonder if it's moonrise yet."

Surprisingly she said, "Oh dear. Moonrise."

Smith did not know why, but for the first time since he had come to the rock, he felt cold. He looked unhappily seaward. A ragged, wistful, handled phrase blew by his consciousness: *save her from herself.* It made him feel unaccountably noble.

She said faintly, "Are you . . . have you . . . I mean, if you don't mind my asking, you don't have to tell me . . ."

"What is it?" he asked gently, moving close to her. She was huddled unhappily on the edge of the shelf. She didn't turn to him, but she didn't move away.

"Married, or anything?" she whispered.

"Oh gosh no. Never. I suppose I had hopes once or twice, but no, oh gosh no."

"Why not?"

"I never met a ... well, they all ... You remember what I said about a touch of strange?"

"Yes, yes ..."

"Nobody had it ... Then I got it, and ... put it this way, I never met a girl I could tell about the mermaid."

The remark stretched itself and lay down comfortably across their laps, warm and increasingly audible, while they sat and regarded it. When he was used to it, he bent his head and turned his face towards where he imagined hers must be, hoping for some glint of expression. He found his lips resting on hers. Not pressing, not cowering. He was still, at first from astonishment, and then in bliss. She sat up straight with her arms braced behind her and her eyes wide until his mouth slid away from hers. It was a very gentle thing.

Mermaids love to kiss. They think it excruciatingly funny. So Smith knew what it was like to kiss one. He was thinking about that while his lips lay still and sweetly on those of Jane Dow. He was thinking that the mermaid's lips were not only cold, but dry and not completely flexible, like the carapace of the soft-shell crab. The mermaid's tongue, suited to the eviction of whelk and the scything of kelp, could draw blood. (It never had, but it could.) And her breath smelt of fish.

He said, when he could, "What were you thinking?"

She answered, but he could not hear her.

"What?"

She murmured into his shoulder, "His teeth all point inwards."

Aha, he thought.

"John," she said suddenly, desperately, "There's one thing you must know now and forever more. I know just how things were between you and *her,* but what you have to understand is that it wasn't the same with me. I want you to know the truth right from the very beginning, and now we don't need to wonder about it or talk about it ever again."

"Oh you're fine," John. Smith choked. "So fine ... Let's go. Let's get out of here before—before moonrise."

Strange how she fell into the wrong and would never know it (for they never discussed it again), and forgave him and drew from that a mightiness; for had she not defeated the most lawless, the loveliest of rivals?

Strange how he fell into the wrong and forgave her, and drew from his forgiveness a lasting pride and a deep certainty of her eternal gratitude.

Strange how the moon had risen long before they left, yet the mermaid and the merman never came at all, feeling things as they strangely do.

And John swam in the dark sea slowly, solicitous, and Jane swam, and they separated on the dark beach and dressed, and met again at John's car, and went to the lights where they saw each other at last; and when it was time, they fell well and truly in love, and surely that is the strangest touch of all.

The Comedian's Children

The quiet third of the Twenty-First Century came to an end at ten o'clock on the morning of May 17, 2034, with the return to earth of a modified Fafnir space cruiser under the command of Capt. Avery Swope. Perhaps in an earlier or a later day, the visitation which began on the above date might have had less effect. But the earth was lulled and content with itself, and for good reason—international rivalries having reverted to the football fields and tennis courts, an intelligent balance of trade and redistribution of agriculture and industry having been achieved.

Captain Swope's mission was to accomplish the twelfth off-earth touchdown, and the body on which he touched was Iapetus (sometimes Japetus), the remarkable eighth satellite of Saturn. All Saturn's satellites are remarkable, each for a different reason. Iapetus' claim to fame is his fluctuating brilliance; he always swings brightly around the eastern limb of the ringed planet, and dwindles dimly behind the western edge. Obviously the little moon is half bright and half dark, and keeps one face turned always to its parent; but why should a moon be half bright and half dark?

It was an intriguing mystery, and it had become the fashion to affect all sorts of decorations which mimicked the fluctuations of the inconstant moonlet: cufflinks and tunic clasps which dimmed and brightened, bread-wrappers and book-jackets in dichotomous motley. Copies were reproduced of the midcentury master Pederson's magnificent oil painting of a space ship aground on one of Saturn's moons, with four suited figures alighting, and it became a sort of colophon for news stories about Swope's achievement and window displays of bi-colored gimcrackery—with everyone marveling at the Twentieth Century artist's unerring prediction of a Fafnir's contours, and no one noticing that the painting could not possibly

93

have been of Iapetus which has no blue sky nor weathered rocks, but must certainly have been the meticulous Pederson's visualization of Titan. Still, everyone thought it was Iapetus, and since it gave no evidence as to why Iapetus changed its brightness, the public embraced the painting as the portrait of a mystery. They told each other that Swope would find out.

Captain Swope found out, but Captain Swope did not tell. Something happened to his Fafnir on Iapetus. His signals were faintly heard through the roar of an electrical disturbance on the parent world, and they were unreadable, and they were the last. Then, voiceless, he returned, took up his braking orbit, and at last came screaming down out of the black into and through the springtime blue. His acquisition of the tail-down attitude so very high—over fifty miles— proved that something was badly wrong. The extreme deliberation with which he came in over White Sands, and the constant yawing, like that of a baseball bat balanced on a fingertip, gave final proof that he was attempting a landing under manual control, something never before attempted with anything the size of a Fafnir. It was superbly done, and may never be equaled, that roaring drift down and down through the miles, over forty-six of them, and never a yaw that the sensitive hands could not compensate, until that last one.

What happened? Did some devil-imp of wind, scampering runt of a hurricane, shoulder against the Fafnir? Or was the tension and strain at last too much for weary muscles which could not, even for a split second, relax and pass the controls to another pair of hands? Whatever it was, it happened at three and six-tenths miles, and she lay over bellowing as her pilot made a last desperate attempt to gain some altitude and perhaps another try.

She gained nothing, she lost a bit, hurtling like a dirigible gone mad, faster and faster, hoping to kick the curve of the earth down and away from her, until, over Arkansas, the forward section of the rocket liner—the one which is mostly inside the ship—disintegrated and she blew off her tail. She turned twice end over end and thundered into a buckwheat field.

Two days afterwards a photographer got a miraculous picture. It was darkly whispered later that he had unforgivably carried the child—the three-year-old Tresak girl from the farm two miles away—into the crash area and had inexcusably posed her there; but this could never be proved, and anyway, how could he have known? Nevertheless, the multiple miracles of a momentary absence of anything at all in the wide clear background, of the shadows which mantled her and of the glitter of the many-sharded metal scrap which reared up behind her to give her a crown but most of all the miracle of the child herself, black-eyed, golden-haired, trusting, fearless, one tender hand resting on some jagged steel which would surely shred her flesh if she were less beautiful—these made one of the decade's most memorable pictures. In a day she was known to the nation, and warmly loved as a sort of infant phoenix rising from the disaster of the roaring bird; the death of the magnificent Swope could not cut the nation quite as painfully because of her, as that cruel ruin could not cut her hand.

The news, then, that on the third day after her contact with the wreck of the ship from Iapetus, the Tresak child had fallen ill of a disfiguring malady never before seen on earth, struck the nation and the world a dreadful and terrifying blow. At first there was only a numbness, but at the appearance of the second, and immediately the third cases of the disease, humanity sprang into action. The first thing it did was to pass seven Acts, an Executive Order and three Conventions against any further off-earth touchdowns; so, until the end of the iapetitis epidemic, there was an end to all but orbital space flight.

"You're going to be all right," she whispered, and bent to kiss the solemn, comic little face. (They said it wasn't contagious; at least, adults didn't get it.) She straightened up and smiled at him, and Billy smiled his half-smile—it was the left half—in response. He said something to her, but by now his words were so blurred that she failed to catch them. She couldn't bear to have him repeat whatever it was; he seemed always so puzzled when people did not understand him, as if he could hear himself quite plainly. So to spare herself the pathetic pucker which would worry the dark half of his face, she only smiled the more and said again, "You're going to be all right," and then she fled. Outside in the corridor she leaned for a moment against the wall and got rid of the smile, the rigid difficult hypocrisy of that smile. There was something standing there on the other side of the scalding blur which replaced the smile; she said, because she had to say it to someone just then: "How could I promise him that?"

"One does," said the man, answering. She shook away the blur and saw that it was Dr. Otis. "I promised him the same thing myself. One just . . . does," he shrugged. "Heri Gonza promises them, too."

"I saw that," she nodded. "He seems to wonder 'How could I?' too."

"He does what he can," said the doctor, indicating, with a motion of his head, the special hospital wing in which they stood, the row of doors behind and beyond, doors to laboratories doors to research and computer rooms, store rooms, staff rooms, all donated by the comedian. "In a way he has more right to make a promise like that than Billy's doctor."

"Or Billy's sister," she agreed tremulously. She turned to walk down the corridor, and the doctor walked with her. "Any new cases?"

"Two."

She shuddered. "Any . . ."

"No," he said quickly, "no deaths." And as if to change the subject, he said, "I understand you're to be congratulated."

"What? Oh," she said wrenching her mind away from the image of Billy's face, half marble, half mobile mahogany. "Oh, the award. Yes, they called me this afternoon. Thank you. Somehow it . . . doesn't mean very much right now."

They stood before his office at the head of the corridor. "I think I understand how you feel," he said. "You'd trade it in a minute for . . ." he nodded down the corridor toward the boy's room.

"I'd even trade it for a reasonable hope," she agreed. "Good night, doctor. You'll call me?"

"I'll call you if anything happens. Including anything good. Don't forget that, will you? I'd hate to have you afraid of the sound of my voice."

"Thank you, Doctor."

"Stay away from the trideo this once. You need some sleep."

"Oh Lord. Tonight's the big effort," she remembered.

"Stay away from it," he said with warm severity. "You don't need to be reminded of iapetitis, or be persuaded to help."

"You sound like Dr. Horowitz."

His smile clicked off. She had meant it as a mild pleasantry; if she had been less tired, less distraught, she would have had better sense. Better taste. Horowitz' name echoed in these of all halls like a blasphemy. Once honored as among the greatest of medical researchers, he had inexplicably turned his back on Heri Gonza and his Foundation, had flatly refused research grants, and had publicly insulted the comedian and his great philanthropy. As a result he had lost his reappointment to the directorship of the Research Institute and a good deal of his professional standing. And like the sullen buffoon he was, he plunged into research—"real research," he inexcusably called it—on iapetitis, attempting single-handedly not only to duplicate the work of the Foundation, but to surpass it: "the only way I know," he had told a reporter, "to pull the pasture out from under that clod and his trained sheep." Heri Gonza's reply was typical: by deft sketches on his programs, he turned Horowitz into an improper noun, defining a horowitz as a sort of sad sack or poor soul, pathetic, mildly despicable, incompetent and always funny— the kind of subhuman who not only asks for, but justly deserves a pie in the face. He backed this up with a widely publicized standing offer to Dr. Horowitz of a no-strings-attached research grant of half a million; which Dr. Horowitz, after his first unprintable refusal (his instructions to the comedian as to what he could do with the money were preceded by the suggestion that he first change it into pennies), ignored.

Therefore the remark, even by a Nobel prizewinner, even by a reasonably handsome woman understandably weary and upset, even by one whose young brother lay helpless in the disfiguring grip of an incurable disease—such a remark could hardly be forgiven, especially when made to the head of the Iapetitis Wing of the Medical Center and local chairman of the Foundation. "I'm sorry, Dr. Otis," she said. "I . . . probably need sleep more than I realized."

"You probably do, Dr. Barran," he said evenly, and went into his office and closed the door.

"Damn," said Iris Barran, and went home.

No one knew precisely how Heri Gonza had run across the idea of
an endurance contest cum public solicitation of funds, or when he
decided to include it in his bag of tricks. He did not invent the idea;
it was a phenomenon of early broadcasting, which erupted briefly
on the marriage of video with audio in a primitive device known as
television. The performances, consisting of up to forty continuous
hours of entertainment interspersed with pleas for aid for one charity or another, were headed by a single celebrity who acted as master of ceremonies and beggar-in-chief. The terminologically bastardized
name for this production was *telethon*, from the Greek root *tele*, to
carry, and the syllable *thon*, meaningless in itself but actually the last
syllable of the word marathon. The telethon, sensational at first, had
rapidly deteriorated, due to its use by numbers of greedy publicists
who, for the price of a phone call, could get large helpings of publicity by pledging donations which, in many cases, they failed to
make, and the large percentage of the citizenry whose impulse to
give did not survive their telephoned promises. And besides, the nov-
elty passed, the public no longer watched. So for nearly eighty years
there were no telethons, and if there had been, a disease to hang on
would have been hard to find. Heart disease, cancer, multiple scle-
rosis, muscular dystrophy—these, and certain other infirmities on
which public appeals had been based, had long since disappeared or
were negligibly present.

Now, however, there was iapetitis.

A disorder of the midbrain and central nervous system, it attacked
children between the ages of three and seven, affecting only one
hemisphere, with no statistical preference for either side. Its mental
effects were slight (which in its way was one of the most tragic aspects
of the disease) being limited to aphasia and sometimes a partial alexia.
It had more drastic effects on the motor system, however, and on
the entire cellular regeneration mechanisms of the affected side, which
would gradually solidify and become inert, immobile. The most spec-
tacular symptom was the superficial pigmentation. The immobilized

side turned white as bleached bone, the other increasingly dark, beginning with a reddening and slowly going through the red-browns to a chocolate in the latter stages. The division was exactly on the median line, and the bicoloration proceeded the same way in all cases, regardless of the original pigmentation.

There was no known cure.

There was no known treatment.

There was only the Foundation—Heri Gonza's Foundation— and all it could do was install expensive equipment and expensive people to operate it . . . and hope. There was nothing anyone else could do which would not merely duplicate the Foundation's efforts, and besides, with one exception the Foundation already had the top people in microbiology, neurology, virology, internal medicine, and virtually every other discipline which might have some bearing on the disease. There were, so far, only 376 known cases, every one of which was in a Foundation hospital.

Heri Gonza had been associated with the disease since the very beginning, when he visited a children's hospital and saw the appalling appearance of the first case, little Linda Tresak of Arkansas. When four more cases appeared in the Arkansas State Hospital after she was a patient there for some months, Heri Gonza moved with characteristic noise and velocity. Within forty-eight hours of his first knowledge of the new cases, all five were ensconced in a specially vacated wing of the Medical Center, and mobilization plans were distributed to centers all over the world, so that new clinics could be set up and duplicate facilities installed the instant the disease showed up. There were at present forty-two such clinics. Each child had been picked up within hours of the first appearance of symptoms, whisked to the hospital, pampered, petted, and observed. No treatment. No cure. The white got whiter, the dark got darker, the white side slowly immobilized, the dark side grew darker but was otherwise unaffected; the speech difficulty grew steadily (but extremely slowly) worse; the prognosis was always negative. Negative by extrapolation: any organism in the throes of such deterioration might survive for a long time, but must ultimately succumb.

In a peaceful world, with economy stabilized, population growing but not running wild any longer, iapetitis was big news. The biggest.

The telethon was, unlike its forebears, not aimed at the public pocket. It was to serve rather as a whip to an already aware world, information to the informed, aimed at earlier and earlier discovery and diagnosis. It was one of the few directions left to medical research. The disease was obviously contagious, but its transmission method was unknown. Some child, somewhere, might be found early enough to display some signs of the point of entry of the disease, something like a fleabite in spotted fever, the mosquito puncture in malaria— some sign which might heal or disappear soon after its occurrence. A faint hope, but it was a hope, and there was little enough of that around.

So, before a wide grey backdrop bearing a forty-foot insignia in the center, the head and shoulders of a crying child vividly done in half silver, half mahogany, Heri Gonza opened his telethon.

Iris Barran got home well after it had started; she had rather over-stayed her hospital visit. She came in wearily and slumped on the divan, thinking detachedly of Billy, thinking of Dr. Otis. The thought of the doctor reminded her of her affront to him, and she felt a flash of annoyance, first at herself for having done it, and immediately another directed at him for being so touchy—and so unforgiving. At the same time she recalled his advice to get some sleep, not to watch the telethon; and in a sudden, almost childish burst of rebellion she slapped the arm of the divan and brought the trideo to life.

The opposite wall of the room, twelve feet high, thirty feet long, seemed to turn to smoke, which cleared to reveal an apparent extension of the floor of the room, back and further back, to Heri Gon-za's great grey backdrop. All around were the sounds, the smells, the pressure of the presence of thousands of massed, rapt people. "... so I looked down and there the horse had caught its silly hoof in my silly stirrup. 'Horse,' I says, 'if you're gettin' on, I'm gettin' off!'"

The laugh was a great soft booming explosion, as usual out of all proportion to the quality of the witticism. Heri Gonza had that rarest of comic skills, the ability to pyramid his effects, so that the mildest of them seemed much funnier than it really was. It was mounted on a rapidly-stacked structure of previous quips and jokes, each with its little store of merriment and all merriment suppressed by the audience for fear of missing not only the next joke, but the entire continuity. When the pyramid was capped, the release was explosive. And yet in that split instant between capper and explosion, he always managed to slip in a clear three or four syllables, "On my way here—" or "When the president—" or "Like the horowitz who—" which, repeated and completed after the big laugh, turned out to be the base brick for the next pyramid.

Watching his face during the big laughs—yocks, the knowledgeable columnists and critics called them—had become a national pastime. Though the contagion of laughter was in his voice and choice of phrase, he played everything deadpan. A small, wiry man with swift nervous movements, he had a face-by-the-million: anybody's face. Its notable characteristics were three: thin lips, masked eyes, impenetrable as onyx, and astonishing jug-handle ears. His voice was totally flexible, capable of almost any timbre, and with the falsetto he frequently affected, his range was slightly over four octaves. He was an accomplished ventriloquist, though he never used the talent with the conventional dummy, but rather to interrupt himself with strange voices. But it was his ordinary, unremarkable, almost immobile face which was his audience's preoccupation. His face never laughed, though in dialogue his voice might. His voice could smile, too, even weep and his face did not. But at the yock, if it was a big yock, a long one, his frozen waiting face would twitch; the thin lips would fill out a trifle: he's going to smile, he's going to smile! Sometimes, when the yock was especially fulsome, his mouth actually would widen a trifle; but then it was always time to go on, and, deadpan he would. What could it matter to anyone whether or not one man in the world smiled? On the face of it, nothing: yet millions of people, most of whom were unaware of it, bent close to their trideo walls and peered raptly, waiting, waiting to see him smile.

As a result, everyone who heard him, heard every word.

Iris found herself grateful, somehow—able to get right out of herself, sweep in with that vast unseen crowd and leave herself, her worrying self, her angry, weary, logical, Nobelprizewinning self asprawl on the divan while she hung on and smiled, hung on and tittered, hung on and exploded with the world.

He built, and he built, and the trideo cameras crept in on him until, before she knew it, he was standing as close to the invisible wall as belief would permit; and still he came closer, so that he seemed in the room with her; and this was a pyramid higher than most, more swiftly and more deftly built, so that the ultimate explosion could contain itself not much longer, not a beat, not a second . . .

And he stopped in mid-sentence, mid-word, even, and, over at the left, fell to one knee and held out his arms to the right. "Come on, honey," he said in a gentle, tear-checked purr.

From the right came a little girl, skipping. She was a beautiful little girl, a picture-book little girl, with old-fashioned bouncing curls, shiny black patent-leather shoes with straps, little white socks, a pale-blue dress with a very wide, very short skirt.

But she wasn't skipping, she was limping. She almost fell, and Heri was there to catch her.

Holding her in his arms, while she looked trustingly up into his face, he walked to center stage, turned, faced the audience. His eyes were on her face; when he raised them abruptly to the audience, they were, by some trick of the light (or of Heri Gonza) unnaturally bright.

And he stood, that's all he did, for a time, stood there with the child in his arms, while the pent-up laughter turned to frustrated annoyance, directed first at the comedian, and slowly, slowly, with a rustle of sighs, at the audience itself by the audience. Ah, to see such a thing and be full of laughter: how awful I am.

I'm sorry. I'm sorry.

One little arm was white, one pink. Between the too-tiny socks and the too-short skirt, the long thin legs were one white, one pink.

"'This is little Koska," he said after an age. The child smiled suddenly at the sound of her name. He shifted her in his elbow so he could stroke her hair. He said softly, "She's a little Esthonian girl, from the far north. She doesn't speak very much English, so she won't mind if we talk about her." A huskiness crept into his voice. "She came to us only yesterday. Her mother is a good woman. She sent her to us the minute she noticed."

Silence again, then he turned the child so their faces were side by side, looking straight into the audience. It was hard to see at first, and then it became all too plain—the excessive pallor of the right side of her face, the too-even flush on the left, and the sharp division between them down the center.

"We'll make you better," he whispered. He said it again in a foreign language, and the child brightened, smiled trustingly into his face, kept her smile as she faced the audience again: and wasn't the smile a tiny bit wider on the pink side than on the white? You couldn't tell . . .

"Help me," said Heri Gonza. "Help her, and the others, help us. Find these children, wherever in the world they might be, and call us. Pick up any telephone in the world and say simply, I . . . F. That's IF, the Iapetitis Foundation. We treat them like little kings and queens. We never cause them any distress. By trideo they are in constant touch with their loved ones." Suddenly, his voice rang. "The call you make may find the child who teaches us what we need to know. Your call—yours!—may find the cure for us."

He knelt and set the child gently on her feet. He knelt holding her hands, looking into her face. He said, "And whoever you are, wherever you might be, you doctors, researchers, students, teachers . . . if anyone, anywhere, has an inkling, an idea, a way to help, any way at all—then call me. Call me now, call here—" He pointed upward and the block letters and figures of the local telephone floated over his head—"and tell me. I'll answer you now, I'll personally speak to anyone who can help. Help, oh, help."

The last word rang and rang in the air. The deep stage behind him slowly darkened, leaving the two figures, the kneeling man and the little golden girl, flooded with light. He released her hands and she turned away from him, smiling timidly, and crossed the wide stage. It seemed to take forever, and as she walked, very slightly she dragged her left foot.

When she was gone, there was nothing left to look at but Heri Gonza. He had not moved, but the lights had changed, making of him a luminous silhouette against the endless black behind him . . .

one kneeling man, a light in the universal dark ... hope ... slowly fading, but there, still there ... no? Oh, there ...

A sound of singing, the palest of pale blue stains in deep center. The singing up, a powerful voice from the past, an ancient, all but forgotten tape of one of the most moving renditions the world has ever known, especially for such a moment as this: Mahalia Jackson singing *The Lord's Prayer,* with the benefit of such audio as had not been dreamed of in her day ... with a cool fresh scent, with inaudible quasihypnotic emanations, with a whispering chorus a chorus of angels might learn from.

Heri Gonza had not said, "Let us pray." He would never do such a thing, not on a global network. There was just the kneeling dimness, and the blue glow far away in the black. And if at the very end the glow looked to some like the sign of the cross, it might have been only a shrouded figure raising its arms; and if this was benediction, surely it was in the eye of the beholder. Whatever it was, no one who saw it completely escaped its spell, or ever forgot it. Iris Barran, for one, exhausted to begin with, heart and mind full to bursting with the tragedy of iapetitis; Iris Barran was wrung out by the spectacle. All she could think of was the last spoken word: *Help!*

She sprang to her phone and waved it active. With trembling fingers she dialed the number which floated in her mind as it had on the trideo wall, and to the composed young lady who appeared in her solido cave, saying, "Trideo, C. A. O. Good evening," she gasped, "Heri Gonza—quickly."

"One moment please," said the vision, and disappeared, to be replaced instantly by another, even more composed, even lovelier, who said, "I.F. Telethon."

"Heri Gonza."

"Yes, of course. Your name?"

"I-Iris Barran. Dr. Iris Barran."

The girl looked up sharply. "Not the ..."

"Yes, I won the Nobel prize. Please—let me speak to Heri Gonza."

"One moment please."

The next one was a young man with curly hair, a bell-like baritone, and an intensely interested face. He was Burcke of the network.

He passed her to a jovial little fat man with shrewd eyes who was with Continuity Acceptance. Iris could have screamed out loud. But a worldwide appeal for calls would jam lines and channels for hours, and obviously a thorough screening process was essential. She was dimly aware that her name and face, only today in all the news, had already carried her to the top. Consciously, she thought of none of this; she held on and drove; wanting only to help ... *help* ... A snatch of the conversation she had had with Dr. Otis drifted across her mind: *I guess you'd trade it for* ... and then a heart-rending picture of Billy's face, trying to smile with half a mouth. *I'd trade it all for a reasonable hope* ... and suddenly she was staring into the face of Heri Gonza. Reflexively she glanced over her shoulder at the trideo wall; Heri Gonza was there too, with a solidophone pillar in center stage, its back to the audience so that only the comedian could see its cave. Light from it flickered on his face.

"I'd know that face anywhere!" he said raspingly.

"Oh," she said faintly, "Mr. ... uh ..." and then remembered that one of his public affectations was never to permit anyone to call him Mister. She said, "Heri Gonza, I ... I'm Iris B-barran, and I—" She realized that her voice could not be heard over the trideo. She was grateful for that.

He said, just as stridently, "I know who you are. I know the story of your life too." Switching to a comic quack, he said "So-o-o?"

"You know I just won the Nobel award. M-uh, Heri Gonza, I want to help, more than anything in the world, I want to help. My brother has it. W-would you like me to give the award money to you ... I mean, to the Foundation?"

She did not know what she expected in exchange for this stunning offer. She had not thought that far ahead. What she did not expect was ...

"You *what?*" he yelled, so loud she drew her head down, gracelessly, turtle-like. "Listen, you, I got along without you before and I can get along without you now. You're getting from me, see, and I'm giving. What you got I don't want. I'm not up here to do *you* no good. I tell you what you got, you *got* a wrong number, and you *are*, s-s-s-s-so," he hissed in a hilarious flatulent stutter, "s-s-so long."

And before she could utter another sound he waved her off and her phone cave went black.

Numb with shock, she slowly turned to the trideo wall, where Heri Gonza was striding downstage to the audience. His expressionless face, his gait, his posture, the inclination of his head, and his tone of voice all added to an amused indignation, with perhaps a shade more anger than mirth. He tossed a thumb at the phone and said, "Wits we got calling, can you imagine? At a time like this. We, got dimwits, half wits, and ..." exactly the right pause; there was one bleat of laughter somewhere in the audience and then a thousand voices to chorus with him—"horowitz!"

Iris sank back in the phone chair and covered her face, pressing so hard against her tired eyes that she saw red speckles. For a time she was shocked completely beyond thought, but at last she was able to move. She rose heavily and went to the divan, arrested her hand as she was about to click off the trideo. Heri Gonza was back at the stage phone, talking eagerly to someone, his voice honey and gentleness. "Oh bless you, brother, and thank you. You may have an idea there, so I tell you what you do. You call the I.F. at Johannesburg and arrange a meeting with the doctors there. They'll listen ... No, brother, collect of course. What's-amatta, brother, you broke? I got news for you, for you-ee are-ee a-ee good-ee man-ee yes-ee indeedy-dee: you ain'ta broka no mo. A man like you? I got a boy on the way this very minute with a bag o' gold for the likes of you brother ... Oh now, don't say thanks, you make me mad. 'Bye."

He waved off, and turned to the audience to intone, "A man with an idea—little one, big one, who knows? But it's to help ... so bless him."

Thunderous applause. Iris let her hand finish the gesture and switched off.

She went and washed her face, and that gave her strength enough to shower and change. After that she could think almost normally.

How *could* he?

She turned over impossible alternatives, explanations. His phone was a dummy: he couldn't see her, didn't know who was on the phone. Or: it was his way, of being funny, and she was too tired to understand. Or ... or ... it was no use: it had really happened, he had known what he was doing, he had a reason.

But what reason? Why? Why?

In her mind she again heard that roar from the audience: Horowitz. With difficulty, because it still stung, she pieced together the conversation and then, moving her forefinger toward her phone and the trideo, back and forth, puzzled out what had gone out over the air and what had not. Only then did she fully understand that Heri Gonza had done what he had done to make it seem that his first call was from Dr. Horowitz. But if he needed that particular gag at that time, why didn't he fake it to a dead phone? Why actually converse with her, cut her down like that?

And he hadn't let her help. That was worse than any of the rudeness, the insult. He wouldn't let her help.

What to do? Making the gesture she had made had not been hard; having it refused was more than she could bear. She must help; she would help. Now of all times, with all this useless money coming to her; she didn't need it, and it might, it just might somehow help, and bring Billy back home.

Well then, expose Heri Gonza. Give him back some of his own humiliation. Call in the newsmen, make a statement. Tell them what she had offered, tell them just who was on the line. He'd *have* to take the money, and apologize to boot.

She stood up; she sat down again. No. He had known what he was doing. He had known who she was; he must have a telltale on his phone to get information on his callers from that screening committee. She knew a lot about Heri Gonza. He seemed so wild, so impulsive; he was not. He ran his many enterprises with a steel fist; he took care of his own money, his own bookings. He did not make mistakes nor take chances. He had refused her and the Foundation would refuse her: the Foundation *was* Heri Gonza. He had his reasons, and if she had any defense at all against what he had done, he would not have done it.

She wasn't allowed to help.

Unless ...

She suddenly ran to the phone. She dialed 5, and the cave lit up with the floating word DIRECTORY. She dialed H, O, R, and touched the Slow button until she had the Horowitzes. There were pathetically few of them. Almost everyone named Horowitz had filed unlisted numbers: many had gone so far as to change their names.

George Rehoboth Horowitz, she remembered.

He wasn't listed.

She dialed Information and asked. The girl gave her a pitying smile and told her the line was unlisted. And of course, it would be. If Dr. Horowitz wasn't the most hated man on earth, he was the next thing to it. A listed phone would be useless to him, never silent.

"Has he screening service?" Iris asked suddenly.

"He has," said the girl, company-polite as always, but now utterly cold. Anyone who *knew* that creature to speak to . . . "Your name, please?"

Iris told her, and added, "Please tell him it's very important."

The cave went dark but for the slowly rotating symbol of the phone company, indicating that the operator was doing her job. Then a man's head appeared and looked her over for a moment, and then said, "Dr. Barran?"

"Dr. Horowitz."

She had not been aware of having formed any idea of the famous (infamous?) Horowitz; yet she must have. His face seemed too gentle to have issued those harsh rejoinders which the news attributed to him; yet perhaps it was gentle enough to be taken for the fumbler, the fool so many people thought he was. His eyes, in some inexplicable way, assured her that his could not be clumsy hands. He wore old-fashioned exterior spectacles; he was losing his hair; he was younger than she had thought, and he was ugly. Crags are ugly, tree-trunks, the hawk's pounce, the bear's foot, if beauty to you is all straight lines and silk. Iris Barran was not repulsed by this kind of ugliness.

She, said, bluntly, "Are you doing any good with the disease?" She did not specify: today, there was only one disease.

He said, in an odd way as if he had known her for a long time and could judge how much she would understand, "I have it all from the top down to the middle, and from the bottom up to about a third. In between—nothing, and no way to get anything."

"Can you go any further?"

"I don't know," he said candidly. "I can go on trying to find ways to go further, and if I find a way, I can try to move along on it."

"Would some money help?"

"It depends on whose it us."

"Mine."

He did not speak, but tilted his head a little to one side and looked at her.

She said, "I won ... I have some money coming in. A good deal of it."

"I heard," he said, and smiled. He seemed to have very strong teeth, not white, not even, just spotless and perfect.

"It's a good deal out of my field, your theoretical physics, and I don't understand it. I'm glad you got it. I really am. You earned it."

She shook her head, denying it, and said, "I was surprised."

"You shouldn't have been. After ninety years of rather frightening confusion, you've restored the concept of parity to science—" he chuckled—"though hardly in the way anyone anticipated."

She had not known that this was her accomplishment; she had never thought of it in those terms. Her demonstration of gravitic flux was a subtle matter to be communicated with wordless symbols, quite past speech. Even to herself she had never made a conversational analog of it; this man had, though, not only easily, but quite accurately.

She thought, if this isn't his field, and he grasps it like that—just how good must he be in his own? She said, "Can you use the money? Will it help?"

"God," he said devoutly, "can I use it.... As to whether it will help, Doctor, I can't answer that. It would help me go on. It may not make me arrive. Why did you think of me?"

Would it hurt him to know? she asked herself, and answered, it would hurt him if I were not honest. She said, "I offered it—to the Foundation. They wouldn't touch it. I don't know why."

"I do," he said, and instantly held up his hand. "Not now," he said, checking her question. He reached somewhere off transmission and came up with a card, on which was lettered, AUDIO TAPPED.

"Who ..."

"The world," he overrode her, "is full of clever amateurs. Tell me, why are you willing to make such a sacrifice?"

"Oh—the money. It isn't a sacrifice. I have enough: I don't need it. And—my baby brother. He has it."

"I didn't know," he said, with compassion. He made a motion with his hands. She did not understand. "What?"

He shook his head, touched his lips, and repeated the motion, beckoning, at himself and the room behind him. Oh. Come where I am.

She nodded, but said only, "It's been a great pleasure talking with you. Perhaps I'll see you soon."

He turned over his card; obviously he had used it many times before. It was a map of a section of the city. She recognized it readily, followed his pointing finger, and nodded eagerly. He said, "I hope it is soon."

She nodded again and rose, to indicate that she was on her way. He smiled and waved off.

It was like a deserted city, or a decimated one; almost everyone was off the streets, watching the telethon. The few people who were about all hurried, as if they were out against their wills and anxious to get back and miss as little as possible. It was known that he intended to go on for at least thirty-six hours, and still they didn't want to miss a minute of him. Wonderful, wonderful, she thought, amazed (not for the first time) at people—just people. Someone had once told her that she was in mathematics because she was so apart from, amazed at, people. It was possible. She was, she knew, very unskilled with people, and she preferred the company of mathematics, which tried so hard to be reasonable, and to say what was really meant ...

She easily found the sporting-goods store he had pointed out on his map, and stepped into the darkened entrance. She looked carefully around and saw no one, then tried the door. It was locked, and she experienced a flash of disappointment of an intensity that surprised her. But even as she felt it, she heard a faint click, tried the door again, and felt it open. She slid inside and closed it, and was gratified to hear it lock again behind her,

Straight ahead a dim, concealed light flickered, enough to show her that there was a clear aisle straight back through the store. When she was almost to the rear wall, the light flickered again, to show her a door at her right, deep in an ell. It clicked as she approached, and opened without trouble. She mounted two flights of stairs, and on the top landing stood Horowitz, his hands out. She took them gladly, and for a wordless moment they stood like that, laughing silently, until he released one of her hands and drew her into his place. He closed the door carefully and then turned and leaned against it.

"Well!" he said. "I'm sorry about the cloak and dagger business."

"It was very exciting." She smiled. "Quite like a mystery story."

"Come in, sit down," he sand, leading the way. "You'll have to excuse the place. I have to do my own housekeeping, and I just don't." He took a test-tube rack and a cracked bunsen tube from an easy chair and nodded her into it. He had to make two circuits of the room before he found somewhere to put them down. "Price of fame," he said sardonically, and sat down on a rope-tied stack of papers bearing the flapping label *Proceedings of the Pan-American Microbiological Society.* "Where that clown makes a joke of Horowitz, other fashionable people make a game of Horowitz. A challenge. Track down Horowitz. Well, if they did, through tapping my phone or following me home, that would satisfy them. Then I would be another kind of challenge. Bother Horowitz. Break in and stir up his lab with a stick. You know."

She shuddered: "People are ... are so ..."

"Don't say that, whatever it was," said Horowitz. "We're living in a quiet time, Doctor, and we haven't evolved too far away from our hunting and tracking appetites. It probably hasn't occurred to you that your kind of math and my kind of biology are hunting and tracking too. Cut away our science bump and we'd probably hunt with the pack too. A big talent is only a means of hunting alone. A little skill is a means of hunting alone some of the time."

"But ... why must they hunt you?"

"Why must you hunt gravitic phenomena?"

"To understand it."

"Which means to end it as a mystery. Cut it down to your size. Conquer it. You happen to be equipped with a rather rarefied type of reason, so you call your conquest understanding. The next guy happens to be equipped with fourteen inches of iron pipe and achieves his conquest with it instead."

"You're amazing," she said openly. "You love your enemies, like—"

"Love thine enemies as thyself. Don't take any piece of that without taking it all. How much I love people is a function off how much I love Horowitz, and you haven't asked me about that . . . Matter of fact, I haven't asked me about that and I don't intend to. My God it's good to talk to somebody again. Do you want a drink?"

"No," she said. "How much do you love Heri Gonza?"

He rose and hit his palm with his fist and sat down again, all his gentleness folded away and put out of sight. "There's the exception. You can understand anything humanity does if you try, but you can't understand the inhumanity of a Heri Gonza. The difference is that he knows what is evil and what isn't and doesn't care. I don't mean any numb by-rote moral knowledge learned at the mother's knee, the kind that afflicts your pipe-wielder a little between blows and a lot when he gets his breath afterward. I mean a clear, analytical, extrapolative, brilliantly intelligent knowledge of each act and each consequence. Don't underestimate that devil."

"He . . . seems to . . . I mean, he does love children," she said fatuously.

"Oh, come on now. He doesn't spend a dime on his precious Foundation that he wouldn't have to give to the government in taxes. Don't you realize that? He doesn't do a thing he doesn't have to do, and he doesn't have to love those kids. He's using those kids. He's using the filthiest affliction mankind has known for a long time just to keep himself front and center."

"But if the Foundation does find a cure, then he . . ."

"Now you've put your finger on the thing that nobody in the world but me seems to understand—why I won't work with the Foundation. Two good reasons. First, I'm 'way ahead of them. I don't need the Foundation and all those fancy facilities. I've got closer to the nature of iapetitis than any of 'em. Second, for all my love for and understanding of people, I don't want to find out what I'm afraid I would find out if I worked there and if a cure was found."

"You mean he'd—he'd withhold it?"

"Maybe not permanently. Maybe he'd sit on it until he'd milked it dry. Years. Some would die by then. Some are pretty close as it is."

She thought of Billy and bit her hand.

"I didn't say he would do that," Horowitz said, more gently. "I said I don't want to be in a position to find out. I don't want to know that any member of my species could do a thing like that. Now you see why I work by myself, whatever it costs. If I can cure iapetitis, I'll say so. I'll do it, I'll prove it. That's why I don't mind his kind of cheap persecution. If I succeed, all that harassment makes it impossible for him to take credit or profit in any way."

"Who are you going to cure?"

"What?"

"He's got them all. He's on trideo right now, a telethon, the biggest show of the last ten years, hammering at people to send him every case the instant it's established." Her eyes were round.

"The logician," he whispered, as round-eyed as she. "Oh my God, I never thought of that." He took a turn around the room and sat down again. His face was white. "But we don't *know* that. Surely he'd give me a patient. Just one."

"It might cost you the cure. You'd have to, you'd just *have* to give it to him, or you'd be the one withholding it!"

"I won't think about it now," he said hoarsely. "I can't think about it now. I'll get the cure. That first."

"Maybe my brother Billy . . ."

"Don't even think about it!" he cried. "He's already got it in for you. Don't get in his way any more. He won't let your Billy out of there and you know it. Try anything and he'll squash you like a beetle."

"What's he got against me?"

"You don't know? You're a Nobel winner—one of the newsiest things there is. A girl, and not bad-looking at all. You're in the public eye, or you will be by noon tomorrow when the reporters get to you. Do you think for a minute he'd let you or anybody climb on his publicity? Listen, iapetitis is his sole property, his monopoly, and he's not going to share it. What'd you expect him to do, announce the gift on his lousy telethon?"

"I—I c-called him on his telethon."

"You didn't !"

"He pretended the call was from you. But . . . but at the same time he told me . . . oh yes, he said, `What you got I don't want. I'm not up here to do you no good.'"

Horowitz spread his hands. "Q.E.D."

"Oh," she said, "how awful."

At that point somebody kicked the door open.

Horowitz sprang to his feet, livid. A big man in an open, flapping topcoat shouldered his way in. He had a long horseface and a blue jaw. His eyes were extremely sad. He said, "Now just relax. Relax and you'll be all right." His hands, as if they had a will of their own, busied themselves about pulling off a tight left-hand glove with wires attached to it and running into his side pocket.

"Flannel!" Horowitz barked. "How did you get in?" He stepped forward, knees slightly bent, head lowering. "You'll get out of here or so help me . . ."

"No!" Iris cried, clutching at Horowitz's forearm. The big man outreached and outweighed the biologist, and certainly would fight rougher and dirtier.

"Don't worry, lady," said the man called Flannel sleepily. He raised a lazy right hand and made a slight motion with it, and a cone-nosed needler glittered in his palm. "He'll be good—won't you, boy? Or I'll put you to bed for two weeks an' a month over."

He sidled past and, never taking his gaze from Horowitz for more than a flickering instant, opened the three doors which led from the laboratory—a bathroom, a bedroom, a storage closet.

"Who is he? You know him?" Iris whispered.

"I know him," growled Horowitz. "He's Heri Gonza's body-guard."

"Nobody but the two of them," said Flannel.

"Good," said a new voice and a second man walked in, throwing off a slouch hat and opening the twin to the long, loose topcoat Flannel wore. "Hi, chillun," said Heri Gonza.

There was a long silence, and then Horowitz plumped down on his pile of *Proceedings,* put his chin in his hands; and said in profound disgust, "Ah, for God's sake."

"Dr. Horowitz," said Heri Gonza pleasantly, nodding, and "Dr. Barran."

Iris said, shakily, "I th-thought you were doing a sh-show."

"Oh, I am, I am. All things are possible if you only know how. At the moment Chitsie Bombom is doing a monolog, and she's good for two encores. After that there's a solido of me sitting way up on the flats in the left rear, oh so whimsically announcing the Player's Pub Players. They have a long one-acter and a pantomime. I've even got a ballet company, in case this takes that long."

"Phoney to the eyeballs, even when you work," said Horowitz. "Quickly and quietly and get the hell out of here, 'scuse me, Dr. Barran."

"Oh, that's all right," she murmured.

"Please," said the comedian softly, "I didn't come here to quarrel with you. I want to end all that. Here and now, and for good."

"We've got something he wants," said Horowitz in a loud aside to Iris.

Heri Gonza closed his eyes and said, "You're making this harder than it has to be. What can I do to make this a peaceful talk?"

"For one thing," said Horowitz, "your simian friend is breathing and it bothers me. Make him stop."

"Flannel," said Heri Gonza, "get out."

Glowering, the big man moved to the door, opened it, and stood on the sill. "All the way," said the comedian. Flannel's broad back was one silent mass of eloquent protest, but he went out and shut the door.

Deftly, with that surprising suddenness of nervous motion which was his stock in trade, Heri Gonza dropped to one knee to bring their faces on a level, and captured Iris's startled hands. "First of all,

Dr. Barran, I came to apologize to you for the way I spoke on the telephone. I had to do it—there was no alternative, as you'll soon understand. I tried to call you back, but you'd already gone."

"You followed me here! Oh, Dr. Horowitz, I'm sorry!"

"I didn't need to follow you. I've had this place spotted since two days before you moved into it, Horowitz. But I'm sorry I had to strongarm my way in."

"I yield to curiosity," said Horowitz. "Why didn't my locks alarm when you opened them? I saw Flannel's palm-print eliminator, but dammit, they should have alarmed."

"The locks were here when you rented the place, right? Well, who do you think had them installed? I'll show you where the cut-off switch is before I leave. Anyhow—grant me this point. Was there any other way I could have gotten in to talk with you?"

"I concede," said Horowitz sourly.

"Now, Dr. Barran. You have my apology, and you'll have the explanation to go with it. Believe me, I'm sorry. The other thing I want to do is to accept, with thanks from the bottom of my heart, your very kind offer of the prize money. I want it, I need it, and it will help more than you can possibly realize."

"No," said Iris flatly. "I've promised it to Dr. Horowitz."

Heri Gonza sighed, got to his feet, and leaned back against the lab bench. He looked down at them sadly.

"Go on," said Horowitz. "Tell us how you need money."

"The only two things I have never expected from you are ignorance and stupidity," said Heri Gonza sharply, "and you're putting up a fine display of both. Do you really think, along with all my millions of ardent fans, that when I land a two-million-dollar contract I somehow put two million dollars in the bank? Don't be childish. My operation is literally too big to hide anything in. I have city, county, state and federal tax vultures picking through my whole operational framework. I'm a corporation and subject to outside accounting. I don't even have a salary; I draw what I need, and I damn well account for it, too. Now, if I'm going to finish what I started with the disease, I'm going to need a lot more money than I can whittle out a chip at a time."

"Then take it out of the Foundation money—that's what it's for."

"I want to do the one thing I'm not allowed to do with it. Which happens to be the one thing that'll break this horrible thing—it has to!"

"The only thing there is like that is a trip to Iapetus."

To this, Heri Gonza said nothing—absolutely nothing at all. He simply waited.

Iris Barran said, "He means it. I think he really means it."

"You're a big wheel," said Horowitz at last, "and there are a lot of corners you can cut, but not that one. There's one thing the government—all governments and all their armed forces—will rise up in wrath to prevent, and that's another landing and return from any place off earth—especially, Iapetus. You're got close to four hundred dying kids on your hands right now, and the whole world is scared."

"Set that aside for a moment." The comedian was earnest, warm-voiced. "Just suppose it could be done. Horowitz, as I understand it you have everything you need on the iapetitis virus but one little link. Is that right?"

"That's right. I can synthesize a surrogate virus from nucleic acids and exactly duplicate the disease. But it dies out of its own accord. There's a difference between my synthetic virus and the natural one, and I don't know what it is. Give me ten hours on Iapetus and half a break, and I'll have the original virus under an electron mike. Then I can synthesize a duplicate, a real self-sustaining virus that can cause the disease. Once I have that, the antigen becomes a factory process, with the techniques we have today. We'll have shots for those kids by the barrel lot inside of a week."

Heri Gonza spread his hands. "There's the problem, then. The law won't allow the flight until we have the cure. We won't have the cure unless we make the flight."

Iris said, "A Nobel prize is an awful lot of money, but it won't buy the shell of a space ship."

"I've got the ship."

For the first time Horowitz straightened up and, spoke with something besides anger and hopelessness. "What kind of a ship? Where is it?"

"A Fafnir. You've seen it, or pictures of it. I use it for globe-trotting mostly, and VIP sightseeing. It's a deepspace craft, crew of twelve, and twelve passenger cabins. But it handles like a dream, and I've got the best pilot in the world. Kearsarge."

"Kearsarge, God yes. But look, what you call deepspace is Mars and Venus. Not Saturn."

"You don't know what's been done to that ship. She'll sleep four now. I have a lab and a shop in her, and all the rest is nothing but power-plant, shielding and fuel. Hell, she'll make Pluto!"

"You mean you've been working on this already?"

"Man, I've been chipping away at my resources for a year and a half now. You don't know what kind of footsie I've been playing with my business managers and the banks and all. I can't squeak out another dime without lighting up the whole project. Dr. Barran, now do you see why I had to treat you like that? You were *the* godsend, with your wonderful offer and your vested interest in Billy. Can you astrogate?"

"I—oh dear. I know the principles well enough. Yes, I could; with a little instruction."

"You'll get it. Now look, I don't want to see that money. You two will go down and inspect the ship tomorrow morning, and then put in everything you'll need beyond what's already there. You've got food, fuel, water and air enough for two trips, let alone one."

"God," said Horowitz.

"I'll arrange for your astrogation, Dr. Barran. You'll have to dream up a story, secret project or long solitary vacation or some such. Horowitz, you can drop out of sight without trouble."

"Oh, sure, thanks to you."

"Dammit, this time you're welcome," said the comedian, and very nearly smiled. "Now, you'll want one more crew member: I'll take care of that before flight time."

"What about the ship? What will you say?"

"Flight test after overhaul. Breakdown in space, repair, return—some such. Leave that to Kearsarge."

"I freely admit," said Horowitz, "that I don't get it. This is one frolic that isn't coming out of taxes, and it's costing you a packet. What's in it, mountebank?"

"You could ask that," said the comedian, sadly. "The kids, that's all."

"You'll get the credit?"

"I won't, I can't, I don't want it. I can't tie in to this jaunt—it would ruin me. Off-earth landings, risking the lives of all earth's kids—you know how they'd talk. No sir: this is your cooky, Horowitz. You disappear, you show up one day with the answer. I eat crow like a hell of a good sport. You get back your directorship if you want it. Happy ending. All the kids get well." He jumped into the air and clicked his heels four times on the way down. "The kids get well," he breathed with sudden sobriety.

Horowitz said gently, "Heri Gonza, what's with you and kids?"

"I like 'em." He buttoned his coat. "Goodnight, Dr. Barran. Please accept my apologies again, and don't think too badly of me."

"I don't," she said smiling, and gave him her hand.

"But why do you like kids that much?" asked Horowitz.

Heri Gonza shrugged easily and laughed his deadpan laugh. "Never had none," he chuckled. He went to the door and stopped facing it, suddenly immobile. His shoulders trembled. He whirled suddenly, and the famous carven face was wet, twisted, the mouth tortured and crooked. "Never can," he whispered, and literally ran out of the room.

The weeks went by, the month. Iapetitis cases underwent some strange undulations, and a hope arose that the off-world virus was losing its strength. Some of the older cases actually improved, and a blessing that was, too; for although overall growth was arrested, there was a tendency for the mobile side to grow faster than the other, and during the improvement phase, the sides seemed to equalize. Then, tragically the improvement would slow; and stop.

Incidence of the disease seemed to be slackening as well. At the last, there had been only three new cases in a year, though they caused a bad flurry, occurring as they did simultaneously in a Belgian village which had had no hint of the disease before.

Heri Gonza still did his weekly stint (less vacation) and still amazed his gigantic audiences with his versatility, acting, singing, dancing, clowning. Sometimes he would make quiet appearances, opening and closing the show and turning it over to a theater or ballet group. During the Old Timer's Celebration he learned to fly a perfect duplicate of a century-old light aircraft with an internal combustion engine, and daringly took his first solo during the show, with a trideo camera occupying the instructor's seat.

At other times he might take up the entire time-segment alone, usually with orchestra and props, once—possibly his most successful show—dressed in sloppy practice clothes on a bare stage, without so much as a chair, and with no assistance but lights and cameras and an occasional invisible touch from the hypnos and the scent generators. Singlehandedly he was a parade, a primary schoolroom, a zoo in an earthquake, and an old lady telling three children, ages five, ten, and fifteen, about sex all at the same time.

And in between (and sometimes during) his shows, he faithfully maintained I. F. He visited his children regularly, every single one of the more than four hundred. He thrilled with their improvements, cheered them in their inevitable relapses. The only time he did not make one of his scheduled shows at all was the time the three cases appeared in Belgium, and then the slot was filled with news-items about the terrifying resurgence, and a world tour of I. F. clinics. He was a great man, a great comic, no question about it, right up to his very last show.

He didn't know it was his last show, which in its way was a pity, because with that knowledge he would have been more than good; he'd have been great. He was that kind of performer.

However, he was good, and was in and out of a vastly amusing variety show, using his old trick of standing offstage and singing with perfect mimicry while top vocalists stood center stage and mouthed the words. He turned out to be one of the Japanese girls who built body-pyramids on their bicycles, and, powered by a spring device under the water, joined a succession of porpoises leaping to take fish out of a keeper's hand.

He played, as he preferred to do, in a large studio without an audience, but playing to the audience-response sound supplied to him. He made his cues well, filled in smoothly with ad-libs when a girl singer ran a chorus short on her arrangement, and did his easy stand-up comedy monologue to close. A pity he didn't smile on that show. When the on-the airs went out and the worklights came on, he threw a sweat-shirt around his shoulder and ambled into the wings, where, as usual, the network man, Burcke, waited for him.

"How'd it look, Burckee ol' turkey?"

"Like never before," said Burcke.

"Aw, you're cute yourself," said the comedian. "Let's have a look." One of his greatest delights—and one reason for his fantastic polish—was the relaxed run-through afterward, where he lounged in the projection-room and looked at the show he had just finished from beginning to end. He and Burcke and a few interested cast members, backstage people, and privileged strangers got arranged in the projection room. Beer was passed around and the small-talk used up. As usual they all deferred to Heri Gonza, and when he waved a negligent hand everybody shut up and the projectionist threw the switch.

Title and credits with moving cloud-blanket background. Credits fade, camera zooms towards clouds, which thin to show mountain range. Down through clouds, hover over huge misty lake. Water begins to heave, to be turbulent, suddenly shores rush together and water squirts high through the clouds in a thick column. Empty lake rises up out of clouds, is discovered to be Heri Gonza's open mouth. Pull back to show full face. Puzzled expression. Hand up, into mouth, extracts live goldfish.

GONZA: Welcome to the Heri Gonza show, this week "As you lake it." *(beat)* Which is all you can expect when you open with a punorama. What ho is *(beat)* What ho is yonder? A mountain. What ho is on the mountain? A mountain goat. What ho is the goat mountain? Why, another moun— Fellers, keep the lens on me, things are gettin' a little blue off camera. Now hear ye, Tom, now hear ye Dick, now hear ye hairy Harry, Heri's here. Hee hee, ho ho, here comes the show.

Soft focus and go to black. Long beat.

Heri took his beer away from his mouth and glared at the wall. "God's sake, you send all that black?"

"Sure did," said Burcke equably.

"Man, you don't do that for anything but the second coming. What you think they expect with all that black? It sucks 'em in, but boy, you got to pay off."

"We paid off," said Burcke. "Here it comes."

"The horse act, right?"

"Wrong," said Burcke.

Dark stage. Desk, pool of light. Zoom in, Burcke, jaw clamped. In a face as sincere and interested as that, the clamped jaw is pretty grim.

BURCKE: Tonight the Heri Gonza show brings you a true story. Although the parts are played by professional actors, and certain scenes are shortened for reasons of time, you may be assured that these are real events and can be proved in every detail.

"What the hell is this?" roared Heri Gonza. "Did you air this? Is this what went out when I was knocking myself out with that horse act?"

"Sit down," said Burcke.

Heri Gonza sat down dazedly.

Burcke at desk. Lifts book and raps it.

BURCKE: This is a ship's rough log, the log of the Fafnir 203. How it comes to be on this desk, on your wall, is, I must warn you, a shocking story. The Fafnir is a twelve-cabin luxury cruiser with a crew of twelve, including stewards and the galley crew. So was the 203, before it was rebuilt. It was redesigned to sleep four with no room over, with two cabins rebuilt as a small-materials shop and a biological laboratory, and all the rest taken up with powerplant, fuel and stores. The ship's complement was Dr. Iris Barran, mathematician—

Fade in foredeck of Fafnir, girl standing by computer.

Dr. George Rehoboth Horowitz, microbiologist—

Bespectacled man enters, crosses to girl, who smiles.

Yeager Kearsarge, pilot first class—

Kearsarge is a midget with a long, bony, hardbitten face. He enters from black foreground and goes to control console.

Sam Flannel, supercargo—

Widen lighting to pass cabin bulkhead, discovering large man strapped in acceleration couch, asleep or unconscious.

"I got it," said Heri Gonza in the projection room. "A rib. It's a rib. Pretty good, fellers."

"It isn't a rib, Heri Gonza," said Burcke. "Sit down, now."

"It's got to be a rib," said Heri Gonza in a low voice. "Slip me a beer I should relax and enjoy the altogether funny joke."

"Here. Now shush."

BURCKE: ... mission totally contrary to law and regulation. Destination: Iapetus. Purpose: collection of the virus, or spores, of the dreaded children's affliction iapetitis, on the theory that examination of these in their natural habitat will reveal their exact internal structure and lead to a cure, or at the very least an immunization. Shipowner and director of mission: *(long beat)* Heri Gonza.

Fourteen hours out.

Fade Burcke and desk and take out. Dolly in to foredeck.

Horowitz crosses to side cabin, looks in on Flannel. Touches Flannel's face. Returns to computer and Iris.

HOROWITZ: He's still out cold. The tough boy is no spaceman.

IRIS: I can't get over his being here at all. Why ever did Heri want him along?

HOROWITZ: Maybe he'll tell us.

Small explosion. High whine.

KEARSARGE: A rock! a rock!

IRIS: *(frightened)* What's a rock?

Kearsarge waddles rapidly to friction hooks on bulkhead, snatches off helmets, throws two to Horowitz and Iris, sprints with two more into cabin. Gets one on Flannel's lolling head, adjusts oxygen valve. Puts on his own. Returns to assist Iris, then Horowitz.

IRIS: What is it?

KEARSARGE: Nothing to worry you, lady. Meteorite. Just a little one. I'll get it patched.

From control console, sudden sharp hiss and cloud of vapor.

IRIS: Oh! And what's *that*?

KEARSARGE: Now you got me.

Kearsarge goes to console kneels, peers underneath. Grunts, fumbles.

HOROWITZ: What is it?

KEARSARGE: Ain't regulation, 'sall I know.

Horowitz kneels beside him and peers.

HOROWITZ: What's this?

KEARSARGE: Bottom of main firing lever. Wire tired to it, pulled that pin when we blasted off.

HOROWITZ: Started this timing mechanism . . . What time did it pop?

KEARSARGE: Just about 14:30 after blastoff.

HOROWITZ: Think you can get it off there? I'd like to test for what was in it.

Kearsarge gets the device off, gives it to Horowitz, who takes it into lab.

Cut to cabin, closeup of Flannel's helmeted face. He opens his eyes, stares blankly. He is very sick, pale, insane with dormant fear. Suddenly fear no longer dormant. With great difficulty raises head, raises strapped-down wrist enough to see watch. Suddenly begins to scream and thrash around. The releases are right by his hands but he can't find them. Iris and Kearsarge run in. Kearsarge stops to take in the situation, then reaches out and pulls releases. Straps fall away; Flannel, howling, leaps for the door, knocking the midget flat and slamming Iris up against edge of door. She screams. Kearsarge scrambles to his feet, takes off after Flannel like a Boston terrier after a bull. Flannel skids to a stop by the lifeboat blister, starts tugging at it.

KEARSARGE: What the hell are you doing?

FLANNEL *(blubbering)*: 14:30 . . . 14:30 . . . I gotta get out, gotta get out . . . (screams)

KEARSARGE: Don't pull on that, y'damn fool! That's not the hatch, it's the release! We got spin on for gravity—you'll pitch the boat a hundred miles off!

FLANNEL: Oh, lemme out, it's too late!

Kearsarge punches upwards with both hands so unexpectedly that Flannel's grip is broken and he pitches over backwards. Kearsarge leaps on him, twists his oxygen valve, and scuttles back out of the way, Flannel staggers over to the boat blister, gets his hands on the wrong lever again, but his knees buckle. Inside the helmet, his face is purpling. Horowitz comes running out of the lab. Kearsarge puts out an arm and holds him back, and together they watch Flannel sag down, fall, roll, writhe. He puts both hands on helmet, tugs at it weakly.

HOROWITZ: Don't for God's sakes let him take off that helmet!

KEARSARGE: Don't worry. He can't.

Flannel slumps and lies still. Kearsarge goes to him and opens valve a little. He beckons Horowitz and together they drag him back to the cabin and with some difficulty get him on the couch and strapped down.

HOROWITZ: What happened? I had my hands full of reagents in there,

KEARSARGE: Space nutty. They get like that sometimes after blackout. He wanted out. Tried to take the boat.

HOROWITZ: He say anything?

KEARSARGE: Buncha junk. Said, 14:30, 14:30. Said it was too late, had to get out.

HOROWITZ; That snivvy under the console popped at 14:30. He knew about it.

KEARSARGE: Did he now. What was it?

HOROWITZ: Cyanide gas. If we hadn't been holed and forced to put the helmets on, we'd've had it.

KEARSARGE: Except him. He figured to be up an' around lookin' at his watch, and when she popped, he'd be in the boat headed home and we'd keep blasting till the pile run dry, som'res out t'ords Algol.

HOROWITZ: Can you fix those releases so he can't reach them?

KEARSARGE: Oh sure.

Fade. Lights pick up Burcke at the side.

BURCKE: *(as narrator)* They got an explanation out of Flannel, and it satisfied none of them. He said he knew nothing of any cyanide. He said that Heri, knowing he was a bad spaceman, had told him that if it got so bad he couldn't stand it, he could always come back in the lifeboat. But if he did that, he'd have to do it before 14:30 after blastoff or there wouldn't be fuel enough to decelerate, start back, and maneuver a landing. He insisted that that was all there was to it. He would not say what he was doing aboard, except to state that Heri Gonza wanted him to look out for Heri's interests.

No amount of discussion made anything clearer. Heri certainly could not have wanted the expedition to fail, nor his ship hurled away from the solar system. They reluctantly concluded that some enemy of Heri Gonza's must have sabotaged them—someone they simply didn't know.

The weeks went by—not easy ones, by any means, in those quarters, without any event except Iris Barran's puzzling discovery that the ship required no astrogator after all: what the veteran Kearsarge couldn't handle in his head was easily treated in the computer. Why, then, had Heri Gonza insisted on her cramming on astrogation?

Zoom in to Saturn until it fills a quadrant. String out the moons.

Heri Gonza watched the bridge sequence, as Saturn swept close and the moons rolled by like broken beads, and little Iapetus swam close. Iapetus is not a moon like most, round or oblate, but a rock, a drifting mountain some 500 miles in diameter. And before them was the solution to the mystery of the changing moonlight. Some unknown cataclysm has cloven Iapetus, so that it has one sheer face, nearly four hundred square miles of flat plain (or cliff, depending on how you look at it) made of pale grey basaltic material. Since Iapetus always maintains one face to Saturn, it always appears brighter as it rounds the eastern limb and dimmer as it goes west, the albedo of the flat face being much higher than the craggy ruin of the rest of its surface.

"Burckee, Burckee, Burckee ol' turkey," murmured the comedian in accents of wonder, "who the hell writes your stuff? Who writes your lousy, lousy stuff?"

Stock shot, Fafnir putting down tail-first on rocky plain, horizon washed out and black space brought down close. Rocks sharp-cornered, uneroded. Long shot, stabilizing jacks extending widest. Ladder out. Two suited figures ride it down, the other two climb down.
Close-up, all four at tail-base.
HOROWITZ: *(filter mike)* Check your radios. Read me?
ALL: Check. Read you fine.
HOROWITZ: Each take a line. Walk straight out with the line as a guide, and when you've passed our scorch area, get a rock scraping every five feet or so until you're far enough away that the horizon's a third of the way up the hull. Got that? No further. *(Beat)* And I can almost tell you now, we aren't going to find one blessed thing. No virus, no spore, no nothing. My God, it's no more than twelve, thirteen degrees K in the shadows here. Anyway . . . let's go.
BURCKE: *(off)* Scratch and hop, scratch and hop. In this gravity, you don't move fast or push hard, or you'll soar away and take minutes to come down again. Shuffle and scratch, scratch and sweep, scratch and hop. It took them hours.
Close-up, Kearsarge, looking down.
KEARSARGE: Here's something.
Close-ups, each of the other three, turning head at the sound of Kearsarge's voice.
HOROWITZ: What is it?
KEARSARGE: Scorch. A regular mess of it. Hell, you know what? Swope toppled his ship. I can see where he came down, where he took off, scraping along to the big edge there.
FLANNEL: Wonder he didn't wreck her.
KEARSARGE: He did. He couldn't hurt the hull any in this gravity, but he, sure as hell wiped off his antennae, because there they are: landing, range, transmission—every one, by God. No wonder he come barreling in the way he did. You can't land a Fafnir on manual, but you can try, and he tried. Poor ol' Swopie.
HOROWITZ: Everybody over there by Kearsarge. Maybe Swope picked up something where he scraped.
Long shot of the four working around long scorch and scrape marks.

BURCKE: *(off, narrating)* They filled their specimen sacks and brought them aboard, and then for seventy-two hours they went through their dust and stones with every test Horowitz could devise.... He had been quite right in his first guess. The moonlet Iapetus is as devoid of life as the inside of an autoclave.

Cut to foredeck set, but upended, the controls at highest point, the floor what was the after bulkhead. Iris moving around with slow shuffle, setting out magnetized plates on a steel table, each one hitting loudly. In background, Flannel fusses with small electron mike, watching screen and moving objective screws. Lifeboat blister open, Kearsarge inside, working.

Airlock cycles, opens, and Horowitz comes in, suited, with sack. He is weary. Iris helps with helmet.

HOROWITZ: I've had it. Let's get home. We can get just so duty-bound.

IRIS: What's this "home"? I don't remember.

HOROWITZ: You for home, Kearsarge?

KEARSARGE: Any time you're through hoein' this rock.

HOROWITZ: What are you doing in there?

KEARSARGE: Just routine. Figured you might want to buzz around the other side with the boat.

HOROWITZ: Nosir. I came close enough on foot. I say we're done here. A man could sit home with a pencil and paper and figure out the density of sub-microscopic growth this place would have to have to bring any back on the hull. We'd be hip deep in it. The iapetitis virus didn't come from Iapetus, and that, friends, is for sure and official.

KEARSARGE: *(off)* Oh my holy mother. *(He pops out, putty-colored.)* George, get over here.

IRIS: (curiously) What is it?

She goes over and disappears for a moment inside the boat, with Kearsarge and Horowitz. Off, she gasps. Then, one by one they climb out and stand looking at Flannel. Sensing the silence, he looks up and meets their eyes.

FLANNEL: What I got, blue horns or something?

HOROWITZ: Show him, Kearsarge.

Kearsarge beckons. There is a strange pucker of grim amusement on his craggy face.

KEARSARGE: Come look, little feller. Then you can join our club.

Reluctantly, the big man goes over to the blister and follows Kearsarge into the lifeboat. Dolly after them, swing in to the instrument panel, under it and look up.

Lashed to the projecting lower end of the main thrust control is a silver can with a small cylinder at the near end.

FLANNEL: *(pointing stupidly)* Is that ... that the same thing that ...

KEARSARGE: A little smaller, but then you don't need as much cyanide for a boat.

FLANNEL: *(angry)* Who the hell put it there? You?

KEARSARGE: Not me, feller. I just found it.

HOROWITZ: It's been there all along, Flannel. Kearsarge is right: you belong to the club too. You sure it was Heri Gonza told you to take the boat?

FLANNEL: Sure it was. He couldn't have nothing to do with this. *(Suddenly it hits him)* Jesus! I mighta ...

HOROWITZ: We'll have plenty of time to talk this over. Let's pack up the testing stuff and haul out of here.

FLANNEL: *(to no one)* Jesus.

Heri Gonza lay back in the projection room and sipped his beer and watched the stock shot of a Fafnir taking off from a rock plain. "You really get all that glop out of that book, Burcke m' boy?"

"Every bit of it," said Burcke, watching the screen.

"You know how it is in space, a fellow's got to do something with his time. Sometimes he writes, and sometimes it's fairy tales, and sometimes you can get a pretty good show out of a fairy tale. But where you do that, you call it a fairy tale. Follow me?"

"Yup."

"This was really what went out on the air tonight?"

"Sure is."

Very, very softly, Heri Gonza said, "Poor Burcke. Poor, poor ol' Burcke."

Close-up, hands turning pages in rough logbook. Pull back to show Burcke with book. He looks up, and when he speaks his voice is solemn.

BURCKE: Time to think, time to talk it over. Time to put all the pieces in the same place at the same time, and push them against each other to see what fits.

Fade to black; but it is not black after all: instead, starry space. Pan across to pick up ship, a silver fish with a scarlet tail. Zoom in fast, dissolve through hull, discovering foredeck. The four lounge around, really relaxed, willing to think before speaking, and to speak carefully. Horowitz and Kearsarge sit at the table ignoring a chessboard. Iris is stretched on the deck with a rolled-up specimen sack under her head. Flannel kneels before a spread of Canfield solitaire. Horowitz is watching him.

HOROWITZ: I like to think about Flannel.

FLANNEL: Think what?

HOROWITZ: Oh ... the alternatives. The "ifs." What would Flannel do if this had been different, or that.

FLANNEL: There's no sense in that kind of thinkin'—if this, if that. This happened, or that happened, and that's all there is to it. You got anything special in mind?

HOROWITZ: I have, as a matter of fact. Given that you had a job to do, namely to cut out and leave us with our cyanide bomb at the start of the trip—

FLANNEL: *(aroused)* I tol' you and *tol'* you that wasn't a job. I didn't know about the damn cyanide.

HOROWITZ: Suppose you had known about it. Would you have come? If you had come, would you have tipped us off about it? And here's the question I thought of: if the first bomb had failed—which it did—and there had been no second bomb to tell you that you were a member of the Exit Club, would you have tried to do the job on the way home?

FLANNEL: I was thinkin' about it, about what to do.

HOROWITZ: And what did you decide?

FLANNEL: Nothin'. You found the bomb in the boat so I just stopped thinkin'.

IRIS: *(suddenly)* Why? Did that really make a difference?

FLANNEL: All the diff'nce in the world. Heri Gonza tol' me to get in the lifeboat before fourteen an' a half hours and come back and tell him how things went. Now if there was just *your* bomb, could be that Heri Gonza wanted you knocked off. There was an accident and it din't knock you off, and here I am working for him and wonderin' if I shoon't take up where the bomb left off.

IRIS: Then we found the second bomb, and you changed your mind. Why?

FLANNEL: *(exasperated)* Whata ya all, simple or somepin? Heri Gonza, *he tol' me to come back and tell him how it went.* If he tells me that an' then plants a bomb on me, how could I get back to tell him? A man's a fool to tell a guy to do somethin' an' then fix it so he can't. He's no fool, Heri Gonza I mean, an' you know it. Well then: if he din't plant my bomb, he din't plant your bomb, because anyone can see they was planted by the same guy. An' if he din't plant your bomb, he don't want you knocked off, so I stopped thinkin' about it. Is that simple enough for ya?

IRIS: I don't know that it's simple, but it sure is beautiful.

HOROWITZ: Well, one of us is satisfied of Heri Gonza's good intentions. Though I still don't see what sense it made to go to all the trouble of putting you aboard just to have you get off and go back right at the start.

FLANNEL: Me neither. But do I have to understand everything he tells me to do? I done lots of things for him I didn't know what they was about. You too, Kearsarge.

KEASARGE: That's right. I drive this can from here to there, and from there to yonder, and I don't notice anything else, but if I notice it I forget it, but if I don't forget it I don't talk about it. That's the way he likes it and we get along fine.

IRIS: *(forcefully)* I think Heri Gonza wanted us all killed.

HOROWITZ: What's that—intuition? And ... shouldn't that read "wants"?

IRIS: "Wants," yes. He wants us all killed. No, it's not intuition. It formulates. Almost. There's a piece missing.

FLANNEL: Ah, y'r out of y'r mind.

KEARSARGE: Doubled.

HOROWITZ: *(good naturedly)* Shut up, both of you. Go on with that, Iris. Maybe by you it formulates, but by me it intuits. Go on.

IRIS: Well, let's use as a working hypothesis that Heri Gonza wants us dead—us four. He wants more than that: he wants us to disappear from the cosmos—no bodies, no graves, no nothing.

KEARSARGE: *But why?*

HOROWITZ: Just you listen. We start with the murders and finish with the why. You'll see.

IRIS: Well then, the ship will do the removal. The cyanide—both cyanides—do the actual killing, and it hits so fast that the ship keeps blasting, out and out until the fuel is gone, and forever after that. We three are on it; Flannel crashes in a small craft and if anybody wonders about it, they don't wonder much. Is there any insignia on that boat, by the way, Kearsarge?

KEARSARGE: Always.

IRIS: Go look, will you? Thanks. Now, what about the traces we leave behind us? Well, we took off illegally so notified no one and filed no clearances. You, George, were already in hiding from Heri Gonza's persecutions; Kearsarge here is so frequently away on indeterminate trips of varying lengths that he would soon be forgotten; Flannel here—no offense, Flannel—I don't think anyone would notice that you're gone for good. As for me, Heri Gonza himself had me plant a story about going off secretly for some solitary research for a year or so. What's the matter, Kearsarge?

KEARSARGE: I wouldn'ta believed it. No insignia. Filed off and sanded smooth and painted. Numbers off the thrust block. Tradename off the dash, even. I . . . I wouldn'ta believed it.

HOROWITZ: Now you'd better listen to the lady.

IRIS: No insignia. So even poor Flannel's little smashup is thoroughly covered. Speaking of Flannel, I say again that it was stretching credibility to put him aboard that way—unless you assume that he was put aboard like the rest of us, to be done away with. I certainly came under false pretenses: Heri Gonza not only told me he needed an astrogator for the trip, which he didn't, but had me bone up on the subject.

Now we can take a quick look at motive. George Horowitz here is the most obvious. He has for a long time been a thorn in the flesh of that comedian. Not only has he concluded that Heri Gonza doesn't really want to find a cure for iapetitis—he says so very loudly and as often as he can. In addition, George is always on the very verge of whipping the disease, something that frightens Heri Gonza so much that he's actually hoarding patients so George can't get to them. Also, he doesn't *like* George.

Why kill Flannel? Is he tired of you, Flannel? Did you boggle something he asked you to do?

FLANNEL: He don't have to kill me, Miss Iris. He could fire me any time. I'd feel real bad, but I wouldn't bother him none. He knows that.

IRIS: Then you must know too much. You must know something about him so dangerous he won't feel safe until you're dead.

FLANNEL: So help me lady, there ain't a single thing like that I know about him. Not one. Not that I know of.

HOROWITZ: There's the key, Iris. He doesn't know he knows it.

KEASARGE: Then that's me too, because if there's a single thing I know that he'd have to kill me for then I don't know what it is.

IRIS: You said "key." Lock and key. A combination of things. Like if you put what Flannel knows with what Kearsarge knows, they will be dangerous to Heri Gonza.

Flannel and Kearsarge gape at each other blankly and simultaneously shrug.

HOROWITZ: I can give you one example of a piece of knowledge we all have that would be dangerous to him. We now know that the disease virus does not originate on Iapetus. Which means that poor Swope was not responsible for bringing it to earth, and, further, the conclusion that the little Tresak girl—the first case— caught it from the wreckage of the space ship, was unwarranted.

FLANNEL: I brung that picture of that little girl standing in the wreck, I brung it to Heri Gonza. He liked it.

IRIS: What made you do that?

FLANNEL: I done it all the time. He told me to.

HOROWITZ: Bring him pictures of little girls?

FLANNEL: Girls, boys ... but pretty ones. I got to know just the ones he would like. He liked to use 'em on his show.

Iris and Horowitz lock glances for one horrified second, and then pounce all but bodily on Flannel.

IRIS: Did you ever show him a picture of any child who later contracted the disease?

FLANNEL: *(startled)* Wh ... I dunno.

IRIS: *(shouting)* Think! Think!

HOROWITZ: *(also shouting)* You did! You did! The Tresak girl—that photograph of her was taken before she had the disease!

FLANNEL: Well yeah, her. And that little blond one he had on the telethon that din't speak no English from Est'onia, but you're not lettin' me think.

FLANNEL: What?

KEARSARGE: I remember that little blond girl. I flew her from Esthonia.

IRIS: Before or after she had the disease?

KEARSARGE: *(shrugging)* The kind of thing I never noticed. She ... she looked all right to me. Real pretty little kid.

IRIS: How long before the telethon was that?

KEARSARGE: Week or so. Wait, I can tell you to the day. *(He rises from the chess table and goes to a locker, from which he brings a notebook. He leafs.)* Here it is. Nine days.

IRIS: *(faintly)* He said, on the telethon, three days ... first symptoms.

HOROWITZ: *(excitedly)* May I see that? *(Takes book, riffles it, throws it on the table, runs to lab, comes back with cardboard file, fans through it, comes up with folder.)* Iris, take Kearsarge's book. Right. Now did he fly to Belem on the ninth of May?

IRIS: The sixth.

HOROWITZ: Rome, around March twelfth.

IRIS: March twelfth, March—here it is. The eleventh.

HOROWITZ: One more. Indianapolis, middle of June.

IRIS: Exactly. The fifteenth. What is that you have there?

He throws it down in front of her.

HOROWITZ: Case files. Arranged chronologically by known or estimated date of first symptom, in an effort to find some pattern of incidence. No wonder there was never any pattern. God in Heaven, if he wanted a clinic in Australia, cases would occur in Australia.

FLANNEL: *(bewildered)* I don't know what you all are talkin' about.

KEARSARGE: *(grimly)* I think I do.

IRIS: Now do you think you're worth murdering—you who can actually place him on the map, at the time some child was stricken, every single time?

KEARSARGE: *(huskily)* I'm worth murdering. I . . . didn't know.

FLANNEL: *(poring over the case file)* Here's that one I seen in Bellefontaine that time, she had on a red dress. And this little guy here, he got his picture in a magazine I found on the street in Little Rock and I had to go clear to St. Louis to find him.

Kearsarge hops up on a chair and kicks Flannel in the head.

FLANNEL: *(howling)* Hooo—wow! What you wanna hafta do that for? Ya little . . .

HOROWITZ: Cut it out, you two. *Cut it out!* That's better. We don't have room for that in here. Leave him alone, Kearsarge. His time will come. Heaven help me, Iris, it's been in front of my nose right from the start, and I didn't see it. I even told you once that I was so close because I could synthesize a virus which would actually cause the disease—but it wouldn't maintain it? I had this *idée fixe* that it was an extra-terrestrial disease. Why? Because it acted like a synthetic *and no natural terran virus does.* Serum from those kids always acted that way—it would cause a form of iapetitis which would fade out in three months or less. *All you have to do to cure the damn thing is to stop injecting it!*

IRIS: Oh, the man, the lovely clever man and his family all over the world, the little darlings, the prettiest ones he could find, whom he never, never failed to visit regularly . . . *(Suddenly, she is crying)* I was so s-sorry for him! Remember the night he . . . tore himself open to tell us he c-couldn't have k-kids of his own?

KEARSARGE: Who you talking about—Heri Gonza? For Pete's sake, he got an ex-wife and three kids he pays money to keep 'em in Spain, and another ex-wife in Paris France with five kids, three his, and that one in Pittsburgh—man, that comedian's always in trouble. He *hates* kids—I mean really hates 'em.

(Iris begins to laugh. Probably hysteria.)

Dissolve to black, then to starry space. To black again, bring up pool of light, resolve it into:

Burcke, sitting at desk. He closes log book.

BURCKE: This is, I regret to say, a true story. The Fafnir 203 came in at night six days ago at a small field some distance from here, and Dr. Horowitz phoned me. After considerable discussion it was decided to present this unhappy story to you in the form written up by the four people who actually experienced it. They are here with me now. And here is a much maligned man, surely one of the greatest medical researchers alive—Dr. Horowitz.

HOROWITZ: Thank you. First I wish to assure everyone within reach of my voice that what has been said here about iapetitis is true: it is a synthetic disorder which is, by its very nature, harmless, and which, if contracted will pass away spontaneously in from two to twelve weeks. Not a single child has died of it, and those who have been its victims the longest—some up to two years—have unquestionably been lavishly treated. A multiple murder was attempted upon my three companions and myself, of course, but it was our greatest desire to see to it that that charge is not pressed.

BURCKE: I wish to express the most heartfelt apologies from myself and all my colleagues for whatever measure of distress this network and its affiliates may have unwittingly brought you, the public. It is as an earnest of this that we suffer, along with you, through the following film clip, taken just two days ago in the I. F. clinic in Montreal. What you see in my hand here is a thin rubber glove, almost invisible on the hand. Fixed to its fingertips is a microscopic forest of tiny sharp steel points, only a few thousandths of an inch long. And this metal box, just large enough to fit unobtrusively in a side pocket, contains a jellied preparation of the synthetic virus.

Fade to:

Wild hilarity in a hospital ward. Children in various stages of

iapetitis, laughing hilariously at the capering, growling, gurgling,
belching funny man as he moves from bed to bed, Peep! at you, peep-
peep at you, and one by one ruffling the little heads at the nape, dip-
ping the fingertips in the side jacket packet between each bed.
    Dissolve, and bring up Burke.
    BURCKE: Good night, ladies, gentlemen, boys and girls ...
I'm sorry.

The lights came up in the projection room. There was nobody there
with Heri Gonza but Burcke: all the others had quietly moved and
watched the last few scenes from the doorway, and slipped away.
    "You did air it?" asked the comedian, making absolutely sure.
"Yes."
    Heri Gonza looked at him without expression and walked toward
the stage door. It opened as he approached, and four people came
in. Flannel, Kearsarge, Horowitz, Iris Barran.
    Without a word Flannel stepped up to the comedian and hit him
in the stomach. Heri Gonza sank slowly to the floor, gasping.
    Horowitz said, "We've spent a lot of time deciding what to do
about you, Heri Gonza. Flannel wanted just one poke at you and
wouldn't settle for anything else. The rest of us felt that killing was
too good for you, but we wanted you dead. So we wrote you that
script. Now you're dead."
    Heri Gonza rose after a moment and walked through the stage
door and out to the middle of acres and acres of stage. He stood
there alone all night, and in the morning was gone.

The Graveyard Reader

The stone was included in the price of the plot; I hadn't known. I hadn't wanted a stone because stones have to say something, and what can you say in a case like this? But unwittingly I'd bought the thing and because I had, the man had put it up—what else? I had anger enough to scatter around heart-deep, but, reasonably, not a flake for the men who had put up the stone.

It was a right and proper stone, I supposed, if one must have one of the things at all: bigger than many of the cheating, bargain sort of stones that stood nearby, and tastefully smaller than the hulking ostentatious ones. *Here lies my wife between poverty and vulgarity.* Now there you go. Have a single elevating thought about that woman and it comes out sounding like that. Soils everything she touches.

The stone called me a liar for that. It was of a whitish granite that would weather whiter still. It had edges of that crinkly texture like matted hair that nothing would stick to because nothing could possibly want to, and a glossy face that nothing would stick to if it wanted nothing else. Whited sepulcher, that's what the hell. The stone is its own epitaph, because look: it's white forever, white and clean, and it has no words—which is to say, nothing. Nothing, and clean, ergo, *Here lies nothing clean.*

What I always say is, there's a way to say anything in the world if you can only think of the way to say it, and I had. I liked this epitaph just fine. There would be no words on this stone, and it had its epitaph.

Laughing out loud is bad form in a graveyard, and stepping down hard on a man's instep is bad form anywhere. This was the moment when, backing off for some perspective on this my masterpiece, I did both these things. The man, apparently, had been standing behind me watching. I whirled and looked him up and down, hoping sincerely that he was offended. There are times in a man's life when he wouldn't want even his friends to like him, and such a time is no time to pay court to the esteem of a stranger.

He wasn't offended. All I got out of him (just then) was a pleasant smile. He had a sort of anybody's face, the like of which you might encounter anywhere, which is to say he had the kind of face you wouldn't be surprised to see visiting a cemetery. I'll say this for him: he was harmonious; his voice and clothing exactly suited his face, and though he wasn't an old man, the things he said weren't hard to figure, coming from a man like that. You could tell he was experienced.

Neither of us said anything right away when I bumped him. He sort of put his hands on my shoulders for a second either to hold one of us up or to keep the other from falling, which gave the gesture a full fifty per cent chance of being selfish, and I am not about to give away a thank-you in the face of those odds. As for an excuse-me, I didn't want to be excused, I wanted to be blamed. So I glared at first, while he smiled, and after those things got used up there was nothing for it but to stand where we were, side by side, looking at my wife's grave because that was straight ahead and we couldn't just go on looking at each other. It was while we were doing this that he said, "Mind if I read it?"

I looked at him. Even if this had been the perfect time and place for joking, a face that looked the way his face looked contained no jests. I looked from him to the bland, uncommunicative sheet of stone and the raw mound with its neat planes still unslumped by wind or water, and I looked back at him. It occurred to me then that maybe his eyes weren't so good, and he honestly didn't know there was nothing on the stone. "Yes," I said as offensively as I could, "I mind."

He put up his hands placatingly, and said in that same good-natured way, "All right, all right! I won't." And he gave me a sort of friendly half-wave and started off.

I looked at the grave and at his retreating back and "Hey!" I called before I realized I wanted to.

He came back, smiling. "Yes?"

I felt robbed, that's why I called him back. I'd realized I wanted to see his face when he got close enough to squint at that unmarked stone. I said, "What I mean is, I'd mind if anyone read anything off that. It would give me the creeps."

He didn't even glance toward the grave, but said patiently, "It's all right. I promised you I wouldn't."

I said, "Oh for God's sake," disgustedly, and with an angry motion beckoned him to follow me. I had that oafish feeling you get when you tell a joke and somebody doesn't get it, so instead of letting the matter drop you lay your ears back and start explaining, knowing perfectly well that when you finally get the point across it isn't going to be funny, either to your victim or to yourself. I ranged up on one side of the grave and he came up and crossed over and stood at the other side, not four feet away from the headstone. He was looking right at it, but didn't say anything, so I barked, "Well?"

"Well," he asked politely, "what?"

The oafish feeling intensified. "Don't you find the language of that epitaph a little on the terse side?" I said sarcastically.

He glanced at it. "There's never very much on the stone," he said, and added, as if to himself, "while it's new."

"New or old," I said, and I guess I showed something of the anger I felt, "the way it is is the way it stays. Anything that gets written on the rock is not going to be written by me."

"Naturally not," he said.

To make it quite clear, I said, "Or by anyone I hire."

"Well," he said comfortingly, "don't worry. I won't read it, now or later."

"You can say that again," I growled. I was finally coming to a certainty about this grave. "The less said about this whole thing, including her *and* her slab, the better. That was her strong point anyway; keeping her mouth shut. At long last, anything she's hiding, she can keep. I don't want to hear it."

"Then you won't," he said peacefully, "and neither will I, because I've promised." After a sort of pause, he added, "I think I ought to warn you, though, that somebody else might come along and read it, not knowing of your objections."

"What are you talking about?"

"I'm not the only one in the world who can read graves."

"I told you—I'm not putting any inscription on. Not a monogram. Not so much as *Hers,* or even—hey, this would be cute: *Her lies.* Not that she was really ever a liar. She just wouldn't *say.*"

"The inscriptions never say very much by themselves," he said in his patient voice, "taken out of context."

"What do you mean, context?"

"I don't think you quite understood me. I didn't say I read gravestones. I said I read graves."

I looked blankly at that tidy, tamped-down mound and the virgin stone, and back at the shovel-patted yellow earth turning grainy in the late warm sunlight, and a more uncommunicative arrangement I had never laid eyes on. It conveyed nothing about her, and for that matter, nothing about anyone else. Me, for instance. No flowers.

"Not this one, you can't," I said finally.

"I wouldn't."

"That promise of yours," I said with a certain amount of smug enmity, "comes in pretty handy, doesn't it? I think I see what you're driving at, and I don't think it's any too funny. You've spent a lot of time ghouling around places like this until you can tell to a dime what the planting cost, how much the survivors give a damn, if any, how long the box has been buried, and how good a job the crew did on the detail. But any time there's a little more than readily meets the eye, like a guy who says he won't have an inscription after paying for a stone, you don't have to risk a wrong guess. You just make a gentlemanly promise, casual-like." I snorted through my nostrils.

He still wouldn't let me annoy him. He simply explained where I was wrong. He said, "It isn't like that at all. There's nothing to deduce, or to guess at. It's all there," he said, nodding at but not looking at the grave, "to be read. I'll admit that it's a little harder to do on a very new grave; you might say that it's all in very fine print and a little hard to see unless you read well. But in time it all comes clear—very clear. As to the promise, it's very obvious that you wouldn't want a stranger like myself to know everything about her."

"Everything?" I laughed bitterly. "Nobody knows everything about *her.*"

"Well, it's all there."

"You know what's happened to me," I said a little too loudly and a little too fast, "I'm a little bit out of my head from all that's happened the last week or so, which makes me stand here listening to you as if you made sense."

He didn't say anything.

"By God," I mumbled, not talking to him or to anyone special at the moment, "it wasn't too long ago I'd given anything you like to know some things about that woman. Only since I made up my mind I don't want to know, I feel much better," I said feeling miserable. "You know what she did, she wasn't home when I got there that night, we'd had a little sort of fight the morning before, and that night she was just gone. No note and she didn't pack anything or take anything but that one green tweed suit and that stupid hat she used to wear with it. If she had any money it wasn't much. Then, nothing for three whole days and nights, until that phone call." My hands got all knotted up and then seemed to get too heavy, pulling my shoulders into a slump. I sat down on the edge of an iron pipe railing at the edge of the next grave and let the heavy hands dangle down between my thighs. I hung my head down so I could watch them while I talked. Watching them didn't tell me anything. "Phone call from the police who found her driver's license in her handbag, the one that matched that stupid hat."

I raised my head and looked across the grave at the man. I couldn't see him too clearly until I hit myself across the eyes with my sleeve. The cuff buttons had got themselves turned around, and it hurt. "Eight hundred miles from home with some guy in a sports car, and all she had on was one of those fancified bathrobes, you know, hostess gown, a good one, I never saw it before. Don't know where the green suit got to or the stupid hat either. Bag was in the car. Car was in an oak tree. No kidding. Upside down in an oak tree fifteen feet off the ground. The police said he had to be going a hundred and twenty to hit as hard as that. I never heard of him before. I don't know how she got there. I don't know why. Well," I said after I thought about it for a minute, "I guess I do know more or less why, but not *exactly why;* not exactly what was in her mind when she did whatever it was she did to get herself into that. I never knew exactly what was in her mind. I could never get her to say. She would . . ."

I guess at that point I stopped talking out loud, because it all turned into a series of swift pictures, one after the other, inside my head, too fast for words, and too detailed. *What's the matter?* I'd be saying, and her, kissing my hands, looking up at me with tears in her eyes: *Can't you see?* And again: me yelling at her, *Well if what I do makes you unhappy, why don't you tell me what you want? Go ahead, write the script, I'll play it.* And the way she'd turn her back when I talked like that, and I'd hear her voice softly: *If you'd only—* and *I just—* and then she'd stall, inarticulate, shake her head. She never talked enough. She never said the things that . . . that . . . World of feeling, spectrum of sensitivity, and no words, no dammit dammit words. Picture of her smiling, looking off, out, a little up; I say *What are you so happy about?*

Oh, she says, coming back into the world, *Oh* . . . and whispers my name four times, smiling. Now what is that—communication?

"I got so there was nothing in the world for me, sleeping or waking or working or mixing a drink," I said aloud to the man, "but *why won't she tell me?* And right to the end, she did that to me. Wondering why she does this or that, why she wears one particular kind of look instead of another, maybe, after all, these things don't matter. But look how she winds up, dead in that new housecoat I didn't buy for her, eight hundred miles from home with a guy I don't know; all in the world I have now is *why? why?* and the idea that she wound it up in the one way where I'd never find out. I mean," I added as soberly as I could, because I was unaccountably out of breath, just from talking to a man, imagine? "I mean, not that I want to find out. Because I don't give a damn any more."

"Well, that's good then," he said, "because you'll save yourself a lot of trouble."

"What trouble?"

"Learning to read graves."

I got enormously tired of this conversation suddenly. "Now what good would it do me to learn a thing like that?"

"None," he said in that pleasant way of his. "You have just finished saying that you don't want to know anything about her, any more."

"It finally sinks in," I said sarcastically, "that what you're trying to tell me is that a person who can read graves can stand in front of one and read it like a book."

"A biography." He nodded.

"And get out of it everything that person ever did."

"Or said, or thought," he agreed.

I looked at the grave, its empty crumbling bare planes, its empty-faced headstone. I looked again, but briefly, at the events that had made it be here just where it was, when it was, containing what, and I wet my lips and said, "You're kidding."

He never seemed to answer what deserved no answer, that man.

I asked him, "Even things nobody ever knew before?"

"Especially those things," he said. "What you can see of a human being is only the outside of the top part of the surface. Now if everything—is there—" he pointed—"to be read—*everything*—then it follows that you can read far more than the most penetrating analysis of anything living." When I had no response to this, he said, "Living things aren't finished, you see. Everything they have ever been in contact with, each thought they have had, each person they have known—these things are still at work in them; nothing's finished."

"And when they're buried, they ... do something to the grave? There's a real difference between one grave and another, or ... a grave would be different if one person or another was buried in it?"

"It has to be that way," he said. Again one of those odd, waiting pauses, which I refused to take for myself. He said, "Surely you've had that feeling that a human being is too much, has too much, means too much just to go out like a light, or be eroded away like the soil of a dust bowl."

I looked at the grave. So new, so raw, so ... blank. In a low voice, I asked, "What do you read?"

He understood what I meant: what are the "letters," the "words," the "grammar"?

He said, "A lot of things. The curve of the mound, the encroachment of growth on it—grass, weeds, mosses. The kind of vegetation that grows there, and the shape of each stem and leaf, even the veining in them. The flight of insects over it, the shadows they cast, the contours of rain rivulets as they form, as they fill, as they dry." He laughed deprecatingly. "It sounds like more than a man could learn, doesn't it?"

I thought it did.

He said, "You are so completely familiar with the act of reading that it never occurs to you how complex an act it is, or how vast is your accomplishment. You take in stride a variety of alphabets—upper case and lower case are very nearly two separate ones, and then upper and lower case in script are quite different from printing or typing. Old English and black-letter faces might slow you down but they won't stop you. Your eye measures light intensities between ink and paper: green letters on a yellow page wouldn't stop you. You select, without effort, just what you read on a page and what you do not. For example, every page of a book might have the book title at the top and a page number at the bottom, and you don't even know they're there. In a magazine or a newspaper, blocks of type might be broken up, carried over, interrupted by pictures or advertisements, and you sail right along reading what you are interested in and nothing else. You might notice a misprint or a misspelling, or even an out-of-context line of type lost in the middle of your paragraph, but in most cases it doesn't bother you much. In addition, you're reading in English—one of the richest of all languages, but also one of the most difficult, with irregular structure, spelling, and some pretty far-fetched semantic shorthand and shortcuts. But all these are the rarefied complications; to get back to basics, what about the letters themselves? The letter 'a' doesn't look like the sound—or several sounds—of 'a.' It's only a most arbitrary symbol, chosen by custom and usage to mean what it means."

"But . . . at least there's a system. I mean, an established alphabet. Accepted spelling. And for all their exceptions, there are rules of grammar and syntax."

Again he said nothing, just waiting for me to come up with something or other. To think, perhaps.

I did, and said, "Oh. You mean there is some such system," I laughed suddenly. "A crooked thorn for the letter 'b,' and a line of mud for past tense?"

He smiled and nodded. "Not those, but things like those. Yes, that's the idea."

"Not as hard as it seems at first, hm?"

"The thing you try to put over to every first grader," he agreed. "But—it is hard. As hard as anything else you can study. Just as hopeless looking at times, too, when the overall pattern just won't emerge and all your work seems useless. Then—it comes clear, and you go on."

I looked at him and said, "I don't know why I believe you."

He waited until I said, "—but I'd like to learn that trick."

"Why?"

I glanced at the bare new grave. "You said . . . '*everything*.' You said I could find out what she did, with whom. And—why."

"That's right."

"So . . . let's go. Where do we start?" I went down on one knee and made an across-the-board gesture at my wife's grave.

"Not here." He smiled. "You don't use Dostoevsky as a first reader."

"Dostoevsky? *Her?*"

"They're all Dostoevskys. They can all express every shade of meaning of every event, and through what they think and feel one can see the meaning of all their world. Isn't that what makes a great writer?"

"I guess it is . . . but . . . great writer? *Her?*"

"She lived," he said. "Now what she was is . . . graven here. Living and feeling are things done by everybody. Writing on their graves is done by everybody. Dostoevsky, now, had what you might term a *previous* skill. He could do it while he was alive. Dead, they can all do it."

This guy made my head spin. I got up slowly and followed him to the "first reader." Like most such volumes, it was a very little one.

I went back every evening, after work, for nearly a year. I learned the meaning of the curl of a leaf and the glisten of wet pebbles, and the special significance of curves and angles. A great deal of the writing was unwritten. Plot three dots on a graph and join them; you now have a curve with certain characteristics. Extend that curve while maintaining the characteristics, and it has meaning, up where no dots are plotted. In just this way I learned to extend the curve of a grass blade and of a protruding root, of the bent edges of wetness on a drying headstone.

I quit smoking so I could sharpen my sense of smell, because the scent of earth after a rain has a clarifying effect on graveyard reading, as if the page were made whiter and the ink darker. I began to listen to the wind, and to the voices of birds and small animals, insects and people, because to the educated ear, every sound is filtered through the story written on graves, and becomes a part of it.

The man met me every day; early or late, he was around. I never asked him anything about himself. Somehow that never came up. He never read anything to me. He would point out the "letters" and occasionally the "letter groups" like (analogously) "-ing" and "-ous" and "un-," and would correct me where I read it wrong. But when I got to where I could read whole sentences, he stopped me. He told me that the one thing I must never do is to read off what I read on a grave, aloud. Not even to him. Those who could read it, would, if they cared to. Those who could not must learn as I was learning, or not know what was written there. "There are reasons enough for not wanting to die," he told me, "without adding the fear that someone like you will go around abusing this privilege."

I would go home at night filled with a gray hope, that at last all the mysteries of that woman would be solved for me, and every sordid, rotten thing she had done and kept secret would be illuminated for me. I didn't sleep very well—I hadn't, since the day she left— and I had lots of time to think over the things she had done to me, and the things she probably had done to me, and the things she was doubtless capable of doing. Maybe this long period of insufficient sleep did something to me; I don't know, but I didn't mind it. I did my work at the office, enough to get along, saving my strength and my brain for the evening; and then I worked at my lessons. I worked.

We went from the "first readers" into more complicated stuff. You can have no idea how complicated a thing like a three-year-old is when you first start. The only thing that took me through this stage was his promise that however hopeless it looked, sooner or later the pattern would emerge and I'd understand and could go on. He was right. He was always right.

I began to learn about people. I began to find out how many were afraid of the same things—afraid of being shut out, of being found out, of being unloved, unwanted, or—worst of all—unneeded. I learned how flimsy were the bases of so many of their fears, and how unimportant, in the long run, were the things on which so many of them pitifully spent their lives. More than anything else, I learned how uncharacteristic of most of them were their cruelties, how excusable their stupidities; in short, how damned decent they were.

I found out the differences between "the truth" and "all the truth." You can know some pretty terrible things about a person, and you can know they're true. But sometimes it makes a huge difference if you know what else is true too. I read something in a book once about an old lady who was walking along the street minding her own business when a young guy came charging along, knocked her down, rolled her in a mud puddle, slapped her head and smeared handsful of wet mud all over her hair. Now what should you do with a guy like that?

But then if you find out that someone had got careless with a drum of gasoline and it ignited and the old lady was splashed with it, and the guy had presence of mind enough to do what he did as fast as he did, and severely burned his hands in the doing of it, then what should you do with him?

Yet everything reported about him is true. The only difference is the amount of truth you tell.

Reading a grave, you read it all. All of the truth makes a difference—but what a difference—in the way you feel about people.

One day the man said to me, "I would say that there are only a half-dozen graves here that are beyond you. I think you're a pretty remarkable student."

I said thanks, but I'd blame the quality of the teaching. "You've taken an awful lot of trouble over me."

He shrugged. "It's what I do," he said inclusively. Then he waited.

I wondered what he was waiting for, and so searched back through what he had been saying. "Oh," I said, and with him, looked up at the north corner of the cemetery where my wife's grave lay. It wasn't sharp-planed any more, or bare. Everything about it had changed ... been changed ... except, of course, that unsoilable headstone. So. "Oh," I said. "I could read it."

"Easily," he said.

I went up there. I don't know if he followed me. I wasn't thinking about him any more. I came to the grave and stood looking at it for a long time. I thought about her, and about the facts I had. Truths. The truth about her. The time I pried her out of a dark corner at a party with a drunk named Wilfred. The time she snatched a letter off the mantel when I came in and threw it into the fire. The time that guy on the boat laughed when her name was mentioned and then shut up when he found I was married to her. More than anything else, the fact of her death in the sports car, the fact of that housecoat, of the missing tweed suit and stupid hat. Now I could know. Now I could know what, where, and how many times. Now I could know why.

I guess I was up there for longer than I realized.

When I came to myself it was almost dark, and growing cold. I almost fell when I started to walk. I walked slowly until my legs woke up and, seeing a light in the caretaker's building, went in to talk to the old fellow for a minute. I didn't see the graveyard reader around anywhere.

I was back the next morning. It was Saturday. The stonecutter was there already, crouched in front of my plot, tick-ticking away. I'd had to agree to time-and-a-half to get him, but I was willing. When at last I decided on an epitaph for that stone, I wanted it put there, and right now.

I walked up there to watch the man work. He knew his trade, that stonecutter, and he had almost finished. After a few minutes I was aware of someone standing next to me, and sure enough, it was the graveyard reader. "Hi."

"How are you?" he asked—not the way anyone else might ask, but meaning it: how was I? what had happened? how did I feel about it? was I all right?

"I'm all right," I said. Also, not the way you'd say it to just anybody.

Silently we watched the man finish up. I nodded to him and said it was fine. He grinned and gathered up his tools and the tarpaulin with the chips in it, and waved and went away. The reader and I stood looking at the inscription.

I said, a little embarrassed, "Not very original."

"But very effective," he answered.

"You think so? You really think so?"

He nodded, and that made me very, very glad. I hadn't meant to tell him, but it slipped out in one great big blurt: "I didn't read it."

"No?"

"No," I said. "I came up here and stood for a long time, thinking about ... all the work I'd done to be able to read it, and about— the truth, what kind of a difference all the truth makes. And I thought a lot about people, and about ... *her*."

"Yes," he said, interested and ... non-prying.

"Yes, about her, the things she'd done, the things she could have done. The way she used to talk to me. Do you know, people like her, who aren't so hot with words—they have ways of talking, if you can read them, almost like a grave has?"

"I think you're right."

"Well, I thought about that too. And my own illiteracy ..." I laughed in some sort of embarrassment and said, "Anyway, the way it wound up, I didn't read it. I went and ordered this epitaph instead."

"Why that particular one?"

We read it over together, and I said, "It's taken me over a year, and a pretty tough year at that, but this is what I wanted to say to her. This is what I want her to know, now and from now on, from me."

He laughed.

I confess to being a little annoyed at that, even after all I had gone through with this fellow. "What's funny?"

"*You're* saying that, to *her?*"

"Something wrong with that?"

"Sure is," he said. And he walked off, and when I called, he just waved, but kept on walking.

I turned to look back at the headstone, with its clean new inscription. I'd put it there because I wanted to say something to her that ...

Me? say something to *her?*

No wonder he had laughed. A guy spends more than a year learning to read a grave, and then gets the silly notion that it's reading him.

So I read it again—not the grave; I would never read that—I read just the inscription. I read what she said to me, now, this morning, new and crisp and for the very first time: *Rest in peace.*

"Thanks, honey," I whispered, "I will," and I went on home and got the first real sleep I'd had since she'd left me.

The Man Who Told Lies

Once there was a man who all the time told lies and everybody hated him and diden't trust him even when he said what time it is they woulden't believe him so one day the craziest thing hapened he was driving his car to work in the morning, and his car slipped on a banana peal only it was reely a whole bunch of banana peals where a garbage truck had a accident and spilled on the road so he cracked a lampost.

The policemen was really mad about it and pinched the man to the courthouse and it took a while to get it all fixed. So when he got to work he was late and his boss said what hapened to you and the man said my car sliped on a banana peal and the boss said you're a liar everybody knows that and if I got any more trouble from you out you go. And no matter what the man said they woulden't beleive him.

So he was walking in the park afterwards and he felt real mean and low and he sat down and a funny little man sat down on the bench too and said whats the matter. And the man said everybody picks on me I am a well known liar and when I get around to telling the truth nobdy believes me anyway: The other man said gosh. I can fix that easy because I am a Magician so the man said he dident beleive in that Magic stuff and the old man said you want people to beleive you you got to start out beleiving me so the man said alright then and the Magician made a spell wich dident hurt.

So he forgot about it for awhile until he met a lady he knew and she said hello hello I'm glad to see you and he was going to say he was glad to see her but he wasen't because he dident reely like her she gave him a pain so what came out of his mouth was Well. Im not glad to see you because you give me a pain so she got so mad she was going to hit him with her pocket book but he ran. So then later he went to dinner were he was invited and the lady said how did you like the dinner and before he could stop he said the meat was tough and the peas taste like garbage which was the truth. So there was one more person who diden't like him.

In the morning the boss was going to give him a raise so he called him in to the ofice and said Well how do you like working here and the man said before he could stop I dont like the work and I dont like you eather wich was the truth. So the boss fired him. Then he went walking in the park again to find the little Magician man. And he found him and said to take off the Magic spell because he said he was a lot better when he was a liar. He said the way it is now I get in trouble every time I open my mouth it seems everybody tells lies to each other all the time like Im glad to see you and I wish you luck and all that when they reely dont mean it. Well the Magician said you just dont know which lies to tell and which not to I hope you learn a lesson but about the spell your out of luck because that spell is pernamet so just work hard and watch what you say.

Then the man got a new job and worked hard as he could and when people asked him anything he just shut his mouth and worked even harder. So when he got home that night his wife said how about the new job is the work hard and he said yes wich it was she said. are you tired and he said tired Im dead so then he droped dead.

—Billy Watson

The Man Who Lost the Sea

Say you're a kid, and one dark night you're running along the cold sand with this helicopter in your hand, saying very fast witchy-witchy-witchy. You pass the sick man and he wants you to shove off with that thing. Maybe he thinks you're too old to play with toys. So you squat next to him in the sand and tell him it isn't a toy, it's a model. You tell him look here, here's something most people don't know about helicopters. You take a blade of the rotor in your fingers and show him how it can move in the hub, up and down a little, back and forth a little, and twist a little, to change pitch. You start to tell him how this flexibility does away with the gyroscopic effect, but he won't listen. He doesn't want to think about flying, about helicopters, or about you, and he most especially does not want explanations about anything by anybody. Not now. Now, he wants to think about the sea. So you go away.

The sick man is buried in the cold sand with only his head and his left arm showing. He is dressed in a pressure suit and looks like a man from Mars. Built into his left sleeve is a combination time-piece and pressure gauge, the gauge with a luminous blue indicator which makes no sense, the clock hands luminous red. He can hear the pounding of surf and the soft swift pulse of his pumps. One time long ago when he was swimming he went too deep and stayed down too long and came up too fast, and when he came to it was like this: they said, "Don't move, boy. You've got the bends. Don't even try to move." He had tried anyway. It hurt. So now, this time, he lies in the sand without moving, without trying.

His head isn't working right. But he knows clearly that it isn't working right, which is a strange thing that happens to people in shock sometimes. Say you were that kid, you could say how it was, because once you woke up lying in the gym office in high school and asked what had happened. They explained how you tried something on the parallel bars and fell on your head. You understood exactly, though you couldn't remember falling. Then a minute later you asked again what had happened and they told you. You understood it. And a minute later ... forty-one times they told you, and you understood. It was just that no matter how many times they pushed it into your head, it wouldn't stick there; but all the while you *knew* that your head would start working again in time. And in time it did.... Of course, if you were that kid, always explaining things to people and to yourself, you wouldn't want to bother the sick man with it now.

Look what you've done already, making him send you away with that angry shrug of the mind (which, with the eyes, are the only things which will move just now). The motionless effort costs him a wave of nausea. He has felt seasick before but he has never *been* seasick, and the formula for that is to keep your eyes on the horizon and stay busy. Now! Then he'd better get busy—now; for there's one place especially not to be seasick in, and that's locked up in a pressure suit. Now!

So he busies himself as best he can, with the seascape, landscape, sky. He lies on high ground, his head propped on a vertical wall of black rock. There is another such outcrop before him, whip-topped with white sand and with smooth flat sand. Beyond and down is valley, salt-flat, estuary; he cannot yet be sure. He is sure of the line of footprints, which begin behind him, pass to his left, disappear in the outcrop shadows, and reappear beyond to vanish at last into the shadows of the valley.

Stretched across the sky is old mourning-cloth, with starlight burning holes in it, and between the holes the black is absolute— wintertime, mountaintop sky-black.

(Far off on the horizon within himself, he sees the swell and crest of approaching nausea; he counters with an undertow of weakness, which meets and rounds and settles the wave before it can break. Get busier. Now.)

Burst in on him, then, with the X-15 model. That'll get him. Hey, how about this for a gimmick? Get too high for the thin air to give you any control, you have these little jets in the wingtips, see? and on the sides of the empennage: bank, roll, yaw, whatever, with squirts of compressed air.

But the sick man curls his sick lip: oh, git, kid, git, will you?—that has nothing to do with the sea. So you git.

Out and out the sick man forces his view, etching all he sees with a meticulous intensity, as if it might be his charge, one day, to duplicate all this. To his left is only starlit sea, windless. In front of him across the valley, rounded hills with dim white epaulettes of light. To his right, the jutting corner of the black wall against which his helmet rests. (He thinks the distant moundings of nausea becalmed, but he will not look yet.) So he scans the sky, black and bright, calling Sirius, calling Pleiades, Polaris, Ursa Minor, calling that ... that ... Why, it *moves*. Watch it: yes, it moves! It is a fleck of light, seeming to be wrinkled, fissured, rather like a chip of boiled cauliflower in the sky. (Of course, he knows better than to trust his own eyes just now.) But that movement ...

As a child he had stood on cold sand in a frosty Cape Cod evening, watching Sputnik's steady spark rise out of the haze (madly, dawning a little north of west); and after that he had sleeplessly wound special coils for his receiver, risked his life restringing high antennas, all for the brief capture of an unreadable *tweetle-eep-tweetle* in his earphones from Vanguard, Explorer, Lunik, Discoverer, Mercury. He knew them all (well, some people collect match-covers, stamps) and he knew especially that unmistakable steady sliding in the sky.

This moving fleck was a satellite, and in a moment, motionless, uninstrumented but for his chronometer and his part-brain, he will know which one. (He is grateful beyond expression—without that sliding chip of light, there were only those footprints, those wandering footprints, to tell a man he was not alone in the world.)

Say you were a kid, eager and challengeable and more than a little bright, you might in a day or so work out a way to measure the period of a satellite with nothing but a timepiece and a brain; you might eventually see that the shadow in the rocks ahead had been there from the first only because of the light from the rising satellite. Now if you check the time exactly at the moment when the shadow on the sand is equal to the height of the outcrop, and time it again when the light is at the zenith and the shadow gone, you will multiply this number of minutes by 8—think why, now: horizon to zenith is one-fourth of the orbit, give or take a little, and halfway up the sky is half that quarter—and you will then know this satellite's period. You know all the periods—ninety minutes, two, two-and-a-half hours; with that and the appearance of this bird, you'll find out which one it is.

But if you were that kid, eager or resourceful or whatever, you wouldn't jabber about it to the sick man, for not only does he not want to be bothered with you, he's thought of all that long since and is even now watching the shadows for that triangular split second of measurement. Now! His eyes drop to the face of his chronometer: 0400, near as makes no never mind.

He has minutes to wait now—ten? . . . thirty? . . . twenty-three?—while this baby moon eats up its slice of shadowpie; and that's too bad, the waiting, for though the inner sea is calm there are currents below, shadows that shift and swim. Be busy. Be busy. He must not swim near that great invisible amoeba, whatever happens: its first cold pseudopod is even now reaching for the vitals.

Being a knowledgeable young fellow, not quite a kid any more, wanting to help the sick man too, you want to tell him everything you know about that cold-in-the-gut, that reaching invisible surrounding implacable amoeba. You know all about it—listen, you want to yell at him, don't let that touch of cold bother you. Just know what it is, that's all. Know what it is that is touching your gut. You want to tell him, listen:

Listen, this is how you met the monster and dissected it. Listen, you were skin-diving in the Grenadines, a hundred tropical shoal-water islands; you had a new blue snorkel mask, the kind with face-plate and breathing-tube all in one, and new blue flippers on your feet, and a new blue spear-gun—all this new because you'd only begun, you see; you were a beginner, aghast with pleasure at your easy intrusion into this underwater otherworld. You'd been out in a boat, you were coming back, you'd just reached the mouth of the little bay, you'd taken the notion to swim the rest of the way. You'd said as much to the boys and slipped into the warm silky water. You brought your gun.

Not far to go at all, but then beginners find wet distances deceiving. For the first five minutes or so it was only delightful, the sun hot on your back and the water so warm it seemed not to have any temperature at all and you were flying. With your face under the water, your mask was not so much attached as part of you, your wide blue flippers trod away yards, your gun rode all but weightless in your hand, the taut rubber sling making an occasional hum as your passage plucked it in the sunlit green. In your ears crooned the breathy monotone of the snorkel tube, and through the invisible disk of plate glass you saw wonders. The bay was shallow—ten, twelve feet or so—and sandy, with great growths of brain-, bone-, and fire-coral, intricate waving sea-fans, and fish—such fish! Scarlet and green and aching azure, gold and rose and slate-color studded with sparks of enamel-blue, pink and peach and silver. And that *thing* got into you, that ... monster.

There were enemies in this otherworld: the sand-colored spotted sea-snake with his big ugly head and turned-down mouth, who would not retreat but lay watching the intruder pass; and the mottled moray with jaws like bolt-cutters; and somewhere around, certainly, the barracuda with his undershot face and teeth turned inward so that he must take away whatever he might strike. There were urchins— the plump white sea-egg with its thick fur of sharp quills and the black ones with the long slender spines that would break off in unwary flesh and fester there for weeks; and file-fish and stone-fish with their poisoned barbs and lethal meat; and the stingaree who could drive his spike through a leg bone. Yet these were not *monsters,* and could not matter to you, the invader churning along above them all. For you were above them in so many ways—armed, rational, comforted by the close shore (ahead the beach, the rocks on each side) and by the presence of the boat not too far behind. Yet you were ... attacked.

At first it was uneasiness, not pressing, but pervasive, a contact quite as intimate as that of the sea; you were sheathed in it. And also there was the touch—the cold inward contact. Aware of it at last, you laughed: for Pete's sake, what's there to be scared of?

The monster, the amoeba.

You raised your head and looked back in air. The boat had edged in to the cliff at the right; someone was giving a last poke around for lobster. You waved at the boat; it was your gun you waved, and emerging from the water it gained its latent ounces so that you sank a bit, and as if you had no snorkel on, you tipped your head back to get a breath. But tipping your head back plunged the end of the tube under water; the valve closed; you drew in a hard lungful of nothing at all. You dropped your face under; up came the tube; you got your air, and along with it a bullet of seawater which struck you somewhere inside the throat. You coughed it out and floundered, sobbing as you sucked in air, inflating your chest until it hurt, and the air you got seemed no good, no good at all, a worthless devitalized inert gas.

You clenched your teeth and headed for the beach, kicking strongly and knowing it was the right thing to do; and then below and to the right you saw a great bulk mounding up out of the sand floor of the sea. You knew it was only the reef, rocks and coral and weed, but the sight of it made you scream; you didn't care what you knew. You turned hard left to avoid it, fought by as if it would reach for you, and you couldn't get air, couldn't get air, for all the unobstructed hooting of your snorkel tube. You couldn't bear the mask, suddenly, not for another second, so you shoved it upward clear of your mouth and rolled over, floating on your back and opening your mouth to the sky and breathing with a quacking noise.

It was then and there that the monster well and truly engulfed you, mantling you round and about within itself—formless, borderless, the illimitable amoeba. The beach, mere yards away, and the rocky arms of the bay, and the not-too-distant boat—these you could identify but no longer distinguish, for they were all one and the same thing ... the thing called unreachable.

You fought that way for a time, on your back, dangling the gun under and behind you and straining to get enough warm sun-stained air into your chest. And in time some particles of sanity began to swirl in the roil of your mind, and to dissolve and tint it. The air pumping in and out of your square-grinned frightened mouth began to be meaningful at last, and the monster relaxed away from you.

You took stock, saw surf, beach, a leaning tree. You felt the new scend of your body as the rollers humped to become breakers. Only a dozen firm kicks brought you to where you could roll over and double up; your shin struck coral with a lovely agony and you stood in foam and waded ashore. You gained the wet sand, hard sand, and ultimately, with two more paces powered by bravado, you crossed high-water mark and lay in the dry sand, unable to move.

You lay in the sand, and before you were able to move or to think, you were able to feel a triumph—a triumph because you were alive and knew that much without thinking at all.

When you were able to think, your first thought was of the gun, and the first move you were able to make was to let go at last of the thing. You had nearly died because you had not let it go before; without it you would not have been burdened and you would not have panicked. You had (you began to understand) kept it because someone else would have had to retrieve it—easily enough—and you could not have stood the laughter. You had almost died because They might laugh at you.

This was the beginning of the dissection, analysis, study of the monster. It began then; it had never finished. Some of what you had learned from it was merely important; some of the rest—vital.

You had learned, for example, never to swim farther with a snorkel than you could swim back without one. You learned never to burden yourself with the unnecessary in an emergency: even a hand or a foot might be as expendable as a gun; pride was expendable, dignity was. You learned never to dive alone, even if They laugh at you, even if you have to shoot a fish yourself and say afterward "we" shot it. Most of all, you learned that fear has many fingers, and one of them—a simple one, made of too great a concentration of carbon dioxide in your blood, as from too-rapid breathing in and out of the same tube—is not really fear at all but feels like fear, and can turn into panic and kill you.

Listen, you want to say, listen, there isn't anything wrong with such an experience or with all the study it leads to, because a man who can learn enough from it could become fit enough, cautious enough, foresighted, unafraid, modest, teachable enough to be chosen, to be qualified for. . . .

You lose the thought, or turn it away, because the sick man feels that cold touch deep inside, feels it right now, feels it beyond ignoring, above and beyond anything that you, with all your experience and certainty, could explain to him even if he would listen, which he won't. Make him, then; tell him the cold touch is some simple explainable thing like anoxia, like gladness even: some triumph that he will be able to appreciate when his head is working right again.

Triumph? Here he's alive after . . . whatever it is, and that doesn't seem to be triumph enough, though it was in the Grenadines, and that other time, when he got the bends, saved his own life, saved two other lives. Now, somehow, it's not the same: there seems to be a reason why just being alive afterward isn't a triumph.

Why not triumph? Because not twelve, not twenty, not even thirty minutes is it taking the satellite to complete its eighth-of-an-orbit: fifty minutes are gone, and still there's a slice of shadow yonder. It is this, this which is placing the cold finger upon his heart, and he doesn't know why, he doesn't know why, he will not know why; he is afraid he shall when his head is working again. . . .

Oh, where's the kid? Where is any way to busy the mind, apply it to something, anything else but the watchhand which outruns the moon? Here, kid: come over here—what you got there?

If you were the kid, then you'd forgive everything and hunker down with your new model, not a toy, not a helicopter or a rocket-plane, but the big one, the one that looks like an overgrown cartridge. It's so big, even as a model, that even an angry sick man wouldn't call it a toy. A giant cartridge, but watch: the lower four-fifths is Alpha—all muscle—over a million pounds thrust. (Snap it off, throw it away.) Half the rest is Beta—all brains—it puts you on your way. (Snap it off, throw it away.) And now look at the polished fraction which is left. Touch a control somewhere and see— see? it has wings—wide triangular wings. This is Gamma, the one with wings, and on its back is a small sausage; it is a moth with a sausage on its back. The sausage (click! it comes free) is Delta. Delta is the last, the smallest: Delta is the way home.

What will they think of next? Quite a toy. Quite a toy. Beat it, kid. The satellite is almost overhead, the sliver of shadow going—going—almost gone and . . . gone.

Check: 0459. Fifty-nine minutes? give or take a few. Times eight . . . 472 . . . is, uh, 7 hours 52 minutes.

Seven hours fifty-two minutes? Why, there isn't a satellite round earth with a period like that. In all the solar system there's only . . .

The cold finger turns fierce, implacable.

The east is paling and the sick man turns to it, wanting the light, the sun, an end to questions whose answers couldn't be looked upon. The sea stretches endlessly out to the growing light, and endlessly, somewhere out of sight, the surf roars. The paling east bleaches the sandy hilltops and throws the line of footprints into aching relief. That would be the buddy, the sick man knows, gone for help. He cannot at the moment recall who the buddy is, but in time he will, and meanwhile the footprints make him less alone.

The sun's upper rim thrusts itself above the horizon with a flash of green, instantly gone. There is no dawn, just the green flash and then a clear white blast of unequivocal sunup. The sea could not be whiter, more still, if it were frozen and snow-blanketed. In the west, stars still blaze, and overhead the crinkled satellite is scarcely abashed by the growing light. A formless jumble in the valley below begins to resolve itself into a sort of tent-city, or installation of some kind, with tubelike and sail-like buildings. This would have meaning for the sick man if his head were working right. Soon, it would. Will. (Oh . . .)

The sea, out on the horizon just under the rising sun, is behaving strangely, for in that place where properly belongs a pool of unbearable brightness, there is instead a notch of brown. It is as if the white fire of the sun is drinking dry the sea—for look, look! the notch becomes a bow and the bow a crescent, racing ahead of the sunlight, white sea ahead of it and behind it a cocoa-dry stain spreading across and down toward where he watches.

Beside the finger of fear which lies on him, another finger places

itself, and another, making ready for that clutch, that grip, that ultimate insane squeeze of panic. Yet beyond that again, past that squeeze
when it comes, to be savored if the squeeze is only fear and not panic,
lies triumph—triumph, and a glory. It is perhaps this which consti-
tutes his whole battle: to fit himself, prepare himself to bear the
utmost that fear could do, for if he can do that, there is a triumph
on the other side. But ... not yet. Please, not yet awhile.

Something flies (or flew, or will fly—he is a little confused on this
point) toward him, from the far right where the stars still shine. It
is not a bird and it is unlike any aircraft on earth, for the aerody-
namics are wrong. Wings so wide and so fragile would be useless,
would melt and tear away in any of earth's atmosphere but the outer
fringes. He sees then (because he prefers to see it so) that it is the
kid's model, or part of it, and for a toy it does very well indeed.

It is the part called Gamma, and it glides in, balancing, parallels
the sand and holds away, holds away slowing, then, settles, all in
slow motion, throwing up graceful sheet-fountains of fine sand from
its skids. And it runs along the ground for an impossible distance,
letting down its weight by the ounce and stingily the ounce, until
look out until a skid *look out* fits itself into a bridged crevasse *look
out, look out!* and still moving on, it settles down to the struts.
Gamma then, tired, digs her wide left wingtip carefully into the racing sand, digs it in hard; and as the wing breaks off, Gamma slews,
sidles, slides slowly, pointing her other triangular tentlike wing at
the sky, and broadside crushes into the rocks at the valley's end.

As she rolls smashing over, there breaks from her broad back the
sausage, the little Delta, which somersaults away to break its back
upon the rocks, and through the broken hull spill smashed shards
of graphite from the moderator of her power-pile. *Look out! Look
out!* and at the same instant from the finally checked mass of Gamma
there explodes a doll, which slides and tumbles into the sand, into
the rocks and smashed hot graphite from the wreck of Delta.

The sick man numbly watches this toy destroy itself: what will they
think of next?—and with a gelid horror prays at the doll lying in
the raging rubble of the atomic pile: *don't stay there, man—get away!*

get away! that's hot, you know? But it seems like a night and a day and half another night before the doll staggers to its feet and, clumsy in its pressure-suit, runs away up the valleyside, climbs a sand-topped outcrop, slips, falls, lies under a slow cascade of cold ancient sand until, but for an arm and the helmet, it is buried.

The sun is high now, high enough to show the sea is not a sea, but brown plain with the frost burned off it, as now it burns away from the hills, diffusing in air and blurring the edges of the sun's disk, so that in a very few minutes there is no sun at all, but only a glare in the east. Then the valley below loses its shadows, and, like an arrangement in a diorama, reveals the form and nature of the wreckage below: no tent city this, no installation, but the true real ruin of Gamma and the eviscerated hulk of Delta. (Alpha was the muscle, Beta the brain; Gamma was a bird, but Delta, Delta was the way home.)

And from it stretches the line of footprints, to and by the sick man, above to the bluff, and gone with the sandslide which had buried him there. Whose footprints?

He knows whose, whether or not he knows that he knows, or wants to or not. He knows what satellite has (give or take a bit) a period like that (want it exactly?—it's 7.66 hours). He knows what world has such a night, and such a frosty glare by day. He knows these things as he knows how spilled radioactives will pour the crash and mutter of surf into a man's earphones.

Say you were that kid: say, instead, at last, that you are the sick man, for they are the same; surely then you can understand why of all things, even while shattered, shocked, sick with radiation calculated (leaving) radiation computed (arriving) and radiation past all bearing (lying in the wreckage of Delta) you would want to think of the sea. For no farmer who fingers the soil with love and knowledge, no poet who sings of it, artist, contractor, engineer, even child bursting into tears at the inexpressible beauty of a field of daffodils—none of these is as intimate with Earth as those who live on, live with, breathe and drift in its seas. So of these things you must think; with these you must dwell until you are less sick and more ready to face the truth.

The truth, then, is that the satellite fading here is Phobos, that those footprints are your own, that there is no sea here, that you have crashed and are killed and will in a moment be dead. The cold hand ready to squeeze and still your heart is not anoxia or even fear, it is death. Now, if there is something more important than this, now is the time for it to show itself.

The sick man looks at the line of his own footprints, which testify that he is alone, and at the wreckage below, which states that there is no way back, and at the white east and the mottled west and the paling flecklike satellite above. Surf sounds in his ears. He hears his pumps. He hears what is left of his breathing. The cold clamps down and folds him round past measuring, past all limit.

Then he speaks, cries out: then with joy he takes his triumph at the other side of death, as one takes a great fish, as one completes a skilled and mighty task, rebalances at the end of some great daring leap; and as he used to say "we shot a fish" he uses no "I":

"God," he cries, dying on Mars, "God, we made it!"

The Man Who Figured Everything

This is about Jim Conlin the Badlands Bookkeeper. He was, according to the journals of the time, a terror, a menace, and a scourge. He was, in the flesh, a mild man, young and balding early, with diffident horizontal lines across his brow.

He hid in the hills with his half-dozen riders, all but one of whom outweighed him, but then that one was only a three-quarter breed Nez Perce, and hardly counted. These men, each to his taste, fought and gambled, drank and wenched, always providing they had Jim Conlin's advance permission and pursued the hobby somewhere away from Jim Conlin's hideout. A long way away. There was a town, Dead Mole Spring, eight miles away as the crow flies, where nobody had ever seen Conlin or any of his crew—a good example of the way the Bookkeeper of the Badlands arranged things.

Jim Conlin figured. He figured everything, the Bookkeeper did. He never moved until he was ready, and when he was ready, it was altogether. In some sleepy mountain town, just when the marshal was out and the sheriff drunk, and the bank heavy with cowpokes' pay and prospectors' dust, Jim Conlin's men would whirl up out of the ground like dust devils and be gone like smoke, the gold with them.

The only similarity between one job and another was that element of perfect planning, perfect timing—the only clue, most of the time, as to who the robbers were. Unless, of course, Conlin wanted it otherwise, like the time he took the Rocky Summit Bank three times in one week, just because everybody was so positive he wouldn't be back.

He would have been caught for sure the time rumors got around that he was going to rob the express between Elwood and Casson's Quarry; the train was loaded with law and the tracks lined on both sides with one of the biggest posses the West had ever seen, which was fine with Conlin, who was busy at the time robbing another train on another railroad.

He would certainly be remembered in large type, like Butch Cassidy and the James boys, if it were not for his concentration on fine detail—this got him only into fine print. As a man, he was colorless to the point of invisibility; as a desperado he was too methodical to be remembered. Probably the largest two reasons his reputation has faded with the newspapers of his day were these: he never killed a lawman, and he was never caught.

There came one night to Jim Conlin's hideout, Arch Scott, invited and escorted. Scott had something of a reputation locally: cautious, sober, with special skills in safes and lockboxes. He could use a gun, and didn't, which was a high recommendation to the Bookkeeper; and Scott's ability to do nine consecutive jobs with the methods of nine different people clinched it.

Although the Bookkeeper occasionally took on a brace or two of drifters for special jobs, letting them go afterwards, he liked to keep a half-dozen regulars with him; and there was a vacancy just now, one Farley Moore having succumbed to romance. (That was Conlin's name for it; actually it was tetanus, contracted after a Rocky Summit housewife, mistaken for a doxie by Moore, removed his ear with an iron skillet.)

So Conlin gave Arch Scott his guided tour and his most careful examination, introducing him around, watching him, making his estimate. He liked Scott—liked him, that is, the way a man likes a well-made saddle or a clean rifle. The Bookkeeper had human feelings, but he had a place for them, and he kept them all there. Which introduces Loretta Harper.

She was the only woman permitted at the hideout, except for a few squaws who washed clothes and swept out. Conlin had found her working in a place she was glad to get out of—especially with a man who knew enough about her to ask no questions and saw to it that she got more of the things she liked than she could hope for working in town. He had something for all her hungers but one, and that one was beyond his comprehension. It was beyond hers, too, until Arch Scott came.

"This here's Loretta," Conlin said when he brought Scott in, and Scott saw a carving come to life, silk and ivory and ice, as out of place here as a leaf from *Godey's Lady's Book* tacked to a haybarn; and Loretta saw a neat man with heavy shoulders and good teeth and eyes you couldn't keep secrets from.

And that should have been that. It would have been, as far as Arch was concerned. He was there on business, and business came first. And Loretta felt nothing, just then; Jim Conlin's men came and went and his steady crew was always there. This was another one, only another one. As Conlin and Scott left she turned back to her mirror, and if anyone had asked her, she probably wouldn't have remembered the new man's name.

Conlin and Arch Scott went down the mountain for fifty yards or so to the cabin and went in. "Henry Little Hawk," said Conlin, nodding at the slight figure squatting by the door.

"Howdy," said Scott. "I'm . . ."

"Yuh," grunted the little man. He looked like an animated piece of mahogany, and seemed to be composed mainly of eyebrows, nose, and sharp shinbones.

Conlin chuckled. "He knows who you are. He's the one found you for me. Or anyway, he's the one who found out it was really you who did the jobs you say you done. He sees everything and everybody, Henry does, and nobody sees him." He went to the back wall of the cabin and put his boot on it. It swung aside. "Havin' Henry around's like having your eyes out on stalks forty mile long," he said, motioning Scott through the opening, then closing it. "Only a misfit Nez Perce breed, but God what a memory! Look at a town he never saw before, ride all night, draw you a map so fine you could go there and jump over a yaller dog blindfold."

They were standing at one end of a section mine tunnel, with the wooden cabin wall behind them and a rockfall at the other end. The long room was fitted out like a bunkhouse, but with a fire in the center, its smoke curling upward to be lost in a fissure overhead. All evidence of the old mine workings had been carefully removed from the outside and the weather-beaten cabin, scarcely large enough for two men, substituted. Any posseman willing to believe the evidence of his own eyes would call you a liar if you told him you had seen a bunch the size of Conlin's disappear into this hillside. Not that a posse had ever been within miles of this place, of course.

"Can sleep eleven here in a pinch," Conlin said. "Ain't but four now—Henry, he don't bunk here. Suit you?"

Scott swept the place with a glance. "Fine, Conlin. I slept in worse and paid money for it. Where's the . . ."

He was interrupted by a blast of language, English and Spanish, profane and obscene, packed tight as grapeshot and twice as loud. A tall man, hidden until now by the end bunks, sprang to his feet, snatching a coiled bullwhip from a peg on the rock wall. He was a blaze of color and fancywork, Mexican weaving and tooled leather. On his shoulder blades, held by an elaborately braided thong, perched a hand-blocked silken felt worth six months of a cowpoke's pay.

He shook out the whip and brought it whistling back, and in that split second Conlin was behind him, grasping the lash. The whip flicked out of the man's hand and Scott, still standing by the wooden wall, had to step aside to avoid the loaded handle.

"Now, Al, you know better'n that," said Conlin quietly. He drew up beside the bunks and looked down. A blanket was spread on the floor, and on it was gold money and a deck of cards. A second giant knelt by the blanket, scowling. His eyes were red, very small, very wide apart, and at the moment full of kill. Conlin's appearance had arrested him halfway to his feet with a nickel-plated .45 halfway out. He came to his feet now, but slowly, and when he stopped moving, his gun was holstered and his hand clear of it.

The man with the fancy hat, Al, began to splutter at Conlin, something about wart-hogs, something about an inside straight, something in Spanish. Conlin shook his head gently, stooped, and picked up most of the cards. Deftly he stacked them, cut them, and tore the pack in two, letting the pieces flutter to the ground.

The two big men watched the pieces fall. The red-eyed man bit his lower lip silently with square yellow teeth. The other one ran out of splutter and simply stood there, breathing hard. If Arch Scott expected anything else to happen, he was disappointed. Conlin motioned to him and said, "Scott, this here's Big Ike Friend." The red-eyed man glowered at the stranger. "And Al Coe."

"Arch Scott. Howdy."

"Howdy," Coe grunted. He walked past the others and went for his whip. He came back, coiling it as he walked, not looking at anybody, and hung it on the peg. "Seen you before, Scott," he said with his back turned.

"Don't think so."

"Ever down Taos way, or 'Dobe?"

"I come from the Dakotas," said Arch Scott quickly, "where folks don't ask questions."

Big Ike Friend produced a harsh brief snicker from the depths of his flat nose.

"Tell you something," said Conlin in a voice so mild in the sudden tension that Scott nearly jumped with shock. "We don't fight among ourselves here. Anybody wants to rassle, go pick on a stranger some place else. You ain't learned that, Scott, and you and Big Ike forgot it, I guess, Al. We don't gamble here, we don't drink—not enough to get drunk on anyways—and there ain't no women allowed. I got nothing against them three things, but they're the three best reasons for fightin', and that kind of fightin' is one thing I ain't got time to keep books on. Scott, you need anything, you ask Big Ike or Al Coe here. I'm going back to the house."

And he did, without so much as a good night, leaving all the makings of a three-sided donnybrook. But then Arch Scott laughed—not at the two big men, but in an indefinable way with them, so that he was no longer a stranger, but part of a crew which had just seen a hundred and forty pounds of mild logic putting out a fire. Big Ike laughed too; Al Coe did not, but he relaxed visibly.

"Where do I bunk?" Scott asked.

Big Ike pointed out the empties. Scott selected one and sat down on it, looking quizzically at the others. "How does he do it?"

"By bein' right," said Al Coe reluctantly.

"Lots of hombres go around being right, nobody listens," said Big Ike.

"Those are the guys that don't pay off," said Coe. "Bein' right is nothin' by itself."

And there it was, in as neat a nutshell as anyone could pack it. There's no point in disagreeing with a man who's always right, who also put money in your sock.

Arch Scott fell asleep that night knowing he wouldn't be bothered.

The horses were corralled in a narrow dry gulch a quarter of a mile away, visible from two places—inside, and straight up. Like the rest of the spread, it was only another scar on the hillside.

Conlin went down there in the morning with Loretta, to cut out a gentle horse for her. It was early, but Arch Scott was already up and about, standing just inside the narrow throat of the gulch, his hands in the back pockets of his Levi's and his hat on the back of his head. "Morning."

Conlin nodded to him. Loretta didn't say anything. Scott glanced at her, then took his hands out of his pockets and removed his hat. His tardiness was understandable. When Loretta rode, the carven goddess was folded up and put away. She wore Levi's and a shirt and a soft leather vest, and her bright hair was hidden under a wide-brimmed man's hat; and from twenty paces she looked like a country boy out to bark squirrels, which was the idea.

She stood by the rails near Scott and waited while Conlin went in with a bridle over his shoulder and a rope on one arm. Scott glanced at her once, but she seemed to be watching Conlin, so he said nothing. He watched Conlin too, and he liked what he saw.

The Bookkeeper did what he had to do without waste motion, and better than anyone he might have ordered to do it for him. He took a roan gelding on the first cast, reeled him in, and had the rope off and the bridle on in what looked like one movement. He led the animal to a shed by the rocky wall of the cut and went in for a saddle.

"Scott."

Arch looked at the woman. She had not moved, and was certainly not looking his way. Her voice had been just loud enough to reach him. He sensed that this was no casual approach to a casual conversation, so he took her cue and stayed where he was. "Ma'am?"

"Waterhole called Green Spring," she said, hardly moving her lips. In spite of its softness she had a surprisingly full voice. "Find it. Be there at two o'clock." Before he could answer or acknowledge, she had slipped through the rails and was walking toward Conlin.

He watched her mount and wheel the horse. He gathered his wits and dropped the bars for her as she rode out. She passed as if he did not exist. Scott replaced the bars without looking after her.

"We're going out on a little job today," Conlin told him when he came up.

"We are?"

"We are—Henry and me and Al and Big Ike. Moko and Gus, that's the two you ain't met yet, they're waiting for us."

"I do something wrong?"

Conlin seemed to think the question quite natural. "Hardly had a chance yet, have you?"

"'What do you want me to do while you're out?"

Conlin swept out his arm in a wide circular motion. "Smell out this spread. I want you to memorize every rock and bush and cut and hogback within ten miles of here. They say a couple big glaciers carved up this country, Scott—I wouldn't know about that myself; but whoever done it was working for us. You'll see. You'll find out that this country can lose a Injun tracker with a pack o' hounds, if you know where to go. Nobody ever trailed us in here, and nobody's about to, because every man of us comes and goes a different way and knows a hundred more. You got to get to know this country like the inside of your front teeth."

"All right," Scott said.

Conlin laughed at his expression. "Don't get yourself so damn' disappointed, Scott. You're about to make the easiest money you'll ever make with us. You get a half share of everything we make, just for stayin' here. The other boys get one share each. I get two and a half. Your pay is free and clear. I got all the expenses. Understand?"

"Sounds fine to me."

"Long as you understand, there ain't nothin' to argue about, with me or anybody. You want to know anything, don't wonder and don't start rumors. Ask."

"All right," said Scott. He wet his lips. "Where you going today?"

Conlin laughed again. "He wants to know where we're goin', Henry."

From midair, apparently, came an amused grunt. Scott whirled and looked right, looked left, then looked up. Henry Little Hawk squatted on a rock ledge ten feet off the ground, toasting his sharp nose and his sharper shinbones in the morning sun. "God!" said Scott. "I never saw him up there."

"I told you before. Henry goes everywhere, nobody ever sees him."

Scott looked again at the little breed, who was slowly coming to life, crabbing sidewise down the bluff. Had he heard Loretta speak to him? And if so—what? Was this her hard luck, or Scott's, or Conlin's? Or maybe it didn't matter. Henry Little Hawk wouldn't be around at two this afternoon anyway.

Scott wrenched his mind away from these thoughts and said, "So where you say you're going?"

Again that amused syllable from Henry Little Hawk. Conlin said, "Tell you what, you ask Big Ike." He turned away and went back to the saddle shed. Scott watched him rope another horse and then went slowly back to the hidden bunkhouse. Al Coe was sitting at a deal table with the guts of one of his pearl-handled .45s spread out on a clean white cloth. For all his fancy-work, this man knew his weapons and treated them right. "Big Ike around?"

"Down to the corral," said Coe.

"I was just there."

Coe shrugged.

"Going to use those today," said Scott about the guns. It was the kind of statement that is a question.

Coe shrugged again and went on working.

Scott said suddenly, "Do I bother you?"

Coe seemed not to hear at all; and then Scott noticed his bands had stopped moving. He sat like that for a long moment, then slowly turned a pair of frozen eyes to take in the newcomer, from his hat to his hands, his holster, the plain strong boot on a bench, the knee on which Scott's crossed forearms rested. In a long, easy half whisper Al Coe said "No-o-o . . ." Scott might have said it the same way if someone had asked him if he was afraid of mice.

Scott smiled and said, "Too bad." He straightened up and went out, not hurrying. He knew that something had started that would have to be finished, and he regretted it; there were plenty of other things to worry him. Being liked or disliked by a jaybird like Al Coe didn't matter; just why, though, might matter very much. One possible reason might matter so much that Arch Scott would wind up dead.

Outside he watched a squaw, a misplaced Pueblo, laboring up the hill toward him from the ramshackle cookhouse, carrying two buckets of what had to be hot breakfast. From the direction of the corral he saw Big Ike swinging along the hillside. Scott let the squaw go on inside and stood where he was, though his stomach wanted to follow her; he was hungry and those buckets smelled good. "Mornin'," he said to the big man when he came up.

Big Ike nodded. Scott said, "Was down to the corral a while back, talked to Conlin."

"Talked to Conlin, did you?"

"Said you were ridin' out today."

"Said that, did he?"

"Asked him where to, he said you'd tell me."

"No, he didn't," said Big Ike. He would have gone on inside, but Scott caught his elbow. Big Ike stopped, freed his arm, and slowly wiped it with his other hand, as if Scott had left mud on it.

Scott said, "You don't want to tell me, Ike, say so."

Big Ike looked surprised. "Hell," he said placatingly, "don't go jumping salty. I wasn't there, but I bet a empty ca'tridge to a dollar that Conlin didn't say no such a thing." As Scott's eyes narrowed he delivered up a surprising, jovial grin and held up both his hands. "Tell you why. Ain't none of us knows where we're goin' till we git there. Conlin he always works like that."

"So why the hell didn't he say so?"

"You know as much about that as I do. He had a reason—he figures everything. Maybe he just wanted you to remember this special."

"The son!" said Scott, rueful and admiring.

"Yeah, he got his ways o' doin' things," chuckled Big Ike. "Now, what was it he reely said?"

"You're right," said Scott. "All he said was, if I want to know where you're ridin' today, ask Big Ike. He didn't say you'd tell me."

"He didn't even say I knew. Come on in and eat. You get a little tetchy when you're hungry, I can see that."

They went in to the buckwheat cakes and muscular black coffee the squaw had laid out. Al Coe had nothing to say to him.

Everybody but Arch Scott rode out at about nine o'clock. They rode east, but in these hills that could mean anything. Scott wished he knew where they were going.

At noon he was picking his way up a creek, crossing and recrossing and letting one of Conlin's surefooted mountain ponies find the route. The Green Spring, he had been told, was the source of this particular stream. He had been told this by the Pueblo, who answered his question in Spanish. He had pretended not to understand her; he didn't want anyone to add his knowledge of Spanish to Al Coe's guess—if it was a guess—about Taos. So she had answered in English and he was now on his way. To what he didn't know, but he had shaved first.

He had to leave the creek at an alder thicket and cut out to open ground. He was well up into the hills now, and could see the rolling country for miles. Ahead of him, a steep slope was capped by a rocky cliff, mostly sheer, in some places overhanging. "That spring better be under the cliff," he muttered. "Sure won't get over it without wings."

He moved back to the stream when he could, and found it boiling along, large as ever. Well, maybe it ran along the base of the cliff . . .

But it didn't. He swore helplessly when he saw how it gushed right out of the rock face and came brawling down the broken slope, with no sign of a spring at all, let alone a green one.

Who was playing games? Loretta? The squaw?

Jokers like to watch their victims. He looked around carefully, angrily. As far as the eye could determine, he had this cliff and this creek to himself, and the whole world to boot.

He looked again at the cliff. Forty, fifty, some places sixty feet. Sharp, almost solid rock, with a few scrubs of jack pine clinging to cracks here and there, a spruce and hemlock at the foot. Up at the top, like as not, it would be flat earth soft as delta country—a giant terrace up to the mountain beyond.

Suddenly he saw an answer—the only possible way that the squaw could be right and Loretta not playing games. Not practical jokes, anyway.

He cast up and back along the face of the cliff until he located a possible break near the top—a long brown scar of spilled earth and the clinging evergreen thick around it. He rode to the foot of it, found shade for the pony, and started to climb a spruce which grew hard by the sheer wall. Near the treetop was a tangle of limbs, part from his tree, part from growth on the cliff. He thrashed his way across and began to crawl upward.

In twenty minutes he was winded and furious. He had been a fly, a mountain goat, a leapfrog, an inchworm. His fingernails were broken and there was dirt in his mouth and grit under his right eyelid. But the last fifteen feet or so were suddenly easy, with a dry wash he had not been able to see before, angling gently up to the right, and he got up it on his hands and knees, and at last reached level ground.

He didn't attempt to get to his feet at first, but stayed there on all fours with his head hanging, blowing like a foundered horse. When at last he raised his head, there was the spring, waiting for him.

It was not, strictly speaking, a spring. Here, too, water appeared out of a hillside. It ran only a hundred feet or so, then widened into a pool overhung by trees and thick bushes. The banks were shadowed and mossy, yet only a few feet away one could stand in the sun and look out over seventy miles of country. Uphill from the pool, the slope became steeper and ended in another, much more formidable cliff. The stream evidently was underground most of the way, and came stitching out just here, to make the pool and disappear again through some fissure in its bottom.

Scott pushed his way through the underbrush to the edge of the water and stood a while, thinking nothing in the world but that this was a mighty nice place to be. Then he scanned the banks and the whole terrace and hillside with a mountain man's instinctive caution; and, seeing nobody, he took off his sweaty shirt and undershirt and doused them in the spring. He spread them on a flat rock to dry in the sun, then washed his head and neck and drank a little. Then he lay down in the mossy shade with his back against a boulder where he could see the whole pool with one flick of the eyes, and settled himself to wait.

He was, he realized with pleasure, early; by the sun, it couldn't be much past one o'clock. From the back pocket of his Levi's he extracted a small leather-bound book, and began to read.

"I never read a book in my life."

For the second time that day a disembodied voice spoke to him. Along with the flash of astonishment, and just as strong, was a surge of irritation. He bounced up and crouched, his eyes everywhere. That all they do between jobs, he thought angrily, make a monkey out of a man?

Then he saw her, and the anger faded, leaving only amazement. She stood in the split trunk of an Engelmann's spruce, her hatless head like a bright flower in the thick growth of mountain laurel which concealed the cleft. He crossed his big arms on his bare chest and said with an odd diffidence, "Beg pardon, ma'am; can't say I saw you there. Let me get my shirt."

She waded through the laurel and stepped out on the bank. "I've seen the like before," she said. "Don't put it on while it's wet. What were you readin'?"

"Cooper."

"What's a cooper?"

"It's a book called *Last of the Mohicans* by a man named Cooper."

"I never read a book in my life," she said again. She looked at the volume where it lay by the boulder, at Scott, at the book again. She seemed to be having a great deal of trouble getting used to the idea of a man reading a book. "What do you read books for?"

Now he laughed, and she flared up at him, "You laughing at me?"

"Lord, no, ma'am. It's just that nobody ever asked me that before." He looked at the still water for a moment, thinking. "Tell you what, suppose you had a friend, he knew a whole lot more than you do. He could tell you things about what people are like all over the world, the way they live, everything. And what folks were like a hundred years ago or even a thousand. He could tell you things that make your hair curl, lose you sleep, or things that make you laugh." He looked up at her swiftly, and away. "Or cry."

He kicked a pebble into the water and watched the sunlight break and break, and heal. "More than that. Suppose you had a friend there waiting for you anytime you wanted him, anyplace. He'd give you all he's got or any part of it, whenever you wanted it. And even more, you could shut him up if you didn't feel like listening. Or if he said something you like, you could get him to say it over a hundred times, and he'd never mind."

He pointed at the book. "And all that you can put in your pocket." Suddenly he faced her. "Talk a heap, don't I?"

"Yes," she said. But there was no objection in the word.

They stood by the water, their eyes trapped. Scott, then Loretta, tugged at the bond and for a moment couldn't break it. They were laughing embarrassedly, and laughing at their own laughter.

She sat down, and he went down beside her, close, but not too close. "How many books've you read?" she asked.

"Lord, I don't know."

"I'd know."

This time he did laugh at her. She looked up into his face without anger. They fell silent again, until he said, "Ma'am . . ."

"Don't call me that. Loretta's my name."

"Yes'm—Loretta. Thanks. Was going to say, I have two-three more books in my bunkroll, you like to read them." He waited a long time for her answer, but there was none. "What's the matter?"

"I guess," she said with difficulty, "I better not borrow a book."

He drew breath to ask her why not, but the strain in her voice warned him away. Something here . . . Conlin didn't like books, or didn't like her borrowing from the bunch . . . or maybe something which didn't concern Conlin at all. He could wait. It would come in time, if it was important. "Any time you change your mind," he said pleasantly.

She moved impatiently. "Don't you wonder why I asked you to come up here?"

He shook his head.

A series of expressions chased themselves across her smooth face—puzzlement, anger, amusement. "I don't know whether to get mad at you for that," she said.

"You shouldn't."

"All right, why did I tell you to meet me?"

"You wanted somebody to talk to," he said immediately.

She made an odd sound, a short, surprised "Hm!" from her nostrils. Reluctantly her eyes met his. "What do you mean?"

"What I said. Someone to talk to," he said carefully. "All the time the same faces saying the same things—Conlin talking business, Al Coe bragging, and in between times," he added shrewdly, "trying on fancy clothes that nobody ever sees you in. Day after day ... and you just naturally got to talk to someone."

"You see a lot!" she blurted, in a voice that should have been banter but came out real.

"I say something wrong?"

She thought about it, honestly searching. Then, "No. You have a way of ... I don't know. I don't know how to say it, I'm just a ... what I mean, it's hard to have secrets from you."

Wisely he said nothing.

"I'll tell you why I wouldn't borrow a book," she blurted. "You see, I don't read so good. If I tried to read one of your books I wouldn't know what the words meant, and you'd think I was ignorant, and that's why." She leaped to her feet.

"Sure you're ignorant," he said, and smiled up at her, watching her face pale and her nostrils arch. "You know what? I'm ignorant too. I can't run a printing press or play the vi'lin or tan a leather hide. You know things I don't know, you've been places I never heard of. Everybody's ignorant, Loretta, one way or another. Should I hold it against you you never happened to read books?"

"I never heard a man talk like you do," she breathed. "I never."

He rose at last, and went and got the book. "Here."

She hesitated, then took it. He said, "About the words, I'll get you a dictionary any time Conlin works a town big enough to find one in. Meanwhile you can write 'em down, or mark them right in the book, and ask me. Eight times out of ten I won't know what they mean either, but that's all right; sooner or later the dictionary'll straighten us out."

He turned away from her; it was kindness not to look at her face just then. He went to the flat rock and shook out his shirt. It was light and warm from the sun, dry and clean. He put it on and went back to her. She stood where he had left her, holding the book against her belt-buckle with both hands. He said, "You didn't climb no cliff to get here."

"No, no, I didn't," she said absently. "Come on, I'll show you how to get back an easier way."

"I have a pony down ..."

"Come on."

They walked southward along the ledge, away from the shadowed pool and across a baking hell of broken rock. The terraced ground narrowed and tilted downward as they rounded the face of the mountain. Just before it turned into a rough trail there was an overhang, and in the shade the roan was tethered.

Loretta swung up on it before Scott could put out a hand to help her, and they continued down the trail. He glanced up at her occasionally; she rode in silence, evidently wrestling with some internal problem. The precipice at their left, which was the one he had climbed, gradually became part of the sidehill, until at last it was fit for a two-legged animal to walk on. She reined in.

"You cut back here, angling down," she said. "You'll be under the bluff then. Just keep going till you get to your pony."

There seemed to be something else that needed saying, but neither could find words. He watched her until she vanished around the face of the mountain, then he watched where she had been. At length he sighed and turned back to find his pony and ride the creek-bed back to the hideout.

A hand on his shoulder, and up he came out of a shining dream of the New Mexican sun glaring off a page of Fenimore Cooper; but it wasn't print, it was a picture of a face with clear skin, hungry with puzzlement. But the thing was gone before he could grasp it. Then the hand touched him again. "Scott!"

He opened his eyes. Someone bent over him. "It's me, Conlin. Come on."

Scott slid into his pants and followed the smaller man through the firelit gloom of the bunkhouse and the falsebacked cabin. He wished he could see Conlin's face.

Conlin led the way to a spot on the trail a short way from the cabin.

"This'll do," he grunted. "Siddown."

They sat on a rock in the shadows. Scott heard the faint scrape of Conlin's holster on the rock, and let himself yearn for his own Colt's.

"How'd you make out?" he asked.

Conlin ignored the question completely. "What did you do with yourself today?"

"Looked around."

"Where at?"

"Yonder."

"By yourself?"

"Mostly."

"All right," said Conlin, "I know you was with Loretta. I know why, too."

Scott remembered how quiet Conlin's voice was when something ugly was going on, like the time he'd walked into the poker game in the bunkhouse. He tried to remember if this quiet was different from Conlin's usual quiet, and he couldn't.

Conlin said, "It's all right. You passed."

"Passed?"

"Some men," said Conlin, "make it to the cliff and turn back. Some bull ahead the way you do and get to the spring. Some cast back and forth along the mountain until they find the easy way. Once one of 'em got lost doing that."

Scott listened, so utterly surprised that he ceased trying to make sense out of any of this.

"Those that get to the top are two kinds—the ones who make mistakes and the ones who don't. You didn't."

It seemed to be time for Scott to say something, so he asked, "You mean you set that up for me, all of it?"

"For you, for everybody. There's some hombres just got to make damn' fools of theirselves first chance they get, and the time to find it out is soon."

"Seems to me . . ." But Scott was learning fast. This was Conlin's method, Conlin's business.

"Spit it out, Scott."

"None of my business, Jim."

"That's all right."

"All right then. Ain't you taking a long chance with Miss Loretta?"

Conlin laughed that quiet chuckle of his. "Not a partickle. First place, ninety-nine out of a hundred wouldn't chance tangling with me on the very first day here. Second place, Loretta can take care of herself. If she can't do it with the back of her hand, she'll do it with the derringer she carries. Third place, if anybody should move too fast or too rough for her, there's Henry Little Hawk on the second bluff, up over the spring, with a long bar'led Winchester and the damnedest eye I seen yet. I seen Henry split a bullet on a knife blade and put out two candles."

Half consciously Scott stroked his breastbone, imagining it suddenly slammed out between his shoulder blades before he could so much as hear the shot. He said, "You figure everything. And I don't know as I like that much, Conlin. I got to tell you that."

"You don't have to like it," said Conlin. "You didn't have to come here and you don't have to stay." The Bookkeeper paused, then said, "Here."

A small heavy cloth bag fell into Scott's slack hand. "All gold, four hundred dollars. Your half share for today."

Scott squeezed the bag and tossed it in his hand. Their shares—his and Conlin's—should come to $2400. The other shares—five if the breed got as much as the rest—brought it to $6400. He whistled.

"Sure you'll stay," said Conlin.

"Why not?"

Conlin chuckled. "Now, Scott, somethin' else. You might as well know right from the start that Loretta don't cotton to you much. You got too much book-learnin' and it scares her. But at the same time them books can be a godsend. She got a lot of time on her hands— I can't be keepin' her happy every single minute—and if you can get her to readin' books you'll be doin' her a favor and me too. Reckon you might loan her some book, somethin' easy to start on?"

I already did! thought Scott, with a vague start of excitement; this was coming through to him like a message from Loretta herself. He said, "If she'll take it."

"She won't at first," Conlin said positively, "but you just nip her along like a cow-dog till she's headed right."

"Can't promise," drawled Scott, "but I'll try."

There was a bang from the cabin—someone kicking open the false wall. "Right on schedule," said Conlin. "We all come back different ways, you know. They'll be driftin' in for the next hour. You go on back to your bunk. Next gold you get, you'll work for."

They got to their feet. "Come on, Henry," said Conlin. And as Scott's heart leaped into his throat, what looked like a rock shadow detached itself from the hillside and said, "Yup," and became Henry Little Hawk.

It was all Scott could do to start for the bunkhouse with an appearance of casualness. If Henry had been on that high bluff, he must have seen Scott give a book to the girl. Now Loretta was telling Conlin how reluctant she was. Was Conlin interested in exactly what lies were being told? Or would the fact of a lie be enough for a bullet out of the dark?

It wasn't until he was back in his bunk that he recaptured the picture of Loretta after he had handed her the book—Loretta pressing it close to her body.

That, he thought as he fell asleep again, is quite one hell of a woman.

The days sped by, easy to lose count of. Some of it was hard to take. On a ranch there's never enough time for all the work. At the hideout there was never enough work. The broken-down buildings, weathered almost to invisibility, had to stay the way they were. The horses could be cared for, shod, watered, fed, and exercised just so much. Conlin permitted a weird kind of poker, which started and finished with chips returned to their box and all tallies canceled out; it was about as satisfying as blowing the head off a glass of branch water. Target shooting and more than a very little game hunting were out; on a still day the shots would be heard for miles. Twice Conlin let men fight; they did it out in the open, starting when Conlin said they could and knocking off when he felt they'd popped off enough steam. It was all worth it, but it wasn't easy.

Most afternoons Scott would amble up to the house and he and Loretta would sit out on the front porch and bone over their books. They stayed in plain sight, without ever discussing the matter first. Sometimes they would sit silently for hours, saying nothing, until a character in Loretta's book "essayed" something or said something "uxorious," at which time she would yell for help.

Scott missed a dictionary; he was a reader, not a scholar, and many a turn of phrase that made sense to him in context were beyond explanation when he tried it word for word. But as the days went by, Loretta learned to hurdle the unfamiliar instead of running into it head on, and increasingly the books began to talk to her instead of fighting back.

Yet sometimes after a long silent period Scott would find himself looking into her eyes. This always made them laugh, and they learned to do it inwardly, without a sound and with barely a change of expression. And sometimes they would look out across the valley and see figures moving; if the figures happened to be Conlin and Henry Little Hawk, things seemed to get said that could come out at no other time; but if the bookkeeper and his little shadow were out of sight, it was sensible to assume that one or the other was within hearing.

It was at one of these times, while Scott was peering down the valley to be sure the group of men he saw breaking a horse included Conlin and the breed, that he heard a slight and disturbing sound and turned quickly to see Loretta crying. He leaned forward and took her hand. "What's the matter?"

She took a long time to find the words, and they came out as if they were hard for her to use. "You," she said. "The way you treat me. You get up when I come in, you tip your hat. If I got something to say, you wait, just like you wait to let me through a door first. All that. It means . . ."

She had to tremble for a while, and then stop trembling. "Arch, don't you know where I come from, where Conlin found me, what I was doing, what I am? Sometimes I think you . . . don't know, and then I feel ashamed, the way you . . . And sometimes I think you do know, and all those things you do, they're making fun of me."

He kept his eye on the horses and let her have it out with herself. When she was quiet, he said, "Loretta, time was when I wasn't more housebroke than a four-week mongrel dog. I used to let my dinner run off my chin and I hadn't the wit to say whoa. Now am I the same Arch Scott? Sure I am. I grew up, that's all, and I don't do those things any more and never will again. Are you going to slap my hand today because I stuck it in a butter churn thirty years ago? Folks are what they are, not what they were."

"Arch," was all she said; but you couldn't write or say how it sounded; you couldn't paint a picture of how it looked.

There were other things said during these brief intervals of open speech between them. Things about past jobs Conlin had pulled, about the way he got his information. About the way he thought. And a good deal about his men. His complete, yet scornful reliance on Henry Little Hawk; how he trusted Big Ike Friend, and his thorough understanding of the Waley brothers, Moko and Gus, whom he had bought and who would sell out at any better offer. And of course, Al Coe.

Al Coe, the big, glittering, braided, pearl-inlaid two-gun-toter, was the only man there who had "failed" the Green Spring test. Conlin had known he would, and he himself had handled the Winchester. His single shot had clipped a boulder right by Coe's head, just the way a Kaintuck rifleman barks a squirrel. He did it, he told Loretta, because he needed the man. He needed his noise and his color and the bragging, wheeling, roaring false front of him when they took a

bank or robbed train passengers. The sight of him would strike terror into many a man who might take an even chance against anyone
as small and ordinary-looking as Conlin, or such saddle tramps as
the Waley brothers. And as Al Coe was only a kind of front, for scaring people who were afraid of rattlesnakes, Big Ike Friend was another
kind, for scaring people who are afraid of grizzly bears.

All this information came out in patches and drabs and small
spurts of reminiscence. Scott never went after it openly, but he never
forgot a word of it.

"Arch," Loretta murmured one afternoon as they leaned together
over a book freckled with her pencil marks, "you got to watch out.
Al Coe's been to Jim about you."

"About you and me?"

"Yes, that's really why, but he wouldn't dare say so—Jim would
kill him. Instead he's trying to make Jim suspicious of you. He says
you're a railroad detective. He says he saw you seven years ago in
New Mexico."

"Yellow," said Scott. "He ever make a play for you?"

"I told you. Only that once, at the spring."

"And he got his ears pinned back. That's what I mean, I tangled
with him the day after I got here, and called him. Only that once.
He's had nothing to say to me ever since. What'd Conlin say when
Al told him that about New Mexico?"

"Told him to go dip his head in the trough. But—you never know
what Jim is thinking."

"What do you think?"

She stepped back from the table and looked at him. "A man is
what he is, not what he was," she said.

He grinned, his mouth dry.

Then one day Arch Scott went to town.

He went, of course, with Conlin's permission and blessing. Conlin was suspicious of men who didn't want an occasional ride to
town; they built up pressures which were unpredictable if they should
explode at the hideout, and Conlin liked to predict. Scott went by
himself, after accepting Conlin's suggestion of company—Big Ike
Friend; Conlin did not want Big Ike to go, but he did want to see

how Scott would take the suggestion, and he was satisfied.

Afterward, Conlin got a full report on what Scott had done at Elwood—from Henry Little Hawk, of course. No, Scott had not seen Henry. The little man had squatted under a blanket outside the rear door of the saloon while Scott drank; he had been in a tree outside Flo Connery's heavily curtained window during Scott's stop at Miz Flagler's honkytonk. He had been sitting in the shadow of a packing case across the street when Scott went into the general store and when Scott came out with the schoolmaster; he had come up the alley by the school just in time to see Scott accept a book from the schoolmaster and leave with it.

Scott had cooked and camped once on the way to Elwood, once on the way back. He had seen and spoken with nobody, either time. Yes, Henry had had a word with Flo Connery and with the bartender at the Last Chance Saloon. Scott had been most discreet and had given no information.

Conlin received all this with satisfaction; he picked his men the way he picked his jobs, with care and forethought. He overlooked only one thing, and that simply because not even Henry Little Hawk could be everywhere. He had no inkling that two hours after Scott's departure the schoolmaster went to the sheriff's office with Scott's carefully drafted map of Casson's Quarry, a neighboring mine and cattle town, complete with the date and time and method of Conlin's next raid.

Before sundown a deputy was on the stage road to Casson's Quarry, where, after some quiet discussion, a welcome was secretly and efficiently prepared. They had more than a week to sew up the details, there at Casson's Quarry, and by the appointed day there were deputies and three sheriffs and railroad men and bank men and even a United States Marshal. Conlin was, indeed, in for a surprise, to discover that a small army knew details possessed, he thought, only by himself and the silent Henry Little Hawk.

And so, for a week after his return, life at the hideout proceeded in its quiet and uneventful way. Scott continued with his bookish visits to Loretta, who was pathetically grateful for the dictionary he brought back with him, and increasingly taken with the worlds she read about—worlds of fashion, adventure, romance, scandal in high places.

She didn't have a chance to say goodbye to Scott. Without advance warning the whole gang, except for Henry Little Hawk who had gone on ahead, assembled two hours before sundown, saddled up, and rode. By the time they camped, most of them had a pretty shrewd idea as to where they were going; but nobody said anything about it until sunup, when they squatted around the fire with their black coffee and fatback and listened to Conlin.

"This here Casson's Quarry," Conlin said, squatting in front of a clean-swept place in the dust, "is hung on the side of a hill. Most of you been there so you know what it's like.

"I want you two who ain't seen it yet to listen even harder; there ain't nothin' clumsier than a man who thinks he knows everything."

He began to draw in the dust.

"This here's the main drag, they call the Stage Road. The town mostly tapers off gradual to the north and west, but here on the east there's a hogback that cuts it off real sharp. The Stage Road runs right down to that hogback, and the bank's spang on the last corner."

"Now, time was when the stage had to turn north a mile, on a road that angled up the hogback, and then switch back south to get down the other side, windin' up not forty yards away from the butt end of the main drag. Somebody got the idea of cuttin' through the hogback so the stage could drive straight through, so they done that, and it's their pride and joy; they opened it with speeches and all that, and everybody in town was drunk for two days.

"But if you go in town that way—and we do—you get through that cut and practic'ly fall into the bank. We don't scatter and we don't filter in, not this time; we go in together, fast and bunched up, and no yippin' an' ki-yi-in', either, hear me, Al? We take the bank and bounce back out again before anyone can so much as start for the sheriff's office—it's way the hell up the other end of the street.

"Coe, Ike, Scott—you three go in with me. Moko, you and your brother ride right past the front and down the alley at the other side and flush out anybody you see there. Go right around the back and around the bank to the front again and cover us—we ought to be out by then.

"Then we bunch up again and out we go through the cut. You all got it straight in your minds how to get back? Six of us—we go back six different ways. Just one thing—if you see Henry Little Hawk settin' on the hitchin' rail at the bank, go on by and don't even look at the place. We'll all go to the Piebald Bar and have a drink and go on home. Is there any questions?"

There were no questions. Conlin stood up and shuffled out the sketch he had made in the dust, and they mounted. They rode west for two miles and then left the trail and entered the woods. It was scramble and duck for a while, and once they had to lead their horses; but at last they emerged on the Stage Road, not a quarter of a mile from the cut.

From the middle of the road they could look through the hogback that barred the way like a high earthen wall, and straight up the main street of Casson's Quarry. It was all but deserted.

"Hey, Jim—bank open now, you reckon?"

"Sure, Ike. Cattle auction today, and payday at the mines."

"Don't see many people around."

"Let me do the worrying," said the Badlands Bookkeeper. "Let's get it done, boys."

They cantered down the road. They had it all to themselves.

Al Coe moved up beside Scott. "All the same to you, perfessor," he growled, "I'll stick by you."

Scott flicked a glance at him. It was the first time since that talk in the bunkhouse that Coe had said more to him than "Pass the salt."

"Help yourself, Coe," drawled Scott, "I ain't afraid to ride next to a target like that pretty hat."

"I don't figure they'll shoot no New Mexico lawman," said Coe.

"You and me," said Scott steadily, "we're going to settle this thing out, right quick."

"That's what I figure," said Coe, and he rode close.

"God," said one of the Waley brothers as they approached the cut, "a ghost town."

"Just early, that's all," said Ike.

"Let's go," said Conlin, and flicked his mount into a lope. They bunched, Al Coe shouldering Scott annoyingly. Scott glared at him, but then they were into the cut and too busy keeping out from under each other to argue.

And suddenly their way was blocked.

A small, tattered figure on a moldy gray mare suddenly appeared at the town end of the cut and ambled toward them. The little brown man seemed to be asleep on his mount.

"Chop 'im down," barked Big Ike to Conlin, who was in the lead.

"Chop hell, that's Henry!" Conlin tried to rein in, but for three, four seconds the idea didn't penetrate to the others and they crowded him at a dead run. "Whoa, dammit!" roared Conlin in the loudest voice Scott had ever heard from him.

They bumped and milled and cussed, and then all hell broke loose.

From the town end of the cut a dozen men appeared. From above, on each side, guns like thunder and lead like hail roared down. There must have been fifty men up there on the ridge, flat on their bellies, watching them come, and now half of them were pouring lead down into the ambush and half were diving and frog-hopping down the eastern slope, to close the trap at the other end.

"Back, get back!" shouted Conlin; but the last word was not a shout. It was an agonized grunt as a .44 slug tore through his thigh and into the side of his horse's neck. The horse screamed and reared, and Conlin fought back, twisting the animal around by brute strength, so that it was headed back through the cut as its forefeet touched tire road.

Moko Waley and his mount were down, kicking and spitting their lives out; Conlin jumped them. His horse screamed again as he lunged forward.

There was a confused motion in front of him—Big Ike leading him pace for pace for an interminable moment; Big Ike, the only one of his crew who'd stick by him, stick for sure, no matter what—then Big Ike throwing his guns up in the air, riding with his hands up and empty, and terror on his face as he swung his head from side to side, hoping someone in the posse would see him surrendering.

To one side was Gus Waley, afoot, hands up too. On the other side was Al Coe, maybe in a panic, crowding Arch Scott to a stand-still against the rock wall.

Then there was nothing ahead of Conlin but a line of men across the road, between him and the badlands, and suddenly he was afloat in the air, his horse gone out from under; and then a jarring, red-hazed impact as he fell, and the wound in his thigh scalding with road grit. He got one foot up, the other knee under him, and wavered there; then there was a thunder of hoofs behind him and Henry Little Hawk landed lightly in the dust. The little breed caught Conlin under the armpits and heaved. It was a desperate, impossible effort; Conlin threw out an arm for balance and felt his hand on a saddle horn.

Then somehow he was lying face down on the back of the breed's gray mare, rushing the line of deputies, riding two of them down.

When Conlin glanced back, he saw Henry Little Hawk lying in the road, one leg twisted crazily. He was propped up on his elbow, waving goodbye like an old woman watching a train pull out of a depot.

There were horsemen at the town end of the cut, but none here; and the cut was full of crazy horses, dead horses, dead and crazy men; so Conlin got clean away on the breed's horse.

Back in the cut Arch Scott was crowded to the wall by Coe and his big black stallion. A man afoot, with a big shiny star pinned to his vest, shouted, "This way, Mr. Scott, this way, I'll cover you."

A hurt-animal sound woke her, and she lay dazedly for a moment, thinking it was part of some unhappy dream. But then she heard it again and flew out of bed and down the narrow stairs.

Out front, on the grass near the door, Jim Conlin lay face down making the noise. A few feet away stood Henry's gray mare, blown and foundered, the reins over her head and a rope of spittle carrying clear from her bloody mouth to the ground.

Loretta got the Bookkeeper inside somehow, and somehow got his clothes off and washed away that special mud made of dust, blood, and sweat, until she could find out where he was hurt. Actually it wasn't much of a wound, as such things go—a little hole here and a large one nearby where the slug had gone through. It had missed the thighbone and had almost stopped bleeding. But it hurt, and maybe it wouldn't heal. She did what she could. She did pretty well.

He didn't talk for a long time. When he did, he said, "All gone. All, all gone. He saved me, Loretta, and he died."

"Big Ike?"

"Big Ike!" he snorted. "Tucked his tail down and threw away his guns."

"Al Coe?"

"Dead. They shot him dead, then they shot him some more.

She had to know, but ... don't ask, don't ask; maybe—"The Waleys?"

"Moko dead. Gus, he and Big Ike quit." Conlin half rose, screwing up his face. "Big Ike surrendered, you know that"" he shouted.

"Shh. Shh. Did ... was it Arch Scott who saved you?" "Damn it, I told you." He sank back. "I always said 'the breed.' Never slept in the bunkhouse with the others. He never asked to, but I tell you, I'd have laughed if he ever did, kicked his butt, the breed. Never ate with us white men, except campin'. He was the one, the only damn one—he saved me, and he died."

"Henry," she identified finally.

"All eyes, all brains. Tried to warn us, then he saved me, then he died."

She hit herself softly on the temples. "Jimmy, for the love of God—"

"All gone. That Coe, crazy as hell. Never tried to fight, never tried to run. Hung on to Scott, watching him every second, then shot him in the head. Then they cut Coe to pieces—crazy ..."

"Scott—dead?"

"All gone," said the Bookkeeper. "All gone."

After a time he said, "Loretta?"

"Get some sleep," she said hoarsely. "You got to get some sleep."

He nodded weakly. "Yuh. Some ... Loretta, they'll be comin'. Big Ike, if he'd quit, he'd bring 'em. And Gus Waley. Always said he'd sell me out for a good enough price. They got the price now—his dirty neck for mine." He breathed painfully for a while. "We'll take all the gold we carry, Loretta. You pack anything you want, and we'll start again some place." He caught up with his breathing again, then opened his eyes and looked around the lamplit room. "Loretta?"

But she was not there.

In the morning Jim Conlin woke up. He had a fever. There was a bottle of water nearby and he drank it all.

There was also a note:

i didn't take nothing but my dictionary i'm going in the morning if you can understand that then i'm going back to work don't try and find me not ever.
L.

"All, all gone," Conlin muttered. He dragged himself upstairs and got fresh clothes. He wondered what had happened. Al Coe had said Scott was a railroad man, but Al was always a trouble-maker. Henry, he'd know what happened.

He found Henry's long Winchester. It made a pretty good crutch. He got to his cache and took as much gold as he could drag. It wasn't much. He inched it down to the corral and caught a gelding and got the gold on. He roped a black, an old one, but the only one that would hold still for the kind of roping he was doing now. He got a saddle on it, led it to the bars, and climbed up on them and fell into the saddle. He rode off, leading the gelding.

They found the gelding, dead, in a ravine a month later. They got that gold and all that was in the cache too. Jim Conlin, the Badlands Bookkeeper, was never caught. Maybe the Mexicans got him, maybe fever. Maybe he's still alive.

Like Young

Here in the moonlit I sit, assigned to write an ode. I won't write an
ode. I'll write ... I'll write what happened instead. I'll never write
another ode. I'm a throwback. I'm a grinning savage, as of this day.
And they won't believe me, and they'll laugh—or they will believe
me, and then by the powers I think I'll laugh. I think I will. I think
I can.

Or cry. I think I can.

I know: I'll write it with all the background, just as if there was
somebody left on earth who hadn't lived with it up to this moment.
I just want to see if one narrative can contain all of an enormity like
this.

The Immune—that's what we're called. But that's a misnomer. We
got it, all of us. It's just that we didn't die of it. So, although Mankind
was dead, we weren't just yet.

Mankind was dead ... Humanity wasn't. I guess these things are
open to definition. There were, by the time we got them all together,
six hundred and four of us left of all the billions. We were all strong
and healthy, and most of us young. We could live, learn, love. We
could not propagate. So much for Mankind.

We were, all of us, devoted to a single idea, and that was that
Humanity should not perish. Humanity in the sense of aspiration,
generosity—if you like, nobility: that was what we were dedicated
to preserve. It was too late for us to use it. We'd only just realized
what it was, when the new encephalitis appeared. Perhaps we realized it *because* the encephalitis appeared. However we came by it,
we had it, and we had to pass it on, or it was all too ludicrous a
tragedy.

We decided to give it to the otters.

Like many another simple truth, the fact that the otters would be the next ones had been obvious and undisclosed. We were bemused by the fact that other animals—dogs, for example, and the higher apes, and (remember how exciting that was?) the contemplative porpoise—they all had intelligences like ours, in kind if not in quality. It was possible to think like a porpoise, or like a dog. It was a high conceit indeed to assume that the Next One would have an intelligence like ours. Once we were ready to discard that cocky notion, it became clear that the otter, a tool-using animal far earlier in its evolution than we had been, and possessed of a much more durable sense of humor, was logically our successor.

We despaired for ourselves; I want to make that quite clear. Our mourning was deep and bitter. But it must be made quite as clear that we passed through this mourning and emerged on the other side, as befit our maturity. We emerged late, and, for ourselves, uselessly; but emerge we did, mature we had become. You see what we were, for all our individual youth. We were the Elders of earth, and carried our insigne with a very real dignity. Too, we were each of us, all of us, wealthy and powerful beyond the wildest imaginings of anyone, ever—there were so few of us, so well trained, with such resources (and no need to save). Any of us could wave a hand and move a mountain. Yet the big thing—the real thing—was that sense of purpose and of dignity we had brought through the terror and the death; a greater purpose, and a dignity more real, than (but for a feeble flicker or two) mankind had ever known before. Proud we were, of course; but pride is a silly little word to use for such a thing. Humbly, we liked ourselves. And it was this above all we were dedicated to keeping alive. The otters would have civilization, with or without us, probably, but the achievement of this ultimate *dignity*— that was something we alone could teach them. Only a Man could reach that height. Death gave us this noble knowledge. Life—the New One's life—gave us this purpose. And now they would have it in their own lifetime.

And what a task it had been! For we were too advanced, and the otters far too primitive, for us to impress anything upon them while we shared the earth with them. We would be dust for many thousands of years before they began to communicate even with one another. We had no intention of speeding up their pre-history. Let them be what they were, strong, adaptable, ubiquitous. Let them content themselves with floating on their backs, holding shellfish on their chests, cracking them open with a stone, until the day came when of their own accord they found that was not enough. Let them kindle their own light.

But we were determined that once it was burning it should never flicker or dim. There would be no dark ages for the otters. We would reduce basic knowledge to its essence, put these in the most understandable form, and leave them like milestones (a statement and a promise, each) along the way.

For the milestones we chose the new alloy 2-chrome-vanadium-prime, which came to be called bicrovalloy. (Ah, what cities that might have built!) Properly fabricated, it could be formed into rods, bars, sheets; once irradiated, it would not, almost could not, change its form or state. This was no molecular lattice, nor even a net of atoms. It can best be described as a matrix of nuclei. Then thirty-foot sheets, supported only at the edges, could bear thousands of pounds at the center without bending more than a few thousandths. A hundred feet of quarter-inch rod, held horizontally by one end, showed no detectable sag. Drawn to a point, it would write on diamond as on wax; plates of it cooled to within a few thousandths of a degree of absolute zero and—or—raised to twenty million degrees, showed only a slight improvement of their finish. And what a finish! Silver-gilt, with a touch of peach ...

On plates of bicrovalloy, then, man's wisdom was scribed. The task was enormous, but it was the only task we had. We had first to amass the necessary knowledge, then to distill it (and distill it again, and again, and again), and finally to codify it in such a way that the new race, the parameters of whose intelligence we could know only vaguely, would when ready for it be able to take and use it. When they had mastered fire, they must have ceramics. When they began working metal, they must have alloying and heat treatment. At a certain point in this mastery, they must be given knowledge of the power of steam. And so on. But nothing, if possible, before they were ready.

Placement of bicrovalloy plates, bearing the pertinent simple illustrations, in pottery-clay pits was self-evident, concealing them in likely lodes of minable metals was not so easy, for they must be hidden far enough down to make sure that their discovery was no accident. We gave language, numbers. And the ultimate secrets—ethical, spiritual as well as technological—these must be triply concealed, so that they would come out as a series of revelations, each a discovery, each a hint of the next, with everything in our power done to ensure they get it neither too soon nor, through over-concealment, not at all.

And so it was that the four equations of Einstein's General Field Theory, together with Heisenberg's addenda, were placed in the most inaccessible vault of all—in the mantle of the earth itself, in the bottom of the great bore under two miles of ocean where, in the twentieth century, we had reached our peak as engineers, seekers after knowledge. I need not go into the details of this ultimate achievement. For all our dedication, our immense resources, and our newer techniques, it was far harder for us to reach the bore than it had been for our forefathers to dig it.

The concealment of this final bicrovalloy plate was (it seemed at the time) our climactic conquest. I look back on those days with affection and sadness. It was a time of contemplative pride. We kept busy, of course, but our work was done. We had, in a fashion, survived our own death. We existed in a timeless moment, neither afterlife nor immortality, after the end of one great flowering and before the beginning of another. Humankind, the very death of humankind—that was behind us. The otters had not even begun; this was eons before their birth as the Next Ones. So in this period we walked proudly, humbly conscious of our true usefulness and nobility. We had carried the torch.

And then—

Then De Wald produced the last equation.

De Wald had worked ceaselessly even before our project had begun, even before the first recorded case of the new encephalitis had claimed the first of its billion of victims. His material was the remarkable mathematical achievements of Heisenberg, and his goal a single expression which would not only encompass Einstein's four, but which would distill even Heisenberg's into something as clear as e=mc².

We had conferences and excited discussions, of course, but they were ritual (we had time for ritual then, and a great liking for it); everyone knew what was to be done. We had known because of the supreme *rightness* of such a discovery at such a time. Some talked about poetic justice and some about God; myself—I am not a scientist—I attributed it to Art. For our kind to end with a whimper, to be proven futile, or to have our work left in any way unfinished— this was Bad Art. De Wald's discovery, on the other hand, coming at just this time, was Art at its peak. One might almost say it justified everything, viewed objectively—even the tragic death of mankind. In a million years, through the eyes of another species, this would be the greatest story ever told ...

Joyfully we set about the sizable task of recovering the now out-dated set of bicrovalloy plates from the very flesh of the earth's body. And meanwhile the new plate was prepared—the old one could not be changed or added to, of course. Oh, it was good, good to be back at work again!

Then we were ready for the final placement. This of all times was the time to have a ceremony, and we planned a beautiful one. Grogerio himself would compose special music, and naturally no one but Fluger would design the dais on which the recovered plate and the ultimate one would lie side by side during the ceremony. And I was not in the least surprised when they came to me for an ode. Not in the least reluctant, either: for if created art comes from inspiration, surely there was enough and to spare in such an assignment.

I requested that I be left alone at the beautiful seaside spot on the night before the ceremony. I had already done a draft of the ode, but I knew what that vigil would do for the final version.

And indeed, the whole mood of the place and the time was perfect for such an effort. The last of the people left late in the afternoon, and I made myself comfortable in a spot where I could, at a glance, take in sea and sky, the silver beach and Fluger's beautiful dais, raised on two of his dizzying, gravity-defying arches. The *rightness* I mentioned earlier—this was a case in point. It has been said many times that neither a Fluger arch nor bicrovalloy could exist without the other.

And the sun went down in a blaze: how right! Even as we . . .

And in the east, a leaching of the firmament, and the loom of the moon . . . to be a new light on earth . . .

Then, wonder of wonders, there was a splash in the whispering surf and a small blackness oozing through the illumined dark. Oh, I thought, awe-struck: it can't be, but . . . yes; nothing could be more right . . . and then the moon struck upward with its metal edge, and cracked the cup of darkness, and I could see I was right in this rightness—it was a large male sea-otter snaking through the sand, working up toward the dais.

Exactly facing me, and not thirty yards way, he froze; had I not known where he was, I might have taken him for a hummock of sand or its deepening shadow. But I did know where he was, and in the growing light I could see the sensitive twitch of his comic mustache. I was not deceived as to the subject of his gaze, either, for I know his kind. An otter never looks directly at anything, any more than a bird does. One eye was regarding his beloved sea, and the other the dais. I, directly ahead of him, was unsuspected. And how perfect a picture this made, in all its symbolisms . . . how very right!

He turned in his quick lithe way and scuttled toward the dais, occasionally stopping in the otter's brief sudden pauses, as if one of his motivating wires were loose at the battery.

Silently, bemused and bemagicked, I followed. For in a moment like this, it must be so; it must be so: I alone—I, possibly the most perfectly qualified person on Earth and in all history to appreciate such a priceless picture, I would see this minion of the far-distant New Ones in the very shrine of all that was highest of Humanity.

And of course I was right—I was right—what could go wrong with such an enchantment? All the Powers of all the Souls of all Good Art would not permit anything, in such a moment, but what was right.

The otter, when at last I had crept round the dais and up behind the curtains and could see him, crouched motionless before and between the two bicrovalloy plates, the one just recovered, bearing

Einstein's and Heisenberg's revelations, and the other which had just been fabricated to replace it.

I thought (a very whisper of a thought, lest I think too loudly and ripple this tableau): Are you praying, little one?

The otter rose suddenly on his hind legs and put his forepaws on the reclaimed plate. He seemed, in his clumsy, fumbling little way, to be caressing its surface. And the strangest feeling came over me, of shame, of that special kind of guilt one feels on having committed a faux pas, a *gaffe,* an in-itself petty kind of social offense which nonetheless it is acutely painful to remember. I felt like an intruder, a spy of the most ignorant and clumsy sort. To spare myself any more to brood on in the future, I removed the one wrong thing in that symphony of rightness—myself. Noiselessly I sank down behind the curtain and slipped into the sand below, and I was congratulating myself on being perhaps alone among men to have such perfect sensibility.

Rather than disturb him at whatever accidental orisons he was performing up there above me, I sat quietly until at last I saw him scampering off toward the sea. He had snatched up some bit of trash or jetsam from somewhere, and I saw him digging at the water's edge with it. I could just make out the two plump clams he unearthed, and then he was gone into the surf. I rose to catch, perhaps just once more, a single last glimpse of this creature, fellow to my most magic moment, and (as was only right) I did. He was floating joyfully on his back in the moonlight, with a clam on his strong chest. He struck it deftly with his crude tool, gulped it from the shattered shell, threw his unwanted trash upward into the moonlight, and was gone beneath the waves.

I gazed after the graceful clever little rascal, loving him ... and turned toward my vigil-spot, all abrim with inspiration ... and had I gone there, I surely should have written one hell, one hell of a *helluva* ode ... but instead I strode back up on the dais, to relive that incredible moment.

In the brilliant moonlight I gazed down at the shrine of humanity, all its dignity and its worth, and at all the meanings of this mighty gesture of faith in the life that had been and the life that was to be,

when my eyes took in ... took in what, some unmeasured time later—
it might have been an hour—my mind was able to take in ...

... just to the right of Einstein's brief immortal perfect statement
of mass-energy conversion, the comment:

WELL, SOMETIMES

written on, *written into the bicrovalloy plate.*

And there were two corrections in the Heisenberg statement,
strikeouts and carelessly scribbled figures which seemed to have been
scribed deep in the impervious metal by a single small foreclaw ...

But it was what had been done to the new De Wald plate that
dealt me that blinding blow, from which I recovered (was it an hour
later?) so slowly. For under that climactic, breathtaking achievement
of intuitive mathematics, that most transcendental of all human statements, the De Wald Synthesis, the otter had scrawled:

NONSENSE!

I write no more odes. As for you who find this, and the plates
which are its proof, do as you will. Have a suicide wave if you like.
Or gather round in chittering groups and make wild surmise about
the true source of the encephalitis which destroyed us, and great agonized guesses as to whether the otter was truly not quite aware of
my presence and the significance of these plates and this whole occasion, and as to whether he and his kind are or are not impatient for
our little remnant, with all our powers and resources, to be broken
and maddened and die and go away. Or send your divers out if you
like, to salvage that which he used to crack a clam—it's out there,
not far—and prove to yourself that it is indeed the corner he broke
off the De Wald plate with his bare paws; pick it up and fit it back
again and pass it around and turn your silly laboratories loose on
it. Maybe some of you will finally begin to roar with laughter, sob
with merriment, as I have done to the point of exhaustion and help-
lessness, unable to get out of your minds the enormity of this one
ridiculous fact: How *childish* is his handwriting! ... so go, do any
of these things, or none of them, or something, out of the vast store
of your pride and knowledge, of your own devising.

But me, I'm a joyful throwback ... I'm one with my eager ances-
tors:—I'm going hunting.

Night Ride

Ninety-four miles an hour. In the back of the bus somebody was dead. In the front of the bus, a scared little guy with thick wrists was going to be dead.

Ninety-six miles an hour. He had a choice to make, he realized as he manhandled the twelve-ton monster through a rocky gap and down around a turn so sharp that loose material from the shoulder sprayed out into space. He had this choice (at a hundred and two miles per hour): He could die alone, blindfolded and strapped to a chair, while a prison chaplain made things easy as he could; or he could just forget to turn the wheel at the next curve, or the one after, and die that way.

Along with thirty-two other guys. Thirty-two innocent guys and a murderer. That, thought little Paul Cahill, half out of his seat to whip the wheel around, that might be worth the price. A good clean finish to the dirty story of Romeo.

The name really was Romeo ... Charley Romeo. Only nobody kidded Romeo about it. That could be because he was just under six five and stood about this wide. Or it could be because he was proud of it. He acted the part, Charley Romeo did, hollering *Watch Me, World* the whole time. He played basketball, and girls. When he made a pass, it stayed made. From any corner—anybody's corner—he sank his shots whenever he felt like it. And if he had to stand taller to do it he'd just as soon stand on somebody's face.

Even Paul Cahill would admit that Charley Romeo was a great basketball player. There was only one thing in all the world that meant more to Paul Cahill than basketball—especially Hill City basketball. He drove the bus at the little mountain school, but he never missed a home game either. The one thing in all his world was

Jenny Cahill, his brand new, late-model wife. Some model. They still make that kind, but not often. Jenny Cahill worked in the school office.

Ever since Charley Romeo came to Hill City, his idea of top comedy was to ride the little bus driver. But when Charley Romeo got a look at Jenny Cahill, and when his first easy hook-shot her way not only missed the hoop but the backboard as well, why, the wisecracks got a little rougher than funny. Romeo never let up on Paul Cahill, nor Jenny either.

Paul Cahill was a little guy; but he was a gutsy little guy, and he wouldn't have held still for much of this if it had not been for "Turk" McGurk, the coach; for the school; for basketball itself. Paul felt deep loyalties to all these, and there was no arguing the fact that in his big fast hands Charley Romeo held the Conference win and the Invitation—things that the little school wanted and needed, things that Paul Cahill wanted for the school almost as much as Coach McGurk. And as for Coach McGurk, if he ever felt anything or thought anything but basketball, he fought it down till it didn't show. That meant that if, to win, Charley Romeo had to pull the wings off flies, Coach McGurk would go catch flies for him.

All this had been going on for too long a time the afternoon the bus started out for Johnson Mesa and the most important game of the year. Win this one, and the Invitation would be a cinch.

Everyone felt good at first, excited and happy. The big new bus was full—all the second-string players were along to see what they could learn, and a couple of guys to report for the school paper, and that weird-o they called Big Dome Craig. (Wherever you found Charley Romeo, you also found Big Dome—nobody knew why. Except it was Romeo's idea. Maybe he thought some of Big Dome's brains would rub off on him.) And of course, Turk McGurk the coach. It was a fine day, and there was some grand country to climb. But really climb—the road wound up and up for eleven and a half miles to a mountain pass nearly seven thousand feet above sea level.

Paul Cahill kept the giant diesel humming along in third and fourth gears in the low range. At first even Paul felt good, in spite of the trouble he knew would come from the big center and his big mouth.

He knew it would come, because it always did on these long hauls. Charley Romeo could look at just so much scenery, and then he'd get bored, and that was when he'd stir up what he called a little fun.

And sure enough, when they were within four miles of the pass, Paul Cahill saw, in the big inside mirror, Romeo suddenly loom up out of his seat. He sat side-saddle on the arm of the seat, about halfway down the aisle, and all the faces from there on back swung toward him.

"Once upon a time—" he bellowed; and all the faces ahead of him swung around to look back.

"Siddown, Romeo," Paul called out peaceably. "You're blocking my view."

"Little man," said Romeo, "drive your bus. *I* am goin' to tell a story. A real old bed-time story."

From the corner of his eye Paul Cahill saw the coach, McGurk, sight down the aisle, look back up at the mirror, and then subside with that give-him-his-head expression. Romeo went on with his yarn, about how "this guy I know"—he meant himself—drew a bead on "a certain chick"—for a bad moment Paul thought he meant ... never mind: he wouldn't even think it ... anyway, the story went on and on. The usual proportion of boneheads who always seem ready to encourage a fool egged Romeo on.

Paul Cahill lost track of the story for a while; he had a job to do. The road was none too wide. Sometimes there were wide flat shoulders, then in a few yards they'd be in a cut with jagged rock walls just far enough apart for two squashed lanes of traffic; then again there would be that queasy feeling that if you hung your chin on the right front fender you could look a blue mile straight down.

But at last he reached that long straight slope that approaches the pass, and happened to glance in the mirror. Romeo was still at it, but what jolted Paul Cahill's attention was the face of young Curtis, white, strained, twisted up on itself with a mixture of held-in anger and disgust; he looked as if he might burst into tears, or throw up, or maybe both. Paul Cahill, driving intently, let himself listen again:

"... but I mean, she had a bedbug on her, but it was pink. Yeah, a pink bedbug, right here." Romeo demonstrated, and the boneheads roared. The reporter, Curtis, bent way down as if he had a shoe to fix or wanted to hide his face.

Suddenly Paul Cahill understood. He'd seen Romeo giving the quick casual rush to Curtis' girlfriend Beth, a squeak-sized upcountry kid who'd be no more able to handle the likes of Romeo than a rock slide. So she happened to have a pink mole some place. And now if Curtis made one move to shut him up, the whole bus would suddenly know just who Romeo was talking about; the whole school would know about her "pink bedbug," yes, and about her and Romeo to boot. Paul Cahill could see Charley Romeo's quick glances down at Curtis. The big fellow was enjoying himself.

Paul Cahill suddenly bellowed, "Now dammit, Romeo, I said get in your seat. I can't see out the back."

Romeo looked around him in stage amazement.

"Any of you fellers hear something?" he said. He made no move to get off his perch. He looked forward, into the big mirror, and that way right into Paul's face. "You mean to say you don't know what goes on behind your back, little man?"

Paul Cahill knotted his jaw and drove his bus. He flicked a glance off the road and saw Romeo's face happy, tense, the flick of his tongue as he wet his lips. He saw McGurk, the coach, looking troubled.

Romeo said, "Tell me something, Shorty, you haul the baseball teams too, don't you?"

Paul Cahill, seeing the coach's face, forcing himself to think of the big game, of the tricky road, did not answer.

"You know what I'm goin' to do," chuckled Romeo, "I'm goin' to stay off the ball team next term. Long as you don't know what goes on behind you, why, every time we have an 'away' game, I'll just stick right around home and—"

Tires crunched heavily, air shrilled as Paul Cahill tramped on the brake, pulled over to the side, set the emergency. All the passengers, but one, sat in surprised silence in the sudden hush: Coach McGurk, however, was on his feet, leaning close over Paul Cahill's shoulder— so close, the little driver could not rise.

McGurk said, pretending to point at the dashboard, "Getting hot?"

Paul Cahill nodded curtly. "A little."

"Listen, boy," said Coach McGurk. "We don't want that."

"Okay, okay," Paul Cahill muttered, and he really meant to stay in line; but then Romeo spoke up, just as Paul Cahill was about to start the bus again.

"Now don't that make y'all go pitty-pat!" Romeo drawled. "Just a mention of her, and he gets all warm."

Paul Cahill was out of his seat and down the aisle before the coach knew he was gone. He stalked up to Charley Romeo, sitting on the arm of his seat in the center of the bus, and looked him in the eye.

"Who's this 'her' you're talking about?" Paul Cahill demanded.

"Your wife I'm talking about. Jenny, I'm talking about. Why?"

Paul Cahill started his swing with the first spoken syllable of his wife's name. Romeo caught his wrist with one easy motion and pulled it past him, fast, snatching Cahill right off his feet. He fell heavily, face down in the aisle, and Romeo slid off the arm of the seat and sat down on him.

"I tell you what I'm goin' to do," Romeo said. "Tonight I'm gonna run up some points, and just so you'll enjoy your favorite game even more, for every one I sink I'm goin' to holler *Hey Jenny!* and since I plan to sink about thirty, that'll give you lots of chances to do something about it."

"Get off him," said Coach McGurk.

"Oh by all means," said Romeo, getting up, laughing. "Time to get up, little man. Get this show on the road."

Wheezing, white with fury, Paul Cahill managed to get back on his feet. Coach McGurk put a hand on his arm but he shook it off.

"Romeo," Paul Cahill said clearly, "I'm going to kill you."

It was a lousy couple of minutes, and even then, some of the boneheads managed to laugh. Paul Cahill, hurt, angry, and humiliated, let in his clutch, kicked off the emergency, and started uphill again. He drove with especial care all the rest of the way.

One of the first-string forwards gaped at the new sign as they rolled into the Mesa.

"*Science* building? What they done with the casaba pavilion?" he asked.

"There's enough hardwood left to choke a hoop," Coach McGurk told him. "Schools all over are making new science buildings out of gyms. Here, they turned the whole north wing over to the science department. But there's still a court."

"Education got a way of creeping up on you in this business," said Romeo. He liked it. He said it three more times.

Paul Cahill shouldered the big bus through the crowded parking lot, and pulled up by the side entrance. The boys bounded out, heading for the dressing rooms, or for the best seats. Paul Cahill stayed a while, gunned his motor once, watching his gauges. He let her idle, switched on the body lights, walked through the bus, sniffed for monoxide around the back, picked up some scraps of paper. In the luggage rack, here and there, were lunch boxes, coffee flasks. He knew them all, who they belonged to; he knew all these guys, what they wanted out of life. He stood a moment, confused by his vague rush of thoughts.

One of the lunches, battered, bright blue, with brass corners, caught his eye. He frowned, picked it up. It was Romeo's. He knew, just as everyone else knew, that the coffee in it was heavily laced with vodka, which doesn't smell on the breath. Coach McGurk alone didn't know it, probably because he didn't want to. Romeo trained carefully, but on the way back from one of those forty-pointers of his, he just had to celebrate.

Paul Cahill sighed, put the box back, and yanking the keys on the way, hopped out of the bus, closed and locked the doors. Somebody was waiting for him out there. Coach McGurk.

"Don't go in there, Paul."

"Don't what?"

Coach McGurk looked, sounded, very tired. "Stay out of the hall," he said wearily. "You know that damn fool Romeo will do what he said. Why get yourself all worked up?"

"Oh," said Paul Cahill, remembering. Romeo was going to yell

Hey Jenny! every time he hit the bucket. He said coldly, "And you wouldn't want me maybe to mess up your ball game."

"It isn't that, Paul—"

"It is that. And . . . for that I got to miss the best game of the year."

"You said it yourself. It's the best game of the year. It's important to all of us. Stay away from it, Paul."

Paul Cahill stood by the bus and watched the coach shamble inside. Then he opened up the bus, flipped up his seat, and fumbled through the tools. After a while he got out again and entered the building. Once inside, he remembered he had not locked up this time. He shrugged and sidled into the noisy gym. No matter what the coach said, this was a game he did not intend to miss.

At the tapoff, Romeo coiled down like a huge steel spring and then didn't jump. The opposing center, caught by surprise, barely tipped the ball. Romeo's long arms snapped up like the business end of a rat trap; he double-palmed the ball and snapped his wrists. The ball took off like a flying saucer, seemingly self-propelled, and flew by itself to the Johnson hoop, where it swished through without touching iron at all. First blood in the first second of play, and Romeo hadn't even moved his feet.

"*Hey Jenny!*" he roared. Blind rage came and went in Paul Cahill. The second time it happened he clenched his fists and turned to go. Then it happened a third time, the roar *Hey Jenny!* and this time Paul Cahill roared with it, a sound without words in it. He rushed forward, a ten-inch box wrench flailing the air. Then something like a railway mail-hook caught his left arm and spun him around, and the wrench disappeared out of his right hand, and he was being hustled in the opposite direction, Coach McGurk on one side of him, young Curtis on the other.

A door opened for them; Big Dome Craig opened it, from inside.

"Sorry, son, but you got to stay in there," said the coach, and they shoved him into a room and the door closed. Through the frosted glass, Paul Cahill could see one of them take up what looked like sentry duty. It had all happened so fast he had stopped thinking.

Hey Jenny! He heard Romeo clearly, and a huge noise from the crowd. He scurried all around the room. There was another door, locked. The windows were hinged vents, high up in a glass ceiling. It had once been part of the gym, he recalled. He saw—now that he looked—that it was a chem lab.

He stood by the glass door after that, listening to the biggest game of the year. *Hey, Jenny!* He thought he would go out of his head. Maybe he did, a little. He heard his wife's name again. He heard the crowd pick it up. He heard that almost thirty times. It was Charley Romeo's big night.

After some hours—months—of this, the door opened and Coach McGurk came in. He spent a moment looking carefully at Paul Cahill's face:

"We won it," he said at last.

Paul Cahill didn't say anything. After a long silence he moved his head tiredly and said, "Let's go."

On the way back, the team was boisterous. Well, they'd won it; that was what they'd come for. Everybody kept patting Romeo on the back. As soon as they were on the road and the lights out, Paul Cahill dimly saw, in his mirror, Romeo's long arm snake up and get his lunch box.

Paul Cahill settled down to his work, and let everything else trickle into a place inside him that had a one-way cork on it.

Therefore he heard the noise a little later than anyone else. It had to filter through to him—a steamboat-whistle kind of *Hoo! Hoo!*

Romeo, of course. Paul Cahill ground his teeth. Then the *Hoo Hoo!* noise turned into a gibbering burble, and a sort of scream so alarming that the boys began to make worried noises. Someone yelled for light and the coach went back. Immediately he called out:

"Stop when you can, Paul." Coach McGurk said it in such a strange tense tone that all Paul Cahill's anger evaporated.

Paul Cahill had to drive nearly half a mile before he could stop, for they were in the pass; still climbing, and they had to get through to the wider road on the other side. But at last he could pull over and stop. He turned on the inside dome lights, and saw his passengers pressing forward from behind, drawing back from around the long figure of Romeo, stretched out in the aisle.

Without the motor, the silence was like a crash.

Then Coach McGurk said, in a weary, puzzled voice:

"Romeo is dead."

"Dead?" they asked each other. "Dead," they kept answering; the word flicked and frothed over them like whitecaps; while they moved under it like waves, craning to look, pressing away.

Somebody said something about getting the police. The remark just lay there.

"Well, what happened to him?" Paul Cahill suddenly barked.

Coach McGurk extended something—a flask—toward him. Paul Cahill started to take it but the coach used it to push his hand away and put it up to his face instead.

Paul Cahill smelled it: sweet bitter coffee smell, and the odor of something else, like ... coffee cake? Sugar buns, the kind with ...

"Almonds," Paul Cahill said.

"Almonds hell, that's arsenic," Coach McGurk said positively.

Paul Cahill made as if to take the flask to sniff, unbelievingly again, but the coach moved it out of his reach, picked up the cover from Romeo's seat, and screwed it down tight. And all the while the Coach kept looking and looking at Paul Cahill out of his tired eyes.

Abruptly Paul Cahill realized what was going through Coach McGurk's mind. He looked at all the other faces and saw the same idea percolate through the crowd.

Who had threatened to kill Romeo?

Who had, with the box-wrench, actually tried?

Who had the best chance, alone in the bus, to put the fatal dose of poison into Romeo's flask?

Paul Cahill said "I—" and again; "I—" and then could only shake his head; and if there were any faces left in the crowd that the idea hadn't reached by then, they got it.

"We can't just sit here ... put Romeo on the long seat at the back," said Coach McGurk.

Nobody wanted to. Finally Paul Cahill and Coach McGurk had to do it. Romeo's eyes were open and he was kind of snarling, all his front teeth bared. No matter what, Paul Cahill was never going to forget that.

Paul Cahill went back to the driver's seat and switched out the domes. Everyone settled down. He started the motor and released the brake. The bus nosed downhill, began to roll immediately. In thirty seconds it was going fifty. In another ten, Coach McGurk sat bolt upright and shouted at him:

"Hey! Take it easy. *Hey!*"

Paul Cahill did not answer. He was too busy picking out the details of the curve ahead, and its one high wall of cliff. Coach McGurk got up and was thrown right down again as Cahill wheeled around the turn.

"Paul! Paul!" the coach shouted.

Hand over hand in the lurching bus, Coach McGurk got up behind Paul Cahill and clutched at his arm. Paul Cahill removed one hand to throw him off, and the back of the bus slewed and nipped the rock wall on the left. At the crash and tearing sound of aluminum skin, one of the boys screamed.

The speedometer needle hit ninety-four. One dead, more dead coming. He could be dead strapped in a chair, with a prison chaplain snaking it as easy as he could. Or he could be dead much quicker than that, just by not taking the next turn, or the one after.

Evidence or not, no matter what anyone had heard him say or seen him do, there was one thing Paul Cahill knew for sure:

He hadn't killed Charley Romeo.

Which meant that someone else had. Someone right here in this bus.

He bellowed, then, at the top of his voice:

"*Listen.* I don't touch the brake until I know who killed Romeo."

"You're crazy!" yelled the coach. "Stop this bus, Paul!"

Paul Cahill yelled back. "Look out!"

Twelve tons of bus entered a turn, sliding, sliding, crossing the pavement to the far side. At the last possible split second the wheels seemed to be taking hold, but there was nothing, nothing at all under the left front—just black dark and distant downward lights.

And as the bus plunged over the edge, the road shook itself and moved under the wheels again, and they went howling down the road again.

"One more like that and we've had it!" Paul Cahill bellowed. "Well?"

The speedometer needle lurched upward.

One hundred and twelve ... fourteen.

"Stop! Stop!" yelled Coach McGurk.

"Shaddup!" Paul Cahill roared at him. "Look!"

Somebody back there began shrieking over and over. The turn beginning to take shape before their headlights was impossible. The shrieking went on and on—more boys started to yell.

Coach McGurk yelled, "For God's sake, Paul. This is murder!"

Paul Cahill didn't answer. He couldn't take his attention for an instant from the approaching turn—a narrow cut, a sharp left with a wall on one side and a precipice on the other, then a right bend to a second cut.

"We'll all die!" wailed a voice that Paul Cahill dimly recognized as belonging to Big Dome Craig.

Then they were into the turn, and were never coming out of it. Coach McGurk got the idea that saved them, temporarily. He put cupped hands around his mouth and shouted:

"Right side, everybody! Get over to the right side! *Jump!*"

As the bus shuddered into the turn, yawing away toward the sharp drop to eternity, thirty-two healthy youngsters—somewhere close to two tons of flesh—flung hard to the right side of the bus.

That did it. The two tons turned the trick, by the narrowest of margins. A giant tire spun on emptiness for a second, but the other tires held the road.

Paul Cahill fought the wheel like a bucking bronc.

Behind him someone started to scream.

"Stop him, somebody! Stop him!"

That was Big Dome Craig again. He was cracking. But nobody made a move to interfere with Paul Cahill at the wheel. They all knew that would speed the moment of annihilation.

Paul Cahill heard, somewhere at his back, a shrieking, sobbing breath, a scuffle. Big Dome Craig had tried to get at him, but the others were holding him back.

Then Big Dome Craig was yelling, "I did it! I DID IT!"

Coach McGurk stumbled up behind Paul Cahill.

"It's Craig, Paul. He says he killed Romeo. For God's sake, hit the brakes! Paul!"

That's when Paul Cahill told him. Even as he swung the wheel as far as it would go and held on, he gritted:

"Brakes gone, coach. Air . . . out. Can't . . . even shift gears . . . air powered."

Coach McGurk wasted no time on a reply. He barked to the others:

"Left, now. Left. *Jump!*"

The two tons dove across to the other seats. That helped—but not enough. In the split second before he swung the wheel, Paul Cahill shifted his grip. There was the tortured rending of aluminum sheathing as the bus slid along the rock wall—enough to slow it. Then the tires kicked gravel out and down into the empty night, and again found the road.

They shot through the cut and, blessedly, ahead of them the road turned up for a half mile before entering the last plunge to the valley. Paul Cahill rode the uphill stretch with the right hand wheels at the very edge of the ditch and, as the bus started to lean, Coach McGurk and the boys shifted again and she settled and ran, and slowed, and not fifty yards from the top of the rise, she stopped.

"Paul," said Coach McGurk. That single word was the finest compliment the little man had ever heard.

Some of the boys began crying, with released tension, crying like the youngsters they were.

Big Dome Craig was crying too, his hands over his face, crying and talking at the same time as the truth poured out of him.

Paul Cahill stood by Coach McGurk and listened. Once, during a break in the confessional, the coach muttered to Paul Cahill:

"I couldn't believe you were doing it on purpose, Paul. Not even when it was happening."

"Thanks," Paul Cahill said.

"Just a coincidence, the brakes going when they did. But I guess I made the most of it." He grinned.

Big Dome Craig was telling now about Romeo and his sister— a long story and a sad one—and how after she had been in that trouble and gone to the doctor, she had still wanted to go live with the big fellow, and the only way Big Dome could stop it was by becoming Romeo's personal valet, doing his school work for him, taking his unending abuse. He had thought of killing Romeo for a long time but he might never have done it, if he hadn't found out about the weekend a month ago, when Romeo went to meet his sister. He only found out about it after his sister had taken the overdose of sleeping pills and had died, and the weekend was the reason. It seems Romeo had waited until the weekend was over before he told her that he didn't intend to see her again. That was Romeo, all right. Take your cake and hand it back, too.

Finally Big Dome Craig ran down and just sat there, strangely relieved.

It was a long time later, after they'd flagged a passing car and were waiting for the tow truck, that Coach McGurk said to Paul Cahill:

"Sorry you had to miss the game, Paul. It was great."

"That's okay," Paul said thoughtfully. "Anyway, we won." They sat quietly, then, thinking about winning.

Need

Some towns seem to defy not only time, but change; when this happens in the far hinterland, one is hardly amazed. Yet, amazingly, it happens all the time quite near some of our largest cities. Occasionally one of these is found by the "project" entrepreneur, and becomes the setting for winding windrows of coops and hutches, alternately "ranch" and "split"; yet not even these, and the prefabricated, alien, chain-driven supercilious superservice shopping centers in symbiosis with them, ever become a part of such towns. Whatever span of years it takes to make the "projects" obsolescent only serves to make these towns themselves more solid, more—in the chemical sense—set. Modernity does not and cannot alter the character of such a place, any more than one might alter a suit of chain mail by topping it with a Panama hat.

In such towns are businesses—shops and services—which live as the unassailable town lives, that is to say, in their own way and forever. Purveyors of the same shoes, sheets and sundries as the multicelled merchandizing mammoths sell go by the board, quite deserving of all that their critics say of them, that they can't keep up with the times, that they're dead and now must lie down. Defiance of time, of change, of anything is, after all, only defiance, and does not in itself guarantee a victory. But certain businesses, by their very nature, may be in a town, may *be* a town and achieve this defiant immortality. Anyone who has reflected with enough detachment on recent history is in a position to realize that, in revolutionary days, there must have been a certain market for genuine antiques made in America of American materials more than a century earlier. No technology advancing or static can eliminate the window-washer, the launderer, the handyman-smith and their establishments. Fashions in invention might change the vestments of their activity, but never their blood and marrow. The boatwright becomes a specialist in wooden station-wagon bodies, and then in mobile-home interiors. The blacksmith trades his leather bellows for a drill-press and a rack of epoxy resins, but he is what he was, and his shop is his permanence and his town's.

The general store has passed into the hands of the chains. It, and they, pursue the grail of *everything,* and since to be able to sell everything is on the face of it impossible, they are as impermanent as a military dictatorship that must expand or die, and that dies expanding. But there is another kind of store that sells, not everything, but *anything.* Its hallmark is that it has no grail at all, and therefore no pursuit. It emphatically does not expand. Its stock is that which has been useful or desirable to some people at some time; its only credo, that anything which has been useful or desirable to some people at some time will again be useful to someone—anything. Here you might find dried flowers under a glass dome, a hand-cranked coffee mill, a toy piano, a two-volume, leather-bound copy of *Dibdin's Journey,* a pair of two-wheel roller skates or a one tube radio set—the tube is a UX-11 and is missing—which tunes with a vario-coupler. You might—you probably would—also find in such a place, a proprietor who could fix almost anything and has the tools to do it with, and who understands that conversation is important and the most important part of it is listening.

Such a town was North Nyack, New York, barely twenty miles from Manhattan, yet—but for superficial scratches—untouched and unchangeable. It contained such a business, the Anything Shoppe—a title that constituted one of the scratches, being a concession to the transient trade, but one that did not bleed—and such a proprietor. His name was Noat, George Noat. G-Note, naturally, to his friends, who were all the people who knew him. He was the ugliest man in town, but that, like the silliness of his concern's name, was only skin-deep.

Why such a trade should be his, or why he was its, might make for some interesting discussion of cause and effect. The fact—which would contribute nothing to the discussion—remained that there was an *anythingness* about G-Note; not only would he buy anything, sell anything or fix anything, he would also listen to anyone, help anyone and, from the depths of a truly extraordinary well of the quality called empathy—the ability to feel with another's fingertips, look out through another pair of eyes—he could understand.

To George Noat, Prop., then, at twenty minutes to three one stormy morning, came Gorwing.

"G-Note!" Gorwing roared, pounding on the front door of the Anything Shoppe with force enough to set adance the two sets of pony harness and the cabbage grater that hung against it. "G-Note, Goddammit!"

A dim light appeared in the back of the shop, and G-Note's grotesque face and one T-shirted shoulder, over which a big square hand was pulling a gallus-strap, appeared at the edge of the baize curtain that separated G-Note's working from G-Note's living—the most partial of barriers, which suited him. He called, "It's open!" semaphored and withdrew.

Gorwing, small, quick, black hair, snapping black voice and eyes, sharp white teeth, slammed into the shop. The vibration set a clothing-dummy, atop which was perched a rubber imp carnival mask, teetering, and it turned as it teetered, bearing round on Gorwing indignantly. He and it stared one another in the eye for an angry moment, and then he cursed and snatched off the head and threw it behind the counter. "G-Note!" he barked.

G-Note shuffled into the shop, shrugging into a shawl-like grey cardigan and, with his heavy lids, wringing sleep out of his eyes. "I got that toilet you wanted yesterday," he mumbled. "Real tall, with pink rosebuds on. I bet there wouldn't be another like it from here to—"

"The hell with it," said Gorwing. "That was yesterday. Come on, willya?"

G-Note blinked at him. "Come?"

"The car, in the car!" Gorwing half cried, in the tones of excessive annoyance applied usually to people who should know by now. It was unfair, because by now G-Note did not know. "Hurry up, willya? What do I hafta do to make you hurry up?"

Gorwing flung open the door, and G-Note peered out into sodden blowing black. "It's raining out."

Gorwing's tight lips emitted a single sibilant explosion, and he raced out, leaving the door open. A moment later there came the sound of a car door slamming. G-Note shrugged and followed, closing the door behind him, and, hunching his shoulders against the driving rain, made his way out to the car. Gorwing had started it and switched on the lights while he was negotiating the puddles, then flung open the door on the driver's side and slid over into the passenger's seat. He shouted something.

"Huh?" G-Note grunted as he came poking and dripping into the car.

"I said Essex Street and Storms Road, right by the traffic light, and get *goin'*, willya?"

G-Note got himself settled and got going. "Gosh, Gorwing," he said, protesting gently.

"Quitcher bitchin'," said Gorwing through clamped teeth and curled lips. "Tromp down on that thing."

"Where we goin'?"

"I told you."

"Yeah, but—"

"You'll see when we get there. There's some money in it. You think I'd come out on a night like this if there wasn't some money in it? Listen, G-Note—" He paused with a mechanical abruptness, as if the machine gun with which he fired his words had jammed.

"What?"

Unjammed as suddenly, Gorwing shot: "You wouldn't let me down."

"No, I won't do that, but I wish I knew what I was 'sposed to do."

They sloshed over the high crown of Storms Hill and down the winding slope on the other side. The slick blacktop showed the loom of lights ahead before they saw the lights themselves—gold tinged with green, suddenly with ruby; the intersection and the traffic signal.

"Cut him out. *Quick!* Don't let'm pick up that guy."

Peering ahead, G-Note saw a car slowing for a waving figure who stood at the far side of the intersection. G-Note seemed not to have heard Gorwing's crackling order, or to have understood; yet it was as if his hands and feet had. The car lurched forward, cut in to the curb at the right of the other, and almost alongside. Startled, the other driver shifted and pulled away up the hill. At Gorwing's grunted order, G-Note stopped at the curb by the sodden and obviously bewildered pedestrian who had been trying to flag the other car. The man bent and tried to peer into the dark interior. Gorwing rolled down his window.

The man said, "Can you give me a lift?"

Gorwing reached back and opened the rear door, and the man plunged in. "Thank God," he panted, slamming the door. "I've got to get home, but I mean quick. You going near Rockland Lake?"

"We're going anywhere you say, mister," said Gorwing. "But it'll cost."

"Oh, that's all right. You're a taxi, hm?"

"We are now." Gorwing's hard hand took G-Note's elbow, squeezed, warned; but, warning or no, G-Note gasped at what came next: "Rockland Lake costs one hundred bucks from here."

G-Note's gasp was quite lost in the newcomer's wordless and indignant sound.

"What's the matter," Gorwing rasped, "can't raise it?"

"What kind of a holdup is this?" squeaked the man.

For the second time Gorwing reached back and swung the rear door open. Then he stretched across G-Note and shut off the motor. In the sudden silence, the sluicing of rain across the roof and the passenger's angry breath seemed too loud. Gorwing said, at a quarter the volume and twice the rasp, "I don't much go for that holdup talk."

The man plunged up and out-half out. He stood, with one foot still in the car, and looked up the road and down the road. Nothing moved but the rain. Clearly, they heard the relay in the traffic light saying *clock, chuck!* as the dim sodden shine of the intersection turned from green to red. To anyone thinking of traffic and transport, it was a persuasive sight. At three in the morning, chances of anything passing before daylight were remote.

He put his head back in. "Look, whoever you are, I've just got to get to Rockland Lake."

"So by now," said Gorwing, "we would be past Hook Mountain Road more'n halfway there. But you want to talk."

The man made his inarticulate sound and got back in. "Go ahead."

Gorwing, with a touch, checked G-Note's move toward the ignition. "A hundred bucks?"

"Yes, damn you!"

Gorwing turned the dome light on. "Take a good careful look at him," he said. Since he might have said it to either of them, they necessarily looked at one another, G-Note twisting around in his seat to look back, the passenger huddled sullen and glaring in the rear corner. G-Note saw a softhanded petulant man in his early thirties, with very fine, rather receding reddish hair and surprisingly bright blue eyes.

G-Note's great ugly head loomed over him like an approaching rockfall. The domelight, almost directly overhead, accentuated the heavy ridges of bone over his eyes, leaving the eyes themselves all but invisible in their caves. It gleamed from the strong fleshy arches that walled his wide nostrils and conceal the soft sensitivity of his thin upper lip while making the most of the muscular protruding underlip.

"You'll pay," said Gorwing, grinning wolfishly and switching off the light. "Drive," he said, nudging G-Note. He laughed. "I got a witness and you ain't," he said cheerfully.

"Just hurry," said the passenger.

G-Note, wondering more than anything else at the first laugh he had ever heard from Gorwing, drove. He said, unhappily, "This ain't a fun one, this time."

"Shut up," Gorwing said.

"Can't you go any faster?" cried the passenger.

He got no response. Only the anxious would feel that this skilled hurtling was not fast enough. No object, including an automobile, was inanimate with G-Note's big hands upon it; this one moved as if it knew its own way and its own weight.

"In here," said the passenger.

"I always wondered," said Gorwing. His meaning was clear. Many must have wondered just who lived behind these stone posts, these arresting NO ADMITTANCE and PRIVATE ROAD, KEEP OUT and NO TURNING and DEAD END ROAD signs. The drive climbed, turning, and in fifty yards one would have thought the arterial road below had ceased to exist. They came to a T. Neat little signs with arrows said SMITH on the left and POLLARD on the right. "Left," said the passenger.

They climbed again, and abruptly the road was manicured, rolled, tended, neat. "This will do."

There was a turn-around; the drive continued, apparently to a garage somewhere. In the howling wet, there was the shadowed white mass of a house. The man opened the door.

"A hundred bucks," Gorwing said.

The man took out his wallet. Gorwing turned on the dome

"I have only twenty here. Twenty-one."

"You got it inside." It could have been a question.

"Damn it!" the man flared. "Four lousy miles!"

"You was in a awful hurry," Gorwing drawled. He took the twenty, and the one, out of the man's hand. "I want the rest of it."

The man got out of the car and backed off into the rain. From about forty feet, he shrieked at them. He meant, undoubtedly, to roar like a lion, but his voice broke and he shrieked. "Well, I won't pay it!" and then he ran like a rabbit.

"Yes you will!" Gorwing bellowed. He slammed the back door of the car, which, if heard by the fleeing man, must have doubled his speed.

"Don't go out in that," said G-Note.

"Oh, I ain't about to," said Gorwing. "He'll pay in the morning. He'll pay you."

"Me?"

"You drop me off home and then come back and park here," said Gorwing. "Don't for Pete's sake go back to bed. You want to sleep any more, you do it right here. When he sees you he'll pay. You won't have to say nothing. Just be here."

G-Note started the car and backed, turning. " Oh, why not just let it go? You got more than it's worth."

Gorwing made a laughing noise. This was not the laugh that had amazed G-Note before; it was the one that G-Note had thought was all the laughter Gorwing had. It was also all the answer Gorwing would offer.

G-Note said, sadly, "You *like* doing this to that fellow."

Gorwing glanced at the road-signs as they pulled out of the driveway. "Private Road," he read aloud, but not very. It was as if to say, "He can afford it."

"Well," said G-Note again, as they neared North Nyack, "This ain't a fun one, this time."

There had been "fun ones." Like the afternoon Gorwing had come roaring and snapping into his place, just as urgently as he had tonight, demanding to know if G-Note had a copy of *Trials and Triumphs, My Forty Years in The Show Business,* by P. T. Barnum; and G-Note had! And they had tumbled it, with a lot of other old books, into two boxes, and had driven out to the end of Carrio Lane, where Gorwing just knew there was somebody who needed the book— not who, not why, just that there was somebody who needed it— and he and G-Note had stood at opposite sides of the lane, each with a box of books, and had bellowed at each other, "You got the P. T. Barnum book over there?" and "I don't know if I have the P. T. Barnum book here; have you got the P. T. Barnum book there?" and "What is the name of the P. T. Barnum book?" and *"Trials and Triumphs, My Forty Years in The Show Business,"* and so on, until, sure enough, a window popped open and a lady called down, "Do one of you men really have Barnum's biography there?" and, when they said they had, she said it was a miracle; she came down and gave them fifteen dollars for it. And that other time, when at Gorwing's urgent behest, G-Note had gone on a hot summer's day to stand blinking in the sun at Broad and Main streets, with a heavy ancient hand-cranked music box unwrapped on his shoulder, and the city man had come running up to him to ask what it played: *"Skater's Waltz,"* G-Note had told him, "and *My Rosary.*" "I'll give you a hundred bucks for it," the man had said, and, when G-Note's jaw dropped and fumbled for an astonished word, he'd made it a hundred and a quarter and had paid it, then and there.

Fun ones, these and others, and it hadn't mattered that the customers (or was it victims?) paid exorbitantly. They did it of their own free will, and they seemed really to *need* whatever it was. How Gorwing knew what was needed, and where—but never by whom or why—was a recurrent mystery; but after a while you stopped asking—because Gorwing wouldn't stand catechizing on the subject—and then you stopped wondering; you just went along with it, the way you do with automatic shifting, the innards of an IBM machine, or, if you happen not to know, precisely what chemicals are put into the head of a match to make it light. You don't *have* to know.

But this man, this passenger they'd charged twenty-five dollars per mile now; it wasn't fun. He was a guy in trouble if ever G-Note had seen one, anxious, worried, even frantic—so anxious he'd say yes to a demand like that, even if he did take it back later; so anxious he was stumbling homeward through the rain at three in the morning. You should help a fellow like that, you shouldn't use his trouble against him. Which didn't seem to bother Gorwing, not one bit: coming into the street-lit area of North Nyack, now, G-Note could glance sidewise at Gorwing's face, see the half grin, the cruel white teeth showing. No, it didn't bother Gorwing.

So . . . you found out new things about people all the time. Such a thing could be surprising, but, if you don't want surprises like that, you just keep away from people. Thus G-Note shrugged away the matter, as he asked, "Where you staying now?" for Gorwing moved around all the time.

"Just drop me off by O'Grady's."

O'Grady's, the poolhall, was across town from G-Note's place, on the same avenue; yet, passing his own shop, G-Note turned right and made the usual wide detour past the hospital. He made a U-turn at the poolhall and stopped. For a good-night, Gorwing had only, "Now you said you wouldn't let me down."

"All right," said G-Note.

"Forty-sixty, you and me," said Gorwing, and turned away.

G-Note drove off.

Eloise Smith hoped Jody wouldn't be mad. His was not the towering rage of this one nor the sullen grumps of that one, but a waspish,
petty, verbose kind of anger, which she had neither the wit nor the
words to cope with. She loved Jody and tried her very best to have
everything the way he wanted it, but it was hard, sometimes, to know
what would annoy him. And when anything did, sometimes she had
to go through an hour or more of his darting, flicking admonish-
ments before she even knew what it was.

She'd broken the telephone. Kicked the wire right out of the
wall—oh, how *clumsy!* But she'd done worse than that from time
to time, and he'd just laughed. Or she'd done much less serious things
and he'd carried on just terrible. Well … she'd just have to wait and
see. She hoped she could stay awake, waiting—goodness, he was
late. Elks nights were always the latest; he was secretary, and was
always left to lock the hall after the meeting. But he usually got home
by two anyway—it was three already, and still no sign of—oh—
there he …

She ran and opened the door. He spun in, dripping, out of breath.
He slammed the door and shot the bolt, and pushed past her to peer
out the front window. Not that anything could be seen out there.
He turned from the window. He looked wild. She stood before him,
clutching her negligee against her breast.

"Eloise … you all right?"

"All right? Why, of course I'm all right!"

"'Thank God?" He pushed past her again, darted to the living
room door, flicked his gaze across and back. "You all alone?"

"Well, not since you got here," she said, in a hopeless attempt to
produce some levity. "Here, you're wet through. Give me your hat.
You poor—"

"It might interest you to know … you've driven me half out …
of my mind," he panted. She had never seen him like this. He might
be a little short of breath from running from the car to the house,
but not this much, and it should be, well, tapering off. It wasn't. It
seemed to get more marked as he talked. He was very pale. His
red-rimmed eyes and the rain running off his bland features gave
him the ludicrous expression of a five-year-old who has bumped his

head and is trying not to cry. She followed him into the living room and rounded on him, to face him, and for the third time he pushed past her, this time to fling open the dining room door. She said timidly, "Jody, I broke the telephone. I mean, I fell over the wire and it came out."

"Oh, you did, did you."

He was still panting. "Jody!" she cried, "whatever is the matter? What's *happened?*"

"Oh, what's happened?" he barked. His eyes were too round. "I call you up and somebody cuts the wire, as far as I know. I rush out of the hall to the car and the door slams behind me, that's all. My keys on the table. Can't get back in, can't start the car. Try my best to get here quickly. Hitchhiking. Get waylaid by a couple of the ugliest hoodlums you ever saw, they *robbed* me."

"Oh dear—did they hurt you, honey?"

"They did not. Matter of fact," he panted, "I told them off, but good. And they better not fool with me again. Not that they will— I guess they learned their lesson." Angrily, proudly, he hitched his shoulders, a gesture that made him aware of his wet coat, which at last he began to remove. She ran to help him. "Oh Jody, Jody darling, but you didn't have to rush back like that . . ."

"Didn't I," he said solemnly, in a tone dripping with meaning, not one whit of which she understood. He pulled himself, glaring, away from her, and, while she stood clutching her negligee to herself again, he ponderously took off the coat, glaring at her.

"Oh, I'm so sorry. You poor dear." She thought, suddenly, of a woman she had seen in the parking lot at the supermarket, whose child had bolted in front of a car. People had shrieked, brakes had squealed, the woman had run out to scoop up her frightened but unharmed youngster—and, in her relief, had whaled the tar out of him.

That was it—Jody had been so terribly worried about her, he'd gotten into all this trouble rushing to help her, and now that he knew she was safe he was, in effect, spanking her.

She grew very tender, very patient. "Oh *Jody* . . ." she said fondly.

"You won't 'Oh Jody' out of this one," he said.

"Well, I'm *sorry!*" she cried, and, "Oh, Jody, what is it? Is it the telephone? Will it be hard to get it fixed?"

"The *telephone* can be fixed," he growled in a voice again inexplicably loaded with meaning. He passed through the dining room into the kitchen, again flicking his glance here, there, up, across. "Got everything put away," he said, looking at the glass cupboard, the dish shelf.

"Well, don't I always?"

"Doubtless," he said bitterly. He opened the refrigerator.

"Let me fix—"

"I'll do it myself," he said.

Her tenderness and patience gave out at that point. She said in a small voice, "I'll go to bed then," and when he did not respond, she went upstairs, lay down and cried.

She managed to be silent, stiff and silent, when he came upstairs, and lay in the dark with her eyes squeezed shut while he undressed and washed and got into his pajamas and into the other bed. She dearly hoped he'd say something, but he didn't. After a long time, she whispered, "Well, good night, Jody." He made a sound which might have been an offensive "Ha!" or just a grunt; she couldn't be sure. She thought he fell asleep after a while, and then she did, too— lightly, troubled.

The glare of her bed lamp awoke her. Up through it, and up through the confusion of puzzlement and sleepiness, she blinked at Jody. Seen so, standing by her bed and glaring down at her, he looked very large. He never had before.

He said, "You'd better tell me all about it right now."

She said, "Wh-what time is it?"

"Now you listen to me, Eloise. I've learned a whole lot of things in the last few hours. About you. About me. About—" Suddenly he raised his voice; at the rim of the glare of light, the vein at the side of his neck swelled. "I'm just too doggoned nice to everybody. When I told off those thugs, I tell you, something happened to me, and from now on I won't stand for it any more!"

"Jody—"

"Two of them, twice my size, and I told *them.*"

"You did?"

In retrospect, Eloise was to look painfully back upon this moment and realize that on it turned everything that subsequently happened between them; she would realize that when she said, "You *did?*" he heard "*You* did?"—a difference in inflection that becomes less subtle the more one thinks about it. Later, she thought a great deal about it; now, however, she could only shrink numbly down into the covers as he roared, "Yes, *I* did! You didn't think I had it in me, did you? Well I did, and from now on nobody puts anything over on me! Including you, you hear?"

"But Jody—I—"

"Who was here when I called you up at two o'clock?"

"Who was—Nobody!"

He sank down to the edge of his bed so their heads were more nearly on a level, and fixed her with a pink-rimmed, weepy, steely gaze. "I . . . heard . . . you," he intoned.

"You mean when you called?"

He simply sat there with his unchanging, unnatural glare. Wonderingly, frightened, she shook her head. "I was watching a movie on TV. It was just ending—the very end; it was a good one. And I— I—"

"You told your . . . your . . ." He could not say the word. "You told whoever it was not to talk. *But I heard you.*"

Dazedly she sat up in bed, a slim, large-eyed, dark-blonde woman in her late twenties—frightened, deeply puzzled, warding off certain hurt. She thought hard, and said, "I spoke to *you*—I said that to you! In the picture, you see, there was this girl that . . . that . . . Oh, never mind; it's just that in that last moment of the picture everything came together, like. And just as you rang and I picked up the phone, it was the last minute of the picture, don't you see? I was sort of into it—you know. So I said to you, 'Don't say anything for a second, honey,' and I—Is that what you heard?"

"That is what I heard," he said coldly.

She laughed with relief. "I said it to you, to you, not to anyone here, you silly! And—well, I was sort of mixed up, coming out of the TV that way, to the phone, and you began to sort of shout at me, and I couldn't hear the TV, and I kind of ran to it to turn it up, just for a second, and I forgot I was holding the phone and the wire caught my ankle and I fell down and the wire pulled out and—*Jody!*" she cried, seeing his face.

"You're a liar, you bitch."

"Jody!" she whispered faintly. Slowly she lay down again. She closed her eyes, and tears crept from beneath her lids. She made no sound.

"I can handle hoodlums and I can handle you," he said flatly, and turned out the light. "And from now on," he added, as if it were a complete statement; he must have thought so, for he said nothing more that night.

Eloise Smith lay trembling, her mind assuring her over and over that none of this was really happening, it couldn't happen. After a useless time of that, she began to piece the thing together, what he'd said, what she'd said ... she recalled suddenly what he had blurted out about the Elks' Hall, and the car, and all ... what was it? Oh: he'd called, apparently to tell her he was on the way; and she'd murmured, "Don't say anything for a second, honey," and he'd thought ... he must have thought oh dear, how *silly* of him! "Jody!" she said, sitting up, and then the sight of his dim rigid form, curled away from her in the other bed, drove her back to silence, and she lay down to think it through some more ... And he'd gotten himself all upset and yelled, and then she'd broken the wire, and probably thought her—*her*—but she could not think the word any more than he had been able to say it—he'd thought that whoever it was had gaily pulled out the wire to, well, stop his interruption. And then apparently Jody had gone all panicky and berserk, had run straight out to the car, got himself locked out of the Elks' Hall with the car keys still inside, had headed north—away from town, and gas stations, and other telephones—and had tried to hitchhike home. And something about hoodlums and being robbed on the way—but then he said he'd driven them off, didn't he?

She gave it up at length. Whatever had happened to him, he obviously felt like a giant, or a giant-killer maybe, for the first time in his life, and he was taking it out on her.

Well, maybe in the morning—

In the morning he was even worse. He hardly spoke to her at all. Just watched her every minute, and once in a while snorted disgustedly. Eloise moved quickly with poached egg, muffin, coffee, marmalade; sleepless, shaken, she would know what to do, take a stand, have a sensible thought, even—later; not now.

Watching her, Jody wiped his lips, threw down his napkin and stood up. "I'm going for the car. If you're thinking of letting anybody in, well, look out, that's all. You don't know when I'll be back."

"Jody, Jody!" she wailed, "I never! I *never*, Jody!"

He walked past her, smiling tightly, and got his other hat. "Oh boy," he said to the cosmos, "I just hope I run across one of those thugs again, that's what I hope." He banged the hat with the edge of his hand, and set it uncharacteristically at a rakish slant on his head. Numbly, she followed him to the door and stood in it, watching him go. He sprang up the steep driveway like a spring lamb. At the top he turned without breaking stride and came straight back—but not springing—scuttling would be the word for it. His face was chalky. He saw her and tried, with some apparent difficulty, to regain his swagger. "Forgot to call the phone company. Get a taxi, too."

"You can't," she said. "I broke the wire."

"I know, I know!" he snapped waspishly, though she felt he had forgotten it. "I'll call from Pollard's." He glanced quickly over his shoulder, up the driveway, and then plunged across the lawn and through the wet shrubbery toward their only neighbor's home.

She looked after him in amazement, and then up the drive. Over its crest, she could see the roof of a car, obviously parked in their turn-around. She was curious, but too much was happening; she would not dare climb the drive to see who it was. Instead she went in and closed the door and climbed upstairs, where she could see from the bedroom windows. From this elevation, the car was plainly visible. It wasn't theirs. Also visible was the ugly giant lounging tiredly against the car, watching the house.

She shrank behind the curtain and put all her left fingers in her mouth.

After a time she saw Jody plunging across the long grass of the vacant acre that lay between their place and Pollard's. He pushed through the shrubs at the edge of the lawn, stopped to paddle uselessly at his damp trouser-legs and then sidled over to the driveway. He peeped around the hollyhocks until he could look up the drive. The ugly man had apparently detected some movement, for he stood up straight and peered. Jody shrank back behind the hollyhocks.

She thought then that he might come in, but instead he crouched there. There was a long—to Eloise, an interminable—wait. Then a taxi pulled in from the road and turned to stop next to the other car. Jody straightened up and began trotting up the drive. The ugly man leaned his elbows on the lower edge of the taxi driver's window— he had to bend nearly double to do it—and began speaking to him. Of course she could not hear a word, but the ugly man and the driver seemed to be laughing. Then the ugly man reached in, slapped the driver cheerfully on the shoulder and stood back. The taxi started up, backed around and pulled out of the drive. Jody, seeing this, for the second time made a U-turn and scuttled back to his hiding place behind the hollyhocks. He looked very little like a man who was overanxious to meet some thugs.

Eloise moved closer to the window in order to see him better, for he was almost straight down beneath her. Perhaps he caught the movement out of the corner of his eye, or perhaps some sixth sense ... anyway, he glanced up, and for a moment looked more miserable than a human being ought, caught like that—chagrined, embarrassed. Then, visibly, he began to grow angry again; it began with her, she could see that. Then he wheeled and marched up the drive like a condemned man ascending the scaffold. The ugly man opened the right front door of his old sedan, and Jody got in.

For a long time Eloise Smith stood in the window, kneading her elbows and frowning. Then, slowly, she went downstairs and began to write a letter.

Smith's posture of pugnacious defiance lasted from the turn-around to the private road he shared with Pollard. Once out of sight of the house, he slumped unhappily into the corner of his seat and stole a quick glance at his captor.

The man was even bigger, and considerably uglier, in daylight than he had been in the dark. He said, "I sent away your taxi. He didn't mind. He's an old buddy of mine."

"Oh," said Jody.

He watched the scenery go by, and thought of how gentle the man's voice was. Very soft and gentle. Into this Jody Smith built vast menace. After a while he said sulkily, "This going to cost me another hundred?"

"Oh gosh no," said the ugly man. "You bought a round trip. Where do you want to go?"

Cat-and-mouse, thought Jody. Trying to get my goat. "Got to get my car at the Elks' Hall."

"Okay," the man said, nodding pleasantly. Deftly, he spun the wheel, turning into what Smith prided himself as being *his* short cut to the Hall. Obviously this creature knew the roads hereabouts.

They came to the built-up area, slid into an alley, crossed two streets and turned sharp right into the crunchy parking yard at the Elks. There were two other cars there; one Smith's, the other obviously the caretaker's, for the doors stood open and the old man was sweeping the step.

Timidly, Smith touched the door handle. The ugly man sat still, big gnarled hands on the wheel, eyes straight ahead. Smith opened the door and said, " ... well—" Then, incredulous, he got out. The ugly man made no attempt to stop him.

Smith actually got two paces away from the car before sheer compulsive curiosity got the better of him. He went back and said, "Look, what about this money? You don't really expect me to pay a hundred dollars for that ride."

"I don't," said the big man, "Gorwing, I guess he does."

"Gorwing. Is that the little ape that—"

"He's a friend of mine," said the giant, not loudly, but just quickly. Smith dropped that tactic, and asked, "You work for him?"

"With, not for. Sometimes."

"But you're doing the collecting."

"Look," said the ugly one, suddenly, "Gorwing, he wants sixty per cent of that money. Well, I wouldn't let him down. For me, I don't want it. Now, how much did he get off you last night?"

"Twenty-one."

"From sixty is thirty-nine. You got thirty-nine bucks?"

"Not on me." Astonished, he looked at the grotesque face. "Tell me something. What would you do if I wouldn't give you another penny?"

The man looked at his gnarled hands, which twisted on the wheel. "I guess I'd just have to put it up myself."

Smith got back in. "Run me over to the bank."

The man made no comment, but started his engine.

"What's your name?" asked Smith as they stopped for a light a block away.

"George Noat."

"Aren't you afraid I'll go to the police?"

"Nope."

Smith recalled then, forcefully, what Gorwing had said: "I got a witness and you haven't." He imagined himself trying to explain what had happened to a desk sergeant, who would be trying to write it all down in a book. Outrageous, certainly—but he had gotten into the car of his own free will, he had agreed to pay.

"How did you happen to come along when you did last night?"

"Just driving by."

Smith found the answer unsatisfying, and he could not say why. He said, sulkily, "Friend or not, I've got to say that your Gorwing is a bandit."

"No he ain't," said George Noat mildly. "Not when all he does is get things people really need. You really need something, you pay for it, right?"

"Yes, I suppose you—"

"And if you need something, and a fellow delivers it, nobody's getting robbed."

At that moment they came to the bank, and the subject was lost.

Jody Smith lived with the letter for a long time.

Dear Jody,

After the way you acted last night I don't know what to do except I have to go away from you. You have to trust a person. I always believed you but why did you make up all that about Mr. Noat I know him a long time and he is about the kindest man who ever lived he wouldn't hurt a fly.

I want you to think about one thing you said a lot about me and some man and all that, well I want you to know that there isn't any man at all and now that means your wife left you and there wasn't even any other man. I bet now you wish there was. I wish there was. No I don't Jody, oh my goodness I wish I could write a letter I never could you know, but I can't stay here any more. Maybe you could find somebody better I guess you better I won't stand in your way because I still want you to be happy.

Eloise

Tell the market not to send the order I sent yesterday. We were supposed to have dinner at the Stewarts Tuesday. I can't think of anything else.

Now Jodham Swaine Smith was a man of independent means—this was the phrase with which on occasion he described himself to himself. His parents had both come from well-to-do families, but Smith was two generations—three, on his mother's side—removed from the kind of fortune-getting that had gotten these fortunes; latterly, it had become the Smith tradition to treat the principal as if it did not exist, and live modestly on the interest.

Independent means. Such independence means all Four Freedoms plus a good many more. Small prep schools—in small towns and with, comparatively, small fees—gray as Groton, followed by tiny, honored colleges on which the ivy, if not the patina, is quite as real as Harvard's, make it possible to grow up in one of the most awesome independencies of all, the freedom from Life. In most cases it takes but six or so post-graduate weeks for trauma and tragedy to set in, and for the discoveries to be made that business is not necessarily conducted on the honor system, that the reward for dutifully reporting the errors of the erring gets you, not a mark toward your Good Citizen Button, but something more like a kick in the teeth, and finally, that the world is full of people who never heard of your family and wouldn't give a damn if they had.

Yet for those few who are enabled by, on the one hand, the effortless accumulation of dividends, and on the other, an absence of personal talent or ambition that might be challenged, it is possible to slip into a surrogate of man's estate in its subjective aspects hardly different from the weatherproof confines of the exclusive neighborhood, the private school and the honored and unheard-of college. Jody Smith was one of these few.

Not that he didn't face the world, just as squarely and as valiantly as he had been taught to do. But it happened that, all unknowing, he gave the world nothing worth abrading, and the world was therefore, as far as he could know, a smooth place to live with. In no sense did he withdraw from life. On the contrary, he sought out the centers of motion, and involved himself as completely as possible with the Elks, the Rotary, the Lions, and the Civic Improvement League. Strangely enough, these gatherings, filled as they were with real people, gave him no evidence of the existence of a real world. Jody Smith was always available for the Thanksgiving Dance Committee and Operation Santa Claus, but did not submit himself, and was somehow never proposed, for any chairmanship. In a word, he wasn't competition for anyone.

And he had gravitated to that same strange other- or no-world in what might laughingly be called his business. He was a philatelist. He ran small classified advertisements in the do-it-yourself and other magazines on a contract basis, and handled the trickle of mail from his little den at home. He made money at it. He also lost money at it. In the aggregate, he probably lost more than he made, but not enough to jeopardize his small but adequate and utterly predictable income.

He had, from time to time, wanted this or that. He had never for a moment *needed,* anything. Eloise, for example—he had wanted her, or perhaps it was to be married to her, but he hadn't needed to. She helped him with his business, typing out some of the correspondence from form letters he had composed, and moistening stamp hinges. But he did not need her help. He did not need her.

Not even when she left. For a while. Weeks, in fact. And even then at first it was want, not need, and even then the want was to create some circumstance that would make her realize how wrong she had been. Then the wants widened, somehow. The television and the stamp hinges seemed after a time to be inadequate to fill the long evenings or to occupy the silence of the house. When no hand but his own moved anything about him, his hat would not go of itself into the closet but remained on hall tables where he himself had put it. And, where at first he had rather admired himself for his cookery, for he was a methodical, meticulous, and, as far as cookbooks were concerned, obedient person, he began slowly to resent the kitchen and even the animal beneath his belt which with such implacability drove him into it. It seemed to him a double burden—that he should have to put in all that time before a meal, and then have nothing ready until he prepared it himself. To do things in order to make lunchtime come seemed ultimately enough, more than enough, for a man to be burdened with. Then to have to do things to make the lunch itself seemed an intolerable injustice.

These matters of convenience—and lack of it—grew into nuisances and then, like the pebble in the shoe, like the inability to turn over even in the most comfortable of beds, into sheer torture.

The breaking point came, oddly enough, not in the long night hours with the empty bed beside his, nor in some dream-wracked and disoriented morning, but in the middle of an otherwise pleasant afternoon. He had just received the new Scott's catalog, and wanted to compare something in it with the 1954 edition. He couldn't find the 1954 edition, and he called out:

"Eloise—"

The sound of his own voice, and of her name, made something happen like the tearing of a membrane. It tore so completely, and with such suddenness and agony, that he grunted aloud and fell back on the couch. He sat there for a moment weaving, and his mouth grew crooked and his eyes pink, and there came a warning sting at the very back of the roof of his mouth that astonishingly informed him, as it hardly had since he was nine years old, that he was about to cry.

He didn't cry, beyond once whimpering, "Eloise?" in a soprano half-whisper; then for a long time he sat silent and stunned, wondering numbly how such a force could have remained coiled so tightly within him, undetected.

When he could, he began to take stock. It was a matter of weeks— six of them, seven—since she had left, and not once had he examined his acts and attitude. He had done nothing about locating her, though in that department there was little to be done—he simply did not know where she was. Her only relative was an aging mother in a rest home out West, and she certainly had not gone there. He had not destroyed her letter, but he hadn't reread it either, nor thought about its contents. He hadn't wanted to think about these things, he now knew. He had thought . . . he hadn't *needed* to.

He needed to now, and he did. The letter gave him nothing at first but a feeling—not quite anger—more like a sullen distaste for himself. And one more thing, slightest of handholds—she apparently, somehow or other, knew George Noat.

And, on that slender evidence, he tore out of the house and got into his car.

Nothing was the way it should be. The trail was not obscure. The taxi-driver—Noat had said he was "an old buddy"—told him immediately where Noat and his business were, and there were no obstacles to his finding the place—it was within three blocks of the Elks' Hall. The fact that never once in Elks or Lions or Rotary had he heard Noat's name was only surprising, not mysterious: such establishments as the Anything Shoppe look back, not forward, and are not found on the lists of forward-looking organizations.

It was only in the subdued light of the shop(pe), with the old-fashioned spring-swung doorbell still jangling behind him, that Jodham Swaine Smith realized that, though intuition and evidence had brought him here, they had not supplied him with the right thing to say. "Mr. Noat!" he bleated urgently, and then dried up altogether.

The proprietor glanced up at him from his work, and said easily, "Oh, hi. Give a hand here, will you?"

Annoyed, which was uncharacteristic of him, and simultaneously much more timid than he ever remembered being, Jody Smith edged around the counter. Noat was squatting before an inverted kitchen chair, painted flat red, with a broken spoke and a split seat-board. "Just grab holt here," he invited. Smith took the legs as indicated and squeezed them together, while Noat drove in corrugated fasteners. "Nothing wrong with the chair," said Noat philosophically between hammer blows. "It's people. People busted this chair. As for fixing it, if people had sense enough to have four arms like this thing has four legs, why, I wouldn't have to call on my neighbors. You like people?"

The direct question startled Smith; he had been about to interrupt, and was only half following what the big man said. He made a weak uncertain laugh, very like that of Sir Laurence in the Graveyard Scene, and said, "Sure. Sure I do."

He stood back while Noat turned the chair upright, set it on the counter and measured the missing spoke with an ancient and frayed dressmaker's tape. "You got to make allowances," Noat said to the tape. "This old thing's stretched, but you see I know just how much it's stretched. 14 inches here is 14 and 17/32nds actual. That's one way to make allowances. Then," he went on, laying the tape against a piece of square stock that was chucked in a highly individual wood lathe, "if the tape says 14 on the chair, and I mark it the same 14 on the lumber, it comes out right and it makes no never mind what it is actual. People," he said, rounding at last on Smith, who prepared himself for some profound truth, "fret too much."

Smith lived for a moment with that feeling one has when mounting ten steps in the dark, then discovers there are only nine stairs. He grasped wildly at what he thought the man had been talking about. "People are all right. I mean, I like people."

Noat considered this, or a turning chisel he had obviously made from an old screwdriver, carefully. Smith could not stand the contemplative silence, and ran on. "Why, I do everything for people.

I join every club or lodge in town that does any good for people, and I work hard at it. I guess I wouldn't do that if I didn't like people."

· "You don't do that for yourself." It was, if a statement, agreement and a compliment; if a question, a searching, even embarrassing one, calling for more insight than Smith had or dared to have. It was voiced as a statement, but so nearly as a question that Smith could not be sure. He was, however, too honest a person to grasp at the compliment . . . and if he rejected it, he must be embarrassed, even insulted, and walk out . . . but he couldn't walk out until he—

"You know my wife, don't you?"

"Sure do. A very nice little lady."

He started the lathe. It made a very strange sound. The power looked like that from an ancient upright vacuum cleaner. Reduction was accomplished through gears that could only have come from one of those hand-operated coffee mills that used, with their great urn-shaped hoppers and scroll-spoked, cast-iron scarlet flywheels, to grace chain markets before they became supered. The frame was that of a treadle-operated sewing machine, complete with treadle, which, never having been disconnected, now disappeared in a blur of oscillation that transferred itself gently to everything in the place. One could not see it, but it was there in the soles of the feet, in the microscopic erection of the fibers in a dusty feather boa, in the way sun-captured dust motes marched instead of wandered. The lathe's spur-center seemed to have been the business end of a planing attachment from some forgotten drill press; it was chucked into a collet that seemed to have been handmade out of rock maple. The cup center, at the other end, turned freely and true in what could be nothing else but a roller-skate wheel. Noat set his ground-down screwdriver on the long tool rest, which was of a size and massiveness that bespoke a history of angle-bracketship aboard a hay wagon. On the white wood a whiter line appeared, and a blizzard of fragrant dust appeared over Noat's heavy wrists. He carried the tool along the rest, and the whiter-upon-white became a band, a sheet. When he had taken it from end to end, he stopped the machine. The wood was still square, but with all its corners rounded. Smith tore his fascinated eyes away from it and asked, wondering if Noat would still know what he was talking about, "How did you happen to know her?"

"Customer."

"Really?"

Noat squinted at the display window over the edge of his chisel. "Garlic press," he said, and pursed his lips. "Swedish cookie mold, by golly, she was here seven times over that. Little lady really gets two bits out of each two dozen pennies." He laughed quietly; he had a good laugh. Smith's solar plexus contained a sudden vacuum at the mention of these homey, Eloise-y things. "And the egg separators—two hundred egg separators."

"*What*? I never saw—"

"Yes, you did. You went away to some kind of convention, and when you came back she'd done over the breakfast nook."

"The textured wall!"

"Yeah, those mash-paper cushions they put between layers in an egg crate. She cut and fit and put 'em up and painted 'em—what she say?" He closed his eyes. "Flat purple with dull gold in the middle of each cup."

"She never told me," Smith informed himself aloud. "She said she'd ... Well, I guess she didn't actually *say*. But I got the idea she saved up from the house money and had it done. She really did it herself?"

Noat nodded gravely.

"I wonder why she didn't tell me," Smith breathed.

"Maybe," said George Noat, "she thought you might live with a textured wall where you wouldn't with egg separators."

There was a meaning here that he could not—would not—see, but that he knew would come to him most distastefully later. He compressed his lips. He had acquired too many things to think about in the last few minutes, and at least two of them might be insults. He glanced doorward, and said in farewell tones, "Well, I—" and then the handle of the chisel pressed into his palm stopped him. "You go on with that. I got to cook some glue."

Smith stared with horror at the chisel. "Me run that machine? I never in my life—"

The giant cupped a hand under his left armpit and propelled him to the machine. "The one wonderful thing about a lathe, you couldn't tell a beginner's first job from Chippendale's last one. Don't ever get all big-eyed over beautiful work—chances are it was real easy to do. What I always say is, a Duncan Phyfe is only a piccoloful of whiskey."

"But—but—"

"Pull this chain, starts it. Rest your chisel here, cut light and slow at first. Anytime you want to see what you've done or feel it, pull the chain again, it stops. That's all there is." He started the machine, took the chisel, and, under its traveling point, the wood drew on a new garment of texture from end to end.

Timidly, Smith took back the chisel and nervously approached the spinning wood. It touched, and he sprang back, but there was a new neat ring around it. Fascinated, he tried it again, and again, and then looked up to ask if that was right: but Noat had confidently retired to the other end of the shop, where a disgraceful-looking glue pot sat upon a gas ring.

Nothing could have given him more assurance than to be trusted with the job like this. For a while, then, he entered the magical, never-quite-to-be-duplicated region of The First Time. You may challenge the world to find anyone who runs a lathe and who also forgets the first cut he ever made.

Disappointingly soon, the square wood was round; but then he realized joyfully that this would be a new spoke for the chair, and must come down quite a bit more. He worked steadily and carefully, until at last his mind was able to watch it while it thought of other things as well—and it thought of Eloise, thought of Eloise in a way unknown to it for oh ... oh, a long time; and for such a brief while, too—there was something deeply sad about that. The day—no, two days—before he had stumblingly asked her to marry him, he had been in a drugstore, just like any other drugstore except for the climactic fact that it was in her neighborhood, the one she always went to, *her* drugstore. He had walked in to get some cough drops and had suddenly realized this incredible thing about the place—that she had many times stood here, had bent over that showcase, had had that prim warm little body cupped there by the padded swivel seats at the soda fountain. She had smiled in this place. Her voice had vibrated the sliding glass over the vitamins, and her little feet must have lightly dotted the floor, from time to time, just after it had been waxed.

And so it was with the Anything Shoppe; her hand had danced the spring-dangling doorbell, and she had bargained here and made plans, and counted money and held it for a moment, while the three fine "thinking" furrows—two long and one short—came between her eyebrows, and went quickly, leaving no mark. She had smiled in this place, and perhaps laughed; and here she had thought of him.

Textured wall.

The turning wood had grown silky, and now seemed to be growing a sheath of mist . . . he withdrew the tool and stood watching it through the blur until a bulky rectangular object on the tool rest distracted him. He blinked, and saw it was a box of tissues. Gratefully he reached for one and blew his nose and wiped his eyes. He gazed guiltily at Noat, but the big man's back was turned and he appeared to be totally absorbed in stirring his stinking glue. Let's not think about how he put the tissues there, or why . . . turn off the machine now.

George Noat found it not necessary to turn to him until he spoke: "Getting a cold, I guess . . . snff . . . time of year. Mr. Noat, have a look at this now."

Noat lumbered back to the lathe and ran his hand along the piece. His hands were those a prep-school boy might see from the windows of the school bus, that a collegian with a school letter on the front of his sweater might see manipulating the mysteries under a car. One seldom noticed the skill of such hands, but ingrained black was dirt and dirt was, vaguely, "them," not "us." The idea does cling, oh yes it does, ingrained, too. Yet for all his distress in this moment, Smith was able to notice how the great grainy leather-brown hand closed all around the stainless new wood, was intimate with it from end to end, left not a mark. To Smith it was an illumination, to see such a hand live so with purity. All this subliminal; still before his stinging eyes was the mist of hurting, and he said aloud, "She left me."

"That's just *fine*," said George Noat. He must have meant one thing or the other—probably he meant ... for he was taking up the red chair. He lifted it high and hung it casually on the handle of a scythe, which, in turn, hung to the beam overhead. An unbroken rung of the chair thereby lay at his eye level. He started the lathe, and with four sure sweeps and five confident pauses, he duplicated the unbroken rung complete to its dowelled ends. He stopped the machine, slapped away collet and tailstock and tried the new rung for size. Freehand, with a keyhole saw, he cut away excess at the tips. It fitted. He took it to the glue pot, dipped the ends, returned and set it in place; then, with simultaneous blows right and left, he drove it home. A war surplus quartermaster's canvas belt plus a suitcase clasp of the over-center type formed a clamp for it. He left it where it hung, and in his strange way—he seemed never to move quickly, but all the same, could loom up over a man in a rush—he rounded on Smith. "You want her back?"

"Oh God," said Jody Smith softly, "I do."

"Hmp." Noat moved to the other end of the counter and gingerly capped the hot glue pot. "You need her," Smith thought he said.

Smith frowned. "Isn't that what I just said?"

"Nope."

Jody Smith's quick petulance evaporated as quickly as it had formed; again he found himself fumbling for whatever it was this creature seemed to mean, or almost meant. "I said I want her back."

"I know. You didn't say you need her."

"It's the same thing."

"No, it ain't."

Half angry, half amused, Smith said, "Oh come on, now. Who'd split hairs about a thing like that?"

"Some people might." He paused, looking at a piece of junk he pulled from a box. "Gorwing, he would."

"Gorwing, he won't," said Smith with some asperity. "Look, I don't want this talked all over with the likes of that Gorwing."

Noat gave a peculiar chuckle. "Gorwing wouldn't talk about it. He'd just *know*."

"I don't get you. He'd just—know? Know what?"

"If you should want something. Or need it."

Smith wagged his head helplessly. "I never know when you're kidding."

"This thing," said Noat soberly, staring at the object in his hand— it seemed to be the ring-shaped, calibrated "card" from a marine compass—"got three hundred and sixty degrees on it. More than any college graduate in the country." Without moving anything but his eyes, he regarded Smith. "Am I kidding?"

In spite of himself, Smith felt moved to laughter. "I don't know." Sobering then, and anxious, "Have you any idea where she might have—"

"I really couldn't say," interjected the proprietor. "Here's Gorwing."

"Oh, for God's sake," Smith muttered.

Gorwing banged in, stopped, stared at Smith. He passed his hand over his eyes and muttered, "Oh, for God's sake."

Then both men turned to Noat, redly regarding his sudden burst of merriment.

"You settin' on a feather?" rasped Gorwing.

"Just listening to the echoes," answered Noat, grinning. Then a quick concern enveloped his features. He leaned forward and watched Gorwing bend his head, gingerly touch the back of his neck. "What is it—him?"

"*Him?*" Gorwing glanced insultingly at Smith. "Him, too, you might say. You doing anything?"

"What do you want?" asked Noat.

"Let's take a ride."

Noat, too, glanced at Smith, but not with insult. "Sure," he said. "Go on out to the car. Be with you soon's I . . . got something to finish."

Gorwing glanced inimically at Smith again. "Don't waste no time, now," he said, and slung out.

Smith made a relieved and disgusted sighing sound like *zhe-e-e-e!* and shrugged like shuddering. Noat came around the counter and stood close, as if his proximity could add a special urgency to what he had to say. "Mister Smith, you want to see your wife again? You want her to come back?"

"I told you—"

"I believe you, especially now. Some other time we'll talk about it all you want. Now if you want to get her back, you go with Gorwing, hear? You drive him where he wants to go."

"*Me?* Not on your life! I want no part of it, and I bet neither does he."

"You just tell him, it's with you or not at all; you tell him I said so."

"Look, I think—"

"Please, Mister Smith, don't think; not now—there isn't time. Just get out there."

"This is the craziest thing I ever heard of."

"You're absolutely right." Noat physically turned Smith around and faced him to the door. Outside, a horn blared. The sound seemed to loop and lock lassolike round the confused and upset Smith. He allowed it to pull him outside. He might then have been frightened if he had been given a chance to think, but Gorwing roared at him: "Where's G-Note?"

"You come in my car or not at all," Smith parrotted, his voice far more harsh than he had intended. He then marched to his car, got in and started the motor.

Livid, Gorwing sprang out of the other car. "G-Note!" he bawled at the unresponsive store front, then cursed and ran to Smith's car and slammed inside.

"Whose stupid idea was this?" he snarled.

White and shaken, but, feeling that in some way he had already tipped over the lip of some long slide, Smith said, "Not mine. You going some place?"

Gorwing hunched back against the door, as far from Smith as he could get. "You know the Thruway exit southbound?"

"All right."

He turned out into the street and right at the main avenue. Once or twice he glanced at his passenger, the slick black hair, the fevered dark eyes, the lips ever curled back from the too-sharp, too-white

teeth. It was a tormented, dangerous kind of face, and the posture—
this had been true as he had seen Gorwing stand, walk, turn, sit—
was always one of imminent attack, like some small furious cornered
animal.

He knew a short cut just here, and was on it before he quite realized he had come so far. He swung the wheel abruptly and turned
into Midland Avenue, and from the corner of his eye, seemed to see
the feral silhouette of his passenger sink and disappear. Astonished,
he glanced at Gorwing, to find him bent almost double, his hands
clasping the back of his neck, his eyes screwed shut.

"You feel sick?" He applied the brakes.

Gorwing unlaced the fingers behind his neck and, without opening his eyes, freed a hand for some violent semaphore. "Just drive,"
came his strained, hissing whisper. Puzzled beyond bearing, Smith
drove. Was Gorwing in pain? Or—could this be it—was he hiding?
Who from? There was a football field and a high school on the left,
a row of houses—mostly nurses' residences for the nearby hospital—
on the right. No one seemed to be paying special attention to the car.

Two blocks further on Gorwing slowly sat up.

"You all right now?"

In a very, very quiet voice, a deathly, a deadly voice, Gorwing
spoke. He tipped the side of his mouth toward Smith as he spoke,
but stared straight ahead. He said, "Don't you ever drive me near
the hospital. Not ever."

Crazy as a coot, thought Smith. "Nobody told me."

"I'm telling you."

They came to the underpass and crossed beneath the Thruway,
and Gorwing came out of himself enough to lean forward and scan
the road and the sides of the road, ahead. Suddenly he pointed.
"There he is. Pull over there."

Smith saw a young man in a grimy flannel suit and a white sport
shirt, standing on the grassy shoulder just by the Thruway exit. There
was a suitcase with a broken clasp on the grass by his feet. Smith
pulled off the pavement and stopped.

The man picked up his suitcase and came toward them, trying
to smile. "Give us a lift into town?"

Gorwing's tongue darted out to wet his lips, and his eyes seemed to grow even brighter. He waited until the man was abreast of the car, was even elevating his suitcase to let it precede him into the back seat, then sprang out and, chest arched, eyes flaming, blocked the man. "Lift hell," he snarled, "this town wouldn't give a cup o' water to the likes of you. Don't you set foot in it. We don't wancha."

The stranger slitted his eyes. "Now wait, Mac, you wait a minute here. Who the hell you think you are? You own this—"

"Git," said Gorwing, and his voice descended to something like the hissing, strained note that Smith had heard in the car. He mouthed his words—spittle ran suddenly from the corner of his mouth. As he spoke he walked, and as he walked the other man backed away. "You gawd ... damn ... junky ... you think you can come here and pick up a fix, well this place is cold turkey for you and you'd better be on your way out of it, never mind who I am, I killed a man once."

The man tried to shout him down, but Gorwing kept talking, kept crouching forward. "We're stayin' right here to see you walk up the pike or down the pike or hitch a ride, I don't care which way, an' don't think you c'n slide into town without my knowin', I got guys spotted all over town and your life ain't worth a bar o' soap if you so much as show your face let alone tryin' to find a pusher. There ain't no pusher an' if you meet another gawd damn hophead you c'n pass the word—" but it was pointless to go on; suitcase and all, the man had turned by then and fled. Gorwing put his thumbs in his belt and watched the hitchhiker, white-faced, scampering to the northbound lane. Then Gorwing sighed, and turned tiredly back to the car.

"What a blistering," breathed the thunderstruck Smith as Gorwing got in and fell back on the seat. "Who was that?"

"Never saw him before in my life," said Gorwing absently. With great tenderness he touched the back of his neck. He looked at Smith by rolling his fevered eyes, as if the neck were too tender to disturb. "I never killed a man," he said. "I just say that to scare 'em."

A thousand questions pressed on Smith's tongue, but he swallowed all but, "You want to go back now?"

"How's our li'l buddy doing?"

Smith peered down the ramp. Through the underpass, he could see the grimy-white of the hitchhiker's clothes. "He's still—no wait, I think he's got a lift."

Gorwing joined him in peering. They saw a green Dodge slow and stop, and the man climb in. "And good riddance," murmured Gorwing.

"I don't think he'll be back," said Smith, for something to say.

"He'll wish he didn't if he does," said Gorwing, so offhandedly that Smith knew the man, the episode, the whole subject was leaving Gorwing's mind; and in a way this was the most extraordinary part of this inexplicable episode, for Smith knew that he himself would never forget it. Gorwing said, "Drive."

Smith made a slightly illegal turn and got the car headed back toward town. When he saw the yellow and black HOSPITAL ENTRANCE—500 FEET sign, he turned left and went into a long detour. Gorwing sat abstractedly, and Smith was certain he had not noticed the special effort he was making, until they turned back again on to Midland Avenue, well past, and Gorwing said, "Hospitals, they give me the creeps."

"Me, too," said Smith, remembering a tonsillectomy when he was fourteen—his only contact with the healing arts in all his life. Gorwing laughed at him—a singularly unpleasant and mirthless laugh. Anything in Smith that was about to formulate conversation—maybe even a question out of his vast perplexity—dried up. Smith's petulant pink underlip protruded, and he drove without speaking until they pulled up in front of the Anything Shoppe. Smith had never been so glad to see anything in his life. He had had, as of now, exactly all he could take of this man.

He swung his door open but "Oh, hell," Gorwing said. He said it in the tones of a man who has conducted a theater party in from the suburbs and finds, under the marquee, that he has forgotten the tickets. In spite of himself, "What's the matter?" asked Smith.

"Shut up," said Gorwing. Suddenly he closed his eyes and said again, "Oh hell." Then he opened his eyes and snapped, "Get goin'. Quick."

Reflexively Smith shut the door, then demanded of himself *why?*

Argumentatively he asked, "Where do you want to go?"

"*Move,* will ya?" He waved vaguely toward Hook Mountain. "Up that way. I'll tell you."

"I don't see—"

Gorwing's words tumbled out so fast they were almost indistinguishable. "Dammit you want somebody should be dead it's your fault you didn't jump when I said jump now *drive!*"

The car was started and heading north before Smith was aware of it, so stunned was he by this hot spurt of language. When a man speaks like that, you want to throw your hands up over your face as if you had seen raging heat through sudden cracks in something you knew, too late, might explode.

A mile later Smith asked timidly, "What do you mean, dead?"

"Your place," Gorwing growled, directing, not responding.

They wheeled into the private road and up the hill. *Dead? My place?* Smith was terrified. "Listen—"

"You got any rope?" Gorwing snapped.

"Rope?" Smith repeated stupidly. He went into his own driveway in a power-slide; he hadn't known he could drive like that. "No, I haven't got any rope. What—"

"Oh, you wouldn't," spat Gorwing. "Chains. You got tire chains?"

"I don't—yes. In the trunk." He braked to a slithering stop in the turnaround. Gorwing was out of the car while it was still sliding, and tugging at the trunk lid. He roared to find it locked. Smith tumbled out with the keys and opened it. Gorwing flung him aside in his dive as he clawed through the trunk, throwing tire iron, jack pedestal, a can of hydraulic fluid behind him like a digging dog. The chains were in a cloth sack; he up-dumped the sack, shook out the chains, hooked the end of one into the end of the other, draped them over his shoulder and sprinted down toward the house.

"Wait, you—" gasped Smith, and trotted after him.

Gorwing passed the house and plunged across the lower lawn into the woods, Smith after him, already panting. "Hey, watch yourself, that's full of poison ivy back there!"

Gorwing was already out of sight in the rank woods below the house.

Stumbling, gasping, Smith floundered after him, until he came to the edge of the cliff that overlooked the broad Hudson. At this point it was sheer about a hundred feet, then slanted down and away in a mass of weed-grown rubble almost to the railroad tracks. For a moment he thought Gorwing must have plunged straight over the edge, but then he saw him working his way along the ragged brink to the right.

"Hang on! Hang on!" Gorwing yelled. Totally perplexed, Smith looked around him for whatever it was he was supposed to hang on to and failed to find it. He shrugged and stumbled after the man. Gorwing kept bellowing to hang on. Suddenly Smith saw him fall to his knees and crawl to the crumbling lip of the precipice. He yelled again, then moved on a couple of feet and hooked a free end of the tire chains to itself around the trunk of a foolhardy pine tree with a ten-inch bole, which grew bravely at the lip of disaster.

At last, Smith reached Gorwing, who had hunkered down with his back to the tree. He had described the man to himself before as "fevered"—he now looked sick as well; there was a difference. "What are you—"

Gorwing motioned toward the drop. "You'll have to do it. I can't stand high places."

"Do what?"

Gorwing pointed again. Smith heard a weak bleating sound that seemed to come from everywhere. But it was specifically outward that Gorwing had pointed. So he fell to his knees and crawled to the edge and looked over.

Eight or ten feet below him he saw the chalk-white, tear-streaked face of a thirteen- or fourteen-year-old boy. The child was hanging by his hands to a protruding root, which angled so sharply downward that it was clear no grip could last too long on it. The boy's toes were dug into loose earth, a fresh damp scar of which surrounded his feet and, widening, showed where to his left a ledge had fallen away. To his right was rock, almost sheer, and without a handhold.

"*Hang on!*" yelled Smith, at least half again as loud and urgently as Gorwing had. He caught up the end of the chain and lowered it carefully down. At its fullest extent it reached about to the boy's belt-line. Smith looked at Gorwing, who looked back out of sick black eyes. "You got to," he said in strained tones, "I tell you I can't. I just can't."

Smith, whose usual activities involved nothing more strenuous than stamp tongs, found himself on his stomach, hanging his legs over, hunting wildly with his toes for the rungs formed by the crosslinks of the tire chain. Then he was stepping down, while the earth and grass of the edge rose up and obscured Gorwing like some crazy inverted theater curtain. "Hang on," he said, and was startled when the boy answered, "Okay ..." because that remark had been for himself.

Tire chains may be roughly the size and shape of a small ladder, but they take unkindly to it. The rungs roll and their parts pinch, and the whole thing swings and bends alarmingly; *you* know they won't break, but do *they?* Too soon the next rung under his seeking foot just—wasn't, and he withdrew the foot from nothing-at-all and stood on the last crosslink, gulping air. He was then of a mind to freeze to his shaky perch and stay there until somebody else figured a way out, but there came a whimper nearby and he saw clods and stones spin sickeningly down and away from the boy's toes. He glanced at the boy's face, saw and would forever see the muddy pallor, the fear-bulged eye, the lips gone whiter than the tanned cheeks. The youngster's foothold was gone, and only his grip on the slanted root held him. Afterward, Smith was to reflect that, if the kid had been standing on anything solid, he would never in life have been able to figure out a way to bring him in; but now he *had* to, so he did.

"Lift your foot!" he screamed. "Give me your foot!"

The foot was already dangling, but for an endless, mindless moment the boy stretched downward with it, trying to make a toe-hold if he could not find one; then Smith screamed again, and the boy brought the foot up slowly, shakily ... and he said, "My hands, I can't ..." but then Smith had the foot, leaning far sidewise to get it; he lifted it, thrust it through the last "rung" down to the knee. One more reach, and he had the skinny upper arm in a grip that astonished both of them. "Let go," he panted, and the boy let go; it may well be that he could not have held on any longer to the root if he had wanted to. With the release, the chains swung nauseatingly sidewise; with one hand Smith ground steel into his own flesh, with the other drove flesh into the arm-bone; but he had the boy, now, thrust the arm through the next rung. "Hold with your arms, not your hands," he said through his teeth.

When they stopped swinging, Smith freed his hand from the boy's biceps. It took a concentrated effort, so clamped, so cramped, was his hysterical hand. "Now rest," he said to both, for both of them. The boy kept whimpering, a past-tears meaningless, habitual kind of sound, dry and probably unfelt. Some measureless time later he helped the boy get his other leg into the little twisted square of chain, so that he sat and whimpered, while Smith stood and panted, for however long it took to be able to think again. Then Smith had the boy stand up inside the circle of his arms, and climb until his buttocks were at the level of Smith's chest. Then they climbed together, Smith urging the boy to sit back on him when he had to, half-lifting him when they got the strength and the courage, each interminable time, to try another rung. And when at last the boy tumbled up and over and was, by Gorwing, snatched back from the edge, Smith had to stop achingly and wearily ponder out what had happened to the weight and presence of him, before he could go on.

Gorwing snatched him, too, away from the edge, where he lay laughing weakly.

"You," said Gorwing darkly, "you real gutsy."

"*Me?*"

"I coudn'. Not ever, I could never do that." He made a sudden vague gesture, startling in its aimlessness, a jolting contrast to his vulpine appearance and harsh voice. "I never had much guts."

Smith held his peace, as does one in the presence of evidence too great for immediate speculation. He thought of Gorwing standing up to him about the hundred-dollar fare, and of Gorwing ravening, tearing, lashing out at the hitchhiking dope addict. Yet there was no mistaking his sincerity in what he said—nor in this frank compliment to him, Smith—a man who had, up until now, stimulated only open disgust. He promised himself he would think about it later. He said to the boy, "How do you feel, kid?"

"Gee, all right." The boy shuddered. "Ain't going to do that again."

"What were you doing?"

"Aw. Bunch of Nyack kids, they bet nobody could climb the cliff. I didn't say nothing, but I thought I could, so I tried it."

Smith stood up, held gingerly to the tree trunk and peered over. "Where are they?"

"Oh gosh, I wouldn't try it when anyone's around. I just wanted to see if I could before I opened my trap about it."

"So no one knew you were there!"

The boy grinned shakily. "You did."

Gorwing and Smith shared a glance; to Smith it meant nothing, but Gorwing rose abruptly and barked, "Let's get out of here." Smith sensed his sudden desire to change the subject, just as he sensed the impact of the boy's refusal to change the subject: "Hey, how *did* you know I was there?"

Gorwing half turned; Smith thought he sensed that glance again, but when he tried to meet it it was gone. "Heard you yellin'," Gorwing said gruffly.

"I live right here," said Smith. It satisfied the boy completely, but for the very first time Smith saw Gorwing look astonished. Yes, and in a way pleased.

They stopped at his house for something cool to drink, and then got in the car to return to Nyack; the boy said he lived on Castle Heights Avenue. There was surprisingly little talk. Neither Gorwing nor Smith seemed to know how to talk to a thirteen-year-old—a rare talent, at best, rare even among thirteen-year-olds—yet what occupied Smith's mind could hardly be discussed in his presence.

Gorwing. This rough, mad, strange, unpredictable Gorwing ... you couldn't like him; and Smith knew he did not. Yet through him, with him, Smith had shared something new—new, yes, and rich. He had ... it was as if he had had a friend for a moment there, working so dangerously together ... and the work was for someone else; that had something to do with it ...

Friend ... Smith knew many people, and he had no enemies, and so he had thought he had had friends; but for a moment now he got a glimpse of the uncomfortable fact that he had no friends. Never had. Even ... even Eloise. Husband and wife they were, lovers they had been—hadn't they?—but could he honestly say that he and Eloise had ever been friends?

He sank for a moment into a viscous caldron of scalding loneliness. *Eloise* ...

"Hey." Gorwing's harsh note crashed into his reverie. "How we get this young feller to keep his mouth shut?"

"Me?" said the boy.

"You better keep your mouth shut, that's all," said Gorwing ominously.

Smith had no experience in talking to boys, but he could see this was the wrong tack. The kid was edging away from Gorwing, and his eyes were too wide. Smith said quickly, "He's right. I don't know your mother, sonny, but I'd say she'd be worried sick if you told her the story. Or maybe just mad."

"Yeah, maybe." He looked warmly at Smith, then timidly at Gorwing. "Yeah, I guess you're right.... Can't I tell *nobody?*"

"I'd as soon you didn't."

"Well, anything you say," said the boy. He swallowed and said again, "Anything ..." and then, "That's my house. The white one."

Smith stopped well away from the house. "Hop out, so no one sees you in the car. So long."

"So long." The boy walked away a slow pace, then turned back. "I don't even know your names."

"Delehanty," said Smith. And Gorwing said solemnly, "Me, too."

"Well," said the boy uneasily, "well, thanks, then," and moved toward the white house.

Smith backed into a nearby driveway and headed back toward the shop.

Gorwing said truculently, "How come you covered for me like that?"

"I had the idea you wanted it that way. Up on the cliff I got that idea."

"Yeah.... You know all the time what people want?"

"I don't think," said Smith slowly, with a frankness that stung his eyes, "I ever tried before."

They rolled along for what seemed a long, companionable moment. Then Smith added, "You don't always help people out for money, do you?"

Gorwing shrugged, rolled down his window, and spat. "Only when I can get it. Oh man, could I use some about now."

"This," said Smith bitterly, "is my taxicab this time."

"Oh, I wasn't asking you for nothing. You watch yourself, Smith. I'm no panhandler."

Smith drove self-consciously, carefully. He knew his face was pink, and he hated himself for it. He wondered if he could say anything to this madman without making him angry. Angrier. He asked, without malice, "What would you do with money?"

"Get drunk," said Gorwing, and immediately glanced at Smith's face. "Oh my God," he said disgustedly, "he believes me. I never drink anything . . . What would I do with money?" he mused. "'Pends how much. Now there's a couple, the old man is dying. I mean, he can't last, not much more. The woman, she stays by him ever minute, don't go out even to buy food. Somebody don't go to the store for 'em, throw 'em a couple skins now and then, they . . . oh, you wouldn't know."

No, Smith wouldn't know. He had never been in need . . . or in danger, before today. Turning into Midland Avenue, he glanced down a side street toward the river, where the wide-lawned pleasant houses gave way to the shabby-decent, the tenement, the shack. He had never done that before, not to *see* them. And then, the need you could see, starting with the shacks, was, when you came to think about it, surely not all the need there was; need comes in so many colors and kinds. He brought the thought back up to the crisp-tended, tree-shaded homes on the Avenue and wondered what it was like to live in this world instead of—of whatever it was he had been doing.

He stopped in front of the Anything Shoppe, and they got out. "Here," Smith said. He took out his wallet and found a twenty-dollar bill. He looked at Gorwing and suddenly took out the ten, too—all he had with him.

Gorwing did not thank him. He took the money and said, "Well, all right!" and marched off.

Smith was still wagging his head as he entered the shop.

"I know how you feel," said G-Note, grinning.

"What is he?"

G-Note grunted. "I never did really know, myself."

"I never thought I'd say this, but I sort of like him." Smith was feeling very warm inside about all this.

Oddly enough, the remark brought no smile this time. "I don't know if you can really *like* Gorwing," said Noat thoughtfully. "He sometimes ... but anyway, tell me what happened."

Smith related his afternoon. Noat nodded sagely. "Junkies," he nodded at one point. "He can't stand 'em. Runs 'em out of town every time."

At the end of his story, Smith told him about the money. "Is that on the level, Mr. Noat? Or will he just go on a toot?"

"No, it's on the level. If he keeps out any for himself, it'll be what he barely needs."

"Doesn't he have a job or something?"

Noat shook his big head. "No job. No home, not what you might call a place of his own. Moves around all the time, furnished rooms, back of the poolhall, here in the shop sometimes. I don't think he ever leaves town, though."

"Mr. Noat, how does he do it?"

Noat cocked his head on one side. "Didn't you ask him?"

Smith laughed weakly. "No." Then, with a sudden surge of candor, "Tell you the truth, I was afraid to."

"Tell you the truth, I'm afraid to, too," said Noat. "He ... well, between you and me, I think he thinks he's some sort of freak. Or, anyway, he's afraid people will think that. He never lets anybody get close to him. He always does what he can to hide how he does what he does. Usually by blowing up in your face."

"He must ... he seems to do a lot of good."

"Yes ..." There was a reservation in the ugly man's voice.

"Well, doggone it, what *is* it he does?"

"He, well, hears when somebody needs something, or maybe you might say smells it. I don't know. I don't know as I care much, except it works. Heck, you don't have to know how everything works—

by the time you did, you'd be too old to work it." He turned away, and Smith thought for a moment he had closed the subject, but he said, without turning around, "Only thing I'm sure of, he knows the difference between wanting something and needing it."

"Want . . . you asked me that!"

"I did. I asked Gorwing, too, although maybe you don't remember."

"Eloise . . . you mean he'd know whether I—need her, or just want her? Him?"

Noat chuckled. "Feels like a sort of invasion of privacy, doesn't it? It is and it isn't . . . what he knows, however he knows it, it isn't like anyone else knowing it. That Gorwing . . . but he does a lot of good, you know."

"I don't doubt it."

"Calla Pincus, she thinks he's some sort of saint."

"Who's she?"

"Girl he—well, she was going to kill herself one time, and he stopped her. She'd do anything for him. So would the Blinker—he's kind of a poolhall rat—and there's old Sarge, that's a track walker for the West Side Line . . . I mean, he has sort of a raggle-taggle army, all through the town, that've learned to ask no questions and jump to do what he says. Sometimes for pay. And Doc Tramble, and one of the teachers at the high school and . . . and me, I guess—"

"And me."

Noat laughed. "So welcome to the fold."

"All these years in this town," Smith marveled, "and I never guessed this was going on. Mr. Noat . . . does he know where my wife is?"

"Did you ask him?"

Smith shook his head. "Somehow I . . . I was afraid to ask him that, too."

"You better. You need her—you know that and I do and he does. I think you should ask him . . . Now can I ask you something?"

"Oh, sure."

"You never went to the police or anything. How come?"

Smith looked down at his hands and closed them, then his eyes.

He said in a low voice, "I guess because . . . You know, she said to me, whatever had happened, she still wanted me to be happy. I imagine I wanted the same thing for her. It was something she had to do; I didn't think I should stop her."

"But you're looking now."

"Not with police."

"Hey, he's coming. Ask him. Go ahead—ask him."

Smith turned eagerly to the door as Gorwing banged in. "Hi!" He felt warm, friendly—pleasurably scared—anticipatory. Gorwing utterly ignored him.

Noat frowned briefly and said, "Hey boy. Smitty there, he's got something to ask you."

"He has?" Gorwing did not even look around.

Smith hesitated, then caught Noat's encouraging nod.

Timidly, he asked, "Mr. Gorwing . . . do you know where my wife is?"

Gorwing flicked him with a black glance and showed his white teeth. "Sure." Then he turned his full cruel smile on Smith and said, "She don't need you."

Smith blinked as if something had flashed before his eyes. His mouth was dry inside, and outside shivery. He wanted to say something but could not.

Noat growled, "That ain't what he asked you, Gorwing. He says do you know where she is."

"Oh sure," said Gorwing easily, and grinned again. "She got a cold-water walk-up over on High Avenue, 'long with the guy she's livin' with."

Smith had never in his life physically attacked anyone, but now he grunted, just as if he had been kicked in the stomach, and rushed Gorwing. He struck out, a wild, round, unpracticed blow, but loaded with hysteria and hate. It never reached Gorwing, but planted itself instead in the region of Noat's left shoulder blade, for Noat, moving with unbelievable speed for so large a man, had vaulted the counter and come between them. He came, obviously, not to protect anyone, but to launch his own attack. "You lousy little rat, you didn't have to do that. Now you get out of here," he rumbled, as with one hand he opened the door and with the other literally threw Gorwing outside. Gorwing tried to keep his balance but could not; he fell heavily, rolled, got up. His face was so white his black hair looked almost blue; still he grinned. Then he was gone.

Noat closed the door and came to Smith. "So now you know."

"El-Eloise is ..." and he began to cough.

"Oh, not that! I mean, now you know about Gorwing. How can you figure it? All he does is take care of what people need ... and there's no kindness in him."

"Eloise is—"

"Your wife is taking care of an old sick man who'll be dead any time now."

"Who?" Smith cried, agonized. "*What* old man?"

"That you just gave the money for."

"I've got to find her," whispered Smith, and then heard what Noat had said. "You mean—*that* old man? Wh-why, he told me it was an old *couple!*"

"I bet he didn't."

"You! *You* know where she is! You knew all the time."

Noat spread his hands unhappily. "You never asked me."

Smith's scorn made him appear a sudden four inches taller. "Quit playing games!"

"Okay ... okay." The big man looked completely miserable. "I just didn't want to hurt you, that's all." At Smith's sharp look, he said "Honest. Honest ... Gorwing, he's right, you know. She doesn't need you. I wish you didn't make me tell you that. I'm sorry." He went back behind the counter, as if he could comfort himself with the tools, the clutter back there.

"You better tell me the whole thing," whispered Smith.

"Well ... she, Mrs. Smith I mean, she came to me that day. She was all ... mixed up. I don't think she meant to spill anything, but she sort of ... couldn't hold it." He put up a swift hand when Smith would have interrupted. "Wait, I'm telling this all wrong. What I'm trying to say, she came here because she just didn't know where else to go to. She said something about 'Anything Shoppe'; she wanted to know if 'anything' meant ... *anything*. She said she had to have a job, something to do. She said never mind the money, just enough to scrape along, but something to *do;* that's what she needed."

"What she needed."

"I know what you're thinking. Yeah, Gorwing knew she needed something, and just what it was, too ... y'see," he said earnestly, "he's always right. Even the lousy things he does sometimes, they're always right. Or at least ... there's always a reason." He stopped, as if to ponder it out for himself.

"Look," said Smith, suddenly, painfully kneading his cheeks, "whatever it is you have to tell me, tell me. I'm all mixed up ... and ... and *where is she?*" Then he opened his blue eyes very wide—oddly like those of the boy he had saved on the cliff, when Gorwing had frightened him—and said piteously, "You mean she really doesn't need me? Gorwing was right?"

G-Note crouched over, elbows on the counter, his big hands holding each other in front of him.

He said, "What she needed, what she needed more than anything in the world, she needed something to take care of. You—well, she tried to take care of you, but—Don't you see what I mean?"

There was silence for a long time. Smith felt that somehow, if he could pull together the churned-up pieces of his mind, he might be able to turn it to this, make some sense out of it. He tried very hard, and at last was able to say, "You mean, when you come right down to it, there ... was never very much for her to do for me."

"Oh, you got it. You got it. You ... well, she told me some things. She cried, I guess she didn't mean to say anything, but I guess—she just had to. She said you could cook better'n she could."

"What?"

"Well, things you liked to eat, you could. And those were all the things you ever wanted. She took care of the house, but you'd 'a done just the same things if she wasn't there. She never felt she really *had* to ..."

"But this old man—who's *he?*"

"One of Gorwing's ... you know. Gorwing found him down by the tracks. Sick, wore out. Needing somebody to take care of him—*needing* it, you see? Not for long ... Doc Tramble, he says he don't know how the old fellow hung on this long."

"God," said Smith, stinging with chagrin, "is that what she needed? Maybe I should be dying—she'd be happy with me then."

"Ah, knock that off. She's only like most people, she has to make a difference to somebody. She makes a difference to that old man, and she knows it."

"She made a difference to me," whispered Smith, and then something lit up inside him. He stared at Noat. "But she never knew it." Suddenly he leaped to his feet, walked up, walked back, sat again bolt upright, holding himself as if he were full of coiled springs. "What's the matter with me? You know what I did, I said she had somebody with her while I was at the Elks' that night, you know, the night you picked me up in the car. That's why she left." He hit himself on the forehead with sharp knuckles. "I know she didn't have anyone, she wouldn't! So what made me think of it? why all of a sudden did I have to think of it, and even when I knew I was wrong, why did I have to go for her, curse at her, call her names the way I did, till she had to leave ... why?" he shouted.

"You really want me to tell you?" Then Noat looked away from Smith's frantic, twisted face and shook his head. "I don't *know*," he said carefully, "I only know what I think. I don't know everything ... I don't know you very much. All right?"

"Yes, I understand that. Go ahead."

"Well, then." Noat watched his big brown hands press and slide on the counter until they squeaked, as if they had ideas under them and could express the words by squeezing. He raised them and looked under them and folded them and looked at Smith. "You hear a lot of glop," he said carefully, "about infantile this and adult that, and acting like a grownup. I've thought a lot about that. Like how you've got to be adult about this or that arrangement with people or the world or your work or something. Like they'd say you never had an adult relationship with the missus. Don't get mad! I don't mean— well, hell, how adult is two rabbits? I don't mean the sex thing." He opened his hands to look for more words, and folded them again. "Most people got the wrong idea about this 'adult' business, this 'grownup' thing they talk about but don't think about. What I'm trying to say, if a thing is alive, it changes all the time. Every single second it changes; it grows or rots or gets bigger or grows hair in its armpits or puts out buds or sheds its skin or something, but when a thing is living, it changes." He looked at Smith, and Smith nodded. He went on:

"What I think about you, I think somewhere along the line you forgot about that, that you had to go on changing. Like when you're little, you keep getting bigger all the time, you get promoted in school; you change; good. But then you get out, you find your spot, you got your house, your wife, your kind of work, then there's nothing around you any more says you have to change. No class to get promoted to. No pants grown too small. You think you can stop now, not change any more." Noat shook his craggy head. "Nothing alive will stand for that, Smitty."

"Well, but why did I think she ... why did I say that about— some man with her, all that?"

Noat shrugged. "I don't know all about you," he said again. "Just sort of guessing, but suppose you'd stopped, you know, *living*. Something's going to kick up about that. It don't have to make a lot of sense; just kick up. Get mad about something. Your wife with some man—now, that's not nice, that's not even true, but it's a *living* kind of thing, you see what I mean? I mean, things change around the house then—but good; altogether; right *now.*"

"My God," Smith breathed.

" 'Course," said Noat, "sooner or later you have to get over it, face things as they really are. Or as they really ain't." He thought again for a time, then said, "Take a tree, starts from a seed, gets to be a stalk, a sapling, on up till it's a hundred feet tall and nine feet through the trunk; it's still growing and changing until one fine day it gets its growth; it's grown up: it's—dead. So the whole thing I'm saying is, this adult relationship stuff they talk about, it's not that at all. It's *growing* up that matters, not *grown*up.... Man can get along alone for quite a long time 'grownup'—taking care of himself. But if he takes in anyone else, he's ... well, he's got to have a piece missing that the other person supplies all the time. He's got to need that, and he's got to have something that's missing in the other person that they need. So then the two of them, they're one thing now ... and still it's got to be like a living thing, it's got to change and grow and be alive. Nothing alive will stand for being stopped. So ... excuse me for butting in, but you thought you could stop it and it blew up on you."

Smith stared silently at the big man, then nodded. "I see. But now what?"

"You want to know where she is?"

"Sure. By the Lord, now I can ..."

"What's the matter?"

Smith looked at him, stricken. "Gorwing said ... she didn't need me."

"Gorwing!" snarled Noat. Then he scratched his head. "I see what he meant. She never could take care of you much, and she awful much needs to take care of somebody. Now she's got the old feller. He needs her, God knows. For a little while yet ... Gorwing ... hey! Why d'ye suppose he tried to make you think—you know—about your wife?"

"You know him better than I do."

"It comes to me," said Noat, inwardly amazed. "I see it. I see it. He makes it his business to take care of what people really need, need real bad. Right? Good. How do you do that?"

"Get 'em what they need, I guess."

"That's one way. Two—" he held up fingers—"you get 'em out of range. Like he does with dope addicts. Right? Then—three. You fix it so they just don't feel they need it any more. I mean, if he was to fix it that you got so mad at your wife you wouldn't want ever to see her again—see?"

"That poor little man! He couldn't do that."

"He just tried. He has a gift, Smitty, but that don't mean he's bright."

"It doesn't?" said Smith in tones of revelation. "It's bright enough. I need her—that's one big need, correct? Now, suppose I go find her, take her away from that poor old man. He starts needing her—and she starts needing to take care of somebody again. So—two big needs. That Gorwing, he knows what he's doing. I—I can't do that, Mr. Noat."

"You mean, to the old man?"

"Well, yes, that. But her ... my wife. I need her. You know that, and I do."

"And Gorwing does."

"Yeah, but she doesn't. God, what do I have to do? Do I really have to be dying?"

"Living," said George Noat.

You're a freak.

Sometimes for days at a time he could content himself with the thought that all the rest of them were freaks. Or that, after all, what does anyone do? When it gets cold, they try to get warm. When they get hungry, they go find something to eat. What people feel, whatever's crowding them, they get out from under the best way they can, right? They duck it or move it or blast it out of the way, or use it on something else that might be bothering them, right? And what bothers people is different, one from the other. Hunger can get to them all and cold and things like that; but look, one wants some music, some special kind of music, more than anything else in life, more than a woman or a drink, while another needs heroin and another to have a roomful of people clapping their hands at him. Or needing, needing like life-and-death, some stupid little thing that would mean nothing to anyone else—something as little as a couple of words, like that Calla girl, about to jump off the Tappan Zee Bridge for wanting somebody to come up to her and say, "Hey, I need you to do something nobody else can do." Or needing to feel safe from some something that lurks inside them, like the Blinker: you'd never guess it to watch him cuss and laugh and make the pass, and chalk the cue, just like anybody, but he was epileptic and he never knew when it was going to hit him. Or needing defense against things lurking outside of them, like Miss Guelph at the high school, crazy afraid of feathers, terrified one might touch her. So the things people need and the things they need to be safe from, they're all kinds of things: it doesn't make one of them a freak if his special need is a little different.

What if you never heard of anyone with a need just like yours?

Does that automatically make you a freak? ... There are lots of people who have to make it alone, who can't share what they have with
anyone. Who can't drive a car for fear that faint-making, aching
cloud will suck them down into it when they don't expect it.

Sometimes, too, you can get to believe that the very thing that's
wrong with you makes you special. Well, it does, too. You have
power over people. Now just how many people in this—or any—
town could tell you a little kid two blocks away was lost, and a
woman three blocks the other way was looking for him? Or look at
the way you found that boy on the cliff—now that boy would be
dead right now.

So if you're so special how come old Noat throws you out on
your ear?

You're a freak.

Now cut it out. You got it made. You got a nice spot. The town's
just big enough so nobody much notices you, just small enough so
when that faintness comes, and that ache, and then the picture in
your head—of a traffic light or a building front or a green fence or
a cliffside—you know just where to go to find the person who has
that big noisy need for something. Remember that trip down to Fort
Lee? So big, so noisy; God, you almost went out of your head. Plank
you down in the middle of New York, say, you'd be dead in a second, all that racket. And the things they need, you'd never know
where to get them in a big place, but here, heck, you know where
to find anything if it's in town. Or old Noat will get it for you.

What he want to throw you out like that for? Just trying to shut
off the shrieking lonesomeness of that squirt Smith; him and his
Eloise, it gave him a headache.

Ow. Here comes one now. Shut your eyes. Ow, my neck. Shut
your eyes tight, now. See ... see a ... see a street, store-front, green
eaves over the window. Felt carpet slippers, a man's belt. That would
be Harry Schein's Haberdashery on Washington Street. Somebody
standing there, needs—what? Sleep, wants to sleep, for God's sake,
gets wide awake soon as hits the sack ... a man. Screaming for sleep,
frantic for sleep. Get some sleeping pills, everything closed now. Hey,
this could be worth a buck. Go call Doc Tramble. Here, phone in

the gas station. NY 7 ... 0 ... 0 ... 5 ...

"Doc? Gorwing here. Got some sleeping pills in your bag? Oh, nothing serious ... yes, I know what's dangerous and what ain't. No, not for me. Oh, five, I guess. I'll send the Blinker or somebody around for 'em, okay?"

Ow. Guy walking toward Broad Street now. Oh boy does he want some sleep. Where's dime ... here. Call poolroom ... 4 ... 7 ... "Hi—Danny? Gorwing. Hey, the Blinker there? Hell ... Who else is around? No ... Nuh, not her. Smith? What Smith—you mean that guy's been hanging around G-Note's? Yeah, put him on."

"Hello—Smitty? Thought you'd be mad. You wouldn't want to do a little job ... you would? Well you'll have to scramble. Get over to Doc Tramble's and say you want the pills for me. Yeah. Then take 'em over to Fordson Alley and North Broad—you know, right by the movie—there's a guy there frantic for 'em. See if you can get a dollar apiece. Sleeping tablets. Yeah. Hurry now ... He's moving, he's ambling up past the movie. I don't know what he looks like. Just look for a guy looks like he needs some sleep. Hurry now. See ya."

Now that's a surprise. I thought I'd botched it up with that Smith but for good. A good boy. Calmed down, too. Wonder if he's going to pull that wife of his away from the old man. Hope not. Set up a hell of a rattle, the two of 'em at once.

So Gorwing ambled through the evening, through the town. He walked in a cloud of, or in a murmur of, or under the pressure of, or through the resistance of the not-mist, not-sound, not-weight, not-fluid presence of human need. Want was there, too, but want of that kind—two teen-agers yearning for a front-drive imported car in a show window, a drowsy child remembering a huge bride-doll in Woolworth's, the susurrus of desire that whispered up in the wake of a white-clad blonde who, with her boy-friend, walked through the lights of the theater marquee—this kind of want was simply there to be noticed if he cared to notice it. But the need ... he watched for it fearfully, yet eagerly—for sometimes it paid off. He hoped that for a while nobody would get hit by a car without getting killed outright, or that some hophead wouldn't suddenly appear with that rasping, edgy scream of demand. Ow. Wish Smitty would get to that guy with the sleeping pills.

Need was a noise to Gorwing. No, not really a noise. Need was an acid cloud, a swirling blindness. Need might mount up out of the nighttime village and make him faint. Need might pay off. Need, other people's need, hurt Gorwing . . . but then each person had one or another difference, one or another talent; this one bad perfect pitch and that one had diabetes, and he wasn't, after all, so different from other people.

You're a freak.

Strangely, it was not too easy to be funereal at this funeral. The flowers were sad, of course, such a scrappy little bunch, and the man was saying all the right things . . . and it was sad how easily the men handled the coffin; poor little old man, so wasted away. But you couldn't feel badly about him now; he'd been glad to go, and it was good that he'd had, for those last weeks, just what he'd yearned for for so many sick lonesome years—someone who sat near and brought him things and listened to him ramble on about all the old places and the friends and family who were passed on, dead and gone and yet waiting eagerly for him, some place. No, it wasn't any tragedy. Sweetly sad, that was it . . . and oh, such a bright beautiful day!

Eloise Smith hadn't been out in the fresh air, the sunshine, since . . . "Eeek!"

It was a small scream, or rather squeak, and really no one noticed. But Jody, oh Jody was standing right next to her in a dark suit, with his hat—the one they called his Other hat—held over his heart, his head bowed. He looked . . . peaceful.

She bowed her head, too, and they stood quite close together until the man finished saying the old simple words, and the handful of earth went *tsk!*—a polite expression of sympathy—on the coffin lid. Then it was over. *"Bye, you old dear,"* she said silently but with her heart full.

Then there was Jody. "Oh, Jody. I don't think I—"

"Shh. Eloise, come home. I need you."

"Jody, you're going to make me sound mean, and I don't want to be mean. But you don't need me or anybody, Jody."

Smith moistened his lips, but loosened no special, just-right winning words; he said, could say, only: "I need you. Come home."

"Wait—there's Mr. Gorwing ... Wait, Jody; I have to speak to him. Will you wait over there, Jody? Please?"

"Let me stay with you."

"Honey," she said, the wifely word slipping out before she realized it, "he's sometimes sort of ... funny. Unpredictable. I wish you'd wait over there and let me talk to—"

"He won't mind. We're old friends."

"You know Mr. Gorwing?"

"Sure."

"Oh dear. I didn't know. He ... he's a kind of saint, you know." When Smith, coolly regarding Gorwing, who was talking to the funeral director, did not answer, she went on nervously—she had to talk, *had* to, oh *why* had he turned up like this, all unexpectedly? "If anyone's in need at all, he has a way of finding it out; he—"

"I'm in need," said Smith. "I need you."

"Jody, *don't*."

"I do, he said softly, earnestly. "You've got to come back. I can't manage without you."

"Oh, that's silly! You have your—"

"I have my nothing, Ellie. I—I gave the money away, almost all of it. I got a job, but I'm only beginning, and the pay isn't much. I'm running a wood lathe in the cabinetmaker's."

"You—*what?*"

"You've got to help; maybe you'll even have to go to work. Would you, if there's no other way? I can't make it without you, Ellie."

What she was going to say through those soft trembling lips he would not know, for Gorwing interrupted. "Miz Smith—you know who he is?"

She flashed a look at her husband and really blushed. Gorwing laughed that wolf's laugh, that barking expression of mirth and hurt, and said, "I'll tell you who he is. He's the only person in the whole world who ever came up to me and asked *me* what *I* needed." He clapped Smith on the shoulder, waved a casual hand at Eloise and walked away toward the cemetery gate. She called him once; he waved his hand but did not turn his face toward them.

"We'll see him again," said Smith. "Ellie ... will you just let me tell you what this is all about?"

"What *is* it all about?"

"Can I tell you all of it?"

"Oh, very well ..."

"It'll take about twenty-three years. Oh Eloise—come home."

"Oh, Jody ..."

The shy man crouched in the hospital stairwell and peered through the crack of the barely-opened door. There were no white-coated figures in the corridor that he could see. He had long ago abandoned the front way, the elevator and all. Slipping in through the fire doors during visiting hours was much better. He pushed the door open far enough to let him into the corridor, and let it swing silently closed.

He gasped.

"Hello, Johnny."

Right behind the door as he opened it, oh God, the doctor. Johnny bit his tongue and stared up into Doc Tramble's face. It blurred.

"Hey now, hold on," said the doctor. "You better come in here and sit down." He took Johnny's forearm—and for a split second they were both acutely aware of Johnny's tearing temptation to snatch it away and run; and of its crushed quelling—and led him across the corridor into an empty private room, where he lowered the sweating visitor into an easy chair. Dr. Tramble pulled up a straight chair and sat close enough to force Johnny's gaze up and into his own.

"I don't know if you can take this, Johnny, all at once, but you're going to have to try."

"I got a second job, nights," said Johnny hollowly. "With that I can catch up some on the bills. Don't put my wife on the charity list, doctor. She couldn't stand it. She—"

"Now you just listen to me, young fella." He reached into the wall, got a paper cup from a dispenser and filled it from the ice-water jet. With his other hand he reached into his side pocket and took out a folded paper, which he planked down on Johnny's knee. "The bill. I want you to look at it."

Painfully, Johnny unfolded it and looked. His jaw dropped. "So much . . ." Then his eyes picked up an additional detail on the paper. "P-p-paid?" he whispered.

"In full," said Dr. Tremble. "That's point one. Point two, Madge gets her operation. MacKinney from the Medical Center got interested in the case. He's going to do it next week. Point three—"

"Her operation . . ."

"Point three," laughed the doctor, "she gets that room to herself now, all paid up, and you have the privilege of telling that to her snide roommate. Point four, here is a check made out to you for five hundred. Drink this," and he pushed the water at him.

Johnny sipped, and over the cup said, "B-but wh-where . . ."

"Let's keep it simple and say it's a special fund for interesting cases from the Medical Center, and you know these endowed institutes—all this money is interest and there's nobody to thank so shut up and get out of here. No—not to see Madge! Not yet. You go down to the office and they'll cash that check for you. Then you grab a taxi and voom down the street and buy flowers and a radio and a big box of dusting powder and a fancy bed jacket. Git!"

Numbly, Johnny walked to the door. Once there, he turned to the doctor, opened his mouth, shook his head, closed his mouth and without a word went for the elevators.

Laughing, the doctor went down the corridor to the telephone booth, dropped a coin, dialed the poolroom.

"Gorwing there?"

"Speaking."

"Tramble. All set."

"Yeah, doc, I know. I know. Oh God, Doc, it's so *quiet* in this town . . ."

How to Kill Aunty

"Little devil," said the old lady admiringly, which was odd, because she detested squirrels, especially when they were after the birdseed and suet set out on the feeder. Birds make a great deal of difference to the bedridden. Yet, "Oh, but you have got a brain in your head," she murmured, for the squirrel, after two futile attempts to climb out to the feeder, was making for the slender branches directly above it.

Squirrels she detested, and unpunctuality, physical sloppiness, rice pudding, greed, advertising (especially TV commercials, of which she saw a great many), dull-wittedness and Hubert. Hubert, her nephew, was not a dish of rice pudding nor a squirrel, but he embodied everything else on the list.

Partly.

Maybe that was it, she thought, admiring the detestable squirrel. Right down the line, from how Hubert looked to what he did (he was an assistant producer—that is, general factotum, bottlewasher, squeezer of shaving cream onto whipped-cream desserts, source of yes-sirs for all the business and all the talent—for a TV commercial packager) Hubert was what she detested—partly. Even mostly. But in no case altogether.

That squirrel now, she thought, leaning out, reaching up over the bed for the brass handle which swung there; that squirrel is all squirrel, the pretty little, speedy little criminal. Letting her weight come on the handle, she reached for the loop of quarter-inch rope which hung from a brass fairlead sunk into the window frame. Holding it carefully, she worked her way back to the center of the bed, let go the brass handle, and sat alertly watching the scene outside. At the very instant the admirable, damnable squirrel dropped from the tree-branches toward the feeding deck, the old lady pulled on the cord, and the feeder, sliding up its guy wires, moved out from under the animal, which snatched vainly at it, then hurtled down spraddle-legged to the lawn. It bounced like a rubber toy, then scampered angrily away, its tail drawing exact trajectories of each long bound.

A little out of breath, the old lady swore cheerfully at it and released the rope, so that the feeder slid back to its resting place among the outer shoots of the birch tree. Like certain other devices around the place, the feeder was her deft idea and Hubert's ham-handed workmanship. There again, she reflected. He wasn't alto-gether three-thumbed. He *could* turn out a job of work. But he got things right only by trying every wrong way first. She shuddered at the memory of the weeks of bully-ragging she'd put him through to get it done. Anyway, it worked, and could be drawn up to her win-dow every morning to be filled.

She glanced at the clock and put her hand under her pillow for the remote control switch of the television. She saw a lot of televi-sion, and, unabashedly, she enjoyed it. Especially now. She enjoyed this particular television set even when it wasn't turned on. Hubert was trying to kill her with this television set, and she was knocking herself out trying to help him.

This was a totally different project from any birdfeeder. That had been done by nag and prod. The TV operation was far more subtle; suggestion, planned convenience, and an imitated stupidity on her part which Hubert was too stupid to know was imitated. And yet—she'd reluctantly admit—there was a certain doggedness about Hubert, this time. Of all the "almost'" things he was, about this one thing he really seemed willing to plug along until he got what he wanted.

He had first tried to kill her—oh, a long time ago, now. It was because of Susie Karina. Well, perhaps there were other things, going back years, but Susie brought it to a head. Susie was a housemaid, and like a fool the old lady had let her live in, never dreaming that Hubert would make a fool of himself over any woman, but if he did, it wouldn't be Susie. Well, she'd been wrong about that. The old lady was never wrong about money or pulleys or birds or bonds or timing-gears, but in the course of her long and lively life, so filled with things to do to keep herself to herself—every dime she had, she had earned—she had bypassed the intricacies of this Thing that seems to be going on between men and women all the time. It was the one area where she could guess wrong, and she certainly did this time. Susie was a small, downcast, black-banged little thing with bite-able lips and a heart full of greed. The old lady was not quite as wrong about Hubert—ordinarily he wouldn't have dared to raise his hat to a doxie on a desert island, so certain was he of his unfailing unattractiveness to women—but neither he nor his aunt reckoned on Susie's barbarous ability to slide out of the camouflage and light fires with damp fuel. Score a man for his technique with women and you've drawn the height of his defenses, give or take a little; so a man like Hubert, whose total experience had been a game of post office when he was ten (by unanimous vote the girls sent him to the dead-letter room) was about as hard to get to as the bottom of a ski slope from halfway down.

It had actually gone on for months, right in her house, right under her nose. Not only was the girl quiet and, at her specialty, clever, not only was the old lady tuned to other wavelengths; Hubert was so benumbed by the experience that even this intimate aunt could not tell his change from the norm. He did not begin to stay out nights, nor sit and moon any more there his usual great deal, and there were no financial flurries at all—Susie coldly set her sights higher than her hat, even a new one.

The old lady, of course, did not know this, even after the silent discovery and quiet excision of the menace. It was quite by accident that she glanced down the stairwell at half-past two one morning and. saw her nephew emerging from, of all places, the dining room, of all things blowing kisses into it. The old lady slipped back into the shadows and had ample opportunity to watch Hubert ascend, grinning fatuously and carrying not only his shoes but his underwear. He passed the thunderstruck watcher all unknowing and entered his room and shut the door, whereupon his aunt, a spry old girl and very fast on her feet, dusted down the stairs like a windblown oatstraw and appeared in the dining-room door.

Four wide solid ancient chairs were placed side by side on the heavy rug, and at the near end of the row hung a dark blouse and a

white brassiere. At the far end, for one brief second full of shock
and scorching hate, stood Susie Karina, clad in the skirt which
matched the blouse. The faint glow from the tiny night light in the
hall was enough to photograph the scene for both of them forever;
then Susie melted backwards into the black shadows and disappeared. Without hesitation the aunt followed—it was the butler's
pantry—and shot the heavy bolt on the dining-room side. She then
stepped round to the kitchen and locked the other pantry door. Not
a word was spoken; save for the snicking of the bolts, there was no
sound.

The aunt made the rounds downstairs, being sure that everything
was locked up tight—except for the pantry window, which opened
easily into the wide wide world—and then, taking the garments from
the dining room between thumb and forefinger and holding them
not quite at arm's length, she took them to the maid's quarters where
she briskly and neatly packed all of the girl's possessions. She secured,
from the wall safe, two weeks' wages, added that to the luggage,
and strapped it up. She took it to the kitchen, unlocked the back
door, set the two suitcases upon and between the garbage cans, went
inside, locked up and went to bed.

She did not know women, but she did know Hubert, and she
knew Susie knew Hubert, and that Hubert's reaction to any scene,
any emergency, would be blindly to do as he was told, and not by
Susie. How long it took Susie to ponder this out she was never to
know, but that Susie got the message was clear the next morning
when the aunt looked out and saw the luggage gone.

Hubert still healthily slept. The aunt prepared breakfast and them
called him commandingly. When, yawning and yapping, he entered
the dining room, she said, "Put the chairs back, Hubert." Hubert
looked once into the kitchen, once at the spectacle of his aunt carrying a tray, and then the blood drained from his face. He put the
chairs back. He sat on one. He ate his breakfast.

Actually the only thing that was ever said directly about the
episode was said two nights later, when, after dinner, he rose casually and sauntered, with all the skilled histrionics of a spear-bearer
on the first night of a high-school play, out to the hall tree where his

hat hung. His aunt then spoke: "A private detective will follow you wherever you go. He reports to Mr. Silverstein." Now it happened that Mr. Silverstein, who was the lawyer who changed bequests in wills and all that, was also the silent and controlling partner in the advertising agency in which Hubert had just then begun.

Hubert paused. His wage was small and his address excellent. His expenses were almost nothing and his comfort considerable. His ability to provide these things—or anything at all—for himself was negligible. He left his hat where it was and went upstairs without a word. In due course they retired for the night.

Now it must be said that up to this point the old lady's actions had most genuinely been motivated by concern for Hubert; he could certainly not pursue his career properly in a town this size in such company as Susie Karina, even if the arrangement were legitimized; he had too much going against him as it was. And she had no intention, then, of punishing him. In her odd way, she felt the stirrings of respect for him—not for his specific acts, the charm of which was lost on her, but for his extraordinary success in pulling wool over her sharp old eyes. For she was, to the bone, an admirer of virtuosity, for its own sweet sake. She admired the music, for example, of Fritz Kreisler, not for its music, but for its fingermanship. She admired the better circus jugglers for the same reason and to the same degree. She owned a piece of jade carved with some symbols which, had she tracked them down, would have led her to a truly remarkable history, but her only interest in it was that it consisted of eight filigree balls, one inside the other, all freed from the same stone; never mind what it represented, where it had been, by whom owned to whom it meant what; just look at that for a clever thing, now! So for this gleam of deftness in her lump of a nephew she was happy to forgive and forget—though she saw no reason to reward him for it. Or to replace what it had cost him.

Mrs. Carstairs, the new maid, certainly did not. She immediately took over Susie's place, space and responsibilities—a weary soul who wore an aura of such a nature that the less the distance from her, by the inverse square law, the more one felt one had been munching saltpeter. Mrs. Carstairs was there asleep—actually, it was only her second night in the house, when it happened.

Again it was in the earliest hours of the morning, and again the big house was illuminated only by the speck of light glowing in the imitation brazier in the hall.

The aunt woke in that sudden, silent fashion which marks alertness to a sound which had now ceased; an opening of the eyelids with a click, a throat-throbbing, instant eagerness to pursue the very last echo of something gone but vitally important. The old lady threw off the covers and rolled to a sitting position and, in spite of the hard difficult thump of her heart, held her breath.

She heard a low, happy, whispering laugh. She barely heard it. It was unvoiced, and came from somewhere indeterminate.

She rose to her feet, and again held her breath.

She heard that childish, effortful sound of someone emphasizing a kiss: mmmm-yuh!

She ran on tiptoe to her door, across from which was the head of the stairs, and stopped again to listen.

What moved her, what sent her moving, sprinting, springing to the stairs was nothing at all. But nothing, not a sound, not a breath. She could have borne anything else, but not this waiting for the next sigh, smack, chuckling tongue-cluck; not this wondering where, wondering who.... How? Mrs. Carstairs, did she know every lock, did ... or was it—and so she sprang.

And her first foot, the right foot, to step off the landing, flew out and up, dragging the other with it, and so she lay in the air. After that the observations, the memories they painted, were not so sharp. She was sure something dark and rectangular flew away, out and down, as she lay in the air, and curved to the steps below: then the cruel crash at the base of her spine and the small of her back (but no no no pain, horribly no pain!) and her elbows; and oh, that was the agony.

It was dark already; it did not grow dark for her; the dark grew black. But in the last clouded second before eclipse, she seemed to see a small someone dart from the dining room, scoop up the rectangular thing, a thing thicker than a briefcase, not as wide or long, and flick away with it. Then a flash of light as Mrs. Carstairs came fumbling into the hall—only a flash because of the greater flash of torture from her elbows, and the black.

Eleven years.

Eleven years she thought about it. You can think a lot in eleven years. You can think a lot in bed. You can think a whole lot in eleven bedridden years.

It doesn't have to drive you crazy, knowing you'll never walk again, not even when you had always walked, yes, run, yes, up until so recently skied, skated, trudged, hiked. (Never danced, though: now, now that was a good thing.)

What happened that night? Was it what she remembered? She could never quite be sure. And what had happened that she did not see or know about? She'd never know. No one, after Mrs. Carstairs and Hubert came tumbling sleepily out (they always claimed they heard nothing but the fall) and the doctors and ambulance and police were in and out, nobody could possibly piece together which doors were locked, or whether the pantry window had been closed. What she said about dark rectangles flying under her feet, about kissings and laughter somewhere—they listened so carefully to the way she talked that they frightened her, and she mentioned them no more. She might have, ten years later when Mrs. Carstairs, grown slow and hobbly, was cleaning out the pantry and found the old-fashioned carpet sweeper thrown far under the big solid maple butcher table. It had no stick and the brushes were worn away, but it had four good wheels and it was just exactly large enough to hide in the shadows, say, on one step of a flight of stairs. But the aunt never saw it, and Mrs. Carstairs never mentioned it; why should she? It wasn't good for anything, and besides, it had a big dent in the top as if it had been stepped on; so she just threw it away; it lay for a day on the garbage cans, looking like a little suitcase.

There was Susie Karina; what ever happened to Susie Karina? Why, she got a better deal from another nothing, name of Smith or something, whose important father owned a car dealership dealing in cars so important they sold themselves; the younger Smith was called the salesman. She married him, and he really loved her, which she didn't fully realize until he shot her as she was about to make a still better deal for herself. So she no longer mattered to Hubert and his aunt if, indeed, she ever really had. The big thing in their lives was each, the other; Susie had just cleaned up the issue.

Bedridden, the aunt now imprisoned him. He had tried to kill her (or the girl had, which was altogether the same thing) and for that she flung her coils around him, coils of business, of banking, of guilt and habit and demand (the threat kind of demand: the sheer nuisance kind of demand). Numb, bound, inarticulate, helpless, he stayed. The only wrinkle in the gelid stream of his life was when he had left the low level of the advertising business which would have lasted the rest of his life had he stayed, for a lower level in television; and anyone but Hubert could see that in some years' time he would elevate himself to about where he had been in advertising, and stay there for the rest of his life.

And what did Hubert think about? It is quite possible he thought not at all; this he was equipped for. But he could feel, and his aunt saw to it that he did. She wasped and prodded him and sat him down and walked him away; she would demand his presence and then not talk to him, but stare into the flat bland silver eye of the television to which she was addicted, and if he shifted his feet she would shush him. And she read aloud to him—car repair manuals, and highly specialized articles on bird food, and legal reviews and murder stories, during all of which he sat mute and moist outside—he was one of those heavyset men with a shiny face—but puckering a bit from some internal drying. Or she would talk to him: "My, Hubert, how little it takes to kill a man, how much sometimes! Why, remember Doc Maginn, so hale and happy, stepped on a needle in the pile of his bedside rug, dead in a week. Yet I've seen basket cases from the First War, Hubert, everything shot away, legs, arms, eyes, voice, hearing; still they live. You can live a long time in a basket, Hubert, in a bed. Keep yourself alert, keep busy doing something, keep your mind alive; have someone to wait on you—why—you can last forever that way, Hubert. Hubert, get up. Sit over there." And Hubert would get up and sit down again over there, moved because she felt like moving him. Oh, she hated him. Oh, she was going to kill him, she was killing him; and the weapon she chose was time and abrasion; she was going to outlast him, she was going to hammer out the length of her life thin and sharp and long, long, and ease it into him up to the hilt till he was dead of it. "Now put me to bed, Hubert, put your old aunty to bed. Close the blinds. Open the window. Hubert," she would snap if he began to decelerate, "pay the rent!" He paid nothing in cash; he never had; he knew what she meant. Earn your keep, do as you're told, be what you're for: pay the rent. So every night he turned the TV to face her bed, he lowered the blinds, opened the drapes, opened or shut the window, checked the heat.

She knew how everything worked; he understood none of it. By how many leaves of the old-fashioned one-pipe steam radiator were hot, she could tell him where to set the thermostat downstairs. By the size of the picture on her TV she could tell how much voltage drop occurred in the line, and by the way it changed, she could tell what caused it, and she knew the difference between the effect of Mrs. Carstairs' ironing downstairs, and the use of the rotisserie in their neighbors' house. She could splice rope, and taught Hubert by the hour because he could not learn: "Worm and parcel with the lay, turn and serve the other way," she'd chant at him, and watch him do it wrong even while he repeated it. She invented things and made him build them. She had him fix a brass handle to a rope from the beam overhead, so she could reach the window sill or turn the TV to face the bed when he wasn't there, or, after the weeks it took him to rig it, the bird-feeder. And a headboard with shelves and a buzzer and light to call him when he was asleep and one to call Mrs. Carstairs. And a sick room tray with a little vise and a rack for hand tools. And inventions on the inventions. A plaited rawhide grip for the brass handle. A floor stand for the workbench so it didn't bounce when she used the jack plane. Remote controls for the TV: on, off, volume, phone jack, in the days before they sold them with sets. She had lived a variegated and busy life, in the long process of doing something instead of the something she did not understand. She was a pioneer of all the Rosie-the-Riveters, going to work in a Liberty engine plant as a young girl; she was tiny then, and the only one in the place with hands small enough to adjust the carburetor heat controls from inside.

She had been the first woman to be called Yachtsman at the Bar Harbor Club, recklessly slamming a Star-class forerunner in the regatta. She was a court reporter and studied law and was a legal secretary— actually running a firm for the figureheads. She made a lot of money and invested skillfully and made more, and hung on to every dime of it. Now she had all this to devote to Hubert. Life was full. Life always had been full.

Then Hubert tried to kill her again. She saw it coming right from the very first, and just watched it come, wondering what on earth he was up to. He was sneaking into her room when she was in the bathroom, doing something, sneaking out. She soon found out what it was. He was loosening the screws in the back of the TV.

It took days. He seemed to be operating on four across the top, three down the side. She said nothing to him about it. He did nothing else differently. He sat and was read to and cut his thumb on a spokeshave, making her laugh, and later, when she came out of the bathroom on her wheelchair—it was more table than chair, for it hurt her to sit up, and she hated it—she would stop and check, and sure enough, he'd slipped in and loosened them a bit more.

She could have stopped him in a second, with a word, but she was fascinated. It went on for five days; on the morning of the sixth, after he had gone to work, she got settled for her morning of TV and found the set wouldn't work. With her ring-on-a-rope holding her up, she reached for the set and swiveled it around on its lazy-susan base. She pulled out three of the loose screws and was able to bend the hardboard back plate far enough to peer inside.

Tubes were gone.

She lay and pondered that. Was he (tender gesture) trying masterfully to help her cut down on her excessive viewing? Or was this just a childish and spiteful annoyance? Surely even Hubert knew better than that! Why, for that he'd pay ... oh Lord, for years he'd pay!

No, it was more than that. He was doing something in his bumbling way. Only there had to be more to it.

"Hubert," she said that evening after she had summoned him (she would not permit him to eat with her), "something's wrong with the TV."

He did not act surprised or try any play-acting, beyond saying with a rehearsed kind of promptness, "All right I'll take it down to be fixed tomorrow," all in a flat uninflected voice; then he sat down where she told him to. She talked to him and read to him; but there was a welcome difference in the air; why, almost half the time she actually realized he was there.

In the morning he grunted and bumped it downstairs, and in the afternoon came bumping and grunting, a colored man helping him, with a new set. A new grey modern streamlined set with a bigger screen than the old one, and a smaller case rather unaccountably designed to offer the least possible resistance to wind. "What on earth is that?"

"The other one is shot," Hubert informed her. "The man said so. I bought this one."

"It's horrible."

"I already bought it," said Hubert with a kind of faint doggedness.

She snorted and told him how to attach two wires to the back and how to stick the plug in the socket. It had a very nice remote control on it, with a station selector as well as volume, and on-off. She was mollified as far as the set was concerned; but what on earth was his play?

She found out the next afternoon when Mrs. Carstairs hobbled up with her arthritis and the mail. Alone with it, she found tucked among the ads and the bills and the magazines, a periodical which she knew, the instant she saw it, was late, though she had not missed it until now. It was a consumer's magazine—one of those outfits which tests goods bought on the open market. The old lady always read the very print off it; she spent her money, she used to say, she didn't throw it away.

Why late? And why had the little semicircular seal that kept it closed in the mail been slit?

Hubert? Had he picked it up, kept it a while, then dropped it in the mailbox on his way to work? *Why?*

She riffled the pages. Soaps, hand-held can openers, table-model TV's, an Italian vs. a French miniature car. ... *Table-model TV!* Oh, that was all. He just wanted to be sure and get one that was recommended.

She looked at the listing. It was there, all right. There was even a picture of it. As to the recommendation—it was heartily, earnestly, explicitly *not*. For this was the make and model, even (she checked this laboriously, swinging perilously at the edge of the bed by her strong right hand holding the ring from the ceiling) within a dozen digits of the serial number—the very same lethal contraption which, ungrounded and suffering slight damage from the overtightening of one hold-down screw between chassis and the metal case, had already killed a man and a boy.

She looked at the picture and the diagrams, and then at the set: "Oh!" she cried in sheerest delight, throwing the magazine high in the air, "How cute!"

Poor precious Hubert, nursing the place inside him where most people keep the embers of hate, but which, in him, must certainly be a clean little barely warm pot of pasteurized mush; oh, how cute! numbly associating her with TV, TV with her, until one day—when was it? four, five months ago, he heard about this set in the news; oh how he must have mumbled and gnashed on the idea; how long must it have taken him to find one? How hard did he have to think before he plotted out the fiendishly clever idea of getting tubes out of her old set and claiming it was finished? Oh, she thought, the little darling. He's really trying.

That night, for the first time in years, his numbed shiny face seemed to move a little from inside, as if some good fluid were soaking the parched places under the moist skin; for she was kind to him. She was unquestionably laughing at him, but she was kind to him.

The next day, after Mrs. Carstairs had cleaned up, Hubert's aunt fumbled through her workbench and tools, and found a lamp socket and some heavy wire. She connected two foot-long leads and screwed, in a bulb after testing it. She chuckled the whole time, even when she underwent the pain of bringing her wheelchair alongside and agonizingly rolling into it. Grunting with pain and chuckling with laughter, she got to the corner and put one wire against the steam pipe and the other against the metal side of the new set.

Nothing.

Using the remote control, she clicked the set on. Again she touched one wire to the set, the other to the pipe.

Still the bulb did not light. There was nothing wrong with this set.

Hubert ... poor, poor old Hubert.

For a limp moment she ignored the pain and lay in the chair, wagging her head from side to side in wordless pity.

This was as far as the poor addlehead could think. Get a set like the one that had killed some people. Get it next to her.... What passed next, in his fogbound mind could only have been, "... and then maybe some way she ..."

She could shake him, the poor darling! Didn't he know that to be electrocuted by house current, the electricity had to flow through the body? Stand in a puddle, preferably with a good iron drain in it, and stick your hand in a fuse box; then maybe. Or hold a water pipe and put a wet thumb in a socket—then perhaps. But he must, with millions of other people, share the notion that you could be killed by, for example, current running from one side of your fingertip to the other side of the same finger ... or maybe the poor thing just didn't have a notion at all.

Back in bed at last, and rested, she began to think of Hubert with pity and tenderness. He'd worked so hard ... and she wasn't thinking of lugging TV sets up and down stairs, either.

And such a clever idea, too, in its way. If he only knew what he was doing.

She thought about it, and about him, all day long; and when at last she knew what she was going to do, it was as if all the clocks in the world had stopped; oh, how she ached for him to be here; oh, how she wanted him near. Suddenly the world was bright again for her who had not realized how dark it had become; here out of the gloom had come the loveliest ... oh, the most wonderful thing to plan, to work on.

Hubert needed help.

He couldn't possibly do this by himself. He had to learn, to plan, to fix, to arrange. And above all he had to feel he was doing it by himself, because he wanted it so; anyone who worked so hard had to want it very much. But it would be no good unless he was sure, all along the line, that it in all its parts was his own doing.

So when he came upstairs that evening, and when she had portrayed enough surliness with him to make him unsuspicious, she began.

"Hubert!" It was said with a slightly rising inflection; in the spectrum of her summonses, this one stood on the line that said, "Get to work." He started uneasily.

"My ring," she said, pointing to her leather-handled, rope-dangled helper. ""That rope stretches all the time."

He looked at it with dim eyes. "Looks okay."

"Well, you don't have to use it. I want you to put up something that won't stretch."

He tried hard. She could see him at it, like a toothless man gumming a steak. "Chain," he said at last.

She argued with him scornfully. Chain was pinchy and noisy. Wire rope would fray after a time, sharp and splintery. And at last she had led him to braided copper cable, which would be handsome, and though it would stretch, it would stretch just so much and no more; and then she led him like Socrates, asking demanding and argumentative question after question, until he had no choice but to devise a big wide ring in the beam above, a second ring in the beam in the corner, and anchorage to something solid there, thus the cable could be taken up as it stretched, until it would stretch no more. Laboriously he wrote down his shopping list, and she spent a delicious night and day anticipating, and two more happy evenings hammering at him until he had it just right. And all the while she savored the delightful, and quite correct, thought that he still did not realize how very beautifully that new cable would fit into "his" sweet little plan. Oh, how she anticipated the moment of revelation! How proud he would be, and hopeful. This, she thought, is living. Where's the woman, she thought (she often compared herself with, categorically, "women") who with all her so-called wiles, who knows what this is like, to lead a poor dear man step by step—no; inch by inch—down the very path you planned for him, and all the while let him think he's the one, he's the one?

She had not felt like this in years. She had never felt like this. She liked it. She liked it so much she let the whole thing rest for two days, while happily she planned the next step the all-powerful male must take.

"Oh ... *Hubert!*" This in descending tones; this was the disappointment, the "how *could* you!" salutation.

"Whuh? Whuh?" he said rapidly, worriedly.

She held up the consumer's magazine. "Of all the TV sets in the whole wide world, why did you buy this one?"

He wet his lips. "Seems pretty okay."

"Here!" she snapped. (Not even "come here.") He rolled to his feet and came, peering at the magazine. She demanded, "What are you trying to do—kill me?"

He opened his mouth, closed it, lifted his hands and let them fall. Finally he said, "Well, I got it awful cheap."

Aloud, she read the account of the deaths. "I don't doubt you got it cheap," she snorted, then looked up. "How cheap?"

He said, "A hundred and twenty off list."

"Oh, well," she said; and inside she hugged herself: oh, what fun! She changed the subject. She said the rawhide on the brass handle hurt her hand, and she made him find her utility knife and cut it away. While he nicked and picked at it, she read aloud the other part of the article, where it said that the set was otherwise very fine. She sounded almost as if she forgave him. Anyway she let up on him, and with her remote unit, turned the set on and they watched a crime show. Or he did. She watched him. At the part in the TV play where the murderer accomplished his evil deed—and it happened to be an old woman—she could have sworn his dull eyes acquired a dim shine. He even stopped picking away at the rawhide and sat down to watch absorbedly. For once she let him, and it was all right; of his own accord he went back to it after the show and finished the job. Oh you sweet boy, she thought, almost fondly, for once in your sloppy life you're altogether something; why you dear, you're just full of this thing.

She turned off the sound—but left the set on—with her control, thereby wrenching him out of the Western which succeeded the murder play. Perforce, he gaped at her. "You *could* have killed me," she said accusingly.

"There has to be something wrong with the set first," he said doggedly. "The set's all right, I tell you."

"That may be," she said. "But look." She reached for the brass handle above the bed and tugged at it. "Look, I'm grounded."

He shook his head, mystified.

"The radiator!" she yelped at him. "Why did you have to anchor the cable to the radiator?"

He scanned the cable, up from her hand, across from one beam to the next, down to the radiator in the corner, behind the TV set. He shrugged, not understanding. "You said anchor it to something solid."

She had said to anchor it to the radiator, but she didn't give him a chance to remember that. "Don't you see?" she shrilled. "Suppose there was a short circuit to the TV case, the way it tells about in the magazine, and suppose I had to touch it, like turn it toward the bed. Don't you see I'd be holding one with the other? Don't you understand *anything*?" She let him watch her cloudily, saw him swing his gaze from her to the cable, the TV set, back to her; saw the stirrings of that moment of revelation she had anticipated so much. "Stupid, stupid, stupid!" she shrilled, "*this* is what I mean!" and she flung her weight on the handle and reached out for the TV set. "See?" she said, slapping it. "See?" she said, turning it on its swivel. She regained the bed.

How shiny his face was. Suddenly she wanted to mop up that dull excitement she could see moistening his parched core. She said coldly, "Well anyway, I guess that proves the set's safe for now."

Through her lashes she watched him. For a split second she thought he was going to cry. Then he slumped dejectedly and stared at the set. She knew what he was thinking as well as if his moist brow had been equipped with one of those electric signs with the moving letters. She knew he was thinking how close he had come, and how never in a thousand years would he be able to figure out the difference between this harmless object and the one he had hoped it would be. She imagined further thoughts—old familiar ones, doubtless, their path trodden smooth by his years of plodding hatred: So bash her head in (but Mrs. Carstairs, downstairs all the time . . .). Feed her a glass of warm milk with—(but he never brought her milk, and she certainly wouldn't touch it if he did).

. . . or maybe these were only her own imaginings; maybe he wasn't thinking at all. He could do that, she was sure. Ha! she'd soon enough turn them on again! She said, batting at the brass handle, and speaking very softly as if to herself, "Couldn't get closer to certain death if you'd planned it," and watching his widening eyes and the slight babyish protrusion of his lower lip, she just knew he was saying to himself, "She knows. Oh my God, I bet she knows."

She felt a thrill of anticipation. Get him scared; oh fine. Fear will make him move. And worry: let's make him worry a little. "Tomorrow," she said, "we'll just have to put up something else besides that copper cable. Just too dangerous." And she saw him look down into his hands and pout miserably. (Was he thinking, *I'll never get a chance like this again.* Sure he was.)

Oh, he looked so miserable! Oh, did any woman ever have such a toy as this? Let's bring back the hope now.

She swatted the magazine explosively, making him jump. "It shouldn't be allowed!"

"Oh," he mumbled, "the factory called them all back in. All they could find."

"I don't mean that," she said, and hit the magazine again. "This thing, with the photographs and diagrams and all. Why, you know what this amounts to, just this one picture of a screw tightened too much? Why, it's instructions, that's what it is; any fool could take a safe set and make a killer out of it, just by reading this. It shouldn't be allowed!" She took the magazine and flung it at his feet, making him jump again. "Take the filthy thing out of here!"

His hands, she gloated, literally trembled as he picked it up. He rolled it and turned it over and over between his hands. It was like a caress. (Oh Hubert, she called silently, if you only knew how wonderful you are!) "Yes, Aunty," he said, his eyes on the magazine. He put it, rolled, into his back pocket, and rose.

"Put your old aunty to bed."

"All right." Preoccupied, he did all the things he had to do with the drapes, the shade, the heat, the TV, her covers, the lights. She was glad when he turned out the lights; it had been hurting her face not to smile openly.

What would he be thinking now? She knew: oh, she knew, especially because—"Hu*bert!*"—because, silhouetted in the door, he already had the magazine out of his pocket, though it was still rolled. Ah, he could barely wait! Imagine—Hubert eager, Hubert dedicated, Hubert excited ... and Hubert certainly wondering how on earth he would get the chance to make that one little change, turn that one screw just far enough to break the insulating washer. "Hubert!"

"Yes, aunty."

"In the morning ask Mrs. Carstairs to turn up the hot water heater right after breakfast. I'm going to have a good long hot soak. Just this once I'm going to soak for a whole hour."

He thought he was answering but his voice was lost in a peculiar abrupt wheeze. Smiling in the darkness, she asked, "What, Hubert?"

"All right, Aunty; I'll tell her."

He went away.

She soaked for more than an hour. She drowsed, almost fell asleep in the tub. In the first place she had been awake almost all night, smiling most of the time, making little bets with herself. Even with a clear photograph and a concise explanation, would Hubert be able to find the right screw? Could there be any guarantee he'd turn it the right way? Would he wait so long for the coast to be clear that he wouldn't have time to do it at all? She had forgotten, at first, about Mrs. Carstairs and the Saturday cleaning, which she would certainly do while the old lady was in the tub. She could all but see poor Hubert in his room down the hall, an ear cocked to the arthritic housekeeper's puttering about in his aunt's room, his eyes glued to the page in the consumer's magazine, reading it, over and over, moving his lips. A killer.

Hubert, Hubert. Dear Hubert. Maybe the silly old thing wouldn't even try to fix the set. Mrs. Carstairs left at last. There was long, long silence. She began to doze.

A sharp sound snapped her out of it, and she literally clapped her soapy hand over her mouth to keep in the burst of shrill laughter that filled her mouth and throat. For dear dedicated worried fearful Hubert, with the bone head and the ham hands, Hubert had dropped his screwdriver. The picture of him, round-eyed and whey-faced, staring in terror at the closed bathroom door, was almost more than she could bear.

More silence, a bit more hot water and another doze. She came to herself with a start, and looked with amused horror at her wrinkled fingerpads; she was as waterlogged as Davy Jones' floor mop. She began the arduous process of draining, drying, dressing, and loading the useless parts of herself onto the agonizing wheelchair. She took as long as possible . . . long enough. He was not in her room when he opened the door.

Back in bed, she composed herself for her Saturday televiewing, and with her hand on the control, remembered. Then: why not? and she laughed and clicked it on.

The sun was out. The birds were out. Hubert was out (she laughed) shopping for rope for her helper-handle, for no matter what, he had his orders. (Oh the fool; what on earth does he think he could with himself without me? But isn't he the one? Isn't he the gutsy boy, though?) The TV was excellent, all of it, even the commercials. She thoroughly enjoyed her afternoon.

At last he came up. She did not greet him; she wondered too much what he would say. She had been philosophizing about murder and the murderer: at what exact point did a man become a murderer? According to the law, when the victim died, be it a microsecond or forty years after the attack. But was that really so? When a man pulls a trigger, and the bullet is on its way, and it's too late for anything but death to happen, is he not already a murderer? Hubert now: Hubert had already pulled his trigger. She might have died any time today. As a matter of fact, she had lain impotently watching a big grey squirrel gobbling up all the suet from the feeder, because she had rather not take hold of that brass handle and swing herself so close to the TV in order to reach the feeder-rope.

And Hubert, out shopping: was he wondering if he would come home to a curious sidewalk and the white wailing of ambulances? She had purposely not called him, and he had delayed downstairs until quite late, doubtless screwing up his courage for the trip upstairs to find—what?—in her room. Surely he had not reckoned on being the one to discover her. She could almost hear his half-articulate complaint: after all he had done, did he have to go through all that too?

She resisted a temptation to arrange herself sprawling on the carpet between the bed and the TV, to lie still until he bent over her, and then to start laughing; a sure instinct told her that this was the way, even with Hubert, to get herself not only murdered, but beaten to death along with it. She contented herself with lying as still and—what was the word? waxen was the word—as possible, with her eyes closed, until he stood over the bed and murmured, "Aunty?"

She opened her eyes and he stepped back two paces and stood, not knowing what to do with his hands. Still she waited, to see what he would say next, and it was (the clumsy, blundering dunderhead), "Watch some TV today, did you?"

She laughed and struggled up, elbow-walking back to her backrest. "Lots, and it was fine. It's late."

"Yes, I . . . think I'll go turn in."

She tilted her head to one side and said, "Had a tough day, Hubert?" and smiled at him. The quick, passing contraction of his features convinced her he was shouting silently to himself, "She knows! She knows!"

"Well," she said, "You're going to put your old aunty to bed first."

Did he hesitate? Did he really? Did he care? He seemed to be ready to turn and walk out . . . or did he turn to remind himself that downstairs the housekeeper kept a living ear, a remembering brain, and there must be no quarrel for her to remember? He said docilely, "All right, aunty."

"I think," she said, "I'll watch the late show tonight. I had a nap."

"The late show, yes," he echoed. He did the window blind and window things, the drape things. Passing the TV, which faced her, he hit it with his hip; it swung to face the door.

She nodded approvingly. She couldn't have done better herself. She said, "Hubert—turn the TV to me."

"All right," he said. But instead he came over and straightened her covers. His face was especially shiny, and she could see the dark marking of damp where his hands touched the bedclothes.

She began to laugh.

For the first, and, the last time in her life, she heard Hubert speak to her in the imperative: "Don't laugh," he said.

She subsided, but she took her time about it, laughing all the way. "Funny boy." Suddenly she cut it dead and said coldly, "Turn that TV to me."

His back was to the set: he stood between it and her. "You can see it all right from there." He held his right wrist hard with his left hand. She could see the shiver of the fabric of his trousers as his knees trembled.

"We don't want a quarrel for Mrs. Carstairs to hear," she said carefully.

"Oh gosh no," he said fervently.

A crazy situation. Extraordinary. Delightful. This, she thought, is living. "'Turn the set, Hubert." She smiled. "It won't bite you. It isn't even on."

He wet his lips, so wet already. His hands were wet, his face and his mouth. His tears were wet, waiting to come. He whispered—she knew he didn't mean to whisper, but it was all he could manage— "You can reach it."

"All right," she said suddenly, gently, with all the tones and overtones of complete capitulation.

"Well I." He said it as if it were a complete and sensible statement, turned and marched to the door.

"Hubert!"

He stopped as if she had roped him. He was in the doorway; he stayed where he was and did not turn. He was like a machine with brakes locked and the clutch disengaged; but one could feel the motor racing; in the split tatter of a second it would be gone from there screaming.

"Please," she said gently (to *Hubert?* Please?) "You forgot to check the heat. You'll do that for me, won't you?"

His shoulders slumped and he turned back into the room. "Oh, sure, I guess," he said wearily. He crossed to the corner and leaned over and felt the radiator. It was the metal top of the TV set that he leaned over. His aunt moved her thumb *that* much on the remote control and turned the set on.

Hubert made the most horrible sound the aunt had ever heard; it was like a particularly raucous sneeze—inward. She had read that sometimes when a jolt first hits them they swallow their tongues, and then suffocate on them. That is what Hubert was doing. One stiff hooked arm rested on the top of the TV set, and the other stiff hooked arm rested on the radiator, and his legs stuck straight out behind him with the toes pointed, and quivered. Through the legs of his trousers, at the calves, could be seen muscle mounding up in cramps like golf-balls.

"Kill me, will you?" croaked the aunt, but the set warmed up just then and roared and drowned her out. She turned the volume down and stared at Hubert's legs and pointing toes sticking out from behind the TV set, and knew with crushing certainty that from the very beginning she had set things up to come out this way. She didn't recall having purposely, consciously done so; she knew only that she must have, that's all. She glared at the legs and said, "But you broke my back!"

All in all, that was a pretty good day. And night. Living; really living. One of the best parts of all had to do with the police, who took all of fifteen seconds to sniff out that there was more to this "accident" than met the eye. There was a young man with two deep measures of vivid intelligence for eyes, and a quick quiet voice; he asked almost exclusively important questions, one right after the other. Who brought that set in here? Who hung that cable from the radiator to a point over the bed? Well, if it was rope before, who substituted woven copper? Who took the leather grip off the brass handle?

Hubert, Hubert, Hubert.

Men came up and brushed fine white dust around the TV, and

took off the back and brushed dust inside, and photographed everything. Whose fingerprints?

Finally, and funniest of all, was the man who regretted the accident, who assured her that the police expert had removed the short circuit, making the set now quite safe, but at the same time warning her to get rid of it, just in case. Lastly, he hemmed and he hawed and he suggested in extremely careful language that she not attempt to bring an action against the set manufacturer in this particular case, in view of certain technicalities which we needn't go into at such a time as this "but I faithfully assure you that if you don't take my advice you will only wish you had, and you will find out at great—ah—trouble to yourself that I was right." In short, it was unanimously agreed to conceal from this little old bedridden lady that her nephew had gotten himself caught in the vicious trap he laid for her. Why bother her with it? The only thing that would ever force her to know it would be if she started lawsuits; lying there like a real little old protected female woman, waxen as possible, she agreed in a faint voice that they were right and she trusted them all. It was grand fun. Her finish didn't come until the next afternoon, when a sniffling Mrs. Carstairs brought her the things out of Hubert's room to sort. There wasn't much, and among the few papers was the copy of the consumer's magazine, still folded back open to the article about the metal-cased TV set. Over this Hubert had pondered and waited, and while waiting, had doodled, filling O's and putting mustaches on the faces of the consumers' electronicians in the photos. He had also written a sentence and a word.

It was as if Hubert had been denied understanding and intelligence and the ability to articulate, all his life, the formless clouds of feeling within him, in just and equal compensation for this single, simple, devastating insight. He had written:

Without me she is nothing but an old woman.

And under that, in very large, careful letters:

OLD

His aunt read this and closed her eyes to consider it, and that was the finish for her. When she opened her eyes again she looked at her hands, skinny and crooken-a-clawed, and she pulled at her sparse white hair, drawing it forward over her face to be able to look at it, through it. All her life she had been too busy to be loved, too busy to be liked. She had been too busy to have a childhood and she had been too busy to be old.

Not any more. The Hubert business was the last thing she had to be busy about; for years it had been everything and the only thing, and now she'd finished it, and though she lingered on for a long while, it was the finish for her.

Tandy's Story

This is Tandy's story. But first, take a recipe: the Canaveral sneeze; the crinkled getter; the Condition adrift; the analogy of the Sahara smash; Hawaii and the missing moon; and the analogy of the profit-sharing plan. There is no discontinuity here, nor is the chain more remarkable than any other. They are all remarkable.

If this were your story, it might compound from the recipe of a letter that never got mailed, a broken galosh clip, a wistful memory of violet eyes, the Malthusian theory and a cheese strudel. However, it is Tandy's.

We begin then with the Canaveral sneeze, delivered by a white-gowned, sterile-gloved man in a germ-free lab, as gently he lifted a gold-plated twenty-three-inch sphere into its ultimate package. Not having a third hand at the time, he was unable to cover his mouth in time. *Gesundheit.*

And now to Tandy's story.

Tandy's brother Robin was an only child for the first two years of his life and he would never get over it. Noël, her sister, was born when Tandy was crossing that high step into consciousness called Three Years Old. (Timothy, the other brother, wasn't until later. Anyway, this isn't his story. This is Tandy's story.)

When Tandy was five, then, it was clear to her that while the older Robin was bigger, stronger, more knowledgeable and smarter (he wasn't, but she hadn't been around long enough to learn that yet) and could push her around at will until she yelled for help—while, to put it another way, she was attacked from above—the sister below was excavating the ground under her feet. Noël unaccountably delighted everyone else, even Robin, for she was a blithe little bundle. But her advent necessarily drained off a good deal of parental attention from Tandy, who lost the household position of The Baby without gaining Robin's altitude as The Firstborn. It didn't seem fair. So she did what she could about it. She yelled for help.

It wasn't any ordinary yell, if an ordinary yell is a kind of punctuation or explosion or communicative change-of-pace. There were times when it wasn't, except for its purpose and figuratively, a yell at all. It was at times a whine—a highly specialized one, not very loud but strident, that could creep in and out of her voice twice in a sentence. Or it might be merely a way of asking for something, and asking and *asking,* so that she couldn't even hear a "yes" and was not aware of the point at which it furiously turned to a "no." Or perhaps an instantaneous approach to tears, complete with filling eyes and twisting mouth, where anyone else might use the mildest emphasis: "It *was* Tuesday I wore the blue dress, not Monday," and the equally instantaneous disappearance of the tears (which, somehow, was the annoying part). Or utter, total, complete, unmoving non-response to an order through the third, the fourth, the fifth repetition, and then a sudden shattering screech: "I *heard* you!"

Tandy had, in short, a talent approaching genius for getting under one's skin and prickling.

This established, it is mere justice to all concerned to report also that Tandy was loved and lovable as well. Her parents took the matter of child-rearing seriously. The reasons (over and above innate talent) for Tandy's more irritating proclivities were quite known to them. And Tandy, long-lashed, supple, with hair the color of buckwheat honey and golden freckles spattered across her straight perfect nose, was an affectionate child, and her parents loved her and showed it very often.

And this did not alter one whit her position as No. Two Child, her distaste for the role, her yelling for help and therefore, for all the love, the concurrent war of abrasion.

There were times when she and Robin got along as contemporaries and splendidly. And of course almost anyone could get along with the biddable Noël. But these times were more wished-for than often. When they occurred, they were so welcome that one is reminded of the lady with the perennially battling children who called out into an unwonted silence one mid-morning: "What are you kids doing'?" From under the porch a young voice replied, "Burning the wrappers off these razorblades with matches, Mommy." "That's nice," she replied, "Don't fight ..."

At such times, in short, they could get away with practically anything, and Tandy's usual occupations were staged alone and away from people.

Yet never completely away.

Perhaps as a result of her crowded loneliness, she liked to be on the outside looking in or on the inside looking on, but not of the group. When the neighborhood gathered on the lawn for hide-and-seek or kickball, and the game was well started, Tandy would be seen forty paces off, squatting by the driveway, making a cake-sized cake of earth, perhaps, and decorating it with pebbles and twigs; or acting out some elaborate dialogue with her doll Luby (whether or not Luby was with her), bowing and mugging and murmuring the while in a number of voices. Tandy spoke beautifully. She had since the beginning, and her command of idiom and tone was too expert to be cute. There were times when it was downright embarrassing, as when the father overheard her demanding of a peonybush, with precisely his own emphasis, *"What the hell are you, hypnotized?"* There were times when these performances at the edge of the activity of others attracted considerable attention. She was surprisingly deft for a five-year-old, being one of these kids who from birth, apparently, can with a single movement draw a closed figure so that you are unable to see where the ends of the line join, and whose structures with blocks never seem jumbled, but quite functional (as indeed, to the fantasy of the moment, they are). Once in a while she drew quite a gallery of the curious with, say, six careful rows of red Japanese maple leaves and deep pink trumpet-vine blossoms alternating on the lawn, before which she would posture severely, murmuring under her breath and pointing to one and another with a stick. At such times she seemed quite oblivious to six or eight children magnetically drawn round her, who watched mystified. Sometimes she would answer and sometimes she would not. Sometimes it would take drastic measures, as for example Robin's shuffling through the careful arrangement of leaves and petals, before it could be learned (the hard way, in this case) that she was teaching school, that the leaves were boys and the trumpets girls, and that she was now going to tell Mama to throw Robin's Erector set into the garbage, and a good deal more—precisely what more, no one knew, for by then the screech would have destroyed intelligibility.

The crinkled getter was placed near the base and inside the metal envelope of an RF amplifier tube in the telemetry circuit of the big rocket's second stage. The getter's function was to absorb the residual gases in the tube and harden the vacuum therein. Its crinkle was an impurity, but so slight as to cause no trouble until the twelfth hour of countdown. Then rarefied gas began to ionize and discharge and ionize and Poop! discharge again.

To replace the tube required that they go back to twenty-four hours and start the countdown again. The extra twelve hours delay enabled sneeze-mist to dry on the sphere, and certain bacilli to die, and others to encyst, and a smear of virus, sub-microscopically, to turn to a leathery, almost crystalline jelly.

Tandy lived in a house in the woods which in turn were in, or nearly in, the very middle of the upstate village, a pleasant accident derived from the land-grabbing, land-holding traditions of three neighbors' fathers, and grandfathers, and great-grandfathers. The three acres on which Tandy's house stood were surrounded by perhaps twenty acres of other people's woods and a small swamp; yet the house was barely ten minutes on foot away from the village green.

Somewhere, then, in house or garden, lawn, swamp or wood, the brownie came to Tandy.

It had that stuffed-toy, left-out-in-the-rain aspect possible only to stuffed toys which have been left out in the rain. It was about nine inches high. Its clothing, or skin (properly, the outside layer was both), was variously khaki-colored and mottled green. The appellation "brownie" derived from what appeared to be a tapered hat, though once the father was heard to remark that it was the damn thing's head that was pointed. The arms and legs were taut and jointless, and looked like sausages on which lived lichens. For hands there were limp yellow-pink leaves of felt, and for feet, what might have been the model for a radical cartoonist's rendering of the knotted moneybags of Old Moneybags. As for a face—well, it was a face. That's all. Black disks for eyes, so faded you couldn't tell whether they were supposed to be open or closed, a ditto-mark for a nose and a streak below which may have been some clumsy whimsy—a smile up on the right scowling downward to the left—or a streak of dirt.

In the light of all that happened, one would think there would be a day of discovery, an hour of revelation, an open-the-package kind of Event. But there wasn't.

The brownie was kicking around the place for weeks, months maybe; they had all seen it, kicked it aside, used it as a peg for that parental sigh, "Got to clean out all this junk sometime . . ." Robin dug a grave for a dead cat once and then couldn't find the cat, so buried the brownie instead. Noël had taken it to bed with her once, and the mother had thrown it out the window during the night. It was one of those things, along with the bent but not quite broken doll carriage, the toy electric motor with the broken brush and Noël's wind-up giraffe, which needed new ears. So the brownie wove its indistinct thread into the tapestry of days, in and out of the margin between toys and trash.

The exact beginnings of Tandy's preoccupation with the brownie were also vague, and even when first her interest was total, it made little impression, because Tandy was . . . Well, for example, the caterpillar. Once when she was four she caught a tent caterpillar and kept him in a coffee can for two days and named him Freddy and fed and watered him and even covered him at night with a doll blanket. During the second night she awoke crying, agonizing after Freddy, inconsolable until the can was found and brought and shown to her. Her grandmother, who was around at the time, said sagely, "That child needs a pet!" and everybody nodded and conversed about pets. The next morning Tandy put Freddy on the flagstones out front "so he could go for a walk." He went for a walk. Altogether.

For half a day people tiptoed around Tandy as if she were full of fulminate and had dined on dynamite.

But not only did she not ask about Freddy, she never even mentioned him. She stumbled over the can and almost fell and kicked it away and did not even glance at it. Thereafter Tandy's preoccupations were beyond judgment or prediction; they might be blood-sistership, like the affair with her doll Luby Cindy, or they might be passing passions like Freddy. The brownie ... well, people became aware not that Tandy had a new one, but that for some indeterminate time she had been orbiting around this artifact. And when Tandy orbited, so did the cosmos or it—all of it—would be accountable to Tandy.

Mention of orbit brings up the Condition adrift. No other name for it will do, and even that is inaccurate. It was ... well, matter; but matter in such a curlicue, so self-involved in stress, that Condition is a better word than Thing. It had been made where it was useful to its makers, and one might say it had a life of its own though it had not used it in some millions of megayears. By a coincidence as unlikely as the existence of the reader of this history or a world to read it on, but as true, the Condition adrift found itself matching course and speed with the golden ball in space. It contacted, interpenetrated, an area of the golden surface four by eight microns, and happily found itself a part of organic material—a dried and frozen virus and two encysted bacteria. The latter it dissected and used. The former it activated, but in a wild reorganizing way so radical its mammy amino wouldn't have recognized it. The Condition became then a Thing (without losing its conditional character) and it scored itself across and divided. And divided again. And that was the end of that, for it had used up its store of a certain substance too technical to mention, but as necessary as number. Such was the nature of this organism that once alive it must grow, but if it could not grow it must cease dividing, and if it ceased dividing it must undergo an elaborate, eons-long cycle before it could come round to being again a mere Condition adrift. But unless it could begin that cycle it must die.

By means known to it, it flowed through the lattices of the sputtered gold, quartered the sphere, searched and probed, and at last stopped.

It turned its attention to the great globe underneath.

Some time or other—it was in the early spring, though Tandy

herself could never remember just when—she got the brownie a house. Actually it was an old basketwork fishing creel she had found behind the garage, but the one thing one learned most quickly about Tandy was that things were what she said they were. Anything else was only your opinion, to which you were not entitled. And there was a certain justice in her attitude, for it did not take long for such an object to lose its creelship and become what she said it was.

She set it against the back wall of the garage, in the tangled ground between the wall and the old stone fence, under the shelter of the adjoining carport—for a wall-less shelter had been hung to the side of the garage to accommodate the second car they hoped for some day. It was a nice sort of outdoors-indoors place. She drove a row of stakes in front of the creel and on it placed a rectangle of discarded plywood—a miniature of the carport—but as time went on she added walls. First they were cardboard. The creel was the bedroom and the rest of it was the living room.

At Easter she saved her basket and it was a bed. She got the brownie up every morning and put him to bed every night, and on weekends he took his nap too.

She fed him.

She had a small table—not a cream cheese box, a table!—for him, and on the table were clamshell plates and an acorn cup, and a pill-bottle—strike that; a flower vase—which, from the time spring first started to show her colors, she kept supplied. But before that she was feeding him snow ice cream, sawdust cereal, mushroom steaks, and wooden bread. She talked to him constantly, sometimes severely. And in that unannounced way of hers, she spent all her free time with him.

No one noticed it especially, in March and almost through April, except perhaps to be grateful for the quiet. A minute spent with the brownie was a minute without Tandy's moaning, whining, sobbing, screeching or otherwise yelling for help. Of course, there had to be minutes spent away from the brownie. Most of them were at school.

School was kindergarten, of course, and it may have been that there was just too much of it for Tandy. Due to factors of distance and necessities of school buses, the kindergarten was not, as is usual for such establishments, a nine-to-noon affair, but instead lasted for the whole school day, ending at three. In spite of a long rest period after lunch, it was the opinion of many that this was asking too much of five-year-olds. It may have been the teacher's opinion as well. It was certainly Tandy's opinion. Her first report card was not resoundingly good, and her second one was somewhat worse. Neither was bad enough to cause concern, but the parents were jolted by the specific items on which she scored worst. Beside the item *Speaks clearly and distinctly* the teacher had marked the symbols which meant "Hardly ever," and beside *Knows right from left* was the mark for "Seldom." The parents looked at one another in amazement, and then the father said, "That can't be right!" and the mother said, "That can't even be Tandy. She's given her the wrong report card!"

But she had not, as the mother found out by visiting the teacher at school one afternoon.

The mother, going in like a lion, came out numb with awe for the teacher's forbearance, and for the second time (Robin had done this to her once, on another matter) suffering that partly amused but nonetheless painful experience of learning how little one knows of one's own. Or as the bemused father put it, "It's a wise father who knows his own child." For, fully documented and with inescapable accuracy, the teacher had described a Tandy they never saw around the house—a Tandy recalcitrant, stubborn, inactive, disobedient and, most incredible of all, talking incessant baby talk. The teacher's ability to see below the surface, to know that the child wasn't *really* as bad as all that, helped the overall picture not at all, because it became manifest that Tandy did not know right from left on purpose; that she spoke baby-talk by choice; that she fell from grace in matters of handkerchiefs and handwashing not because she forgot, but because she remembered.

Above and beyond everything else was that the degree of this behavior was by no means excessive. She had never once been subjected to the routine punishment of being made to stand out in the hall. She could always stop just short of outright delinquency. She was the foot that drags, the pressure which is not quite toothache, the discomfort which is not yet heartburn.

The parents conferred unhappily with each other and then with Tandy, who answered every "Why?" with "I just—" and an infuriating shrug, rolling upward of the eyes, flinging the hands out and down to flap helplessly against the thighs. It was the mother's exact gesture, which of course is precisely why it was infuriating.

So the father, his anger at last arriving, drew a bead on Tandy with his long forefinger and declared, "This is a *rule*. No more brownie."

The analogy of the Sahara smash is the anecdote of one of the desert crashes of a B-17 in Africa. Unlike tragic others, this one had a happy ending, and this is why: the crew made no attempt to trek out of there in a body, but instead assigned one man to march out and get help. The significant thing is that he carried with him not only a compass, but almost their entire water supply. The rest of the crew rationed themselves down to three tablespoons a day and lay as still as possible buried in the sand under the broken fuselage. So it was that the organism on the golden satellite told one of itself to ooze patiently out to the tip of one of the whip antennae; then, by means known to it—for as related, it contained unheard-of stresses, neatly curled up and intertwined—it bent the whip double and released it, and out into the emptiness, in the opposite direction from orbital motion, was snapped this infinitesimal fleck of substance. It tracked along with the satellite for a long time, but separating always, until it was lost in the glittering emptiness. But with it it carried all but a fraction of the organic substance available to the whole. Three parts were left quiescent, waiting moveless to die or be saved. The fourth fell toward Earth, which took—as long as it took ...

Now there is a school of control-by-giving (hits in the head or ice cream) and a school of taking away, and the father, when aroused, tended to the latter. In extreme cases a child can learn never to express preference or fondness for anything lest he qualify it for the disciplinary list. This was not that extreme. It would not be because of the mother, who despised this kind of thing and whose reactions were very fast. One glimpse of Tandy's stricken face at this "No more brownie!" dictum and she added. " ... if you go on making people unhappy." And, ignoring the father's stifled cry of rage, she went on,

"Now you run on out and talk it over with the brownie."

Tandy did as she was told, leaving her parents to instruct one another about child-rearing, and communed with the brownie; and perhaps this was the real beginning of it all.

For she had done a great deal for this brownie. Now, for the first time, she had made it clear that there were things that needed doing for her.

If things changed at school, it was naturally not immediately apparent at home. Things at home did not change. That is, the busy-ness with the brownie continued to use up the whining time, the screeching time, the opportunities for chance medley and battle royal with Noël and Robin.

One weekday morning the mother had hung out a line-full of clothes and, being face to face with the garage, was moved to go round and see how Tandy was coming along with Project Brownie. She hadn't seen it for some weeks. She recalled vaguely that the cardboard sides had been replaced, and she knew that the tiny flower-vase had borne violets, and baby's breath, and alyssum. And she recalled the time she had turned out her sewing basket and the kitchen gadget drawer and rearranged them, all in one morning, and had given the detritus to Tandy for her brownie. Time was when Tandy would have gathered up such a treasure-trove with a shrill shriek of joy, would have fought selfishly and jealously with the other children over the ownership of every ribbon-end, every old cork and worn-out baby-bottle nipple, only to leave bits and pieces exasperatingly all over the house and yard within the next couple of hours. But this time she had spread the whole clutter out on the living room table, darted her deft small hands in and out of the pile, and in a few seconds had selected the blunt end of a broken nutpick, the china handle of a Wedgewood pitcher, a small tangle of pale blue nylon-and-wool yarn, and a brass wing-nut. "He wants these," she said positively. "That's all?" the mother had asked, astonished. And Tandy had replied, precisely mimicking the father, "Now what would a brownie want with all that junk?" It wasn't so much the modesty of Tandy's wants that had surprised the mother. It was the absolute and unhesitating certainty with which she chose.

Thinking of this, the mother rounded the garage and saw the brownie's house.

The old creel was still the bedroom, but the rest of the structure had vastly altered. The cardboard walls had been replaced with wood—some ends of shiplap that used to lie under the sleeping porch—and since the mother had heard nothing of any carpentry by or for Tandy, she could see that the stony ground had been carefully and laboriously dug to various depths so that the little boards, buried upright, could present an even eaveline. On one side were two small square window-openings, glazed with cellophane; on the other was a longer opening like a picture-window. The roof, still the castoff piece of plywood, had been covered with a layer of earth, and smoothly, brilliantly, it was thatched with living star-moss.

The mother knelt to look inside. The floor of the house was covered with a blinding-white powder of some kind. She took a pinch of it and felt it and smelt it and even tasted it a little without recognizing it; she'd ask Tandy later. The table was covered with a cloth which had once been part of a dust-rag which had once been one of the mother's dresses; it was spotlessly clean—it seemed to have been ironed—and was so folded and placed that the torn edges were out of sight. On the table was the pill-bottle flower-vase, just half full of clean water, in which stood a single stem and blossom of bleeding-heart. The effect was simple, tasteful, sort of Japanese-y. And further inside was the creel bedroom, with an oval dresser (despite the neat cloth cover and skirt, she recognized the lines of an inverted sardine tin) over which was the mirror which had been in Tandy's birthday pocketbook, and before which was a handsome little round chair, made of a bit of cardboard glued to a large wooden thread-spool, also covered and skirted with a scrap of material matching the dresser. And in bed was the brownie.

The mother had to go down almost flat on her stomach to see what it was which covered his pillow so whitely, so clean and thick-textured. A luxury material indeed—dogwood petals. He was covered with a quilt (she couldn't bring herself to call it one of her old pot-holders) and he was sleeping.

She chuckled at herself. How were those round black painted

eyes to look open or closed? . . . and she looked again and thought they were open. She almost said "Excuse me!" and she actually did blush at disturbing his nap. Wagging her head, she backed away and stood up.

Between her and the old stone fence was usually a carpet of weeds. There was no pretense of making lawn or garden out of the stony soil here. Actually, the front lawn had been grown on trucked-in topsoil. Yet—

Yet this area was now planted. A row of early marigolds between the brownie's house and the onetime weed-bed. And, from there to the fence, a dark-green plant, low, spidery, in rows. She did not recognize the plant except perhaps as just another weed.

Speechless, she returned to the house.

Trouble on the school bus that day; Robin came home bloody and triumphant.

Mother had meant to talk about brownie, but it was some time before events sorted themselves out. It appeared that a "big kid" had started chanting the well-known chant about "I seen Tandy's underwear," and Robin had punched him and gotten clobbered for it. The bus monitor broke it up, and in spite of Robin's having gotten the worst of it, he came home bursting with pride and Tandy awash with admiration.

The mother felt both. It was the first time Robin had ever brought arms to bear in defense of his sister, and after the question and cross-question and verbal jigsaw-puzzling which is always necessary to get an anecdote out of a child, and the awkward telephone conversation with the parent of the party of the other part, she found herself alone not with Tandy, but with Robin, Tandy having escaped to her preoccupation behind the garage.

"Robin, I don't like fighting but I must say, I like the way you took up for Tandy."

"Aw, she's okay," said Robin, not noticing how the mother of what he usually called that little tattletale, that squeaky wheel, that pushfaced squint-eyed bow-legged stoop . . . how the mother of this repulsive sibling let drop her jaw, and slumped into a chair.

She was still sitting there, trying to recover her strength, while

Robin pedaled away on his bicycle and while, a moment later, Tandy came in. She came totteringly, mounded down with clean laundry. The mother leapt up to help her get the screen door open and then had to sit down again: "Tandy!" she cried.

"Well, they was all dry, Mommy, so I brought them in."

"They *were*," said the mother weakly.

"Sure they were. Mommy . . ."

She was going to ask for something. If it was a diamond tiara, the mother thought, she'd get her one if she had to murder for it. "Yes, honey."

"Mommy, would you teach me how to set the table? I could do it every day while you get dinner."

So for the time being the mother utterly forgot to ask any questions about the brownie.

The mother thought about the brownie a good deal, although—perhaps it was a remnant of her comical embarrassment at having caught him in bed—she seldom went back there to look at the house. But one afternoon, thinking about the neatness of the little table, the dresser and chair and mirror, the shining white floor (what *was* that stuff, anyway?) it occurred to her that the three-year-old Noël would find that arrangement back there irresistible, and she shuddered at the mental picture of Noël bellying delightedly into the careful structure, churning up the white floor, leaning too hard on the cheese-box table, tumbling the mossy roof. "Noël . . ."

"?"

"Noël, we've all got to be specially careful of Tandy's brownie house. You wouldn't ever play with it unless she asked you to, would you?"

Noël gravely shook her helmet of tight curls. "I not allowed."

The mother tipped her head to one side and regarded the child. There were a number of things Noël was not allowed to do which she . . . "But all the same, you won't go back there by yourself."

"I not *allowed*," said Noël with great emphasis, and simultaneously the mother thought (a) that she'd like Tandy's formula for not allowing if it worked like this and (b) let's keep an eye on Noël all the same.

It was demonstrated, about ten days later, just how unnecessary it was to stand guard over the brownie's house. It was a Saturday. The father was home, Robin was off somewhere on his bicycle, and Tandy was slaving happily away behind the garage. The father, from the front of the house, called out, "Do you know what happened to the hand cultivator?"

The mother's photographic memory saw it lying beside a row of green. Oh, of course. "Noël, darling, run out behind the garage and get the cultivator. Tandy'll show you."

Pleadingly, "No, Mommy!"

"Noël!"

"I not *allowed* to!" said Noël, and incredibly, for she was a cheerful child, she began to cry.

The first impulse was to lay on some muscle and authority, the next a deep sympathy for the little one. "Oh ... Noël ..."

"I gon' *hide!*" shrieked Noël in something very like Tandy's special rasping shriek; and go she did, hide she did, ineffectively (the mother knew she was in the baby's blue chiffonier) but with great purpose. Apparently her "not allowed" was big enough to make it worth while defying the giants. Sighing, the mother went to the back door. "Tandy!"

"Yes, Mommy ..."

"Bring Daddy's cultivator to him, he needs it!"

"The handle-fingers?"

"That's right, dear."

She watched Tandy, in a yellow dress, bounding from behind the garage and heading for the front lawn. She waited until she saw the flash of yellow again and called her to the back steps.

"Tandy, you must have been terribly rough to Noël about not playing with your brownie. She's afraid to go back there because you said she's not allowed."

"No, I didn't, Mommy."

"Tandy!" (The explosion of the name alone was the mother's favorite curb.)

For the first time in many weeks Tandy began to pucker up, the eyes grew bright, the mouth trembled. "I reely, reely, reely ..."

Moving on impulse, the mother stepped forward and took Tandy's wrist. "Shh, honey. Take me out and show me what you're doing."

Tandy immediately shut it all off and they went back of the garage, Tandy skipping. The mother was prepared to be complimentary as one normally is, multiplied by the wonder of what she had seen before; but she was not prepared for what she found.

One wall had been removed from the little house, the shiplap scraps unearthed and tossed aside. The roof was still supported by the other side and the top of the creel. A heap of flat stones lay near, and a small sack of readymixed concrete. A seed-flat was doing service as a miniature mortar-board, and a discarded pancake-turner as a trowel.

Tandy was composedly replacing the wooden wall with one of fieldstone.

"Tandy! Why, I never ... who taught you to do this?"

"I asked Mr. Holmes-the-gym-teacher." (Tandy's teachers' names were all compounded like this.)

"But-but ... where did you get the concrete?"

"I boughted it. I saved my 'lowance money and all my ice-cream money. That's all right, isn't it? I didn't go into town, Robin did on his bicycle." She slopped water from a toy sand-bucket and began to mix the concrete.

"Robin never told me," said the mother faintly.

"I guess you never asked him, Mommy."

"I guess I never." The mother wet her lips. "Tandy, how did you ever think of all this?"

"I didn't think of it. I just did it, that's all." She picked up a slather of cement and ladled it on to the top course of her new wall. "You wouldn't expect a brownie to go on living in a ol' wood house, now, would you?" she demanded in grandmotherly tones.

"No, I—I suppose not ... Tandy, I saw the dresser and the little chair and the tablecloth. They're lovely. Tandy, did someone iron the tablecloth for you?"

"Oh, it irons itself," said Tandy. "You wash it an' rinse it and stick it on a window an' when it's dry it's ironed."

"What's that lovely white floor?"

Tandy selected and hefted a stone, then carefully laid it on the course. "Borax," she said.

"And you bought that with your ice-cream money too?"

"Sure. Brownies like borax and the little lumps off roots and that stuff there." She pointed to the rows of dark green weed.

"What is that?"

"The brownie's farm."

"I mean, the plant."

"I don't know what the real name is. I found it through the woods there, there's a whole patch. I call it brownie spinach. Look, over there's the lumps. It's like candy to a brownie." She pointed to a heap of roots, from some legume or other—the mother couldn't tell, for the leaves were gone; but the root-hairs had clusters of the typical nitrogenous nodules. "Tandy, how on earth do you know so much about brownies?"

Tandy gave her an impish glance. "I guess the same way you know about little girls."

The mother laughed. "Oh, but I had little girls of my own!"

Tandy just nodded: "Mm-hm."

The mother laughed again. When she left Tandy was fitting a whiskey-bottle—the three-sided "pinch" bottle—full of water, into the wall she was building, taking infinite pains to have it slant just so.

The mother wasn't laughing, though, later when she told her husband about it. As such things occasionally do, these developments had come about invisibly to him, having shown themselves mostly when he was away during the day. He listened, frowning thoughtfully, and when the children were glued to the television set the parents went out to look at the brownie house. All he said—all he could find to say, over and over, was: "Well, how about that."

When they left he snapped off a sprig of the dark green weed and put it in his pocket.

"And she sets the table every night," breathed the mother.

After she finished the fieldstone house (even the roof was stone, laid over the plywood from which the mossy earth had been swept away) Tandy seemed to abandon the brownie and his house altogether. She went back to one of her earlier passions, modeling clay, and spent her time studiously working it. But not ducks, not elephants. She would make thick rectangular slabs of it, and draw, or score, deeply into it. Some of the channels she cut were deeper than others, some curved, some straight but cut with her stylus at an acute angle, so that portions were undercut. "Looks like a three-dimensional Mondrian," said the father one night when the kids were asleep. He worked in a museum and knew a great many things, and had access to a great many more. That plant, for example. "It's *astralagus vetch,*" he told his wife. "And I knew I'd read something about it somewhere, so I looked it up again. It's a pretty ordinary sort of vegetable except for some reason it has a fantastic appetite for selenium. So much so that proposals have been made to mine selenium—and you know, that's that light-sensitive element they use in TV tubes and photocells and the like—by planting the vetch where selenium is known to be in the soil, harvesting the whole plant, burning it and recovering selenium from the ash. All of which is beside the point—what on earth made the little fuzzhead pick the stuff up and plant it?"

"Brownies like it," the mother said, and smiled.

It was the very next morning that Tandy was missing from the breakfast table.

There was only a small flurry about it; the mother knew just where to look. The child was busily packing armloads of vetch and tangles of knobby roots into a hole in the solid front of the brownie house. The brownie himself sat against the garage, its face turned toward her, its not-closed, not-open eyes seeming to watch. "I'm sorry, Mommy," Tandy said brightly, "but I'm not late for school, am I?"

"No, dear, but your breakfast is ready. What on earth are you doing to the brownie's house?"

"It isn't a house any more," said Tandy, in the tones of one explaining the self-evident to one who should know better without asking, "it's a factory." She put both hands in the hole and pushed hard. Apparently the house was baled full of weeds and roots. She daubed mortar around the opening quickly.

"Come, dear."

"Just finished, Mommy." She took a flat stone and set it into the opening, which must have been prepared for it, for it seemed a perfect fit. Another slap of mortar and she was up smiling. "I'm sorry, Mommy, but this is the day I had to do that."

"For the brownie."

"For the brownie." They went back to the house.

In Hawaii, a specialist, who should have been but was not more than a sergeant at the missile tracking station, grunted and straightened away from the high definition screen. "Lost it." He pulled a tablet toward him, glanced at the clock, and started filling in the log.

Nobody saw the faint swift streak as the satellite died. But if there had been a witness to that death—placed not to see faint swift streaks, but right on the scene, with a high-speed stroboscopic viewing device, he would have had some remarkable pictures.

As the golden sphere surrendered to the ravening attack of fractional heat, in that all but immeasurable fragment of time wherein parts became malleable, plastic, useful—they were used. Selenium from the solar cells, nitrogen from the pressurized interior, borosilicates ripped from refractory parts, were gleaned and garnered and formed and conformed. For a brief time (but quite long enough) there existed a device of molten alloy bars and threads surrounding a throat, or gate, which was composed of a pulsing, brilliant blue non-substance.

Anything placed within this blue area would cease to exist—not destroyed in any ordinary sense, but utterly eliminated. And the laws of the universe being what they are, such eliminated matter must reappear elsewhere. Exactly where, depends of course on circumstances.

That morning the mother was hanging clothes when a flash of light caught her eye. She put down her clothesbasket and went to the back of the garage.

The brownie sat with his back to the garage, staring glumly at the torn-up remnants of his "farm." The midmorning sunlight, warm and bright in this clear dry day, struck down through a gap in the trees and poured itself on and over the pinch bottle, half in and half out of the near wall of the little house. The colors were, she found

by screening her vision through her eyelashes, lovely and very bright—
flame-orange and white—why, the bottle itself seemed to be alight.

Or was it the inside of the little house?

There was a violent, sudden hiss as the bottle, full of water, popped
its cork and sent a gout of water inside the little stone structure.
Steam rolled up and then disappeared, and she took a pace back
from the sudden wave of heat. Terrified, she began to think of hose,
or extinguisher . . . the garage, all these trees, the house . . . and then
she saw that the side of the brownie's house which adjoined the
wooden garage was fieldstone too. The heat, whatever it was, was
contained.

It seemed to diminish a little. Then the glass bottle wavered, soft-
ened, slumped and fell inside. Heat blasted out again and again
diminished.

She stepped closer and peered down through the hole left by the
bottle. She could clearly see, lying on the floor of the stone chamber, the clay slab Tandy had made, with its odd, geometrical system
of ditches and scorings. But they seemed filled with some quivering
liquid, which even as she watched turned from yellow to silver and
then dulled to what could only be called a chalky pewter. The lines
and ditches, filled with this almost-metal, made a sort of screen, but
not exactly. It was too tangled for that. Say an irregular frame about
an irregular opening in the center of the slab. And this center area
began to turn blue and then purple, and then throb in some way she
would never be able to describe. She had to turn her eyes away.

Looking away seemed to snap the thread of fascination with
which she had leashed fear. She fled to the house, dialed the telephone, got her husband. "Quick," she said, and stopped to pant,
alarming him mightily. "Come home."

It was all she could manage. She hung up and sank into a couch.
She was therefore unaware of Noël, who came trotting across the
back of the house and straight and fearlessly behind the garage. She
stood for a while with a red lollipop in her mouth and pink hands
behind her, watching the heat-flickers over the stones, then circled
them carefully to windward and squatted down where she could
peer inside. Carefully then, and much more steadily than even a deft

three-year-old might be expected to move, she reached down with her delicate lollipop and probed the molten slag.

"Oh, don't, don't!" the mother said later back of the garage, as the father stabbed angrily at the hot stones with a crowbar. "Tandy might . . . she might . . . oh, it's meant so much to her . . ."

"I don't care, I don't care," he growled, stabbing and slashing and ruining. "I don't like it. Just say it's about fire, like playing with matches. We won't punish her or anything."

"No?" she said woefully, looking at the ruins.

"And this," he said, "damn devilish thing." He scooped up the brownie and thrust it among the scorching rocks. It flamed up easily. The last thing to go was the pair of dull eyes. The mother was at last sure they had been open the whole time. "Just tell her we almost had a fire," growled the father.

. . . which was the selfsame day Tandy brought back her report card, the absolutely perfect report card, and the note:

> . . . *truly the first absolutely perfect report card I have ever made out in my twenty-eight years of teaching school. The change in Tandy is quite beyond anything I have ever seen. She is an absolute delight, and I think it is safe to say that probably she always was; her previous behavior was, perhaps, a protest against something which she has now accepted. I shall never be able to express my gratitude to you for coming in for that talk, nor my admiration of you for your handling of the child (whatever that was!). It might be gracious of you to say that perhaps I had something to do with this; I would like to forestall that compliment. I did nothing special, nothing extra. It is you who have wrought the most pleasant kind of miracle.*

It was signed by her teacher, and it left them numb. Then the mother kissed Tandy and exclaimed, "Oh darling, whoever in the world magicked you!"

Exclamation or no, Tandy took it as a question and answered it directly: "The brownie."

There was a heavy silence, and then the mother took Tandy's hand. "You have to know about something," she said, and ungently to the father, "You come too."

They went out behind the garage, the woman touching Tandy's shoulders with ready mother hands. "There was a fire, honey. It all burned up. The brownie burned too."

The father, watching Tandy's face, which had not changed at the sight of the ruin (was this that un-seeing you read about, when people in shock deny to themselves what they see?) said suddenly and hoarsely, "It was an accident."

"No, it wasn't," Tandy said. She looked at her father and her mother but they were both looking at their feet. "And anyway *he* isn't burned up, he wasn't in that fire."

"He was," said the father, but she ignored him. "Anyway," the mother said, "I'm terribly sorry about your pretty little house, Tandy."

Tandy poked out her lips briefly. "It wasn't a house, it was a factory, I told you," she said. "And anyway it's all finished with anyway."

"You better understand," said the father doggedly, "that brownie did burn."

"You remember. You left him sitting right there," said the mother.

"Oh," said Tandy, "*that* wasn't a brownie! You can't see a brownie, silly. I've got the brownie. Don't you know that? Didn't you see the 'port card?"

"How did the . . ." She couldn't say it.

"It was easy. Any time I got to do something, I think about should I or not, and if I should, how I should do it; when I think of the right way, something inside here goes *bwoop-eee!*" (she made a startlingly electronic sound, the first syllable glissading upward and the second flat and unmusical, like a "pure" tone) "and I know that's what I should do. It's easy, And that's the brownie."

"Inside you."

"Mm-hm. That dirty old doll, that was just a way to get some fun out of all that hard work. I couldn't've done it without having some sort of fun. So I made it easy for brownies to live in this whole world and they make it easy for me."

317

The mother thought about a metallic twisted thing with a purple mystery atremble in it. It was like looking through a window into a—another place. Or a door.

"Tandy," she said, moved as she sometimes was by sheer impulse, "how many brownies came through the door?"

"Four," said Tandy blithely, and began to skip. "One for me, one for Robin, one for Noël and one for the baby. Could I have some juice?"

They walked back to the house. Robin was home. He was giving Noël back her lollipop and saying "Thank you" the way they always wished he would. Noël always was a generous child. She had already given the baby a lick.

The analogy of the profit-sharing plan appears as we imagine a self-satisfied tycoon at his desk and a bright-eyed junior exec sprinting in bearing mimeographed sheets. "Gosh, J. G., this is that first look I had at the new plan. You're doing a lot for your people here, J. G., a whole lot." And homiletically the great man inclines his head, accepting the tribute, and says "A happy worker is a loyal worker, my boy." And while bobbing his head, the junior executive is thinking. "Yeah, and what's good for the happy workers is good for management, how about that?"

Yet enlightened and cooperative self-interest is not always to be sneered at. Ask any symbiote. Whatever it was that bubbled up out of that blue orifice had been designed simply and solely to adapt a host fully to its environment, in order to induce that cardinal harmony called joy.

Not satisfaction, not contentment, not pleasure. These can be had in other ways, and by using less than all of the environment. A surge of joy within the host created that special substance on which the symbiote fed, and it was as simple as that. Oh happy worker. Oh happy management . . .

"Well, thank God anyway she's back to normal," said the father. He came in from the porch where he and the mother had stood watching the neighborhood kids and Robin and Tandy playing on the lawn. The mother did not point out to him that Tandy, in and of the whole group now, may have been playing normally, but she wasn't back to it; she'd come to it. The mother stood watching, silent, happy, and frightened.

Inside, the father picked up his newspaper and threw it down again when he heard one of those special in-group code sounds which come to families like secret ciphers. This one was the click of heavy glass against hardwood, and meant that the baby, who had been put down in the crib in the master bedroom, had lashed out with a strong left hook in his random way and belted his bottle out of his mouth and up against the crib bars.

The father stopped just inside the bedroom. His jaw dropped, and all he could do was slowly to raise a hand to his chin and close it and hold it closed. For the baby, the six-months-old Timothy, who only yesterday could hopelessly lose a bottle five-eighths of an inch away from his hungry face, pulled himself to a sitting position by the bars, half-turned to the left and pulled the pillow on which the bottle had been perched away from the side of the crib and up to a formal position across the end of the mattress; half-turned to the right to grasp the bottle, then lay back.

He not only took the bottle firmly in his two hands; he not only got his mouth on it; he also elevated it so it would flow freely.

And for a long moment there was no sound but his suckings, his rhythmic murmurs of sheer joy, and the faint susurrus of tiny bubbles valving back into the bottle; for the father was holding his breath. At last the father inhaled and opened his mouth to call his wife witness to this miracle. He then thought better of it, closed his mouth, wagged his head and quietly left the room.

As he entered by one door, Robin, the firstborn, bounded in at the front. The screen door went to the stretch, and uncorked a curve that promised to tear out the moldings when it hit. The father squinched up his face and eyes in preparation for the crash, but Robin, for the first time in his life—a boy has to be at least eleven before he stops slamming screen-doors, and Robin was only eight—Robin reached behind him without looking and buffered the door with his fingertips, so it closed with a whisper and a click. He galloped past the unthunderstruck father and went into the kitchen; a moment later he was seen, all unbidden, lugging the garbage out.

The father fell weakly back into the big wicker chair.

"Daddy ..."

He put down his paper. Noël came to him with a long cardboard box stretching her three-year-old arms out almost straight. She pleaded, "You wanna play chest with me?"

He looked at her for a long moment. Many times they had sat on the carpet and made soldier-parades with the chessmen. But now he—he ...

He shuddered. He tried to control it but he couldn't. "No, Noël," he said. "I don't want to play chest with you ..." But oh, that's Noël's story, not Tandy's.

Story Notes

By Paul Williams

"A Crime for Llewellyn": first published in *Mike Shayne Mystery Magazine*, October 1957. Probably written spring or summer 1957. In August 1957, in a proposal sent to Doubleday editor Walter Bradbury describing the stories that could be included in a new Sturgeon collection (*A Touch of Strange*) he hoped Doubleday would publish, TS said of this story: *In spite of its title and its berth* [the magazine it was already scheduled to be published in], *it is not a crime or mystery story in the usual sense; call it rather an off-trail, straight fiction story.*

In chapter 7 ("Art and Artistry") of her 1981 book/monograph *Theodore Sturgeon,* Lucy Menger identifies a subcategory of Sturgeon's writing as "his portrait stories," and says, "In these, the protagonist's subjective experience provides the framework and tone for the narrative." She cites as examples "Scars," "A Way Home," "Bright Segment," "Bulkhead," "And Now the News," "To Here and the Easel," "The Man Who Lost the Sea," and "It's You!" Menger writes, "Sturgeon's portrait stories are the most powerful and moving of his works. Only one of these tales ['Bulkhead'] is also science fiction.... These portrait stories show what the author can do when not constrained by the strictures of speculative fiction."

After a brief discussion of how plot functions in speculative fiction (science fiction), Menger writes: "In most other types of fiction, both genre and mainstream, human character is the basis of plot. A plot may involve conflicts between humans or between one or more humans and circumstances, or within a human, etc., but in every instance, the plot explores the ramifications of the human character. This is what Sturgeon's portrait stories do. They are journeys of discovery into man himself.

"These journeys follow many paths," Menger continues. "Two of Sturgeon's portrait stories, 'How to Kill Aunty' and 'A Crime for Llewellyn,' involve crimes. In this pair, however, as in life, the crime is only a symptom. In 'A Crime for Llewellyn,' the subject is the problems of a human who, like the protagonist in 'Bright Segment,' can only marginally cope."

"It Opens the Sky": first published in *Venture Science Fiction,* November 1957. In his 8/13/57 proposal for Doubleday, TS described this one as *written only a few days ago and too new for evaluation. It's space opera cum personal regeneration.*

Interesting that years before writing "Tandy's Story," Sturgeon used his three-year-old daughter's name as the name of his attractive, idealistic teenage heroine in this space adventure about moral values.

"A Touch of Strange": first published in *The Magazine of Fantasy and Science Fiction,* January 1958. In the 8/13/57 proposal, Sturgeon said of this: *Contemporary sci-fantasy. Sold only a few days ago to* Fantasy & Science Fiction.

TS, in his introduction to a 1982 book called *The Eureka Years, Boucher and McComas's The Magazine of Fantasy and Science Fiction 1949–1954,* without identifying this story by name, talked about his nervous reaction to "A Touch of Strange" when he first read it: *I shall close with what, to me, is the definitive Boucher anecdote.*

The editors had asked me for a story, and had, in time, pressed a little by telling me there was a spot for it in the upcoming issue, but it had to be in by such-and-such. Finding just the right story to tell wasn't easy, and the calendar and then the clock began to run awfully fast, and finally I sat down with my head as blank as the paper and started to put out words more or less at random, until some thirty sleepless, eatless, even coffee-less hours had gone by. Somehow I got it into the mail and then fell over sidewise. In due course I convalesced, and sat down to read my carbon.

I was horrified. I felt that I had violated one of the most cardinal edicts of story. I felt that the manuscript was too long, the story too thin, and the whole thing totally unprofessional and unworthy of the magazine.

I tottered to the typewriter and banged out (as I remember) five single-spaced pages saying all the above in much greater detail, begging the editors to fill my slot with someone else's story, pleading for advice as to how to fix this one if it could be fixed, or giving me some sort of plot or idea or springboard for another story that I could get out in the next four weeks before deadline. All but weeping, I fired this moany missive off to California [where Boucher lived].

By return mail I got the only airmail, special delivery post card *I have ever seen. It read:*

   Dear Ted:

    I love you.

   You write such beautiful stories.

       Tony

Editor's introduction to this story (above the title) in the original magazine appearance: "A reviewer can't win for losing. If he doesn't write, the reviewed will exclaim, 'Who's he to talk? He's not a writer.' And if he *is* a writer, they'll say, 'Who's he to talk? Look at his own stuff!' The book reviewer of *Venture Science Fiction* is at least safer than most in this respect; for Theodore Sturgeon's own stuff is, as a rule, just about the best science-fantasy being written today. I hope that reviewing remains only an avocation with him: the shrewdest criticism ever achieved in s.f. would be small repayment for the loss of such stories as this one, with a title that could fit the *Collected Works* of Sturgeon." The story did indeed give its title to Sturgeon's fifth story collection, *A Touch of Strange* (Doubleday, 1958).

"The Comedian's Children": first published in *Venture Science Fiction,* May 1958. The comedian protagonist (or antagonist) of this story, Heri Gonza, was of course inspired by Sturgeon watching Jerry Lewis conduct early versions of his fund-raising "telethons" for the Muscular Dystrophy Association and children with neuromuscular diseases.

I'd like to mention that Gonza in this story joins a short list of very memorable and hate-inspiring villains in Sturgeon stories, including the narrator of "When You're Smiling" and Costello in "Mr. Costello, Hero" and the Maneater in *The Dreaming Jewels.* These characters, like Gonza, have an unusual power over their fellow men that can be described as "charm" and that seems characteristic of the modern psychological archetype known as the psychopath or sociopath.

I'd also like to quote myself. In a biographical profile called "Theodore Sturgeon" in *The Berkley Showcase, Vol. 3* (1981), I wrote: "'The Comedian's Children,' about a manipulative TV personality, was another impossible triumph—that story tore me into little pieces when I was twelve years old, and it remains one of the most powerful pieces of fiction I've ever read."

"The Graveyard Reader": first published in an anthology edited by Groff Conklin called *The Graveyard Reader* and published by Ballantine Books in 1958.

In 1958 one of my dearest friends, the late Groff Conklin, sent me a permission form to enable him to include a story of mine in a new anthology, as he did for almost every one of the many anthologies he produced. I forget what story he asked for, but I recall thinking that it wasn't suitable altogether for this book, which was to be called The Graveyard Reader. *In a rush of gratitude for the many kindnesses that remarkable man had done for me, I sat down and wrote him an original story with the same title as his book. I wrote it without getting up from the type-writer, and gave it to him. I mean, I really gave it, asking him not to send me a check, an offer which he subsequently and forcefully refused, though he cried when he read it. Just by the way, the first time I read it in public, I did too. And it wasn't until I began compiling this special book* [*Maturity*, 1979; this quote is from the introduction to that collection] *that it came to me that this story expresses a highly refined aspect of maturity that isn't even hinted at in the two preceding it* ["Maturity" and "Bulkhead"]: *Words are by no means the best means of communication, and they need all the help they can get.*

"The Man Who Told Lies": first published in *The Magazine of Fantasy and Science Fiction,* September 1959, under the pseudonym "Billy Watson" as part of a feature called "Quintet." "Quintet" consisted of three short-short stories and two poems, all credited to names unfamiliar to the magazine's readers. The editor's introduction to the feature read as follows:

"The imaginative eye of a child sees without the blinders of culture and sophistication, and the result, in the case of a truly creative child, is a fresh and different kind of art which an adult cannot easily duplicate.... Or can he? That is the question at hand. At least one of the following pieces was written by a child under 12; at least one was written by either Damon Knight, Jane Rice, Theodore Sturgeon, or Alfred Bester—all of whom are, shall we say, over 35. All of the pieces are, we think, worth reading on any grounds; we offer the additional piquancy of asking you to guess which of the following bylines are the actual names of creative children, and which hide the identities of professional writers. To give you adequate time to think about it, we withhold the answers till next month."

"The Man Who Lost the Sea": first published in *The Magazine of Fantasy and Science Fiction,* October 1959.

In his introduction to "The Man Who Lost the Sea" in the 1979 collection *The Golden Helix,* Sturgeon wrote:

In 1959 I left for the West Indies seeking a balmy climate and a low-rent district. For the first time in my life I worked eight hours a day, seven days a week on a regular schedule. And in practically every way it turned into a disaster. I just couldn't make a story jell. I finally got going on a space-travel story and ground out words, one after the other, until I had a start, a middle, a finish. It was awful—wordy and slow and muzzy.

So literally for months I cut. I cut until the story and I bled. I cut it from 21,000 words down to 5,000, and at last called it finished. I showed it to my wife and she couldn't understand it. I showed it to my mother, who was alive at the time, and she couldn't understand it. I had completely lost perspective on it, and I returned to the States, bloody and very much bowed.

Shortly afterward Bob Mills called and wanted a story for an All-Star issue of F&SF. I told him that all I had was this, but that if I sent it, I never wanted to see it again. I did, and he read it, and called back to say it was okay, he guessed—but it needed cutting!

I guess I got a little hysterical I told him to burn it. But he bought it, and ran it, and it wound up in that year's Martha Foley Award Anthology as one of the best short stories of the year. Moral: Don't believe what everybody tells you, even if everybody is your mother.

"The Man Who Lost the Sea" did in fact get selected for Martha Foley's prestigious annual anthology *Best American Short Stories,* possibly the first time a story first published in a science fiction magazine was awarded that honor. And it is described as "perhaps his most-praised story" on the back of the year 2000 Vintage Books Sturgeon collection, *Selected Stories.*

On March 31, 1959, Sturgeon mailed "The Man Who Lost the Sea" to his New York literary agent from Grenada Island accompanied by a letter that began: *Here at last is the story on which I have worked so hard for so long—longer, as a consecutive effort, than anything else I have ever written. It has been profoundly researched: if anyone ever wants to know, I will supply a formidable bibliography. Everything in it, the landscape, the sky phenomena, the ship design, the suit, the sickness, even the special kind of in-shock mental aberration suffered by the protagonist, is in accord with the best references I have or can lay my hands on.*

Yet I am profoundly discouraged with it. What I have been trying to do—what has taken me so long—is to hit the top slick markets with a kind of s-f which is truly scientific, but not the ultra-ultra of wild distant worlds and phantastic beasties. What I want is the future of the day after tomorrow, clearly linked to today's headlines. I see clearly that I ought not to change my style or approach, but simply go on with what I've done all along, if only because Ray Russell [of Playboy]*, among others, is willing to list already published stuff as items he would have bought, as is. But I have been unable to do this, since I regard my association with you as a profound break with all that has gone before, and a new career in new places. Perhaps I should go back to the same as before, and rely on you to throw it high and let it find its own level. Maybe you'll have a word of advice for me on this.*

To be specific, I feel that in this story I have aimed at a market which requires less "science," not more: more direct, simple-minded clarity, not less. But what I've produced is an elaborate switching of points-of-view, tense, and locale, self-consciously "skillful" to the point of obscuration.

I'd like to rewrite it and will if you say so: and I'll do it quickly, by the way—don't worry about that! I have it all blocked out. I think the very worst fault of this version is similar to that I detected in "Ride In, Ride Out" [a not-yet-published Sturgeon/Ward story]—a protagonist who does virtually nothing, but lounges along letting things happen to him. I think in the rewrite this problem of the "sick man" should be a fight, a battle every inch of the way, until at the end, he wins. He still dies, but he wins his particular battle, which is to figure out where he is—an act which is obscured to him, in his sickness, by his subconscious mind's unwillingness to face the fact that he is not only dying but more alone than anyone has ever been before. So bit by bit, piece by piece, he gathers the evidence before him until he has the truth, then transcends it in his triumphant last line. So that instead of the current, supine waiting for it all to clear up for him, he makes it clear up—surely the essence of good narrative.

"The Man Who Lost the Sea" was nominated for a Hugo Award for best science fiction short story of the year 1959.

In her discussion of "portrait stories" (mentioned above in the note to "A Crime for Llewellyn"), Lucy Menger wrote: "Despite an exotic locale, 'The Man Who Lost the Sea' is not, by Sturgeon's own definition

[A good science fiction story is a story with a human problem, and a human solution, which would not have happened at all without its science content], science fiction because its scientific elements could be replaced by relative commonplaces. Told in an unusual manner, it is the drama of a man becoming aware of his own circumstances and realizing that his defeat is only one facet of a larger victory." Menger notes that the Sturgeon definition she quotes is from page 10 of a 1962 book edited by Damon Knight called *A Century of Science Fiction*.

Sturgeon's daughter Noël has said, "one of the things that has always struck me about this story is how it turned out, eerily, to be a description of how he [TS] died, slowly losing the ability to breathe."

"The Man Who Figured Everything" by Theodore Sturgeon and Don Ward; first published in *Ellery Queen's Mystery Magazine*, January 1960.

Editor's introduction to this story from the original magazine appearance:

"An unorthodox Western detective story—unorthodox because it not only breaks the rules of Westerns but of crime fiction as well. As a matter of fact, the authors, messrs. Sturgeon and Ward, deliberately set out to write a Western that departed from tradition and formula—and they succeeded.

"So meet Arch Scott, a Western law man, and the Badlands Bookkeeper, a Western bad man, who play their usual roles in unusual ways ..."

TS in 1956 described the process of collaboration between himself and Ward: *Don dreams 'em up and I write 'em my way and submit them without his seeing them.* Ward in his introduction to their 1973 collection, *Sturgeon's West*, described the collaboration as "my contribution minor, his major."

"Like Young": first published in *The Magazine of Fantasy and Science Fiction*, March 1960.

There is a half-page, 19 single-spaced lines, typed note among Sturgeon's papers found at his former home in Woodstock, that is clearly the genesis not just of this story's idea but of some of its language: *They called us the Immune, but that was a misnomer. We'd all had it. It's just that we hadn't died of it. Mankind was dead; we weren't, just yet.*

Humanity wasn't.... I guess these things are open to definition. There were six hundred and four of us left alive, and we'd all grown up to a long lifetime devoted to the single idea of seeing to it that with mankind dead, humanity would survive—humanity in the sense of aspiration, generosity—if you like, nobility.

We were going to give it to the otters.

Ever since the first man observed with delight the playfulness of the otters, ever since they had been seen using tools—the sea otter always has, you know, floating on his back, bracing a shellfish against his chest, cracking it with a stone—the evidence had been before us that the Otters were the next Ones. Adaptable, intelligent, humorful in the way that only humans had been humorful, continuing it all their lives, while other species got grim at adulthood—wonderfully able to survive in arctic or tropics, highland and low—it had always been obvious that the otters would be Next.

Experiments in accelerating their development were made, of course, but without success except in the extrapolative, statistical sense; it became obvious that they would advance to civilized status, but not in our lifetimes.

When the narrator says, near the middle of this story, *"For our kind to end with a whimper . . . this was Bad Art"* I hear echoes of these lines from the closing pages of Sturgeon's first novel, *The Dreaming Jewels*: *She has given her life for an alien caste . . . It might be that "justice" and "mercy" are relative terms; but nothing can alter the fact that her death, upon earning her right to survive, is bad art.* I asked Sturgeon about these lines in 1978 when I was writing an introduction for a reprint of that novel. He told me: *I think I derived that from an early Heinlein story, which one I don't remember. where a real nuts-and-bolts engineering type was asked if he believed in life after death, and he said immediately and without hesitation, of course I do. And this girl was really astonished and says, why is that? And he says "It has to be that way, otherwise it would be bad art." That impressed me tremendously, it really did.*

"Night Ride": first published in *Keyhole Mystery Magazine*, June 1960. Editor's blurb from the first page of the original magazine appearance: THE RUNAWAY BUS WAS CARRYING A STRANGE GROUP ON ITS ONE-WAY PLUNGE TO DOOM. THERE WERE 32 LIVE PASSENGERS—AND ONE CORPSE!

"**Need**": first published in the Sturgeon collection *Beyond* (Avon paperbacks, July 1960).

"Need" was nominated for a Hugo Award for best science fiction novelette of the year 1960.

In a letter to Damon Knight dated Nov. 13, 1959, TS wrote: *I sold a new book to Avon in the summer. They wouldn't play unless I promised a new novelette to go with it. I get $750 if I send them 10–15M* [10 to 15 thousand words]. *I can't write the 10–15M.* [This in the context of describing a bout of writer's block that had started in the West Indies.] This letter to Knight is also interesting for a paragraph in which he reports his recollection of how long it took him to write certain stories and novels that he wrote relatively quickly (and easily) as opposed to the long struggle he was having with "Need": *I wrote "Saucer of Loneliness" in four hours, "The Pod in the Barrier" in one day, "Drusilla Strange" in three, "Killdozer!" in nine, I, Libertine in 22. More than Human took five weeks total.*

There are ten pages of "maundering" notes among Sturgeon's papers, trying to develop this story idea, several of them headed "Gorwing." The following passages (from one single-spaced sheet of typing) suggest that TS had already written the opening scene (or had pictured it, thought about it) and was using that plus presumably a basic idea of a story about a guy (Gorwing) who has a telepathic ability (and, sometimes, curse) to be aware of people in need and of what they seem to be feeling a need for:

It seems to me that perhaps the best narrator is the first (taxi) victim. This guy is really burning at being taken this way; yet overriding that is a growing curiosity as to how the hell Gorwing did it. He goes to work on the one weak link—Noat. What happens when the plug-ugly is treated well, covered for his boss, treated as a real human being with real problems? Perhaps he's always been underprivileged and warms to this. GLIMMERING of a sequence where Smith almost learns the trick, walking about under the stars and sensing the crying, yearning, hungry hopeful masses around him ... but my Machine won't produce this until it has a clear Build to the yarn ... Hm ... THIS MUST BE TRUE: If I keep whanging away at this plot it will yield. And then—think of it! All I'll have to do then is to write what moves me, about anyone, anywhere— and the hell with sf & f... I wonder if I could write the Sylvana story in a week once the draft is done? I bet I could. And oh then the lovely

*money ... GALAXY and then Doubleday or Farrar, Strauss, and later,
Gold Medal or Dell ... but I can't do any of that until this ruddy Avon
chore is done with ... so let's go: Gorwing has a talent. Marvelous as it
is, it profits him little because too seldom does anyone close enough need
anything he has to offer. He enlists the aid of a mass of muscles nzmed
George Noat, known as G-note. One episode has to do with $100 asked
demanded for a one-way ride from Nyack to Congers, victim, one Smith.
With this as the basis, get right to work and build a good reader-identifi-
cation plot.*

*Character is the key. Plot springs from character. I have a "talented"
but rather frantic and insecure Gorwing, a big good-natured physically
ugly ape, Noat, and Smith, who could be anybody ... would I be in too
much of a pocket if I just started out with the taxi incident and went on
from there? ... Noat narrating: I was in front of the pool hall when Gorwing pulled up in his Dodge. Do you want to make a big buck? I said
sure. So I got in and he tore off. All he told me was to keep my eyes open,
especially the ears, and my mouth shut. We pulled up by the traffic light
on 9W and there was this anxious-looking guy pacing it on the road. Gorwing says, "Taxi, mister?" and laughs a dirty laugh. The guy jumps in
and Gorwing pulls right over to the side and shuts the motor off. The guy
gets frantic. Gorwing puts it to him: how much? The guy says, whatever
you say, but get going. Gorwing says, I say a hundred. The guy screams.
Gorwing opens the door. The guy closes it and says drive then. We go to
Congers, the guy fires out into a house. Gorwing starts to lean on the
horn. The guy comes out with a twenty and says push off. Gorwing turns
the flashlight on my face and says G-Note here will collect in the morning. Then I begin to haunt the house. Pretty soon the guy stops being
tough at me and begins to be nice. I fall for it and finally settle for Gorwing's cut: Gorwing never knows the difference. But after that I see a lot
of this Smith.*

*G-Note could be a charming character who believes everything any-
one tells him and has an alarming ability to rationalize the irreducible.
He believes Gorwing and then he believes Smith, and in his own mind
sees nothing difficult about believing both. Keep it in mind but don't make
it signal.*

*Wonder if I'm overlooking my Woodford after all these years. Seven
elements: Problem, character, obstacle, complication, crisis, climax, denoue-
ment. BOY that was a meaty thought! Do you mean after all these years*

I got plot trouble? That's it, tho'—at least as far as this beast is concerned. Because tho' I have characters, my Noat is only an observer, Smith a motivator, and really, only Gorwing has a problem—and that's not much of a problem; it's only that of making a living like the rest of us . . . which may be the crucial thing here after all. How about a domestic picture of Gorwing in trouble—his story after all—in why he pulls Noat into it. At first seeming hard, taciturn, unsympathetic, he is revealed as a guy crying inside with the clamor of demand on him: for his own survival he can't sympathize with anyone . . . the undertone of the story, then, can be a study of values. He has to get liquor, say, for an alcoholic wife whom he really loves . . . or food for the baby, for that matter . . . and in the course of the story, he does. The big switch is in the reader's re-estimate of him, which he shares with Smith. . . . Maybe Smith is looking for a hard guy and in a way appreciates this ploy . . . or Noat could wander through the story in his dim way trying to show each what a nice guy the other is . . .

This is quite a portrait of an author getting ready to let a story come through him. Interesting that he says, early on: *my Machine won't produce this until it has a clear Build to the yarn,* as though his experience is that there is a mechanism inside him that seems to write the stories itself once he gives it sufficient fodder and momentum. The comment *All I'll have to do then is to write what moves me . . . and the hell with sf & f . . .* suggests that the editor at Avon has let him know that this new story for the book didn't have to be science fiction or fantasy (perhaps the editor was aware of what a valuable addition "Bright Segment" was to *Caviar,* without being sf or fantasy).

The line in the above "maundering" *Wonder if I'm overlooking my Woodford after all these years* is of much interest to students of Sturgeon's work. Jack Woodford's first book on writing, *Trial and Error: A Key to the Secret of Writing and Selling* was published in 1933, five years before Sturgeon began writing professionally. It seems possible that the "Woodford" Sturgeon is referring to here (indicating clearly that he's studied and practiced Woodford's guidelines in past years) is Woodford's 1939 book *PLOTTING: How to Have a Brain Child.*

"How to Kill Aunty": first published in *Mike Shayne Mystery Magazine,* March 1961. Editor's blurb from the first page of the original magazine appearance (where the story was titled "How to Kill Your Aunty"; Sturgeon changed the title when the story was included in his 1966 collection

Starshine): A CAT MAY PLAY WITH A MOUSE A LONG TIME BEFORE KILLING IT. AND MURDER IS CAT PLAY TO SOME. Below this blurb and under the author's name atop the story was this line: A MYSTERY NOVELET OF DARK VIOLENCE

As mentioned above in the note to "A Crime for Llewellyn," Lucy Menger in her book *Theodore Sturgeon* describes "How to Kill Aunty" as one of Sturgeon's "portrait stories," "journeys of discovery into man himself."

In 1962, this story was included in Brett Halliday's annual collection *Best Detective Stories of the Year.*

"Tandy's Story": first published in *Galaxy Science Fiction*, April 1961. Editor's blurb above the title from the first page of the original magazine appearance: BORAX FOR BROWNIES AND THE MOONWATCHER WHO MISSED—THE CRINKLED GETTER AND THE CANAVERAL SNEEZE—THESE ARE THE THINGS THAT MAKE UP—

In his introduction to "Tandy's Story" in the 1979 collection *The Stars Are the Styx,* Sturgeon wrote:

One is conditioned to be austere and objective—I don't know why, or who started it; somehow it's not supposed to be "appropriate" (a word I hate a lot) to bring oneself and one's bloodstream into public view.

Well, I say the hell with it. Most of what I write is written by the simple process of opening a vein and dripping it (all too slowly) into the typewriter. My research has always been people, and more often than not, it's the people closest to me that I can research most conveniently. And the process of compiling such a collection as this must of necessity bring a sharp focus on the environment in which they are written.

Tandy's Story was designed to be the first in a series, ultimately to be collected as a book of short stories and novelettes, to be called The Family. *There would be this, and Noël's, and Timothy's (he's the baby mentioned in these pages) and Robin's, and then* The Mother's Story *and finally* The Father's Story.

But then one of those great winds that sweep across our biographies arose, and I was separated from these people by some thousands of miles and days, and here I am a week away from having watched Noël graduate from college and "the baby" Timothy whack his head against a six-foot door lintel. Robin has been celebrated elsewhere in my work, and Noël's turn is coming some day soon, I'm sure, as is something special for Tim, but these can't happen in the same matrix as this one. Nostalgia is often tinged with regret; mine is not. But at the same time I am poignantly aware that in a contiguous universe there is a volume called The Family *which will not and cannot be written. I'd like to read it.*

In the December 1962 issue of a science fiction writers' journal called *PITFCS* (*Proceedings of the Institute for Twenty-First Century Sudies*), Frederik Pohl, Horace Gold's successor as editor of *Galaxy*, wrote, "One of the best stories Horace ever bought—the last he worked on before he had to give up and go to the hospital—was Theodore Sturgeon's "Tandy's Story." I know for a fact that he converted it from a passable bit into an excellent job by demanding and getting considerable revision."

"Tandy's Story" is included in *The Norton Book of Science Fiction: North American Science Fiction, 1960–1990*, edited by Ursula K. Le Guin and Brian Attebery.

Further bibliographic and biographical notes

During the time when Sturgeon wrote the stories included in this volume, mid-1957 to the end of 1960, he published five books, and lived in four different towns in several different parts of the world. *A Touch of Strange* (August 1958) was a hardcover collection of nine stories, three of which are included in this volume of *The Complete Stories of Theodore Sturgeon*.

The Cosmic Rape was a novel, published as an original paperback in August 1958, four years after Sturgeon had contracted to write it and had indicated that he could produce it quickly; the delay led his editor to remark to a mutual acquaintance, Judith Merril: "I know Sturgeon can write a novel in three days, but *which three days?*" The August 1958 issue of *Galaxy* included a short novel by Sturgeon called "To Marry Medusa," which is actually a condensed or edited-down version of *The Cosmic Rape,* probably prepared by the magazine's editor. I have not chosen to include "To Marry Medusa" in *The Complete Stories of Theodore Sturgeon* because I believe it is not a story but a shortened version of an already completed novel, possibly put together by someone other than Sturgeon.

In 1959, Sturgeon published a new paperback collection called *Aliens 4*, made up of four short novels: "The Comedian's Children," "Killdozer!" (slightly revised), "Cactus Dance," and "The [Widget], The [Wadget], and Boff."

In September 1960, Sturgeon published an original paperback novel called *Venus Plus X*. In July 1960, he published a new paperback collection called *Beyond,* which included "Need" and "Like Young."

For the first part of 1957, Theodore and Marion Sturgeon and their children Robin, Tandy and Noël continued to live in Congers in Rockland County, New York, just northwest of New York City. Sometime in the second half of 1957, the Sturgeons moved to a house in Truro, Massachusetts, near the tip of Cape Cod. "The Comedian's Children" and much of *The Cosmic Rape* were probably written in Truro.

"But the Cape was cold and lonely," I wrote in my biographical profile (published in 1981 in *The Berkley Showcase, vol. 3* and currently available online at the Sturgeon Literary Trust page whose address is in the Editor's Note at the front of this volume), "and the Sturgeon family decided they could live cheaper and happier in the West Indies. Ted's mother was teaching on St. Vincent, and she found them a place on the island of Bequi. They arrived and the house was too small, noisy, no privacy ... so they began months of island-hopping, searching for a home. They ended up on Grenada. Ted had no place to write during all this, but he kept trying. He was working on a story called 'The Man Who Lost the Sea.'"

In mid-1959 the Sturgeons left the West Indies and returned to New York state, eventually settling in the "artists' colony" town of Woodstock, where they would live happily for the next six or seven years.

Corrections and addenda

Series reader Jim Wilson has found and kindly supplied us with a further comment by Sturgeon on "A Saucer of Loneliness" (volume VII). This is from a 1968 paperback anthology edited by Robert P. Mills, called *The Worlds of Science Fiction,* in which authors were asked to choose their personal favorite among their stories and to write a brief rubric explaining why they chose that particular story. TS wrote:

"Not one writer in twenty thousand," a knowledgeable agent once told me, "is competent to judge his own product." This may well be true; could I judge him and his sweeping statements? Be that as it may, I have good and sufficient reasons for my special fondness for "Saucer." It was written in about four hours, one of those profoundly satisfying creations, which simply lays itself out, word after word, "feeling" right all the way. In addition, it is one of the stories which bears out something that I have been formulating for some time; that good science fiction is good to the extent that it is fable; that is, stories about foxes and grapes are not dubi-

ous accounts of improbably herbivorous foxes impossibly making spoken conclusions; they mean other things in other contexts. As such, "Saucer" is a fable, an explication of that endemic disease called loneliness. Finally, the story pleases me with its opening; few things I have ever done have so exploded onto the page.